The Collected Supernatural and Weird Fiction of Grant Allen Volume 1

The Collected Supernatural and Weird Fiction of Grant Allen Volume 1

One Novel 'Kalee's Shrine', and Nine
Short Stories of the Strange and Unusual
Including 'Our Scientific Observations on a
Ghost', 'Pallinghurst Barrow' and 'My New
Year's Eve Among the Mummies'

Grant Allen

LEONAUR

The Collected
Supernatural and Weird
Fiction of
Grant Allen
Volume 1
One Novel 'Kalee's Shrine', and Nine Short Stories of the Strange and Unusual
Including 'Our Scientific Observations on a Ghost', 'Pallinghurst Barrow' and 'My
New Year's Eve Among the Mummies'
by Grant Allen

FIRST EDITION

Leonaur is an imprint of Oakpast Ltd

Copyright in this form © 2019 Oakpast Ltd

ISBN: 978-1-78282-868-6 (hardcover)
ISBN: 978-1-78282-869-3 (softcover)

http://www.leonaur.com

Contents

Our Scientific Observations on a Ghost

"Then nothing would convince you of the existence of ghosts, Harry," I said, "except seeing one."

"Not even seeing one, my dear Jim," said Harry. "Nothing on earth would make me believe in them, unless I were turned into a ghost myself."

So saying, Harry drained his glass of whisky toddy, shook out the last ashes from his pipe, and went off upstairs to bed. I sat for a while over the remnants of my cigar, and ruminated upon the subject of our conversation. For my own part, I was as little inclined to believe in ghosts as anybody; but Harry seemed to go one degree beyond me in scepticism. His argument amounted in brief to this,—that a ghost was by definition the spirit of a dead man in a visible form here on earth; but however strange might be the apparition which a ghost-seer thought he had observed, there was no evidence possible or actual to connect such apparition with any dead person whatsoever.

It might resemble the deceased in face and figure, but so, said Harry, does a portrait. It might resemble him in voice and manner, but so does an actor or a mimic. It might resemble him in every possible particular, but even then, we should only be justified in saying that it formed a close counterpart of the person in question, not that it was bis ghost or spirit. In short, Harry maintained, with considerable show of reason, that nobody could ever have any scientific ground for identifying any external object, whether shadowy or material, with a past human existence of any sort. According to him, a man might conceivably see a phantom, but could not possibly know that he saw a ghost.

Harry and I were two Oxford bachelors, studying at the time for our degree in Medicine, and with an ardent love for the scientific

7

side of our future profession. Indeed, we took a greater interest in comparative physiology and anatomy than in physic proper; and at this particular moment we were stopping in a very comfortable farmhouse on the coast of Flintshire for our long vacation, with the special object of observing histologically a peculiar sea-side organism, the Thingumbobbum Whatumaycallianum, which is found so plentifully on the shores of North Wales, and which has been identified by Professor Haeckel with the larva of that famous marine ascidian from whom the Professor himself and the remainder of humanity generally are supposed to be undoubtedly descended. We had brought with us a full complement of lancets and scalpels, chemicals and test-tubes, galvanic batteries and thermo-electric piles; and we were splendidly equipped for a thorough-going scientific campaign of the first water.

The farmhouse in which we lodged had formerly belonged to the county family of the Egertons; and though an Elizabethan manor replaced the ancient defensive building which had been wisely dismantled by Henry VIII., the modern farmhouse into which it had finally degenerated still bore the name of Egerton Castle.

The whole house had a reputation in the neighbourhood for being haunted by the ghost of one Algernon Egerton, who was beheaded under James II. for his participation, or rather his intention to participate, in Monmouth's rebellion. A wretched portrait of the hapless Protestant hero hung upon the wall of our joint sitting-room, having been left behind when the family moved to their new seat in Cheshire, as being unworthy of a place in the present baronet's splendid apartments. It was a few remarks upon the subject of Algernon's ghost which had introduced the question of ghosts in general; and after Harry had left the room, I sat for a while slowly finishing my cigar, and contemplating the battered features of the deceased gentleman.

As I did so, I was somewhat startled to hear a voice at my side observe in a bland and graceful tone, not unmixed with aristocratic *hauteur*, "You have been speaking of me, I believe,—in fact, I have unavoidably overheard your conversation,—and I have decided to assume the visible form and make a few remarks upon what seems to me a very hasty decision on your friend's part."

I turned round at once, and saw, in the easy-chair which Harry had just vacated, a shadowy shape, which grew clearer and clearer the longer I looked at it. It was that of a man of forty, fashionably dressed in the costume of the year 1685 or thereabouts, and bearing a close resemblance to the faded portrait on the wall just opposite. But the striking point about the object was this, that it evidently did not consist of any ordinary material substance, as its outline seemed vague and wavy, like that of a photograph where the sitter has moved; while all the objects behind it, such as the back of the chair and the clock in the corner, showed through the filmly head and body, in the very manner which painters have always adopted in representing a ghost. I saw at once that whatever else the object before might be, it certainly formed a fine specimen of the orthodox and old-fashioned apparition. In dress, appearance, and every other particular, it distinctly answered to what the unscientific mind would unhesitatingly have called the ghost of Algernon Egerton.

Here was a piece of extraordinary luck! In a house with two trained observers, supplied with every instrument of modern experimental research, we had lighted upon an undoubted specimen of the common spectre, which had so long eluded the scientific grasp. I was beside myself with delight. "Really, sir," I said, cheerfully, "it is most kind of you to pay us this visit, and I'm sure my friend will be only too happy to hear your remarks. Of course, you will permit me to call him?"

The apparition appeared somewhat surprised at the philosophic manner in which I received his advances; for ghosts are accustomed to find people faint away or scream with terror at their first appearance; but for my own part I regarded him merely in the light of a very interesting phenomenon, which required immediate observation by two independent witnesses. However, he smothered his chagrin—for I believe he was really disappointed at my cool deportment—and answered that he would be very glad to see my friend if I wished it, though he had specially intended this visit for myself alone.

I ran upstairs hastily and found Harry in his dressing-gown, on the point of removing his nether garments. "Harry," I cried breathlessly, "you must come downstairs at once. Algernon Egerton's ghost wants to speak to you."

Harry held up the candle and looked in my face with great deliberation. "Jim, my boy," he said quietly, "you've been having too much whisky."

"Not a bit of it," I answered, angrily. "Come downstairs and see. I swear to you positively that a Thing, the very counterpart of Algernon Egerton's picture, is sitting in your easy-chair downstairs, anxious to convert you to a belief in ghosts."

It took about three minutes to induce Harry to leave his room; but at last, merely to satisfy himself that I was demented, he gave way and accompanied me into the sitting-room. I was half afraid that the spectre would have taken umbrage at my long delay, and gone off in a huff and a blue flame; but when we reached the room, there he was, *in propriâ personâ*, gazing at his own portrait—or should I rather say his counterpart?—on the wall, with the utmost composure.

"Well, Harry," I said, "what do you call that?"

Harry put up his eyeglass, peered suspiciously at the phantom, and answered in a mollified tone, "It certainly is a most interesting phenomenon. It looks like a case of fluorescence; but you say the object can talk?"

"Decidedly," I answered, "it can talk as well as you or me. Allow me to introduce you to one another, gentlemen:—Mr. Henry Stevens, Mr. Algernon Egerton; for though you didn't mention your name, Mr. Egerton, I presume from what you said that I am right in my conjecture."

"Quite right," replied the phantom, rising as it spoke, and making a low bow to Harry from the waist upward. "I suppose your friend is one of the Lincolnshire Stevenses, sir?"

"Upon my soul," said Harry, "I haven't the faintest conception where my family came from. My grandfather, who made what little money we have got, was a cotton-spinner at Rochdale, but he might have come from heaven knows where. I only know he was a very honest old gentleman, and he remembered me handsomely in his will."

"Indeed, sir," said the apparition coldly. "*My* family were the Egertons of Egerton Castle, in the county of Flint, Armigeri; whose ancestor, Radulphus de Egerton, is mentioned in Domesday as one of the esquires of Hugh Lupus, Earl Palatine of Chester. Radulphus de Egerton had a son—"

"Whose history," said Harry, anxious to cut short these genealogical details, "I have read in the *Annals of Flintshire*, which lies in the next room, with the name you give as yours on the fly-leaf. But it seems, sir, you are anxious to converse with me on the subject of ghosts. As that question interests us all at present, much more than family descent, will you kindly begin by telling us whether you yourself lay claim to be a ghost? "

"Undoubtedly I do," replied the phantom.

"The ghost of Algernon Egerton, formerly of Egerton Castle?" I interposed.

"Formerly and now," said the phantom, in correction. "I have long

10

inhabited, and I still habitually inhabit, by night at least, the room in which we are at present seated."

"The deuce you do," said Harry warmly. "This is a most illegal and unconstitutional proceeding. The house belongs to our landlord, Mr. Hay: and my friend here and myself have hired it for the summer, sharing the expenses, and claiming the sole title to the use of the rooms." (Harry omitted to mention that he took the best bedroom himself and put me off with a shabby little closet, while we divided the rent on equal terms.)

"True," said the spectre good-humouredly; "but you can't eject a ghost, you know You may get a writ of *habeas corpus*, but the English law doesn't supply you with a writ of *habeas animam*. The infamous Jeffreys left me that at least. I am sure the enlightened nineteenth century wouldn't seek to deprive me of it."

"Well," said Harry, relenting, "provided you don't interfere with the experiments, or make away with the tea and sugar, I'm sure I have no objection. But if you are anxious to prove to us the existence of ghosts, perhaps you will kindly allow us to make a few simple observations?"

"With all the pleasure in death," answered the apparition courteously. "Such, in fact, is the very object for which I've assumed visibility."

"In that case, Harry," I said, "the correct thing will be to get out some paper, and draw up a running report which we may both attest afterwards. A few simple notes on the chemical and physical properties of a spectre will be an interesting novelty for the Royal Society, and they ought all to be jotted down in black and white at once."

This course having been unanimously determined upon as strictly regular, I laid a large folio of foolscap on the writing-table, and the apparition proceeded to put itself in an attitude for careful inspection.

"The first point to decide," said I, "is obviously the physical properties of our visitor. Mr. Egerton, will you kindly allow us to feel your hand?"

"You may *try* to feel it if you like," said the phantom quietly, "but I doubt if you will succeed to any brilliant extent." As he spoke, he held out his arm. Harry and I endeavoured successively to grasp it: our fingers slipped through the faintly luminous object as though it were air or shadow. The phantom bowed forward his head; we attempted to touch it, but our hands once more passed unopposed across the whole face and shoulders, without finding any trace whatsoever of mechani-

11

cal resistance.

"Experience the first," said Harry; "the apparition has no tangible material substratum." I seized the pen and jotted down the words as he spoke them. This was really turning out a very full-blown specimen of the ordinary ghost!

"The next question to settle," I said, "is that of gravity—Harry, give me a hand out here with the weighing-machine—Mr. Egerton, will you be good enough to step upon this board?"

Mirabile dictu! The board remained steady as ever. Not a tremor of the steelyard betrayed the weight of its shadowy occupant. "Experience the second," cried Harry, in his cool, scientific way: "the apparition has the specific gravity of atmospheric air." I jotted down this note also, and quietly prepared for the next observation.

"Wouldn't it be well," I inquired of Harry, "to try the weight in vacuo? It is possible that, while the specific gravity in air is equal to that of the atmosphere, the specific gravity in vacuo may be zero. The apparition—pray excuse me, Mr. Egerton, if the terms in which I allude to you seem disrespectful, but to call you a ghost would be to prejudge the point at issue—the apparition may have no proper weight of its own at all."

"It would be very inconvenient, though," said Harry, "to put the whole apparition under a bell-glass: in fact, we have none big enough. Besides, suppose we were to find that by exhausting the air we got rid of the object altogether, as is very possible, that would awkwardly interfere with the future prosecution of our researches into its nature and properties."

"Permit me to make a suggestion," interposed the phantom, "if a person whom you choose to relegate to the neuter gender may be allowed to have a voice in so scientific a question. My friend, the ingenious Mr. Boyle, has lately explained to me the construction of his air-pump, which we saw at one of the Friday evenings at the Royal Institution. It seems to me that your object would be attained if I were to put one hand only on the scale under the bell-glass, and permit the air to be exhausted."

"Capital," said Harry: and we got the air-pump in readiness accordingly. The spectre then put his right hand into the scale, and we plumped the bell-glass on top of it. The connecting portion of the arm shone through the severing glass, exactly as though the spectre consisted merely of an immaterial light. In a few minutes the air was exhausted, and the scales remained evenly balanced as before.

"This experiment," said Harry judicially, "slightly modifies the opinion which we formed from the preceding one. The specific gravity evidently amounts in itself to nothing, being as air in air, and as vacuum in vacuo. Jot down the result, Jim, will you?"

I did so faithfully, and then turning to the spectre I observed, "You mentioned a Mr. Boyle, sir, just now. You allude, I suppose, to the father of chemistry?"

"And uncle of the Earl of Cork," replied the apparition, promptly filling up the well-known quotation. "Exactly so. I knew Mr. Boyle slightly during our lifetime, and I have known him intimately ever since he joined the majority."

"May I ask, while my friend makes the necessary preparations for the spectrum analysis and the chemical investigation, whether you are in the habit of associating much with—er—well, with other ghosts?"

"Oh yes, I see a good deal of society."

"Contemporaries of your own, or persons of earlier and later dates? "

"Dates really matter very little to us. We may have Socrates and Bacon chatting in the same group. For my own part, I prefer modern society—I may say, the society of the latest arrivals."

"That's exactly why I asked," said I. "The excessively modern tone of your language and idioms struck me, so to speak, as a sort of anachronism with your Restoration costume—an anachronism which I fancy I have noticed in many printed accounts of gentlemen from your portion of the universe."

"Your observation is quite true," replied the apparition. "We continue always to wear the clothes which were in fashion at the time of our decease; but we pick up from new-comers the latest additions to the English language, and even, I may say, to the slang dictionary. I know many ghosts who talk familiarly of 'awfully jolly hops,' and allude to their progenitors as 'the governor.' Indeed, it is considered quite behind the times to describe a lady as 'vastly pretty,' and poor Mr. Pepys, who still preserves the antiquated idiom of his diary, is looked upon among us as a dreadfully slow old fogey."

"But why, then," said I, "do you wear your old costumes for ever? Why not imitate the latest fashions from Poole's and Worth's, as well as the latest cant phrase from the popular novels?"

"Why, my dear sir," answered the phantom, "we must have something to mark our original period. Besides, most people to whom we appear know something about costume, while very few know anything about changes in idiom,"—that I must say seemed to me, in passing, a powerful argument indeed—"and so we all preserve the dress which we habitually wore during our lifetime."

"Then," said Harry irreverently, looking up from his chemicals, "the society in your part of the country must closely resemble a fancy-dress ball."

"Without the tinsel and vulgarity, we flatter ourselves," answered the phantom.

By this time the preparations were complete, and Harry inquired whether the apparition would object to our putting out the lights in order to obtain definite results with the spectroscope. Our visitor politely replied that he was better accustomed to darkness than to the painful glare of our paraffin candles. "In fact," he added, "only the strong desire which I felt to convince you of our existence as ghosts could have induced me to present myself in so blight a room. Light is very trying to the eyes of spirits, and we generally take our constitutionals between eleven at night and four in the morning, stopping at home entirely during the moonlit half of the month."

"Ah, yes," said Harry, extinguishing the candles; "I've read, of course, that your authorities exactly reverse our own Oxford rules. You are all gated, I believe, from dawn to sunset, instead of from sunset to dawn, and have to run away helter-skelter at the first streaks of daylight, for fear of being too late for admission without a fine of two pence. But you will allow that your usual habit of showing yourselves only in the very darkest places and seasons naturally militates somewhat against the credibility of your existence.

"If all apparitions would only follow your sensible example by coming out before two scientific people in a well-lighted room, they would stand a much better chance of getting believed: though even in the present case I must allow that I should have felt far more confidence in your positive reality if you'd presented yourself in broad daylight, when Jim and I hadn't punished the whisky quite as fully as we've done this evening."

When the candles were out, our apparition still retained its fluorescent, luminous appearance, and seemed to burn with a faint bluish light of its own. We projected a pencil through the spectroscope, and obtained, for the first time in the history of science, the spectrum of a spectre. The result was a startling one indeed. We had expected to find lines indicating the presence of sulphur or phosphorus: instead of that, we obtained a continuous band of pale luminosity, clearly pointing to the fact that the apparition had no known terrestrial element in its composition. Though we felt rather surprised at this discovery, we simply noted it down on our paper, and proceeded to verify it by chemical analysis.

The phantom obligingly allowed us to fill a small phial with the luminous matter, which Harry immediately proceeded to test with all the resources at our disposal. For purposes of comparison I filled a corresponding phial with air from another part of the room, which I subjected to precisely similar tests. At the end of half an hour we had completed our examination—the spectre meanwhile watching us with mingled curiosity and amusement; and we laid our written quantitative results side by side. They agreed to a decimal. The table, being interesting, deserves a place in this memoir. It ran as follows:—

Chemical Analysis of an Apparition.

Atmospheric air	96.45	*per cent.*
Aqueous vapour	2.31	,,
Carbonic acid	1.08	,,
Tobacco smoke	0.16	,,
Volatile alcohol	A trace	
	———	
	100.00	

The alcohol Harry plausibly attributed to the presence of glasses which had contained whisky toddy. The other constituents would have been normally present in the atmosphere of a room where two fellows had been smoking uninterruptedly ever since dinner. This important experiment clearly showed that the apparition had no proper chemical constitution of its own, but consisted entirely of the same materials as the surrounding air.

"Only one thing remains to be done now, Jim," said Harry, glancing significantly at a plain deal table in the corner, with whose uses we were both familiar; "but then the question arises, does this gentleman come within the meaning of the Act? I don't feel certain about it in my own mind, and with the present unsettled state of public opinion on this subject, our first duty is to obey the law."

"Within the meaning of the Act?" I answered; "decidedly not. The words of the forty-second section say distinctly 'any *living* animal.' Now, Mr. Egerton, according to his own account is a ghost, and has been dead for some two hundred years or thereabouts: so that we needn't have the slightest scruple on *that* account."

"Quite so," said Harry, in a tone of relief. "Well then, sir," turning to the apparition, "may I ask you whether you would object to our vivisecting you? "

"Mortuisecting, you mean, Harry," I interposed parenthetically. "Let us keep ourselves strictly within the utmost letter of the law."

"Vivisecting? Mortuisecting?" exclaimed the spectre, with some amusement. "Really, the proposal is so very novel that I hardly know how to answer it. I don't think you will find it a very practicable undertaking: but still, if you like, yes, you may try your hands upon me."

We were both much gratified at this generous readiness to further the cause of science, for which, to say the truth, we had hardly felt prepared. No doubt, we were constantly in the habit of maintaining that vivisection didn't really hurt, and that rabbits or dogs rather enjoyed the process than otherwise; still, we did not quite expect an apparition in human form to accede in this gentlemanly manner to a personal request which after all is rather a startling one.

I seized our new friend's hand with warmth and effusion (though my emotion was somewhat checked by finding it slip through my fingers immaterially), and observed in a voice trembling with admiration, "Sir, you display a spirit of self-sacrifice which does honour to your head and heart. Your total freedom from prejudice is perfectly refreshing to the anatomical mind. If all 'subjects' were equally ready to be vivisected—no, I mean mortuisected—oh,—well,—there," I added (for I began to perceive that my argument didn't hang together, as "subjects" usually accepted mortuisection with the utmost resignation), "perhaps it wouldn't make much difference after all."

Meanwhile Harry had pulled the table into the centre of the room, and arranged the necessary instruments at one end. The bright steel had a most charming and scientific appearance, which added greatly to the general effect. I saw myself already in imagination drawing up an elaborate report for the Royal Society, and delivering a Croonian Oration, with diagrams and sections complete, in illustration of the *Vascular System of a Ghost*. But alas, it was not to be. A preliminary difficulty, slight in itself, yet enormous in its preventive effects, unhappily defeated our well-made plans.

"Before you lay yourself on the table," said Harry, gracefully indicating that article of furniture to the spectre with his lancet, "may I ask you to oblige me by removing your clothes? It is usual in all these operations to—ahem—in short, to proceed *in puris naturalibus*. As you have been so very kind in allowing us to operate upon you, of course you won't object to this minor but indispensable accompaniment."

"Well, really, sir," answered the ghost, "I should have no personal objection whatsoever; but I'm rather afraid it can't be done. To tell you the truth, my clothes are an integral part of myself. Indeed, I consist chiefly of clothes, with only a head and hands protruding at the principal extremities. You must have noticed that all persons of my sort about whom you have read or heard were fully clothed in the fashion of their own day. I fear it would be quite impossible to remove these clothes. For example, how very absurd it would be to see the shadowy outline of a ghostly coat hanging up on a peg behind a door. The bare notion would be sufficient to cast ridicule upon the whole community. No, gentlemen, much as I should like to gratify you, I fear the thing's impossible. And, to let the whole secret out, I'm inclined to think, for my part, that I haven't got any independent body whatsoever."

"But, surely," I interposed, "you must have some internal economy, or else how can you walk and talk? For example, have you a heart? "

"Most certainly, my dear sir, and I humbly trust it is in the right place."

"You misunderstand me," I repeated: "I am speaking literally, not figuratively. Have you a central vascular organ on your left-hand side, with two auricles and ventricles, a mitral and a tricuspid valve, and the usual accompaniment of aorta, pulmonary vein, pulmonary artery, systole and diastole, and so forth? "

"Upon my soul, sir," replied the spectre with an air of bewilderment, "I have never even heard the names of these various objects to which you refer, and so I am quite unable to answer your question. But if you mean to ask whether I have something beating just under my fob (excuse the antiquated word, but as I wear the thing in question, I must necessarily use the name), why then, most undoubtedly I have."

"Will you oblige me, sir," said Harry, "by showing me your wrist? It is true I can't *feel* your pulse, owing to what you must acknowledge as a very unpleasant tenuity in your component tissues: but perhaps I may succeed in seeing it."

The apparition held out its arm. Harry instinctively endeavoured to balance the wrist in his hand, but of course failed in catching it. We were both amused throughout to observe how difficult it remained, after several experiences, to realize the fact that this visible object had no material and tangible background underlying it. Harry put up his eyeglass and gazed steadily at the phantom arm; not a trace of veins or arteries could anywhere be seen. "Upon my word," he muttered, "I believe it's true, and the subject has no internal economy at all. This is really very interesting."

"As it is quite impossible to undress you," I observed, turning to our visitor, "may I venture to make a section through your chest, in order, if practicable, to satisfy myself as to your organs generally?"

"Certainly," replied the good-humoured spectre; "I am quite at your service."

I took my longest lancet from its case and made a very neat cut, right across the sternum, so as to pass directly through all the principal viscera. The effect, I regret to say, was absolutely nugatory. The two halves of the body reunited instantaneously behind the instrument, just as a mass of mercury reunites behind a knife. Evidently there was no chance of getting at the anatomical details, if any existed, underneath that brocaded waistcoat of phantasmagoric satin. We gave up the attempt in despair.

"And now," said the shadowy form, with a smile of conscious triumph, flinging itself easily but noiselessly into a comfortable armchair, "I hope you are convinced that ghosts really do exist. I think I have pretty fully demonstrated to you my own purely spiritual and immaterial nature."

"Excuse me," said Harry, seating himself in his turn on the ottoman: "I regret to say that I remain as sceptical as at the beginning. You have merely convinced me that a certain visible shape exists apparently unaccompanied by any tangible properties. With this phenomenon I am already familiar in the case of phosphorescent gaseous effluvia. You also seem to utter audible words without the aid of a proper larynx or other muscular apparatus; but the telephone has taught me that sounds exactly resembling those of the human voice may be produced by a very simple membrane. You have afforded us probably the best opportunity ever given for examining a so-called ghost, and my private conviction at the end of it is that you are very likely an egregious humbug."

I confess I was rather surprised at this energetic conclusion, for my own faith had been rapidly expanding under the strange experiences of that memorable evening. But the visitor himself seemed much hurt and distressed. "Surely," he said, "you won't doubt my word when I tell you plainly that I am the authentic ghost of Algernon Egerton. The word of an Egerton of Egerton Castle was always better than another man's oath, and it is so still, I hope. Besides, my frank and courteous conduct to you both tonight, and the readiness with which I have met all your proposals for scientific examination, certainly entitle me to better treatment at your hands."

I must beg ten thousand pardons," Harry replied, "for the plain language which I am compelled to use. But let us look at the case in a different point of view. During your occasional visits to the world of living men; you may sometimes have travelled in a railway carriage in your invisible form."

"I have taken a trip now and then (by a night train, of course), just to see what the invention was like."

"Exactly so. Well, now, you must have noticed that a guard insisted from time to time upon waking up the sleepy passengers for no other purpose than to look at their tickets. Such a precaution might be resented, say by an Egerton of Egerton Castle, as an insult to his veracity and his honesty. But, you see, the guard doesn't know an Egerton from a Muggins: and the mere word of a passenger to the effect that he belongs to that distinguished family is in itself of no more value than his personal assertion that his ticket is perfectly *en règle*."

"I see your analogy, and I must allow its remarkable force."

"Not only so," continued Harry firmly, "but you must remember that in the case I have put, the guard is dealing with known beings of the ordinary human type. Now, when a living person introduces himself to me as Egerton of Egerton Castle, or Sir Roger Tichborne of Alresford, I accept his statement with a certain amount of doubt, proportionate to the natural improbability of the circumstances. But when a gentleman of shadowy appearance and immaterial substance, like yourself, makes a similar assertion, to the effect that he is Algernon Egerton who died two hundred years ago, then I am reluctantly compelled to acknowledge, even at the risk of hurting that gentleman's susceptible feelings, that I can form no proper opinion whatsoever of his probable veracity.

" Even men, whose habits and constitution I familiarly understand, cannot always be trusted to tell me the truth: and how then can I expect implicitly to believe a being whose very existence contradicts all my previous experiences, and whose properties give the lie to all my scientific conceptions—a being who moves without muscles and speaks without lungs? Look at the possible alternatives, and then you will see that I am guilty of no personal rudeness when I respectfully decline to accept your uncorroborated assertions. You may be Mr. Algernon Egerton, it is true, and your general style of dress and appearance certainly bears out that supposition; but then you may equally well be his Satanic Majesty in person—in which case you can hardly expect me to credit your character for implicit truthfulness.

"Or again, you may be a mere hallucination of my fancy: I may be suddenly gone mad, or I may be totally drunk—and now that I look at the bottle, Jim, we must certainly allow that we have fully appreciated the excellent qualities of your capital Glenlivat. In short, a number of alternatives exist, any one of which is quite as probable as the supposition of your being a genuine ghost; which supposition I must therefore lay aside as a mere matter for the exercise of a suspended judgment."

I thought Harry had him on the hip, there: and the spectre evidently thought so too; for he rose at once and said rather stiffly, "I fear, sir, you are a confirmed sceptic upon this point, and further argument might only result in one or the other of us losing his temper. Perhaps it would be better for me to withdraw. I have the honour to wish you both a very good evening." He spoke once more with the hauteur and grand mannerism of the old school, besides bowing very low at each of us separately as he wished us goodnight.

"Stop a moment," said Harry rather hastily. "I wouldn't for the world be guilty of any inhospitality, and least of all to a gentleman, however indefinite in his outline, who has been so anxious to afford us every chance of settling an interesting question as you have. Won't you take a glass of whisky and water before you go, just to show there's no animosity?"

"I thank you," answered the apparition, in the same chilly tone; "I cannot accept your kind offer. My visit has already extended to a very unusual length, and I have no doubt I shall be blamed as it is by more reticent ghosts for the excessive openness with which I have conversed upon subjects generally kept back from the living world. Once more," with another ceremonious bow, "I have the honour to wish you a pleasant evening."

As he said these words, the fluorescent light brightened for a second, and then faded entirely away. A slightly unpleasant odour also accompanied the departure of our guest. In a moment, spectre and scent alike disappeared; but careful examination with a delicate test exhibited a faint reaction which proved the presence of sulphur in small quantities. The ghost had evidently vanished quite according to established precedent.

We filled our glasses once more, drained them off meditatively, and turned into our bedrooms as the clock was striking four.

Next morning, Harry and I drew up a formal account of the whole circumstance, which we sent to the Royal Society, with a request that they would publish it in their Transactions. To our great surprise, that learned body refused the paper, I may say with contumely. We next applied to the Anthropological Institute, where, strange to tell, we met with a like inexplicable rebuff. Nothing daunted by our double failure, we despatched a copy of our analysis to the Chemical Society; but the only acknowledgment accorded to us was a letter from the secretary, who stated that "such a sorry joke was at once impertinent and undignified." In short, the scientific world utterly refuses to credit our simple and straightforward narrative; so that we are compelled to throw ourselves for justice upon the general reading public at large.

As the latter invariably peruse the pages of *Belgravia*, I have ventured to appeal to them in the present article, confident that they will redress our wrongs, and accept this valuable contribution to a great scientific question at its proper worth. It may be many years before another chance occurs for watching an undoubted and interesting Apparition under such favourable circumstances for careful observation; and all the above information may be regarded as absolutely correct, down to five places of decimals.

Still, it must be borne in mind that unless an apparition had been scientifically observed as we two independent witnesses observed this one, the grounds for believing in its existence would have been next to none. And even after the clear evidence which we obtained of its immaterial nature, we yet remain entirely in the dark as to its objective reality, and we have not the faintest reason for believing it to have been a genuine unadulterated ghost. At the best we can only say that we saw and heard Something, and that this Something differed very widely from almost any other object we had ever seen and heard before. To leap at the conclusion that the Something was therefore a ghost, would be, I venture humbly to submit, without offence to the Psychical Research Society, a most unscientific and illogical specimen of that peculiar fallacy known as Begging the Question.

My One Gorilla

I looked up from my beetles. The night was warm.

A naked little black girl crossed the dusty main street of the village just in front of my hut, carrying in her hand what seemed to me in the gloaming the largest blossom I had ever observed since my arrival in Africa. That *was* a blossom. It looked like an orchid, pale cream-colour in hue, and very fantastic and bizarre in shape; but what specially attracted my attention at first was its peculiar shining and glistening effect, like luminous paint, which made it glow in the grey dusk with a sort of phosphorescent light such as one observes in tropical seas on calm summer evenings.

To a naturalist, of course, such a vision as that was simply irresistible. "Hullo, there, little girl!" I cried out in Fantee, which I had learned by that time to speak pretty fluently; "let me look at your flower, will you? Where on earth did you get it?"

But instead of answering me civilly, like a Christian child, the scared little savage, alarmed at my white face, set up a wild howl of terror and amazement, and bolted off down the street at the top of her speed, as fast as her small bandy legs would carry her.

Well, science is science. I wasn't to be balked of a unique specimen for my great collection by a trick like that. So, flinging away my cigarette and darting out of my hut, I gave chase incontinently, and rushed, full pelt, down the main street of Tulamba, helter-skelter and devil-take-the-hindmost, in pursuit of my ten-year old.

But I reckoned without my host. Children of the Gaboon beat the record for the quarter-mile. I was quite pumped out and panting for breath before I ran that girl to the earth at last, by her mother's door at the far end of the village. A dozen more of the negroes, loitering about on their backs in the dust of the street, had joined the hue and cry with great gusto by that time. They didn't know, to be sure, what the fuss was about; but given a white man—bestower of rum and money—rushing in mad pursuit, and a poor little frightened black girl scampering away for dear life at the top of her speed, in abject bodily terror, and you may confidently reckon on the chivalry of the Gaboon to range itself automatically on the side of the stronger, and to drive the unhappy small child hopelessly into a very bad corner.

When at last I got up with the object of my quest, she was so alarmed and blown with her headlong career that I felt thoroughly ashamed of myself. Even the pursuit of science, I will frankly admit, hardly justified me in so chivvying that frightened little mortal, ten negroes strong, through the street of Tulamba. However, a bright English sixpence, a red silk pocket-handkerchief, and the promise of a box of European sweets from the old half-caste Portuguese trader's shop in the village, soon restored her confidence.

Unhappily, it did not restore that broken and draggled, but priceless, orchid. In her headlong flight, the child had crumpled it hopelessly up in her hand, and distorted it almost beyond the possibility of scientific recognition. All I could make out with certainty now was that the orchid belonged to a new and hitherto undescribed species; that it was large and luminous and extremely beautiful; and that if only I could succeed in securing a plant of it, my name was made as a scientific explorer.

The natives crowded round with disinterested advice, and eyed the torn and draggled blossom curiously. "It's a moon-flower," they said in their own dialect. "Very rare. Hard to get. Comes from the deep shades in the great forest."

"How did you come by it, my child?" I asked, coaxingly, of my sobbing little ten-year old.

"My father brought it in," the child answered, with a burst. "He gave it to me a week ago. He was out in the country of the dwarfs, doing trade. He went for ivory, and he brought this back to me."

"Boys," I cried to the negroes who crowded round, looking on, "do you know where it lives? I want to get one. A good English rifle to any man in Tulamba who guides me to the spot where I can pick a live moon-flower!"

The men shook their heads and shrugged their shoulders dubiously.

"Oh, no," they all answered, like supers at the theatre, with one accord. "Too far! Too dangerous!"

"Why dangerous?" I cried, laughing. "The moon-flower won't bite

24

you. Who says danger in picking a flower?"

My head guide and hunter stood out from the crowd, and looked across at me, awe-struck. "Oh, excellency," he said, in a hushed and frightened voice, "the moon-flower is rare; it is very scarce; it grows only in the dark forest of the inner land where the *Ngina* dwells. No man dare pick it for fear of the *Ngina*."

"Oho," said I. "Is that so, my friend? Then I'm not astonished." For *Ngina*, as no doubt you're already aware, is the native West African name for the gorilla.

Well, I took home the poor draggled blossom to my hut, dissected it carefully, and made what scientific study was possible of its unhappy remains in their much-tattered condition. But for the next ten days, as you can readily believe, I could think and talk and dream of nothing but moon-flowers. You can't think what a fascination it exerts on a naturalist explorer's mind—a new orchid like that, as big round as a dessert plate, and marked by so extraordinary and hitherto unknown a peculiarity in plants as phosphorescence. For the moon-flower was phosphorescent; of that I had now not the shadow of a doubt. Its petals gave out by night a faint and dreamy luminousness, which must have made it shine like a moon indeed in the dense dark shade of a tropical African forest.

The more I inquired of the natives about this new plant, the more was my curiosity piqued to possess one. I longed to bring a root of the marvellous bloom to Europe. For the natives all spoke of it with a certain hushed awe or superstitious respect: "It is *Ngina's* flower," they said. "It grows in dark places—the gardens of *Ngina*. If any man breaks one off, that is very bad luck; the *Ngina* will surely overtake and destroy him."

This superstitious awe only inflamed my desire to possess a root. The negroes' stories showed the moon-flower to be really a most unique species. I gathered from what they told me that the blossom had a very long spur or sac, containing honey at its base in great quantities; that it was fertilised and rifled by a huge evening moth, whose proboscis was exactly adapted in length to the spur and its nectary; that it was creamy white in order to attract the insect's eyes in the grey shades of dusk; and that, for the self-same reason, its petals were endowed with the strange quality of phosphorescence, till now unknown in the vegetable kingdom; while it exhaled by night a delicious perfume, strong enough to be perceived at some twenty yards' distance. So great a prize to a man of my tastes was simply irresistible.

I made up my mind that, come what might, I must, could and would possess a tuber of the moon-flower.

One fortnight sufficed for me to make my final plans. Heavy bribes overcame the scruples of the negroes. The promise of a good rifle induced the first finder of the first specimen to take service with me as a guide. Fully equipped for a week's march, and well attended with followers all armed to the teeth, I made my start at last for the home of the moon-flower.

To cut a long story short, we went for three days into the primeval shade of the great equatorial African forest. Dense roofs of foliage shut out the light of day; underfoot, the ground was encumbered with thick, tropical brushwood. We crept along cautiously, hacking our way at times among the brake with our cutlasses, and crawling at others through the deep tangle of the underbrush on all fours like monkeys. During all those three days we never caught sight of a single moon-flower. They were growing very rare nowadays, my guide explained in most voluble Fantee. When he was a mere boy, his father found dozens of them; but now, why, you must go miles and miles through the depths of the forest and never so much as light on a specimen.

At last, about noon on the fourth day out, we came upon a torrent, rushing with great velocity among huge boulders, and sending up the spray of its boiling rapids into the trees of the neighbourhood. I sat down to rest, meaning to mix the water from the cool, fresh stream with a spoonful or two of cognac from the flask in my pocket. As I drank it, I tossed back my head and looked up. Something on one of the trees hard by attracted my eyes strangely. A parasite stood out boldly from a fork of the branches, bearing a long, lithe spray of huge luminous flowers as big as dessert-plates. My heart gave a bound; the prize was within sight. I pointed my finger in silence to the tree. All the negroes with one voice raised a loud shout of triumph. Their words rent the air: "The moon-flower—the moon-flower!"

I felt myself for a moment a perfect Stanley or Du Chaillu. I had discovered the most marvellous and beautiful orchid known to science.

In a moment I had tossed off my brandy, laid down my rifle, and mounting on the back of one of my negro porters, was swinging myself up to the lowest branch of the tree where my new treasure shone resplendent in its own dim phosphorescence. I couldn't have trusted any hand but my own to pick or egg out that glorious tuber. I meant to cut it bodily from the bark as it stood, and bear it back in triumph in my own arms to Tulamba.

I had climbed the tree cautiously, and was standing almost within grasp of the prize, when a sudden shout among my followers below startled and discomposed me. I looked down and hesitated. My brain reeled and sickened. A strange sight met my eyes. My negroes, one and all, had taken to their feet down the bed of the stream at the very top of their speed, and were making a most unanimous and inexplicable stampede toward the direction of Tulamba.

For a moment I couldn't imagine what had happened to discon-cert them; the, casting my glance casually towards the spot where I had flung down my rifle, I became aware at once of the cause of this commotion. Their retreat was well-timed. By the moss-clad boulders which filled the bed of the torrent, somebody with a big, black face and huge grinning teeth, was standing erect, looking up at me and laughing. I had never seen the somebody's awful features before, but I had no need, for all that, to ask myself his name. I paused face to face with a live male gorilla.

For a moment or two, the creature gazed up at me and grinned. Then he raised my rifle in his arms; held it clumsily before him; and, to my intense surprise, taking a very bad aim, or, rather pointing it aim-lessly in the air, pulled both triggers with one hand, and discharged the two barrels at me with one pull, simultaneously. The bullets whizzed past me some ten yards off. They knocked off the twigs beyond my precious moon-flower.

Well, I don't deny, as I say, that I was in a state of blue funk at the creature's gigantic and almost supernatural powers. But still, the moon-flower was at stake, and I wouldn't desert it. I was so horribly fright-ened that I don't believe wife, or child, or fatherland, or freedom would have induced me to stay one moment alone in such dire extremities. But when it comes to orchids! Well, I say no more than that I am above all things a scientific explorer; each of us has his weakness; and mine is a flower. That touches my heart. For that alone can I be wrought up to the utmost pitch of daring conceivable or possible for me.

So, I looked at the huge brute, and I looked at the moon-flower. Slowly and cautiously, gazing down all the time as I went to watch the creature's face, I crept along the branch, took my knife from my pocket, and began to loosen the bark all round the spot where the glorious parasite was all a-growing and all a-blowing. The gorilla, from below, stood watching me and roaring. His roar seemed like an invi-tation to come down and fight. I never in my life heard anything so awfully human in its deep bass roll. It reminded me of the lowest notes of the stage villain in the Italian operas, magnified, so to speak, two hundred diameters.

Presently, as I went on cutting away the bark, as if for dear life, and loosening the precious tuber, my gorilla, who still remained motionless by his moss-clad boulder, left off his roaring, and appeared to grow interested in the process of the operation. A change came o'er the spirit of his dream. He looked up and wondered, with vague brute curiosity, not unmixed with a certain strange air of low cunning and intelligence. It was clear to me as mud that he was saying to himself inwardly, "Why doesn't the fellow cut and run for his life? Does he think I don't know how to climb a tree? Does he imagine that I couldn't be up there in a jiffy if I liked—to choke or scrag him? What the dickens does he go on hacking away at the bark so quietly like that for, when he ought to be all agog to save his own bacon?"

I despaired of explaining to so rude a creature the imperative nature of scientific need. So, with one eye on the orchid and one on the brute, at the risk of contracting a permanent squint for life, I continued to egg out that magnificent moon-flower, root and branch and tuber.

The longer I went on, the closer and more attentively did the gorilla take stock of all my acts and movements. "Well, I declare," I could see him say to himself in the gorilla tongue, opening wide his huge eyes and elevating in surprise his shaggy, brown eyebrows, "such an animal as this I never yet did come across. He isn't one bit afraid, apparently of *me*, the redoubtable and redoubted king of the great Gaboon forest."

But I *was*, most consumedly, for all that, though I pretended not to be. Nothing but the presence before my eyes of that magnificent plant would have induced me for one moment to face or confront the unspeakable brute there.

At last I had finished, and held my specimen in my hands entire. The next question now was what to do with it.

I walked slowly and cautiously along the branch of the tree. The gorilla, with his eyes now fixed curiously on the moon-flower, put forth one hairy leg in front of the other, and grinning with a sort of diabolical, brutish good-humour, walked, step for step, on the ground, just as cautiously beneath me.

I came to the end of the bough, and reached the point where interlacing branches enabled me to get on to another tree. I did so somewhat clumsily, for I was handicapped by the moon-flower. The gorilla, still grinning, looked up, and remarked in his own tongue, "I could do that lot, I can tell you, a jolly sight better than you do."

As he smiled those words, I half lost my balance, and, clinging still to my moon-flower in my last chance for life, lowered myself slowly, hand over hand, to the ground in front of him.

With a frightful roar, the creature sprang upon me—and made a wild grab at my precious moon-flower. That was more than human scientific human nature could stand. I turned and fled, carrying my specimen with me. But my pursuer was too quick. He caught me up in a moment. His scowling black face was ghastly to behold; his huge, white teeth gleamed fierce and hideous; his brawny, thick hands could have crushed me to a jelly. I panted and paused. My heart fluttered fast, the stood still within me. There was a second's suspense. At its end, to my infinite horror, he seized—not me-oh no, not me—I might have put up with *that*—but the priceless moon-flower!

I was helpless to defend myself. Helpless to secure or safeguard my treasure. He took it from me with a grin. I could see through those sunken eyes what was passing in the creature's dim and brutal brain. He was saying to himself, like men at his own low grade of cunning, "If that tuber was worth so much pains to *him* to get it, it must be worth just as much to me to keep. So, by your leave, my friend, if you'll excuse me, I'll take it."

I stood appalled and gazed at him. The brute snatched that unique specimen of a dying or almost extinct genus in his swarthy, hairy hands of his—raised it bodily to his mouth, crushing and tearing the beautiful petals in his coarse grasp as he went—ate it slowly through, tuber, stem, spray, blossom—and swallowed it conscientiously, with a hideous grimace, to the very last morsel. I had but one grain of consolation or revenge. It was clear the taste was exceedingly nasty.

Then he looked in my face and burst into a loud, discordant laugh. That laugh was hideous.

"Aha!" it said in effect, "so *that's* all you've got, my fine fellow, after all, for all your pains, and care, and trouble!"

I shut my eyes and waited. *My* turn would come next. He would rend me in his rage for the nastiness of the taste. I stood still and shuddered. But, alas, he meant only to eat the moon-flower.

When I opened my eyes again, the brute had turned his back without one word of apology, and was walking off at a leisurely pace in contemptuous triumph, shrugging his shoulders as he went, and chuckling low to himself in his vulgar dog-in-the-manger joy and malignancy.

It was four days before I straggled alone, half dead, into Tulamba. I never came across another of those orchids. And that is why at Kew they have still no moon-flower.

The Search Party's Find

I can stand it no longer. I must put down my confession on paper, since there is no living creature left to whom I can confess it.

The snow is drifting fiercer than ever today against the cabin; the last biscuit is almost finished; my fingers are so pinched with cold I can hardly grasp the pen to write with. But I *will* write, I must write, and I am writing. I cannot die with the dreadful story unconfessed upon my conscience.

It was only an accident, most of you who read this confession perhaps will say; but in my own heart I know better than that—I know it was a murder, a wicked murder.

Still, though my hands are very numb, and my head swimming wildly with delirium, I will try to be coherent, and to tell my story clearly and collectedly.

★★★★★★

I was appointed surgeon of the *Cotopaxi* in June, 1880. I had reasons of my own—sad reasons—for wishing to join an Arctic expedition. I didn't join it, as most of the other men did, from pure love of danger and adventure. I am not a man to care for that sort of thing on its own account. I joined it because of a terrible disappointment.

For two years I had been engaged to Dora—I needn't call her anything but Dora; my brother, to whom I wish this paper sent, but whom I daren't address as "Dear Arthur"—how could I, a murderer?—will know well enough who I mean; and as to other people, it isn't needful they should know anything about it. But whoever you are, whoever finds this paper, I beg of you, I implore you, I adjure you, do not tell a word of it to Dora. I cannot die unconfessed, but I cannot let the confession reach *her*; if it does, I know the double shock will kill her. Keep it from her. Tell her only he is dead—dead at his post, like a brave man, on the *Cotopaxi* exploring expedition. For mercy's

31

sake don't tell her that he was murdered, and that I murdered him.

I had been engaged, I said, two years to Dora. She lived in Arthur's parish, and I loved her—yes, in those days I loved her purely, devotedly, innocently. I was innocent then myself, and I really believe good and well-meaning. I should have been genuinely horrified and indignant if anybody had ventured to say that I should end by committing a murder.

It was a great grief to me when I had to leave Arthur's parish, and my father's parish before him, to go up to London and take a post as surgeon to a small hospital. I couldn't bear being so far away from Dora. And at first Dora wrote to me almost every day with the greatest affection. (Heaven forgive me, if I still venture to call her Dora! her, so good and pure and beautiful, and I, a murderer.) But, after a while, I noticed slowly that Dora's tone seemed to grow colder and colder, and her letters less and less frequent. Why she should have begun to cease loving me, I cannot imagine; perhaps she had a premonition of what possibility of wickedness was really in me.

At any rate, her coldness grew at last so marked that I wrote and asked Arthur whether he could explain it. Arthur answered me, a little regretfully, and with brotherly affection (he is a good fellow, Arthur), that he thought he could. He feared—it was painful to say so—but he feared Dora was beginning to love a newer lover. A young man had lately come to the village of whom she had seen a great deal, and who was very handsome and brave and fascinating. Arthur was afraid he could not conceal from me his impression that Dora and the stranger were very much taken with one another.

At last, one morning, a letter came to me from Dora. I can put it in here, because I carried it away with me when I went to Hammerfest to join the *Cotopaxi*, and ever since I have kept it sadly in my private pocket-book.

> Dear Ernest (she had always called me Ernest since we had been children together, and she couldn't leave it off even now when she was writing to let me know she no longer loved me),
> Can you forgive me for what I am going to tell you? I thought I loved you till lately; but then I had never discovered what love really meant. I have discovered it now, and I find that, after all, I only liked you very sincerely. You will have guessed before this that I love somebody else, who loves me in return with all the strength of his whole nature. I have made a grievous mistake,

which I know will render you terribly unhappy. But it is better so than to marry a man whom I do not really love with all my heart and soul and affection; better in the end, I am sure, for both of us. I am too much ashamed of myself to write more to you. Can you forgive me?

Yours,

Dora.

I could not forgive her then, though I loved her too much to be angry; I was only broken-hearted—thoroughly stunned and broken-hearted. I can forgive her now, but she can never forgive me, Heaven help me!

I only wanted to get away, anywhere, anywhere, and forget all about it in a life of danger. So, I asked for the post of surgeon to Sir Paxton Bateman's *Cotopaxi* expedition a few weeks afterwards. They wanted a man who knew something about natural history and deep-sea dredging, and they took me on at once, on the recommendation of a well-known man of science!

The very day I joined the ship at Hammerfest, in August, I noticed immediately there was one man on board whose mere face and bearing and manner were at first sight excessively objectionable to me. He was a handsome young fellow enough—one Harry Lemarchant, who had been a planter in Queensland, and who, after being burned up with three years of tropical sunshine was anxious to cool himself apparently by a long winter of Arctic gloom. Handsome as he was, with his black moustache and big dark eyes rolling restlessly, I took an instantaneous dislike to his cruel thin lip and cold proud mouth the moment I looked upon him. If I had been wise, I would have drawn back from the expedition at once. It is a foolish thing to bind one's self down to a voyage of that sort unless you are perfectly sure beforehand that you have at least no instinctive hatred of any one among your messmates in that long, forced companionship. But I wasn't wise, and I went on with him.

From the first moment, even before I had spoken to him, I disliked Lemarchant; very soon I grew to hate him. He seemed to me the most recklessly cruel and devilish creature (God forgive me that I should say it!) I had ever met with in my whole lifetime. On an Arctic expedition, a man's true nature soon comes out—mine did certainly—and he lets his companions know more about his inner self in six weeks than they could possibly learn about him in years of intercourse under other circumstances. And the second night I was on board the *Cotopaxi* I learnt enough to make my blood run cold about Harry Lemarchant's ideas and feelings.

We were all sitting on deck together, those of us who were not on duty, and listening to yarns from one another, as idle men will, when the conversation happened accidentally to turn on Queensland, and Lemarchant began to enlighten us about his own doings when he was in the colony. He boasted a great deal about his prowess as a disperser of the black fellows, which he seemed to consider a very noble sort of occupation. There was nobody in the colony, he said, who had ever dispersed so many blacks as he had; and he'd like to be back there, dispersing again, for, in the matter of sport, it beat kangaroo-hunting, or any other kind of shooting he had ever yet tried his hand at, all to pieces.

The second-lieutenant, Hepworth Paterson, a nice kind-hearted young Scotchman, looked up at him a little curiously, and said, "Why, what do you mean by dispersing, Lemarchant? Driving them off into the bush, I suppose: isn't that it? Not much fun in that, that I can see, scattering a lot of poor helpless black naked savages."

Lemarchant curled his lip contemptuously (he didn't think much of Paterson, because his father was said to be a Glasgow grocer), and answered in his rapid, dare-devil fashion: "No fun! Isn't there, just! that's all you know about it, my good fellow. Now I'll give you one example. One day, the inspector came in and told us there were a lot of blacks camping out on our estate down by the Warramidgee River. So, we jumped on our horses like a shot, went down there immediately, and began dispersing them.

We didn't fire at them, because the grass and ferns and things were very high, and we might have wasted our ammunition; but we went at them with native spears, just for all the world like pig-sticking. You should have seen those black fellows run for their lives through the long grass—men, women, and little ones together. We rode after them, full pelt; and as we came up with them, one by one, we just rolled them over, helter-skelter, as if they'd been antelopes or bears or something. By-and-by, after a good long charge or two, we'd cleared the place of the big blacks altogether; but the gins and the children, some of them, lay lurking in among the grass, you know, and wouldn't come out and give us fair sport, as they ought to have done, out in the open: children will pack, you see, whenever they're hard driven, exactly like grouse, after a month or two's steady shooting. Well, to make them start and show game, of course we just put a match to the grass; and in a minute the whole thing was in a blaze, right down the corner to the two rivers.

So we turned our horses into the stream, and rode alongside, half a dozen of us on each river; and every now and then, one of the young ones would break cover, and slide out quietly into the stream, and try to swim across without being perceived, and get clean away into the back country. Then we just made a dash at them with the pig-spears; and sometimes they'd dive—and precious good divers they are, too, those Queenslanders, I can tell you; but we waited around till they came up again, and then we stuck them as sure as houses. That's what we call dispersing the natives over in Queensland: extending the blessings of civilization to the unsettled parts of the back country."

He laughed a pleasant laugh to himself quietly as he finished this atrocious, devilish story, and showed his white teeth all in a row, as if he thought the whole reminiscence exceedingly amusing.

Of course, we were all simply speechless with horror and astonishment. Such deliberate brutal murderousness—gracious heavens! what am I saying? I had half-forgotten for the moment that I, too, am a murderer.

"But what had the black fellows done to you?" Paterson asked with a tone of natural loathing, after we had all sat silent and horror-stricken in a circle for a moment. "I suppose they'd been behaving awfully badly to some white people somewhere—massacring women or something—to get your blood up to such a horrid piece of butchery."

Lemarchant laughed again, a quiet chuckle of conscious superiority, and only answered: "Behaving badly! Massacring white women! Lord bless your heart, I'd like to see them! Why, the wretched creatures wouldn't ever dare to do it. Oh, no, nothing of that sort, I can tell you. And our blood wasn't up either. We went in for it just by way of something to do, and to keep our hands in. Of course, you can't allow a lot of lazy hulking blacks to go knocking around in the neighbourhood of an estate, stealing your fowls and fruit and so forth, without let or hindrance. It's the custom in Queensland to disperse the black fellows. I've often been out riding with a friend, and I've seen a n——r skulking about somewhere down in a hollow among the tree-ferns; and I've just drawn my six-shooter, and said to my friend, 'You see me disperse that confounded n——r!' and I've dispersed him right off—into little pieces, too, you may take your oath upon it."

"But do you mean to tell me, Mr. Lemarchant," Paterson said, looking a deal more puzzled and shocked, "that these poor creatures had been doing absolutely nothing?"

"Well, now, that's the way of all you home-sticking sentimentalists," Lemarchant went on, with an ugly simper. "You want to push on the outskirts of civilization and to see the world colonised, but you're too squeamish to listen to anything about the only practicable civilizing and colonizing agencies. It's the struggle for existence, don't you see: the plain outcome of all the best modern scientific theories. The black man has got to go to the wall; the white man, with his superior moral and intellectual nature, has got to push him there. At bottom, it's nothing more than civilization. Shoot 'em off at once, I say, and get rid of 'em forthwith and for ever."

"Why," I said, looking at him, with my disgust speaking in my face (Heaven forgive me!), "I call it nothing less than murder."

Lemarchant laughed, and lit his cigar; but after that, somehow, the other men didn't much care to talk to him in an ordinary way more than was necessary for the carrying out of the ship's business.

And yet he was a very gentlemanly fellow, I must admit, and well-read and decently educated. Only there seemed to be a certain natural brutality about him, under a thin veneer of culture and good breeding, that repelled us all dreadfully from the moment we saw him. I dare say we shouldn't have noticed it so much if we hadn't been thrown together so closely as men are on an Arctic voyage, but then and there it was positively unendurable. We none of us held any communications with him whenever we could help it; and he soon saw that we all of us thoroughly disliked and distrusted him.

That only made him reckless and defiant. He knew he was bound to go the journey through with us now, and he set to work deliberately to shock and horrify us. Whether all the stories he told us by the ward-room fire in the evenings were true or not, I can't tell you—I don't believe they all were; but at any rate he made them seem as brutal and disgusting as the most loathsome details could possibly make them. He was always apologising—nay, glorying—in bloodshed and slaughter, which he used to defend with a show of cultivated reasoning that made the naked brutality of his stories seem all the more awful and unpardonable at bottom.

And yet one couldn't deny, all the time, that there was a grace of manner and a show of polite feeling about him which gave him a certain external pleasantness, in spite of everything. He was always boasting that women liked him; and I could easily understand how a great many women who saw him only with his company manners might even think him brave and handsome and very chivalrous.

I won't go into the details of the expedition. They will be found fully and officially narrated in the log, which I have hidden in the captain's box in the hut beside the captain's body. I need only mention here the circumstances immediately connected with the main matter of this confession.

★★★★★★

One day, a little while before we got jammed into the ice off the Liakov Islands, Lemarchant was up on deck with me, helping me to remove from the net the creatures that we had dredged up in our shallow soundings. As he stooped to pick out a *Leptocardium boreale*, I happened to observe that a gold locket had fallen out of the front of his waistcoat, and showed a lock of hair on its exposed surface. Lemarchant noticed it too, and with an awkward laugh put it back hurriedly. "My little girl's keepsake!" he said in a tone that seemed to me disagreeably flippant about such a subject. "She gave it to me just before I set off on my way to Hammerfest."

I started in some astonishment. He had a little girl then—a sweetheart he meant, obviously. If so, Heaven help her! poor soul, Heaven help her! For any woman to be tied for life to such a creature as that was really quite too horrible. I didn't even like to think upon it.

I don't know what devil prompted me, for I seldom spoke to him, even when we were told off on duty together; but I said at last, after a moment's pause, "If you are engaged to be married, as I suppose you are from what you say, I wonder you could bear to come away on such a long business as this, when you couldn't get a word or a letter from the lady you're engaged to for a whole winter."

He went on picking out the shells and weeds as he answered in a careless, jaunty tone, "Why, to tell you the truth, doctor, that was just about the very meaning of it. We're going to be married next summer, you see, and for reasons of her papa's—the deuce knows what!—my little girl couldn't possibly be allowed to marry one week sooner. There I'd been, knocking about and spooning with her violently for three months nearly; and the more I spooned, and the more tired I got of it, the more she expected me to go on spooning. Well, I'm not the sort of man to stand billing and cooing for a whole year together. At last the thing grew monotonous.

"I wanted to get an excuse to go off somewhere, where there was some sort of fun going on, till summer came, and we could get spliced properly (for she's got some tin, too, and I didn't want to throw her over); but I felt that if I'd got to keep on spooning and spooning for a whole winter, without intermission, the thing would really be one too many for me, and I should have to give it up from sheer weariness. So I heard of this precious expedition, which is just the sort of adventure I like; I wrote and volunteered for it; and then I managed to make my little girl and her dear papa believe that as I was an officer in the naval reserve I was compelled to go when asked, willy-nilly. 'It's only for half a year, you know, darling,' and all that sort of thing—you understand the line of country; and meanwhile I'm saved the bother of ever writing to her, or getting any letters from her either, which is almost in its way an equal nuisance."

"I see," said I shortly. "Not to put too fine a point upon it, you simply lied to her."

"Upon my soul," he answered, showing his teeth again, but this time by no means pleasantly, "you fellows on the *Cotopaxi* are really the sternest set of moralists I ever met with outside a book of sermons or a Surrey melodrama. You ought all to have been parsons, every man Jack of you; that's just about what you're fit for."

★★★★★★

On the fourteenth of September we got jammed in the ice, and the *Cotopaxi* went to pieces. You will find in the captain's log how part of us walked across the pack to the Liakov Islands, and settled ourselves here on Point Sibiriakoff in winter quarters. As to what became of the other party, which went southwards to the mouth of the Lena, I know nothing.

It was a hard winter, but by the aid of our stores and an occasional walrus shot by one of the blue-jackets, we managed to get along till March without serious illness. Then, one day, after a spell of terrible frost and snow, the captain came to me, and said, "Doctor, I wish you'd come and see Lemarchant, in the other hut here. I'm afraid he's got a bad fever."

I went to see him. So he had. A raging fever.

Fumbling about among his clothes to lay him down comfortably on the bearskin (for of course we had saved no bedding from the wreck), I happened to knock out once more the same locket that I had seen when he was emptying the drag-net. There was a photograph in it of a young lady. The seal-oil lamp didn't give very much light in the dark hut (it was still the long winter night on the Liakov Islands), but even so I couldn't help seeing and recognizing the young lady's features. Great Heaven support me! uphold me! I reeled with horror and amazement. It was Dora.

Yes; his little girl, that he spoke of so carelessly, that he lied to so easily, that he meant to marry so cruelly, was my Dora.

I had pitied the woman who was to be Harry Lemarchant's wife even when I didn't know who she was in any way; I pitied her terribly, with all my heart, when I knew that she was Dora—my own Dora. If I have become a murderer, after all, it was to save Dora—to save Dora from that unutterable, abominable ruffian.

I clutched the photograph in the locket eagerly, and held it up to the man's eyes. He opened them dreamily. "Is that the lady you are going to marry?" I asked him, with all the boiling indignation of that terrible discovery seething and burning in my very face.

He smiled, and took it all in in half a minute. "It is," he answered, in spite of the fever, with all his old dare-devil carelessness. "And now I recollect they told me the fellow she was engaged to was a doctor in London, and a brother of the parson. By Jove, I never thought of it before that your name, too, was actually Robinson. That's the worst of having such a deuced common name as yours; no one ever dreams of recognising your relations. Hang it all, if you're the man, I suppose now, out of revenge, you'll be wanting next to go and poison me."

"You judge others by yourself, I'm afraid," I answered sternly. Oh, how the words seem to rise up in judgment against me at last, now the dreadful thing is all over!

I doctored him as well as I was able, hoping all the time in my inmost soul (for I will confess all now) that he would never recover. Already in wish I had become a murderer. It was too horrible to think that such a man as that should marry Dora. I had loved her once and I loved her still; I love her now; I shall always love her. Murderer as I am, I say it nevertheless, I shall always love her.

But at last, to my grief and disappointment, the man began to mend and get better. My doctoring had done him good; and the sailors, though even they did not love him, had shot him once or twice a small bird, of which we made fresh soup that seemed to revive him. Yes, yes, he was coming round; and my cursed medicines had done it all. He was getting well, and he would still go back to marry Dora.

The very idea put me into such a fever of terror and excitement that at last I began to exhibit the same symptoms as Lemarchant himself had done. The captain saw I was sickening, and feared the fever might prove an epidemic. It wasn't: I knew that. Mine was brain,

Lemarchant's was intermittent; but the captain insisted upon disbelieving me. So, he put me and Lemarchant into the same hut, and made all the others clear out, so as to turn it into a sort of temporary hospital.

Every night I put out from the medicine-chest two quinine powders apiece, for myself and Lemarchant.

One night, it was the 7th of April (I can't forget it), I woke feebly from my feverish sleep, and noticed in a faint sort of fashion that Lemarchant was moving about restlessly in the cabin.

"Lemarchant," I cried authoritatively (for as surgeon I was, of course, responsible for the health of the expedition), "go back and lie down upon your bearskin this minute! You're a great deal too weak to go getting anything for yourself as yet. Go back this minute, sir, and if you want anything, I'll pull the string, and Paterson'll come and see what you're after." For we had fixed up a string between the two huts, tied to a box at the end, as a rough means of communication.

"All right, old fellow," he answered, more cordially than I had ever yet heard him speak to me. "It's all square, I assure you. I was only seeing whether you were quite warm and comfortable on your rug there."

"Perhaps," I thought, "the care I've taken of him has made him really feel a little grateful to me." So, I dozed off and thought nothing more at the moment about it.

Presently, I heard a noise again, and woke up quietly, without starting, but just opened my eyes and peered about as well as the dim light of the little oil-lamp would allow me.

To my great surprise, I could make out somehow that Lemarchant was meddling with the bottles in the medicine-chest.

"Perhaps," thought I again, "he wants another dose of quinine. Anyhow, I'm too tired and sleepy to ask him anything just now about it."

I knew he hated me, and I knew he was unscrupulous, but it didn't occur to me to think he would poison the man who had just helped him through a dangerous fever.

At four I woke, as I always did, and proceeded to take one of my powders. Curiously enough, before I tasted it, the grain appeared to me to be rather coarser and more granular than the quinine I had originally put there. I took a pinch between my finger and thumb, and placed it on my tongue by way of testing it. Instead of being bitter, the powder, I found, was insipid and almost tasteless.

Could I possibly in my fever and delirium (though I had not consciously been delirious) have put some other powder instead of the quinine into the two papers? The bare idea made me tremble with horror. If so, I might have poisoned Lemarchant, who had taken one of his powders already, and was now sleeping quietly upon his bearskin. At least, I thought so.

Glancing accidentally to his place that moment, I was vaguely conscious that he was not really sleeping, but lying with his eyes held half open, gazing at me cautiously and furtively through his closed eyelids.

Then the horrid truth flashed suddenly across me. Lemarchant was trying to poison me.

Yes, he had always hated me; and now that he knew I was Dora's discarded lover, he hated me worse than ever. He had got up and taken a bottle from the medicine-chest, I felt certain, and put something else instead of my quinine inside my paper.

I knew his eyes were fixed upon me then, and for the moment I dissembled. I turned round and pretended to swallow the contents of the packet, and then lay down upon my rug as if nothing unusual had happened. The fever was burning me fiercely, but I lay awake, kept up by the excitement, till I saw that he was really asleep, and then I once more undid the paper.

Looking at it closely by the light of the lamp, I saw a finer powder sticking closely to the folded edges. I wetted my finger, put it down and tasted it. Yes, that was quite bitter. That was quinine, not a doubt about it.

I saw at once what Lemarchant had done. He had emptied out the quinine and replaced it by some other white powder, probably arsenic. But a little of the quinine still adhered to the folds in the paper, because he had been obliged to substitute it hurriedly; and that at once proved that it was no mistake of my own, but that Lemarchant had really made the deliberate attempt to poison me.

This is a confession, and a confession only, so I shall make no effort in any way to exculpate myself for the horrid crime I committed the next moment. True, I was wild with fever and delirium; I was maddened with the thought that this wretched man would marry Dora; I was horrified at the idea of sleeping in the same room with him any longer. But still, I acknowledge it now, face to face with a lonely death upon this frozen island, it was murder—wilful murder. I meant to poison him, and I did it.

"He has set this powder for me, the villain," I said to myself, "and now I shall make him take it without knowing it. How do I know that it's arsenic or anything else to do him any harm? His blood be upon his own head, for aught I know about it. What I put there was simply quinine. If anybody has changed it, he has changed it himself. The pit that he dug for another, he himself shall fall therein."

I wouldn't even test it, for fear I should find it was arsenic, and be unable to give it to him innocently and harmlessly.

I rose up and went over to Lemarchant's side. Horror of horrors, he was sleeping soundly! Yes, the man had tried to poison me; and when he thought he had seen me swallow his poisonous powder, so callous and hardened was his nature that he didn't even lie awake to watch the effect of it. He had dropped off soundly, as if nothing had happened, and was sleeping now, to all appearance, the sleep of innocence. Being convalescent, in fact, and therefore in need of rest, he slept with unusual soundness.

I laid the altered powder quietly by his pillow, took away his that I had laid out in readiness for him, and crept back to my own place noiselessly. There I lay awake, hot and feverish, wondering to myself hour after hour when he would ever wake and take it.

At last he woke, and looked over towards me with unusual interest. "Hullo, Doctor," he said quite genially, "how are you this morning, eh? getting on well, I hope." It was the first time during all my illness that he had ever inquired after me.

I lied to him deliberately to keep the delusion up. "I have a terrible grinding pain in my chest," I said, pretending to writhe. I had sunk to his level, it seems. I was a liar and a murderer.

He looked quite gay over it, and laughed. "It's nothing," he said, grinning horribly. "It's a good symptom. I felt just like that myself, my dear fellow, when I was beginning to recover."

Then I knew he had tried to poison me, and I felt no remorse for my terrible action. It was a good deed to prevent such a man as that from ever carrying away Dora—my Dora—into a horrid slavery. Sooner than that he should marry Dora, I would poison him—I would poison him a thousand times over.

He sat up, took the spoon full of treacle, and poured the powder as usual into the very middle of it. I watched him take it off at a single gulp without perceiving the difference, and then I sank back exhausted upon my roll of sealskins.

★★★★★★

All that day I was very ill; and Lemarchant, lying tossing beside me, groaned and moaned in a fearful fashion. At last the truth seemed to

42

dawn upon him gradually, and he cried aloud to me: "Doctor, Doctor, quick, for Heaven's sake! you must get me out an antidote. The powders must have got mixed up somehow, and you've given me arsenic instead of quinine, I'm certain."

"Not a bit of it, Lemarchant," I said, with some devilish malice; "I've given you one of my own packets, that was lying here beside my pillow."

He turned as white as a sheet the moment he heard that, and gasped out horribly, "That—that—why, that was arsenic!" But he never explained in a single word how he knew it, or where it came from. I knew. I needed no explanation, and I wanted no lies, so I didn't question him.

I treated him as well as I could for arsenic poisoning, without saying a word to the captain and the other men about it; for if he died, I said, it would be by his own act, and if my skill could still avail, he should have the benefit of it; but the poison had had full time to work before I gave him the antidote, and he died by seven o'clock that night in fearful agonies.

Then I knew that I was really a murderer.

My fingers are beginning to get horribly numb, and I'm afraid I shan't be able to write much longer. I must be quick about it, if I want to finish this confession.

★★★★★★

After that came my retribution. I have been punished for it, and punished terribly.

As soon as they all heard Lemarchant was dead—a severe relapse, I called it—they set to work to carry him out and lay him somewhere. Then for the first time the idea flashed across my mind that they couldn't possibly bury him. The ice was too deep everywhere, and underneath it lay the solid rock of the bare granite islands. There was no snow even, for the wind swept it away as it fell, and we couldn't so much as decently cover him. There was nothing for it but to lay him out upon the icy surface.

So, we carried the stark frozen body, with its hideous staring eyes wide open, out by the jutting point of rock behind the hut, and there we placed it, dressed and upright. We stood it up against the point exactly as if it were alive, and by-and-by the snow came and froze it to the rock; and there it stands to this moment, glaring for ever fiercely upon me.

Whenever I went in or out of the hut, for three long months, that hideous thing stood there staring me in the face with mute indignation. At night, when I tried to sleep, the murdered man stood there still in the darkness beside me. O God! I dared not say a word to anybody: but I trembled every time I passed it, and I knew what it was to be a murderer.

In May, the sun came back again, but still no open water for our one boat. In June, we had the long day, but no open water. The captain began to get impatient and despondent, as you will read in the log: he was afraid now we might never get a chance of making the mouth of the Lena.

By-and-by, the scurvy came (I have no time now for details, my hands are so cramped with cold), and then we began to run short of provisions. Soon I had them all down upon my hands, and presently we had to place Paterson's corpse beside Lemarchant's on the little headland. Then they sank, one after another—sank of cold and hunger, as you will read in the log—till I alone, who wanted least to live, was the last left living.

I was left alone with those nine corpses propped up awfully against the naked rock, and one of the nine the man I had murdered.

May Heaven forgive me for that terrible crime; and for pity's sake, whoever you may be, keep it from Dora—keep it from Dora!

My brother's address is in my pocket-book.

The fever and remorse alone have given me strength to hold the pen. My hands are quite numbed now. I can write no longer.

★★★★★★

There the manuscript ended. Heaven knows what effect it may have upon all of you, who read it quietly at home in your own easy-chairs in England; but we of the search party, who took those almost illegible sheets of shaky writing from the cold fingers of the one solitary corpse within the frozen cabin on the Liakov Islands—we read them through with such a mingled thrill of awe and horror and sympathy and pity as no one can fully understand who has not been upon an Arctic expedition. And when we gathered our sad burdens up to take them off for burial at home, the corpse to which we gave the most reverent attention was certainly that of the self-accused murderer.

Dick Prothero's Luck

1

That farm in Manitoba was always an unlucky one. From the very first day when Dick Prothero left the West Cornwall Rangers, and took him a wife, determined to settle down to agricultural retirement in the Far West, a fatal ill-fortune seemed to dog and pursue him with merciless persistence. At least, so Dick said; though people who knew Manitoba better, doubted within themselves whether the discipline of the messroom in a crack regiment, where Dick had stood junior captain on the list, was quite the sort of thing to prepare a man beforehand for becoming a vigorous and successful farmer in a raw community.

At any rate, things somehow didn't seem to prosper with Dick Prothero. The horses were always getting glanders at unhappy moments; the cows were always poisoning themselves with uncanny prairie weeds; the rain was always rough on the standing hay; the fall wheat was always getting nipped by the first sharp frosts of a Canadian springtide. Dick worked as hard, to be sure, as a man could work; but he didn't work the right way on, so experts said—all his energy and good will were quite thrown away through his want of knowledge of practical farming.

The worst of it was, too, Manitoba didn't agree with Bertha, and that was Dick's greatest cross of all. For himself, he didn't much mind the small frame house, the long cold winter when the grouse was on the wing, or the changeable spring with its teal and wild duck. A strong and hearty young man, with a sound constitution and a natural love of outdoor sport, can put up with roughing it for himself very well, in those wild west countries. But to see his pretty young English wife, delicately bred and nurtured in a Devonshire Rectory, shrinking from the privations of the frozen prairie—that was the sort of thing that makes a man regret he hadn't invested his money instead at two and three-quarters *per cent*, in the munificent hands of the Right Honourable the Chancellor of the Exchequer. If Dick could have done it, he'd have sold his farm; but it's always easier to buy land anywhere in the world than sell it; so, Dick had to hang on as best he might, hoping for better times and a turn in the real estate market.

Still, if it hadn't been for little Daisy and his brother Archie, Dick, who was a sentimental, rather melodramatically-minded young man (in spite of his Sandhurst training), would sometimes have sat down despondent in the frame house, with a fixed determination to blow his unlucky brains out. But little Daisy, thank heaven, was as strong as a toy Shetland pony; and Archie, good fellow, was always helpful and always cheery, even when the rain came and spoiled the harvest. Archie was the best brother any man in this world ever had; nobody could help being cheered and helped on by that dear, good Archie.

The frame house where they all lived together—Dick and his wife, and little Daisy, and Archie—was situated a good many miles from anywhere, and at a great distance from Winnipeg, the centre of mushroom civilization in the Canadian Northwest at the present moment. It was altogether about as dreary a place as any fellow could well ask a young English wife to settle in. It stood alone upon the wide-open prairie, a square, bare box, just perched upon the soil, with doors and windows like those of a German toy house, and with not a tree or shrub standing anywhere in sight of it. In front you looked out upon the waving plain of grass and cornfield—monotonous, arid, as far as the eye could reach, with only a few more equally square and bare little wooden shanties dotted about here and there to relieve its utter blank of sameness and dreariness.

Sometimes in dry weather the whole unvaried plain caught fire at once, from some careless pipe or match, and then the smoke of it went up to heaven in a great dusky column, and the flames marched abreast like an army over the land, and the farmers defended their own houses and yards as best they might by cutting down and wetting the grass all round; and next morning nothing remained of the year's labours but a vast black desert, smoking dismal and grey to the lurid sky, where yesterday had been whole acres of corn and meadow land. Those are the chances of war in the great Northwest—the chances of that terrible pioneer warfare which man wages single-handed with valorous heart against the fierce, blind powers of unconscious nature.

And in this bare, bleak house, with its unlovely surroundings, gentle and delicately nurtured English Bertha had to live by herself, for the most part servantless. Now and then, to be sure, some raw Irish lass, fresh out from the Ould Counthry, with a bright red face, and a fine, rich brogue, would accept for a week or two a situation as general help, to assist in the cooking and take care of Daisy. But at the end of a fortnight the help usually came in and informed Bertha, with tears in her eyes, that she found it "lonesome," and that if Bertha would "suit herself" when the month was up, she'd like to go back to a place in Winnipeg. Bertha, as a rule, did not succeed at all in suiting herself; so, she had to do all the cooking, and washing, and nursing, and mending, more than half her time for those two strong men and for little Daisy.

Dick, being a tender-hearted, sentimental fellow, could have cried his eyes out (only that he was ashamed), when he thought of the sort of life, he had brought that sweet, pretty little English wife to. There are plenty more of his sort in the West. Young man, stop East. Don't you go and be fooled by delusive promises into following his example.

2

That summer was very hot and dry, and things went even worse with the Protheros than usual. In the hay season Bertha fell ill with fever, and as she was then in her chronic servantless condition, for weeks Dick had hard work to nurse and tend her. At last, however, she began to come round again; and one sunny morning in the August drought, she rose and lay on the sofa in the little living-room, by the open window, looking out upon all the view there was—the great blank prairie and the desolate cornfields. Dick brought little Daisy and placed her by her side; and Bertha, though still too weak to walk, seemed so cheerful and happy at the mere sight of the fields, that Dick almost felt as if that long-expected turn in his luck were coming at last, and things were going to mend in Manitoba. He made everything snug in the bare small parlour for poor pale Bertha, and then he saddled his horse and rode off, better pleased, to see how business looked after so many days absence in the dip by the river.

When he got there the corn was certainly most promising, and all was going well with the ripening crops for the agricultural interest. By a rare chance, too, he met a neighbour by the stream, and they stopped long chatting about the Boom at Regina and the Chicago futures, and the probability of an advance in spring wheat next Winnipeg market. The neighbour was hopeful, like Dick himself. Land was on the rise, he said, in their own section, and a great development, a great development, sir, was, as sure as fate, in store for Manitoba. A magnificent country, and it was going to be developed.

Dick hoped so in his heart, and that land would rise till he could get his own price back again for his own farm, take Bertha home to her native shores, show little Daisy what was meant by a decent road, and leave the development of that magnificent country to the more capable hands and arms of others.

At last he wheeled round his horse once more, and after riding about for a couple of hours, surveying the soil, he made towards home across the open prairie.

As he did so, a sickening horror seized upon his soul. He looked in front of him and shaded his eyes, incredulous. Great heavens, what he saw was all too true. No farmhouse visible.

Other houses were there, to be sure, each standing in its place over the vast plain, at wide intervals, and each marked by a long blue line of smoke, where the "smudges" or fly-dispersers were burning in front of them to keep off the mosquitoes. A smudge, in North-western parlance, is a fire of turf kept alight in a sort of standing iron cage or basket, which smoulders away for hours at a time, and is peculiarly offensive to the senses of insects. But though the smudge still smoked in front of the place where his own house had once stood, not a sign of the house itself remained anywhere visible. Dick shaded his eyes and looked in vain. It had melted from the scene as if by magic.

At the sight the strong man's heart sank down with horror and awe within him. He knew what it meant; he was too old a hand, indeed, in the ways of Manitoba not to realize at a glance what a terrible, unspeakable thing had happened. The house had been burnt down to the ground in his absence.

And Bertha? And Daisy? He grew pale with terror. Unless Archie had saved them, heaven only knew what nameless misfortune might have fallen upon them. And Archie was away in the Swale with the wagon.

With a wild cry of despair, the unhappy man urged his horse forward, and never paused for breath till he drew rein at last by the smouldering remains of the charred and desolate farmhouse.

There, the whole truth came upon him in all its awful vividness.

In front of the yard, the smudge lay on the ground, overturned, and still feebly burning. From the smudge to the spot where the house once stood, a path of fire lay traced on the dry grass, widening from windward. Even in the first burst of his horror and grief, the poor trembling husband and father felt instinctively just what had occurred. Rollo, the pointer, had upset the smudge, and the fire had run from it before the wind through the parched grass, and set in a blaze the frail timber tenement.

The rest was obvious. Those frame houses of the West, when once alight, burn to the ground with awful rapidity in a few brief minutes. Constructed as they are of light pitch pine, all wooden throughout, and slight into the bargain, they leave at the end of a quarter of an hour nothing to mark the spot where they once stood, save a pile of grey and smouldering ashes.

That was all that remained of Dick Prothero's home. And Bertha, and Daisy, must have been burnt or smothered before they could move from the sofa by the window.

Unmanned with horror, Dick leaped from his horse, and strode over to the smouldering, smoking ruins. For a minute or two he was stupefied by the awful suddenness of that crushing blow. He sat down on the ground, with his head in his hands, and rocked himself idly to and fro in the first full bitterness of his speechless agony.

And the very last words little Daisy had said to him as he rode away were, "Turn back soon, Papa. Daisy wants to play with 'oo."

3

Ten minutes after Dick had left the house Archie had driven up in front of the door, and seeing Bertha lying on the sofa at the open window, had cried out to her cheerily, in his good-humoured fashion, "Come along, Bertha; you're convalescent now. A bit of fresh air'll do you all the good in the world, I bet you. I'm going to drive in to the post office at Swaleborough. You may as well come with me."

"Oh, Archie, I couldn't," Bertha cried, all aghast. "I'm only just up out of bed today, and the wagon's so dreadfully, dreadfully jolty."

"Nonsense," Archie answered, jumping down and coming over to her. " I'll fetch down the mattress out of the servants' room—it don't get much slept upon; lay it in the wagon with a couple of pillows; carry you out and set you in comfortably; and there you are at once fixed up, as the Yankees say, as well as you'd be in an English victoria."

"Oh, do!" Daisy cried, clapping her little hands. "Oh, do, mamma, for it amuses Daisy."

So, in three minutes more, with Archie's strong arms to help, the thing was done. Bertha, wrapped round in a big buffalo skin, was laid in the wagon; Daisy was installed on a pillow by her side, and the three drove off, laughing and talking, with fresh hope in their hearts, as merry as crickets.

"Where's Rollo, Uncle Archie?" Daisy asked, as they jolted along over the rough plain, though Archie drove as carefully as he could to save Bertha any unnecessary shaking.

"Oh, he's all right," Archie answered, smiling. "He'll come along soon. Here, Rollo, Rollo!"

At the word, Rollo leaped up from the mat where he was dozing in the sun, and followed the wagon with a bound of delight. They didn't notice, however, that as he came, he had upset the smudge, and that the turves were smoking on the dry grass in front of the window.

Bertha had never enjoyed a drive so much. In spite of the wagon and the jolting road, it was so delightful to be out in the fresh air once more, and to feel the motion and the free breeze of heaven. Little Daisy enjoyed it all so thoroughly, too, and made her mother's heart more glad by sympathy. And when at last, after their long drive, they got to the post, there were letters from home, such cheerful letters, with talk of Bertha's shares in that unfortunate concern at the Cape (which her uncle had left her), going up at last, so that perhaps they might in time be able to return to dear old England. Bertha turned to go back, feeling ever so much better, and longing to tell the good news to dear Dick, who had been so terribly down on his luck just lately.

4

But Dick, among the smouldering ruins of his lost house, was sitting still, in an agony of despair, rocking himself to and fro with his head in his hands, and overwhelmed with this awful fate of Bertha and Daisy.

For a long time, he sat there, incapable of thought or act, or motion; sat there like one dazed by his terrible loss, holding his face between his palms in his misery, and incapable even of realizing his own desolate position. But at last he rose, determined to know the worst, and began with a pick that was lying near to turn ever the hot ashes, in the vain attempt to find some charred and mangled remains of his wife and child, if anything was left of them. He turned the ashes over carefully, but the fire had indeed done its work well. Not a stick or plank, not a beam or rafter, not a leg of chair, or sofa or table, remained distinguishable among all that heap of grey and calcined relics. Only the frames of the iron bedsteads and a few castors and other metal objects were to be found in any recognisable shape. The rest was mere cinder or white powdery ashes.

In the depths of his despair Dick looked around for Archie. But Archie, too, was nowhere to be seen, and Dick remembered he had talked in the morning about going into Swaleborough. The first apathy of grief had worn off now, and Dick had reached that second active stage of wild despondency when a man feels he must go at once and maim or kill himself. As he fumbled among the ashes, digging deeper and deeper, a weird idea seemed to frame itself within him. Since all that remained of Bertha and Daisy lay there in those ashes, he would dig a grave on the very spot where they had died—those two that were dearest to him—throw the ashes into it, and then shoot himself there above the relics of his loved ones. When Archie came back with the wagon from Swaleborough, he would find no house, but an open grave, and his brother's dead body, stark and bleeding within it.

It was one of those awful melodramatic ideas which sometimes occur with irresistible force to such minds as Dick Prothero's at a great crisis in their lives; and its very weirdness commended it to his inflamed fancy. He proceeded at once, with the energy of despair, to carry the mad notion into actual practice. He took up the spade which lay in the back yard, untouched by the fire, and began to dig and dig, to drown his misery for a while in the mere act of digging. If Archie had been there, he might have groaned and cried; but in his utter solitude, alone with the prairie and his vanished wife and child, he dug and dug, with feverish energy, for very need of some violent occupation. He dug as he never knew he could dig before, with the wild maniac strength of a terrible sorrow.

As he dug, the ashes and the smoke blinded his eyes, and the fumes from the fire rose up and choked him. But still he dug on, going deeper and deeper, and flinging out the earth with fierce and frantic eagerness. He must get it all done before Archie came back; and at the very first sound of Archie's wheels in the distance, he must pull out his revolver, finished or not finished, and shoot himself dead before Archie's eyes in the grave he had dug himself.

He had got down now into a deep subsoil, thick and clayey, and hard to cut through; but he went on nevertheless, digging it square and even, and taking care to throw the clay well out of the way, where it wouldn't interfere with those sacred ashes. His eyes were blinded with tears and smoke and the dust from the pile; but still he continued. He came across little stones in the clay now and again. His spade struck against them from time to time, or even cut into them, for they were mere soft nodules. But he shovelled them out with the rest of the dirt, and went blindly on at his ghastly occupation.

Presently, as he worked, the sound of distant wheels fell on his ear. It was Archie coming back! It he meant to carry his scheme into execution he must make haste now. There was no time to be lost. If Archie arrived, he would disarm him and prevent him. Frantic with grief he pulled out his revolver and held it close to his left temple. For one awful second he paused and prayed. He knew he was mad—what man would not go mad in face of such a blow?—but, all the same, he prayed wildly for forgiveness. Then he snapped the trigger right against his brow, and waited to know he was really dying.

A terrible moment of suspense followed. What had gone wrong? The revolver had clearly hung fire somehow! He had never known that trusty weapon serve him such a trick in his life before. He took it down and looked at it carefully. As he did so the cartridge went off in his hands, and the bullet buried itself in the deep clay bottom. What luck, to be sure!

The very powers of inanimate nature seemed to fight against him! Why, he couldn't even succeed in killing himself comfortably when he tried to do so. He raised the pistol angrily to his head once more. This time, at least, he'd take care it didn't miss and disappoint him.

But before he could fire again a terrible thrill ran through his brain; a thrill that made him drop the revolver in his amazement. For he heard, from the direction where the wagon was advancing, a cry of surprise—a child's cry of simple wonder and astonishment. The cry went through him like a flash of pain. But it was joy that unnerved him! Then, Daisy, at least, was safe! Daisy had gone with Archie in the wagon! It was Daisy's voice; and for Daisy's sake, at any rate, he dared not kill himself.

He raised himself to the top of that strange grave on both his elbows and looked around with dim vision to see what had happened. His eyes were still blinded by the smoke and ash, and he could hardly make out who was in the wagon. Then with another wild burst of gratitude and joy he heard another voice he had never expected to hear again. Contrary to all probability, all possibility almost, Bertha was there as well as Daisy and Archie.

He flung down the spade in a strange access of delight and rushed to the wagon. To the rest, it was a moment of surprise and terror, to see the house burnt down, and that gaunt, wan man in his grimy shirt sleeves, all stained with smoke and dirt, darting wildly out like some madman to greet them. But to Dick, it was a moment of unspeakable joy. House and land were forgotten altogether in the sudden revulsion of intense delight with which he saw his wife and child brought back to him from the dead again.

It was some minutes before each party could understand exactly what had happened, for at first Dick could only look on and laugh and cry like a maniac, and take Daisy up in his arms over and over again, and lay Bertha down on the ground, crying, upon her mattress. But after a while they grew more calm, and in broken words explained how things had fared on either side with either of them. As to the grave and the revolver. Indeed, Dick remained for the moment discreetly silent; but the rest, he told as well as he was able in brief sobbing sentences. Then they kissed one another once more, that husband and wife, so strangely restored, and wept with thankfulness, all houseless and homeless, alone on the prairie.

Presently Archie broke the solemn silence.

"We must take Bertha somewhere for tonight," he said gazing round ruefully. "Perhaps they could give us a bed at McDougall's."

They raised the mattress into the wagon again, and were going to lay Bertha back on her improvised invalid's couch, when Bertha cried out, "Oh, look at Daisy, Dick; what's that she's doing over there on that dirt-heap yonder?"

Dick turned round, and with his bloodshot eyes, saw dimly that Daisy was trying to suck one of the roundish pebbles he had struck his spade against so often in digging. It was a pebble as big as a hen's egg, and he was afraid the child would fairly choke herself with it. But he would not go near that open grave himself, from which he had been preserved almost by a miracle. It fairly daunted him.

"Go over and fetch her, Archie," he cried in a tone of command. And Archie went to her.

But Daisy didn't want to be deprived of her pebble.

"It's pretty," she said, and went on sucking at it.

Archie snatched it from her. "Why, Dick," he exclaimed, looking close at the rough lump, and pressing it with his nail, "what on earth's this? It's as soft as lead, and as yellow as a guinea!"

Then he burst into a sudden loud laugh of triumph. Dick stared at him in amazement, thinking the painful drama of the last two hours must have fairly made Archie lose his senses. But Archie waved the pebble frantically round his head with a strange air of victory. "Dick, Dick," he cried, in his joy, "luck's turned at last; they're nuggets! they're nuggets!"

And that's just how Dick Prothero found the first rich paying plac-er of alluvial gold that ever was discovered in Manitoba.

Dr. Greatrex's Engagement

Everybody knows by name at least the celebrated Dr. Greatrex, the discoverer of that abstruse molecular theory of the interrelations of forces and energies. He is a comparatively young man still, as times go, for a person of such scientific distinction, for he is now barely forty; but to look at his tall, spare, earnest figure, and his clear-cut, delicate, intellectual face, you would scarcely imagine that he had once been the hero of a singularly strange and romantic story. Yet there have been few lives more romantic than Arthur Greatrex's, and few histories stranger in their way than this of his engagement. After all, why should not a scientific light have a romance of his own as well as other people?

Fifteen years ago, Arthur Greatrex, then a young Cambridge fellow, had just come up to begin his medical studies at a London hospital. He was tall in those days, of course, but not nearly so slender or so pale as now; for he had rowed seven in his college boat, and was a fine, athletic young man of the true English university pattern. Handsome, too, then and always, but with a more human looking and ordinary handsomeness when he was young than in these latter times of his scientific eminence. Indeed, anyone who met Arthur Greatrex at that time would merely have noticed him as a fine, intelligent young English gentleman, with a marked taste for manly sports, and a decided opinion of his own about most passing matters of public interest.

Already, even in those days, the young medical student was very deeply engaged in recondite speculations on the question of energy. His active mind, always dwelling upon wide points of cosmical significance, had hit upon the germ of that great revolutionary idea which was afterwards to change the whole course of modern physics. But, as often happens with young men of twenty-five, there was another subject which divided his attention with the grand theory of his life:

and that subject was the pretty daughter of his friend and instructor, Dr. Abury, the eminent authority on the treatment of the insane. In all London you couldn't have found a sweeter or prettier girl than Hetty Abury. Young Greatrex thought her clever, too; and, though that is perhaps saying rather too much, she was certainly a good deal above the average of ordinary London girls in intellect and accomplishments.

"They say, Arthur," she said to him on the day after their formal engagement, "that the course of true love never did run smooth; and yet it seems somehow as if ours was wonderfully smoothed over for us by everybody and everything. I am the happiest and proudest girl in all the world to have won the love of such a man as you for my future husband."

Arthur Greatrex stroked the back of her white little hand with his, and answered gently, "I hope nothing will ever arise to make the course of our love run any the rougher; for certainly we do seem to have every happiness laid out most temptingly before us. It almost feels to me as if my paradise had been too easily won, and I ought to have something harder to do before I enter it."

"Don't say that, Arthur," Hetty put in hastily. "It sounds too much like an evil omen."

"You superstitious little woman!" the young doctor replied with a smile. "Talking to a scientific man about signs and portents!" And he kissed her wee hand tenderly, and went home to his bachelor lodging with that strange exhilaration in heart and step which only the ecstasy of first love can ever bring one.

" No," he thought to himself, as he sat down in his own easy-chair, and lighted his cigar; "I don't believe any cloud can ever arise between me and Hetty. We have everything in our favour—means to live upon, love for one another, a mutual respect, kind relations, and hearts that were meant by nature each for the other. Hetty is certainly the very sweetest little girl that ever lived; and she's as good as she's sweet, and as loving as she's beautiful. What a dreadful thing it is for a man in love to have to read up medicine for his next examination!" And he took a medical book down from the shelf with a sigh, and pretended to be deeply interested in the diagnosis of scarlet fever till his cigar was finished.

But, if the truth must be told, the words really swam before him, and all the letters on the page apparently conspired together to make up but a single name a thousand times over—Hetty, Hetty, Hetty, Hetty. At last he laid the volume down as hopeless, and turned dreamily into his bedroom, only to lie awake half the night and think perpetually on that one theme of Hetty.

Next day was Dr. Abury's weekly lecture on diseases of the brain and nervous system; and Arthur Greatrex, convinced that he really must make an effort, went to hear it. The subject was one that always interested him; and partly by dint of mental attention, partly out of sheer desire to master the matter, he managed to hear it through, and even take in the greater part of its import. As he left the room to go down the hospital stairs, he had his mind fairly distracted between the premonitory symptoms of insanity and Hetty Abury. "Was there ever such an unfortunate profession as medicine for a man in love?" he asked himself, half angrily. "Why didn't I go and be a parson or a barrister, or anything else that would have kept me from mixing up such incongruous associations? And yet, when one comes to think of it, too, there's no particular natural connection after all between 'Chitty on Contract' and dearest Hetty."

Musing thus, he turned to walk down the great central staircase of the hospital. As he did so, his attention was attracted for a moment by a singular person who was descending the opposite stair towards the same landing. This person was tall and not ill-looking; but, as he came down the steps, he kept pursing up his mouth and cheeks into the most extraordinary and hideous grimaces; in fact, he was obviously making insulting faces at Arthur Greatrex. Arthur was so much preoccupied at the moment, however, that he hardly had time to notice the eccentric stranger; and, as he took him for one of the harmless lunatic patients in the mental-diseases ward, he would have passed on without further observing the man but for an odd circumstance which occurred as they both reached the great central landing together. Arthur happened to drop the book he was carrying from under his arm, and instinctively stooped to pick it up. At the same moment the grimacing stranger dropped his own book also, not in imitation, but by obvious coincidence, and stooped to pick it up with the self-same gesture. Struck by the oddity of the situation, Arthur turned to look at the curious patient. To his utter horror and surprise, he discovered that the man he had been observing was his own reflection.

In one second the real state of the case flashed like lightning across his bewildered brain. There was no opposite staircase, as he knew very well, for he had been down those steps a hundred times before: nothing but a big mirror, which reflected and doubled the one-sided flight from top to bottom. It was only his momentary preoccupation which had made him for a minute fall into the obvious delusion. The man whom he saw descending towards him was really himself, Arthur Greatrex.

Even so, he did not at once grasp the full strangeness of the scene he had just witnessed. It was only as he turned to descend again that he caught another glimpse of himself in the big mirror, and saw that he was still making the most horrible and ghastliest grimaces—grimaces such as he had never seen equalled save by the monkeys at the Zoo, and (horridest thought of all!) by the worst patients in the mental-disease ward. He pulled himself up in speechless horror, and looked once more into the big mirror. Yes, there was positively no mistaking the fact: it was he, Arthur Greatrex, fellow of Catherine's, who was making these hideous and meaningless distortions of his own countenance.

With a terrible effort of will he pulled his face quite straight again, and assumed his usual grave and quiet demeanour. For a full minute he stood looking at himself in the glass; and then, fearful that someone else would come and surprise him, he hurried down the remaining steps, and rushed out into the streets of London. Which way he turned he did not know or care; all he knew was that he was repressing by sheer force of muscular strain a deadly impulse to pucker up his mouth and draw down the corners of his lips into one-sided grimaces. As he passed down the streets, he watched his own image faintly reflected in the panes of the windows, and saw that he was maintaining outward decorum, but only with a conscious and evident struggle.

At one doorstep a little child was playing with a kitten; Arthur Greatrex, who was a naturally kindly man, looked down at her and smiled, in spite of his preoccupation: instead of smiling back, the child uttered a scream of terror, and rushed back into the house to hide her face in her mother's apron. He felt instinctively that, in place of smiling, he had looked at the child with one of his awful faces. It was horrible, unendurable, and he walked on through the streets and across the bridges, pulling himself together all the time, till at last, half-unconsciously, he found himself near Pimlico, where the Aburys were then living.

Looking around him, he saw that he had come nearly to the corner where Hetty's little drawing-room faced the road. The accustomed place seemed to draw him off for a moment from thinking of himself, and he remembered that he had promised Hetty to come in for luncheon. But dare he go in such a state of mind and body as he then found himself in? Well, Hetty would be expecting him; Hetty would be disappointed if he didn't come; he certainly mustn't break his engagement with dear little Hetty. After all, he began to say to himself, what was it but a mere twitching of his face, probably a slight nervous affection? Young doctors are always nervous about themselves, they say; they find all their own symptoms accurately described in all the text-books. His face wasn't twitching now, of that he was certain; the nearer he got to Hetty's, the calmer he grew, and the more he was conscious he could relax his attention without finding his muscles were playing tricks upon him. He would turn in and have luncheon, and soon forget all about it.

Hetty saw him coming, and ran lightly to open the door for him, and as he took his seat beside her at the table, he forgot straightway his whole trouble, and found himself at once in Paradise once more. All through lunch they talked about other things—happy plans for the future, and the small prettinesses that lovers find so perennially delightful; and long before Arthur went away the twitching in his face had altogether ceased to trouble him. Once or twice, indeed, in the course of the afternoon he happened to glance casually at the looking-glass above the drawing-room fireplace (those were the pre-Morrisian days when over-mantels as yet were not), and he saw to his great comfort that his face was resting in its usual handsome repose and peacefulness. A bright, earnest, strong face it was, with all the promise of greatness already in it; and so Hetty thought as she looked up at it from the low footstool where she sat by his side and half whispered into his ear the little timid confidences of early betrothal.

Five o'clock tea came all too soon, and then Arthur felt he must really be going and must get home to do a little reading. On his way, he fancied once he saw a street boy start in evident surprise as he approached him, but it might be fancy; and when the street boy stuck his tongue into the corner of his cheek and uttered derisive shouts from a safe distance, Arthur concluded he was only doing after the manner of his kind out of pure gratuitous insolence. He went home to his lodgings and sat down to an hour's work; but after he had read up several pages more of *Stuckey on Gout*, he laid down the book in disgust, and took out Helmholtz and Joule instead, indulging himself with a little desultory reading in his favourite study of the higher physics.

As he read and read the theory of correlation, the great idea as to the real nature of energy, which had escaped all these learned physicists, and which was then slowly forming itself in his own mind, grew gradually clearer and clearer still before his mental vision. Helmholtz was wrong here, because he had not thoroughly appreciated the disjunctive nature of electric energy; Joule was wrong there, because he had failed to understand the real antithesis between potential and kinetic. He laid down the books, paced up and down the room thoughtfully, and beheld the whole concrete theory of interrelation embodying itself visibly before his very eyes. At last he grew tired with the stupendous grandeur of his own conception, seized a quire of foolscap, and sat down eagerly at the table to give written form to the splendid phantom that was floating before him in so distinct a fashion. He would make a great name, for Hetty's sake; and, when he had made it, his dearest reward would be to know that Hetty was proud of him.

Hour after hour he sat and wrote, as if inspired, at his little table. The landlady knocked at the door to tell him dinner was ready, but he would have none of it, he said; let her bring him up a good cup of strong tea and a few plain biscuits. So, he wrote and wrote in feverish haste, drinking cup after cup of tea, and turning off page after page of foolscap, till long past midnight. The whole theory had come up so distinctly before his mind's eye, under the exceptional exaltation of first love, and the powerful stimulus of the day's excitement, that he wrote it off as though he had it by heart; omitting only the mathematical calculations, which he left blank, not because he had not got them clearly in his head, but because he would not stop his flying pen to copy them all out then and there at full length, for fear of losing the main thread of his argument. When he had finished, about forty sheets of foolscap lay huddled together on the table before him, written in a hasty hand, and scarcely legible; but they contained the first rough draft and central principle of that immortal work, the *Transcendental Dynamics*.

Arthur Greatrex rose from the table, where his grand discovery was first formulated, well satisfied with himself and his theory, and fully determined to submit it shortly to the critical judgment of the Royal Society. As he took up his bedroom candle, however, he went over to the mantelpiece to kiss Hetty's photograph, as he always did (for even men of science are human) every evening before retiring. He lifted the portrait reverently to his lips, and was just about to kiss it, when suddenly in the mirror before him he saw the same horrible mocking face which bad greeted him so unexpectedly that morning on the hospital staircase. It was a face of inhuman devilry; the face of a mediaeval demon, a hideous, grinning, distorted ghoul, a very caricature and insult upon the features of humanity.

In his dismay he dropped the frame and the photograph, shivering the glass that covered it into a thousand atoms. Summoning up all his resolution, he looked again. Yes, there was no mistaking it: a face was gibing and jeering at him from the mirror with diabolical ingenuity of distorted hideousness; a disgusting face which even the direct evidence of his senses would scarcely permit him to believe was really the reflection of his own features. It was overpowering, it was awful, it was wholly incredible; and, utterly unmanned by the sight, he sank back into his easy-chair and buried his face bitterly between the shelter of his trembling hands.

At that moment Arthur Greatrex felt sure he knew the real meaning of the horror that surrounded him. He was going mad.

For ten minutes or more he sat there motionless, hot tears boiling up from his eyes and falling silently between his fingers. Then at last he rose nervously from his seat, and reached down a volume from the shelf behind him. It was Prang's *Treatise on the Physiology of the Brain*. He turned it over hurriedly for a few pages, till he came to the passage he was looking for.

"Ah, I thought so," he said to himself, half aloud: "'Premonitory symptoms: facial distortions; infirmity of the will; inability to distinguish muscular movements.' Let's see what Prang has to say about it. 'A not uncommon concomitant of these early stages'—Great heavens, how calmly the man talks about losing your reason!—'is an unconscious or semi-conscious tendency to produce a series of extraordinary facial distortions. At times, the sufferer is not aware of the movements thus initiated; at other times they are quite voluntary, and are accompanied by bodily gestures of contempt or derision for passing strangers.' Why, that's what must have happened with that boy this morning! 'Symptoms of this character usually result from excessive activity of the brain, and are most frequent among mathematicians or scholars who have overworked their intellectual faculties. They may be regarded as the immediate precursors of acute dementia.' Acute dementia! Oh, Hetty! Oh, heavens! What have I done to deserve such a blow as this?"

He laid his face between his hands once more, and sobbed like a broken-hearted child for a few minutes. Then he turned accidentally towards his tumbled manuscript. "No, no," he said to himself, reassuringly; "I can't be going mad. My brain was never clearer in my life. I couldn't have done a piece of good work like that, bristling with equations and figures and formulas, if my head was really giving way. I seemed to grasp the subject as I never grasped it in my life before. I never worked so well at Cambridge; this is a discovery, a genuine discovery. It's impossible that a man who was going mad could ever see anything so visibly and distinctly as I see that universal principle. Let's look again at what Prang has to say upon that subject."

He turned over the volume a few pages further, and glanced lightly at the contents at the head of each chapter, till at last a few words in the title struck his eye, and he hurried on to the paragraph they indicated, with feverish eagerness. As he did so, these were the words which met his bewildered gaze.

"In certain cases, especially among men of unusual intelligence and high attainments, the exaltation of incipient madness takes rather the guise of a scientific or philosophic enthusiasm. Instead of imagining himself the possessor of untold wealth, or the absolute despot of a servile people, the patient deludes himself with the belief that he has made a great discovery or lighted upon a splendid generalization of the deepest and most universal importance. He sees new truths crowding upon him with the most startling and vivid objectivity. He perceives intimate relations of things which he never before suspected. He destroys at one blow the Newtonian theory of gravitation; he discovers obvious flaws in the nebular hypothesis of Laplace; he gives a scholar's-mate to Kant in the very fundamental points of the *Critique of Pure Reason.*

The more serious the attack, the more utterly convinced is the patient of the exceptional clearness of his own intelligence at that particular moment. He writes pamphlets whose scientific value he ridiculously over-estimates; and he is sure to be very angry with anyone who tries rationally to combat his newly found authority. Mathematical reasoners are especially liable to this form of incipient mental disease, which, when combined with the facial distortions already alluded to in a previous section, is peculiarly apt to terminate in acute dementia."

"Acute dementia again!" Arthur Greatrex cried with a gesture of horror, flinging the book from him as if it were a poisonous serpent. "Acute dementia, acute dementia, acute dementia; nothing but acute dementia ahead of me, whichever way I happen to turn. Oh, this is too horrible! I shall never be able to marry Hetty! And yet I shall never be able to break it to Hetty! Great heavens, that such a phantom as this should have risen between me and paradise only since this very morning!"

In his agony he caught up the papers on which he had written the rough draft of his grand discovery, and crumpled them up fiercely in his fingers. "The cursed things!" he groaned between his teeth, tossing them with a gesture of impatient disgust into the waste-paper basket; "how could I ever have deluded myself into thinking I had hit offhand upon a grand truth which had escaped such men as Helmholtz, and Mayer, and Joule, and Thomson! The thing's preposterous upon the very face of it; I must be going mad, indeed, ever to have dreamt of it!"

He took up his candle once more, kissed the portrait in the broken frame with intense fervour a dozen times over, and then went up gloomily into his own bedroom. There he did not attempt to undress, but merely pulled off his boots, lay down in his clothes upon the bed, and hastily blew out the candle. For a long time he lay tossing and turning in unspeakable terror; but at last, after perhaps two hours or so, he fell into a troubled sleep, and dreamed a hideous nightmare, in which somebody or other in shadowy outlines was trying perpetually to tear him away by main force from poor pale and weeping Hetty.

It was daylight when Arthur woke again, and he lay for some time upon his bed, thinking over his last night's scare, which seemed much less serious, as such things always do, now that the sun had risen upon it. After a while his mind got round to the energy question; and, as he thought it over once more, the conviction forced itself afresh upon him that he was right upon the matter after all, and that if he was going mad there was at least method in his madness. So firmly was he convinced upon this point now (though he recognised that that very certainty might be merely a symptom of his coming malady) that he got up hurriedly, before the lodging-house servant came to clean up his little sitting-room, so as to rescue his crumpled foolscap from the waste-paper basket. After that, a bath and breakfast almost made him laugh at his evening terrors.

All the morning Arthur Greatrex sat down at his table again, working in the algebraical calculations which he had omitted from his paper overnight, and finishing it in full form as if for presentation to a learned society. But he did not mean now to offer it to any society: he had a far deeper and more personal interest in the matter at present than that. He wanted to settle first of all the question whether he was going mad or not. Afterwards, there would be plenty of time to settle such minor theoretical problems as the general physical constitution of the universe.

As soon as he had finished his calculations, he took the paper in his hands, and went out with it to make two calls on scientific acquaintances. The first man he called upon was that distinguished specialist, Professor Linklight, one of the greatest authorities of his own day on all questions of molecular physics. Poor man! he is almost forgotten now, for he died ten years ago; and his scientific reputation was, after all, of that flashy sort which bases itself chiefly upon giving good dinners to leading fellows of the Royal Society. But fifteen years ago, Professor Linklight, with his cut-and-dried dogmatic notions, and his narrow technical accuracy, was universally considered the principal physical philosopher in all England. To him, then, Arthur Greatrex—a far deeper and clearer thinker—took in all humility the first manuscript of his marvellous discovery; not to ask him whether it was true or not, but to find out whether it was physical science at all or pure insanity.

The professor received him kindly; and when Arthur, who had of course his own reasons for attempting a little modest concealment, asked him to look over a friend's paper for him, with a view to its presentation to the Royal Society, he cheerfully promised to do his best. "Though you will admit, my dear Mr. Greatrex," he said with his blandest smile, "that your friend's manuscript certainly does not err on the side of excessive brevity."

Prom Linklight's, Arthur walked on tremulously to the house of another great scientific magnate, Dr. Warminster, who shared with his friendly rival, Abury, the reputation of being the first living authority on the treatment of the insane in the United Kingdom. Before Dr. Warminster, Arthur made no attempt to conceal his apprehensions. He told out all his symptoms and fears without reserve, even exaggerating them a little, as a man is prone to do through over-anxiety not to put too favourable a face upon his own ailments. Dr. Warminster listened attentively and with a gathering interest to all that Arthur told him, and at the end of his account he shook his head gloomily, and answered in a very grave and sympathetic tone.

"My dear Greatrex," he said gently, holding his arm with a kindly pressure, "I should be dealing wrongly with you if I did not candidly tell you that your case gives ground for very serious apprehensions. You are a young man, and with steady attention to curative means and surroundings, it is possible that you may ward off this threatened danger. Society, amusement, relaxation, complete cessation of scientific work, absence, as far as possible, of mental anxiety in any form, may enable you to tide over the turning point. But that there is danger threatened, it would be unkind and untrue not to warn you. It is very unusual for a patient to consult us in person about these matters. More often it is the friends who notice the coming change; but, as you ask me directly for an opinion, I can't help telling you that I regard your case as not without real cause for the strictest care and for a preventive regimen."

Arthur thanked him for the numerous directions he gave as to things which should be done or things which should be avoided, and hurried out into the street with his brain swimming and reeling. "Absence of mental anxiety!" he said to himself bitterly. "How calmly they talk about mental anxiety! How can I possibly be free from anxiety when I know I may go mad at any moment, and that the blow would kill Hetty outright? For myself, I should not care a farthing; but for Hetty! It is too terrible."

He had not the heart to call at the Aburys' that afternoon, though he had promised to do so; and he tortured himself with the thought that Hetty would think him neglectful. He could not call again while the present suspense lasted; and if his worst fears were confirmed he could never call again, except once, to take leave of Hetty for ever. For, deeply as Arthur Greatrex loved her, he loved her too well ever to dream of marrying her if the possible shadow of madness was to cloud her future life with its perpetual presence. Better she should bear the shock, even if it killed her at once, than that both should live in ceaseless apprehension of that horrible possibility, and should become the parents of children upon whom that hereditary curse might rest for a lifetime, reflecting itself back with the added sting of conscientious remorse on the father who had brought them into the world against his own clear judgment of right and justice.

Next morning Arthur went round once more to Professor Linklight's. The professor had promised to read through the paper immediately, and give his opinion of its chances for presentation to the Royal Society. He was sitting at his breakfast-table, in his flowered dressing-gown and slippers, when Arthur called upon him, and, with a cup of coffee in one hand, was actually skimming the last few pages through his critical eye-glass as his visitor entered.

"Good-morning, Mr. Greatrex!" he said, with one of his most gracious smiles, indicative of the warm welcome extended by acknowledged wisdom towards rising talent. "You see I have been reading your friend's paper, as I promised. Well, my dear sir, not to put too fine a point, upon it, it won't hold water. In fact, it's a mere rigmarole. Excuse my asking you, Greatrex, but have you any idea, my dear fellow, whether your friend is inclined to be a little cracky?"

Arthur swallowed a groan with the greatest difficulty, and answered in as unconcerned a tone as possible, "Well, to tell you the truth, Mr. Linklight, some doubts have been cast upon his perfect sanity."

"Ah, I should have thought so," the professor went on in his airiest manner; "I should have thought so. The fact is, this paper is fitter for the Transactions of the Colney Hatch Academy than for those of the Royal Society. It has a delusive outer appearance of physical thinking, but there's no real meaning in it of any sort. It's gassy, unsubstantial, purely imaginative." And the professor waved his hand in the air to indicate its utter gaseousness. "If you were to ask my own opinion about it, I should say it's the sort of thing that might be produced by a young man of some mathematical training with a very superficial knowledge of modern physics, just as he was on the point of lapsing into complete insanity. It's the maddest bit of writing that has ever yet fallen under my critical notice."

"Your opinion is of course conclusive," Arthur answered with unfeigned humility, his eyes almost bursting with the tears he would not let come to the surface. "It will be a great disappointment to my friend, but I have no doubt he will accept your verdict."

"Not a bit of it, my dear sir," the professor put in quickly. "Not a bit of it. These crazy fellows always stick to their own opinions, and think you a perfect fool for disagreeing with them. Mark my words, Mr. Greatrex, your friend will still go on believing, in spite of everything, that his roundabout reasoning upon that preposterous square-root-of-Pi theorem is sound mathematics."

And Arthur, looking within, felt with a glow of horror that the theorem in question seemed to him at that moment more obviously true and certain in all its deductions than it had ever done before since the first day that he conceived it. How very mad he must be after all.

He thanked Professor Linklight as well as he was able for his kindness in looking over the paper, and groped his way blindly through the passage to the front door and out into the square. Thence he staggered home wearily, convinced that it was all over between him and Hetty, and that he must make up his mind forthwith to his horrible destiny.

If he had only known at that moment that forty years earlier Professor Linklight had used almost the same words about Young's theory of undulations, and had since used them about every new discovery from that day to the one on which he then saw him, he might have attached less importance than he actually did to this supposed final proof of his own insanity.

As Arthur entered his lodgings, he hung his hat up on the stand in the passage. There was a little strip of mirror in the middle of the stand, and glancing at it casually he saw once more that awful face—his own—distorted and almost diabolical, which he had learnt so soon to hate instinctively as if it were a felon's and a murderer's. He rushed away wildly into his little sitting-room, and flung his manuscript on the table, almost without observing that his friend Freeling, the rising physiologist, was quietly seated on the sofa opposite.

"What's this, Arthur?" Freeling asked, taking it up carelessly and glancing at the title. "You don't mean to say that you've finally written out that splendid idea of yours about the interrelations of energy?"

"Yes, I have, Harry: I have, and I wish to heaven I hadn't, for it's all mad and silly and foolish and meaningless!"

"If it is, then I'm mad too, my dear fellow, for I think it's the most convincing thing in physics I ever listened to. Let me have the manuscript to look over, and see how you've worked out those beautiful calculations about the square root of Pi, will you?"

"Take the thing, for heaven's sake, and leave me, Harry, for if I'm not left alone, I shall break down and cry before you." And as he spoke, he buried his head in his arm and sobbed like a woman.

Dr. Freeling knew Arthur was in love, and was aware that people sometimes act very unaccountably under such circumstances; so, he did the wisest thing to be done then and there: he grasped his friend's arm gently with his hand, spoke never a word, and, taking up his hat and the manuscript, walked quietly out into the passage. Then he told the landlady to make Mr. Greatrex a strong cup of tea, with a dash of brandy in it, and turned away, leaving Arthur to solitude and his own reflections.;

That evening's post brought Arthur Greatrex two letters, which finally completed his utter prostration. The first he opened was from Dr. Abury. He broke the envelope with a terrible misgiving, and read the letter through with a deepening and sickening feeling of horror. It was not he alone, then, who had distorted the secret of his own incipient insanity. Dr. Abury's practised eye had also detected the rising symptoms. The doctor wrote kindly and with evident grief; but there was no mistaking the firm purport of his intentions. Conferring this morning with his professional friend Warminster, a case had been mentioned to him, without a name, which he at once recognized as Arthur's. He recalled certain symptoms he had himself observed, and his suspicions were thus vividly aroused.

Happening accidentally to follow Arthur in the street he was convinced that his surmise was correct, and he thought it his duty both to inform Arthur of the danger that encompassed him, and to assure him that, deeply as it grieved him to withdraw the consent he had so gladly given, he could not allow his only daughter to marry a man bearing on his face the evident marks of an insane tendency. The letter contained much more of regret and condolence; but that was the pith that Arthur Greatrex picked out of it all through the blinding tears that dimmed his vision.

The second letter was from Hetty. Half guessing its contents, he had left it purposely till the last, and he tore it open now with a fearful sinking feeling in his bosom. It was indeed a heart-broken, heart-breaking letter. What could be the secret which papa would not tell her? Why had not Arthur come yesterday? Why could she never marry him? Why was papa so cruel as not to tell her the reason? He couldn't have done anything in the slightest degree dishonourable, far less anything wicked: of that she felt sure; but, if not, what could be this horrible, mysterious, unknown barrier that was so suddenly raised between them?

"Do write, dearest Arthur, and relieve me from this terrible, incomprehensible suspense; do let me know what has happened to make papa so determined against you. I could bear to lose you—at least I could bear it as other women have done—but I can't bear this awful uncertainty, this awful doubt as to your love or your constancy. For heaven's sake, darling, send me a note somehow! send me a line to tell me you love me. Your heart-broken

"Hetty."

Arthur took his hat, and, unable to endure this agony, set out at once for the Aburys'. When he reached the door, the servant who answered his ring at the bell told him he could not see the doctor; he was engaged with two other doctors in a consultation about Miss Hetty. What was the matter with Miss Hetty, then? What, didn't he know that? Oh, Miss Hetty had had a fit, and Dr. Freeling and Dr. MacKinlay had been called in to see her. Arthur did not wait for a moment, but walked upstairs unannounced, and into the consulting room.

Was it a very serious matter? Yes, Freeling answered, very serious.

It seemed Miss Abury had had a great shock—a great shock to her affections—which, he added in a lower voice, "you yourself can perhaps best explain to me. She will certainly have a long illness. Perhaps she may never recover."

"Come out into the conservatory, Harry," said Arthur to his friend. "I can tell you there what it is all about."

In a few words Arthur told him the nature of the shock, but without describing the particular symptoms on which the opinion of his supposed approaching insanity was based. Freeling listened with an incredulous smile, and at the end he said to his friend gently, "My dear Arthur, I wish you had told me all this before. If you had done so, we might have saved Miss Abury a shock which may perhaps be fatal. You are no more going mad than I am; on the contrary, you're about the sanest and most clear-headed fellow of my acquaintance. But these mad-doctors are always finding madness everywhere. If you had come to me and told me the symptoms that troubled you, I should soon have set you right again in your own opinion. To have gone to Warminster was most unfortunate, but it can't be helped now. What we have to do at present is to take care of Miss Abury."

Arthur shook his head sadly. "Ah," he said, "you don't know the real gravity of the symptoms I am suffering from. I shall tell you all about them some other time. However, as you say, what we have to think about now is Hetty. Can you let me see her? I am sure if I could see her it would reassure her and do her good."

Dr. Abury was at first very unwilling to let Arthur visit Hetty, who was now lying unconscious on the sofa in her own *boudoir*; but Freeling's opinion that it might possibly do her good at last prevailed with him, and he gave his permission grudgingly.

Arthur went into the room silently and took his seat beside the low couch where the motherless girl was lying. Her face was very white, and her hands pale and bloodless. He took one hand in his: the pulse was hardly perceptible. He laid it down upon her breast, and leaned back to watch for any sign of returning life in her pallid cheek and closed eyelids.

For hours and hours, he sat there watching, and no sign came. Dr. Abury sat at the bottom of the couch, watching with him; and as they watched, Arthur felt from time to time that his face was again twitching horribly. However, he had only thoughts for one thing now: would Hetty die or would she recover? The servants brought them a little cake and wine. They sat and drank in silence, looking at one another, but each absorbed in his own thoughts, and speaking never a word for good or evil.

At last Hatty's eyes opened. Arthur noticed the change first, and took her hand in his gently. Her staring gaze fell upon him for a moment, and she asked feebly, "Arthur, Arthur, do you still love me?"

"Love you, Hetty? With all my heart and soul, as I have always loved you!"

She smiled, and said nothing. Dr. Abury gave her a little wine in a teaspoon, and she drank it quietly. Then she shut her eyes again, but this time she was sleeping.

All night Arthur watched still by the bedside where they put her a little later, and Dr. Abury and a nurse watched with him. In the morning she woke slightly better, and when she saw Arthur still there, she smiled again, and said that if he was with her, she was happy. When Freeling came to inquire after the patient, he found her so much stronger, and Arthur so worn with fear and sleeplessness, that he insisted upon carrying off his friend in his brougham to his own house, and giving him a slight restorative. He might come back at once, he said; but only after he had had a dose of mixture, a glass of brandy and seltzer, and at least a mouthful of something for breakfast.

As Freeling was drawing the cork of the seltzer, Arthur's eye happened to light on a monkey, which was chained to a post in the little area plot outside the consulting-room. Arthur was accustomed to see monkeys there, for Freeling often had invalids from the Zoo to observe side by side with human patients; but this particular monkey fascinated him even in his present shattered state of nerves, because there was a something in its face which seemed strangely and horribly familiar to him. As he looked, he recognized with a feeling of unspeakable aversion what it was of which the monkey reminded him. It was making a series of hideous and apparently mocking grimaces—the very self-same grimaces which he had seen on his own features in the mirror during the last day or two! Horrible idea! He was descending to the level of the very monkeys!

The more he watched, the more absolutely identical the two sets of grimaces appeared to him to be. Could it be fancy or was it reality? Or might it be one more delusion, showing that his brain was now giving way entirely? He rubbed his eyes, steadied his attention, and looked again with the deepest interest. No, he could not be mistaken. The monkey was acting in every respect precisely as he himself had acted.

"Harry," he said, in a low and frightened tone, "look at this monkey. Is he mad? Tell me."

"My dear Arthur," replied his friend, with just a shade of expostu-
lation in his voice, "you have really got madness on the brain at present. No, he isn't mad at all. He's as sane as you are, and that's saying a
good deal, I can assure you."

"But, Harry, you can't have seen what he's doing. He's grimacing
and contorting himself in the most extraordinary fashion."

"Well, monkeys often do grimace, don't they?" Harry Freeling answered coolly. "Take this brandy and you'll soon feel better."

"But they don't grimace like this one," Arthur persisted.

"No, not like this one, certainly. That's why I've got him here. I'm
going to operate upon him for it under chloroform, and cure him
immediately."

Arthur leaped from his seat like one demented. "Operate upon
him, cure him!" he cried hastily. "What on earth do you mean, Harry?"

"My dear boy, don't be so excited," said Freeling. "This suspense
and sleeplessness have been too much for you. This is antivivisection
carried *ad absurdum*. You don't mean to say you object to operations
upon a monkey for his own benefit, do you? If I don't cut a nerve,
tetanus will finally set in, and he'll die of it in great agony. Drink off
your brandy, and you'll feel better after it."

"But, Harry, what's the matter with the monkey? For heaven's sake,
tell me!"

Harry Freeling looked at his friend for the first time a little suspiciously. Could Warminster be right after all, and could Arthur really
be going mad? It was so ridiculous of him to get into such a state of
flurry about the ailments of a tame monkey, and at such a moment,
too! "Well," he answered slowly, "the monkey has got facial distortions
due to a slight local paralysis of the inhibitory nerves supplied to the
buccal and pharyngeal muscles, with a tendency to end in tetanus. If I
cut a small ganglion behind the ear, and exhibit santonin, the muscles
will be relaxed; and though they won't act so freely as before, they
won't jerk and grimace any longer."

"Does it ever occur in human beings?" Arthur asked eagerly.

"Occur in human beings? Bless my soul, yes! I've seen dozens of
cases. Why, goodness gracious, Arthur, it's positively occurring in your
own face at this very moment!"

"I know it is," Arthur answered in an agony of suspense. "Do you
think this twitching of mine is due to a local paralysis of the inhibito-
ries, such as you speak of?"

71

"Excuse my laughing, my dear fellow; you really do look so absurdly comical. No, I don't think anything about it. I know it is."

"Then you believe Warminster was wrong in taking it for a symptom of incipient insanity?"

It was Freeling's turn now to jump up in surprise. "You don't mean to tell me, Arthur, that that was the sole ground on which that old fool, Warminster, thought you were going crazy?"

"He didn't see it himself," answered Arthur, with a sigh of unspeakable relief. "I only described it to him, and he drew his inference from what I told him. But the real question is this, Harry: Do you feel quite sure that there's nothing more than that the matter with me?"

"Absolutely certain, my dear fellow. I can cure you in half an hour. I've done it dozens of times before, and know the thing as well as you know an ordinary case of scarlet fever."

Arthur sighed again. "And perhaps," he said bitterly, "this terrible mistake may cost dear Hetty her life!"

He drank off the brandy, ate a few mouthfuls of food as best he might, and hastened back to the Aburys' When he got there, he learned from the servant that Hetty was at least no worse; and with that negative comfort he had for the moment to content himself.

Hetty's illness was long and serious; but before it was over Freeling was able to convince Dr. Abury of his own and his colleague's error, and to prove by a simple piece of surgery that Arthur's hideous grimaces were due to nothing worse than a purely physical impediment. The operation was quite a successful one; but though Greatrex's face has never since been liable to these curious contortions, the consequent relaxation of the muscles has given his features that peculiarly calm and almost impassive expression which everybody must have noticed upon them at the present day, even in moments of the greatest animation. The difficulty was how to break the cause of the temporary mistake to Hetty, and this they were unable to do until she was to a great extent convalescent. When once the needful explanation was over, and Arthur was able once more to kiss her with perfect freedom from any tinge of suspicion on her part, he felt that his paradise was at last attained.

A few days before the deferred date fixed for their wedding, Freeling came into the doctor's drawing-room, where Hetty and Arthur were sitting together, and threw a letter with a French official stamp on its face down upon the table.

"There," he said, "I find all the members of the Académie des Sciences at Paris are madmen also!"

Hetty smiled faintly, and said with a little earnestness in her tone, "Ah, Dr. Freeling, that subject has been far too serious a one for both of us to make it pleasant jesting."

"Oh, but look here, Miss Abury," said Freeling; "I have to apologise to Arthur for a great liberty I have ventured to take, and I think it best to begin by explaining to you wherein it consisted. The fact is, before you were ill, Arthur had just written a paper on the interrelations of energy, which he showed to that pompous old nincompoop, Professor Linklight. Well, Linklight being one of those men who can never see an inch beyond his own nose, had the incomprehensible stupidity to tell him there was nothing in it. Thereupon your future husband, who is a modest and self-depreciating sort of fellow, was minded to throw it incontinently into the waste-paper basket.

"But a friend of his, Harry Freeling, who flatters himself that he can see an inch or two beyond his own nose, read it over, and recognised that it was a brilliant discovery. So, what does he go and do— here comes in the apologetic matter—but get this memoir quietly translated into French, affix a motto to it, put it in an envelope, and send it in for the gold medal competition of the Académie. Strange to say, the members of the Académie turned out to be every bit as mad as the author and his friend; for I have just received this letter, addressed to Arthur at my house (which I have taken the further liberty of opening), and it informs me that the Académie decrees its gold medal for physical discovery to M. Arthur Greatrex, of London, which is a subject of congratulation for us three, and a regular slap in the face for pompous old Linklight."

Hetty seized Freeling's two hands in hers. "You have been our good genius, Dr. Freeling," she said with brimming eyes. "I owe Arthur to you; and Arthur owes me to you; and now we both owe you this. What can we ever do to thank you sufficiently?"

Since those days Hetty and Arthur have long been married, and Dr. Greatrex's famous work (in its enlarged form) has been translated into all the civilized languages of the world, as well as into German; but to this moment, happy as they both are, you can read in their faces the lasting marks of that one terrible anxiety. To many of their friends it seemed afterwards a mere laughing matter; but to those two, who went through it, and especially to Arthur Greatrex, it is a memory too painful to be looked back upon even now without a thrill of terrible recollection.

John Cann's Treasure

Cecil Mitford sat at a desk in the Record Office with a stained and tattered sheet of dark dirty-brown antique paper spread before him in triumph, and with an eager air of anxious inquiry speaking forth from every line in his white face and every convulsive twitch at the irrepressible corners of his firm pallid mouth. Yes, there was no doubt at all about it; the piece of torn and greasy paper which he had at last discovered was nothing more or less than John Cann's missing letter. For two years Cecil Mitford had given up all his spare time, day and night, to the search for that lost fragment of crabbed seventeenth-century handwriting; and now at length, after so many disappointments and so much fruitless anxious hunting, the clue to the secret of John Cann's treasure was lying there positively before him. The young man's hand trembled violently as he held the paper fast, unopened in his feverish grasp, and read upon its back the autograph endorsement of Charles the Second's Secretary of State—

Letter in cypher from Io. Cann, the noted buccaneer, to his brother Willm., intercepted at Port Royal by his Matie's command, and despatched by General Ed. D'Oyley, his Matie's Captain-Gen'l and Governor-in-Chief of the Island of Jamaica, to me, H. Nicholas.

That was it, beyond the shadow of a doubt; and though Cecil Mitford had still to apply to the cypher John Cann's own written key, and to find out the precise import of the directions it contained, he felt at that moment that the secret was now at last virtually discovered, and that John Cann's untold thousands of buried wealth were potentially his very own already.

He was only a clerk in the Colonial Office, was Cecil Mitford, on a beggarly income of a hundred and eighty a year—how small it seemed now, when John Cann's money was actually floating before his mind's-eye; but he had brains and industry and enterprise after a fitful adventurous fashion of his own; and he had made up his mind years before that he would find out the secret of John Cann's buried treasure, if he had to spend half a lifetime on the almost hopeless quest. As a boy, Cecil Mitford had been brought up at his father's rectory on the slopes of Dartmoor, and there he had played from his babyhood upward among the rugged granite boulders of John Cann's rocks, and had heard from the farm labourers and the other children around the romantic but perfectly historical legend of John Cann's treasure.

Unknown and incredible sums in Mexican *doubloons* and Spanish dollars lay guarded by a strong oaken chest in a cavern on the hilltop, long since filled up with flints and mould from the neighbouring summits. To that secure hiding-place the great buccaneer had committed the hoard gathered in his numberless piratical expeditions, burying all together under the shadow of a petty porphyritic tor that overhangs the green valley of Bovey Tracy. Beside the bare rocks that mark the site, a perfectly distinct pathway is worn by footsteps into the granite platform underfoot; and that path, little Cecil Mitford had heard with childish awe and wonder, was cut out by the pacing up and down of old John Cann himself, mounting guard in the darkness and solitude over the countless treasure that he had hidden away in the recesses of the pixies' hole beneath.

As young Mitford grew up to man's estate, this story of John Cann's treasure haunted his quick imagination for many years with wonderful vividness. When he first came up to London, after his father's death, and took his paltry clerkship in the Colonial Office—how he hated the place, with its monotonous drudgery, while John Cann's wealth was only waiting for him to take it and floating visibly before his prophetic eyes!—the story began for a while to fade out under the disillusioning realities of respectable poverty and a petty Government post.

But before he had been many months in the West India department (he had a small room on the third floor, overlooking Downing Street) a casual discovery made in overhauling the archives of the office suddenly revived the boyish dream with all the added realism and cool intensity of maturer years. He came across a letter from John Cann himself to the Protector Oliver, detailing the particulars of a fierce irregular engagement with a Spanish privateer, in which the Spaniard had been captured with much booty, and his vessel duly sold to the highest bidder in Port Royal harbour.

This curious coincidence gave a great shock of surprise to young Mitford. John Cann, then, was no mythical prehistoric hero, no fairy-king or pixy or barrow-haunter of the popular fancy, but an actual genuine historical figure, who corresponded about his daring exploits with no less a personage than Oliver himself! From that moment forth, Cecil Mitford gave himself up almost entirely to tracing out the forgotten history of the old buccaneer. He allowed no peace to the learned person who took care of the State Papers of the Commonwealth at the Record Office, and he established private relations, by letter, with two or three clerks in the Colonial Secretary's Office at Kingston, Jamaica, whom he induced to help him in reconstructing the lost story of John Cann's life.

Bit by bit Cecil Mitford had slowly pieced together a wonderful mass of information, buried under piles of ragged manuscript and weary reams of dusty documents, about the days and doings of that ancient terror of the Spanish Main. John Cann was a Devonshire lad, of the rollicking, roving seventeenth century, born and bred at Bovey Tracy, on the flanks of Dartmoor, the last survivor of those sea-dogs of Devon who had sallied forth to conquer and explore a new Continent under the guidance of Drake, and Raleigh, and Frobisher, and Hawkins.

As a boy, he had sailed with his father in a ship that bore the queen's letters of marque and reprisal against the Spanish galleons; in his middle life, he had lived a strange roaming existence—half pirate and half privateer, intent upon securing the Protestant religion and punishing the king's enemies by robbing wealthy Spanish skippers and cutting off the recusant noses of vile Papistical Cuban slave-traders; in his latter days, the fierce, half-savage old mariner had relapsed into sheer robbery, and had been hunted down as a public enemy by the Lord Protector's servants, or later still by the Captains-General and Governors-in-Chief of his Most Sacred Majesty's Dominions in the West Indies. For what was legitimate warfare in the spacious days of great Elizabeth, had come to be regarded in the degenerate reign of Charles II. as rank piracy.

One other thing Cecil Mitford had discovered, with absolute certainty; and that was that in the summer of 1660, 'the year of His Majesty's most happy restoration,' as John Cann himself phrased it, the persecuted and much misunderstood old buccaneer had paid a secret visit to England, and had brought with him the whole hoard which he had accumulated during sixty years of lawful or unlawful piracy in the West Indies and the Spanish Main. Concerning this hoard, which he had concealed somewhere in Devonshire, he kept up a brisk vernacular correspondence in cypher with his brother William, at Tavistock; and the key to that cypher, marked outside 'A clew to my Bro. Iohn's secret writing,' Cecil Mitford had been fortunate enough to unearth among the undigested masses of the Record Office.

But one letter, the last and most important of the whole series, containing as he believed the actual statement of the hiding-place, had long evaded all his research: and that was the letter which, now at last, after months and months of patient inquiry, lay unfolded before his dazzled eyes on the little desk in his accustomed corner. It had somehow been folded up by mistake in the papers relating to the charge against Cyriack Skinner, of complicity in the Rye House Plot. How it got there nobody knows, and probably nobody but Cecil Mitford himself could ever have succeeded in solving the mystery.

As he gazed, trembling, at the precious piece of dusty much-creased paper, scribbled over in the unlettered schoolboy hand of the wild old sea-dog, Cecil Mitford could hardly restrain himself for a moment from uttering a cry. Untold wealth swam before his eyes: he could marry Ethel now, and let her drive in her own carriage! Ah, what he would give if he might only shout in his triumph. He couldn't even read the words, he was so excited. But after a minute or two, he recovered his composure sufficiently to begin deciphering the crabbed writing, which constant practice and familiarity with the system enabled him to do immediately, without even referring to the key. And this was what, with a few minutes' inspection, Cecil Mitford slowly spelled out of the dirty manuscript:—

From Jamaica. This 23rd day of Jany.
in the Yeare of our Lord 1663.

My deare Bro.,—I did not think to have written you againe, after the scurvie Trick you have played me in disclosing my Affairs to that meddlesome Knight that calls himself the King's Secretary: but in truth your last Letter hath so moved me by your Vileness that I must needs reply thereto with all Expedicion. These are to assure you, then, that let you pray how you may, or gloze over your base treatment with fine cozening Words and fair Promises, you shall have neither lot nor scot in my Threasure, which is indeed as you surmise hidden away in

England, but the Secret whereof I shall impart neither to you nor to no man. I have give commands, therefore, that the Paper whereunto I have committed the place of its hiding shall be buried with my own Body (when God please) in the grave-yarde at Port Royal in this Island: so that you shall never be bettered one Penny by your most Damnable Treachery and Double-facedness. For I know you, my deare Bro., in very truth for a prating Coxcomb, a scurvie cowardlie Knave, and a lying Thief of other Men's Reputations. Therefore, no more here-with from your very humble Servt. and Loving Bro.,

Iohn Cann, Captn.

Cecil Mitford laid the paper down as he finished reading it with a face even whiter and paler than before, and with the muscles of his mouth trembling violently with suppressed emotion. At the exact second when he felt sure he had discovered the momentous secret, it had slipped mysteriously through his very fingers, and seemed now to float away into the remote distance, almost as far from his eager grasp as ever. Even there, in the musty Record Office, before all the clerks and scholars who were sitting about working carelessly at their desks at mere dilettante historical problems—the stupid prigs, how he hated them!—he could hardly restrain the expression of his pent-up feelings at that bitter disappointment in the very hour of his fancied triumph. Jamaica! How absolutely distant and unapproachable it sounded!

How hopeless the attempt to follow up the clue! How utterly his daydream had been dashed to the ground in those three minutes of silent deciphering! He felt as if the solid earth was reeling beneath him, and he would have given the whole world if he could have put his face between his two hands on the desk and cried like a woman before the whole Record Office.

For half an hour by the clock he sat there dazed and motionless, gazing in a blank disappointed fashion at the sheet of coffee-coloured paper in front of him. It was late, and workers were dropping away one after another from the scantily peopled desks. But Cecil Mitford took no notice of them: he merely sat with his arms folded, and gazed abstractedly at that disappointing, disheartening, irretrievable piece of crabbed writing. At last an assistant came up and gently touched his arm. 'We're going to close now, sir,' he said in his unfeeling of-ficial tone—just as if it were a mere bit of historical inquiry he was after—'and I shall be obliged if you'll put back the manuscripts you've been consulting into F. 27' Cecil Mitford rose mechanically and sorted out the Cyriack Skinner papers into their proper places. Then he laid them quietly on the shelf, and walked out into the streets of London, for the moment a broken-hearted man.

But as he walked home alone that clear warm summer evening, and felt the cool breeze blowing against his forehead, he began to reflect to himself that, after all, all was not lost; that in fact things really stood better with him now than they had stood that very morning, before he lighted upon John Cann's last letter. He had not discovered the actual hiding-place of the hoard, to be sure, but he now knew on John Cann's own indisputable authority, first, that there really was a hidden treasure; second, that the hiding-place was really in England; and third, that full particulars as to the spot where it was buried might be found in John Cann's own coffin at Port Royal, Jamaica.

It was a risky and difficult thing to open a coffin, no doubt; but it was not impossible. No, not impossible. On the whole, putting one thing with another, in spite of his terrible galling disappointment, he was really nearer to the recovery of the treasure now than he had ever been in his life before. Till today, the final clue was missing; today, it had been found. It was a difficult and dangerous clue to follow, but still it had been found.

And yet, setting aside the question of desecrating a grave, how all but impossible it was for him to get to Jamaica! His small funds had long ago been exhausted in prosecuting the research, and he had nothing on earth to live upon now but his wretched salary. Even if he could get three or six months' leave from the Colonial Office, which was highly improbable, how could he ever raise the necessary money for his passage out and home, as well as for the delicate and doubtful operation of searching for documents in John Cann's coffin? It was tantalising, it was horrible, it was unendurable; but here, with the secret actually luring him on to discover it, he was to be foiled and baffled at the last moment by a mere paltry, petty, foolish consideration of two hundred pounds! Two hundred pounds!

How utterly ludicrous! Why, John Cann's treasure would make him a man of fabulous wealth for a whole lifetime, and he was to be prevented from realising it by a wretched matter of two hundred pounds! He would do anything to get it—for a loan, a mere loan; to be repaid with cent. *per cent.* interest; but where in the world, where in the world, was he ever to get it from?

And then, quick as lightning, the true solution of the whole difficulty flashed at once across his excited brain. He could borrow all the money if he chose from Ethel! Poor little Ethel; she hadn't much of her own; but she had just enough to live very quietly upon with her Aunt Emily; and, thank Heaven, it wasn't tied up with any of those bothering, meddling three-*per-cent.*-loving trustees! She had her little all at her own disposal, and he could surely get two or three hundred pounds from her to secure for them both the boundless buried wealth of John Cann's treasure.

Should he make her a confidante outright, and tell her what it was that he wanted the money for? No, that would be impossible; for though she had heard all about John Cann over and over again, she had not faith enough in the treasure—women are so unpractical—to hazard her little scrap of money on it; of that he felt certain. She would go and ask old Mr. Cartwright's opinion; and old Mr. Cartwright was one of those penny-wise, purblind, unimaginative old gentlemen who will never believe in anything until they've seen it.

Yet here was John Cann's money going a-begging, so to speak, and only waiting for him and Ethel to come and enjoy it. Cecil had no patience with those stupid, stick-in-the-mud, timid people who can see no further than their own noses. For Ethel's own sake he would borrow two or three hundred pounds from her, one way or another, and she would easily forgive him the harmless little deception when he paid her back a hundredfold out of John Cann's boundless treasure.

2

That very evening, without a minute's delay, Cecil determined to go round and have a talk with Ethel Sutherland. 'Strike while the iron's hot,' he said to himself. 'There isn't a minute to be lost; for who knows but somebody else may find John Cann's treasure before I do?'

Ethel opened the door to him herself; theirs was an old engagement of long standing, after the usual Government clerk's fashion; and Aunt Emily didn't stand out so stiffly as many old maids do for the regular proprieties. Very pretty Ethel looked with her pale face and the red ribbon in her hair; very pretty, but Cecil feared, as he looked into her dark hazel eyes, a little wearied and worn-out, for it was her music-lesson day, as he well remembered. Her music-lesson day! Ethel Sutherland to give music-lessons to some wretched squealing children at the West-End, when all John Cann's wealth was lying there, uncounted, only waiting for him and her to take it and enjoy it! The bare thought was a perfect purgatory to him. He must get that two hundred pounds tonight, or give up the enterprise altogether.

'Well, Ethel darling,' he said tenderly, taking her pretty little hand in his; 'you look tired, dearest. Those horrid children have been bothering you again. How I wish we were married, and you were well out of it!'

Ethel smiled a quiet smile of resignation. 'They *are* rather trying, Cecil,' she said gently, 'especially on days when one has got a headache; but, after all, I'm very glad to have the work to do; it helps such a lot to eke out our little income. We have so *very* little, you know, even for two lonely women to live upon in simple little lodgings like these, that I'm thankful I can do something to help dear Aunt Emily, who's really goodness itself. You see, after all, I get very well paid indeed for the lessons.'

'Ethel,' Cecil Mitford said suddenly, thinking it better to dash at once into the midst of business; 'I've come round this evening to talk with you about a means by which you can add a great deal with perfect safety to your little income. Not by lessons, Ethel darling; not by lessons. I can't bear to see you working away the pretty tips off those dear little fingers of yours with strumming scales on the piano for a lot of stupid, gawky schoolgirls; it's by a much simpler way than that; I know of a perfectly safe investment for that three hundred that you've got in New Zealand Four *per cents*. Can you not have heard that New Zealand securities are in a very shaky way just at present?'

'Very shaky, Cecil?' Ethel answered in surprise. 'Why, Mr. Cartwright told me only a week ago they were as safe as the Bank of England!'

'Mr. Cartwright's an ignorant old martinet,' Cecil replied vigorously. 'He thinks because the stock's inscribed and the dividends are payable in Threadneedle Street, that the colony of New Zealand's perfectly solvent. Now, I'm in the Colonial Office, and I know a great deal better than that. New Zealand has over-borrowed, I assure you; quite over-borrowed; and a serious fall is certain to come sooner or later. Mark my words, Ethel darling; if you don't sell out those New Zealand Fours, you'll find your three hundred has sunk to a hundred and fifty in rather less than half no time!'

Ethel hesitated, and looked at him in astonishment. 'That's very queer,' she said, 'for Mr. Cartwright wants me to sell out my little bit of Midland and put it all into the same New Zealands. He says they're so safe and pay so well.'

'Mr. Cartwright indeed!' Cecil cried contemptuously. 'What means on earth has he of knowing? Didn't he advise you to buy nothing but three *per cents.*, and then let you get some Portuguese Threes at fifty, which are really sixes, and exceedingly doubtful securities? What's the use of trusting a man like that, I should like to know? No, Ethel, if you'll be guided by me—and I have special opportunities of knowing about these things at the Colonial Office—you'll sell out your New Zealands, and put them into a much better investment that I can tell you about. And if I were you, I'd say nothing about it to Mr. Cartwright.'

'But, Cecil, I never did anything in business before without consulting him! I should be afraid of going quite wrong.'

Cecil took her hand in his with real tenderness. Though he was trying to deceive her—for her own good—he loved her dearly in his heart of hearts, and hated himself for the deception he was remorsefully practising upon her. Yet, for her sake, he would go through with it. 'You must get accustomed to trusting *me* instead of him, darling,' he said softly. 'When you are mine for ever, as I hope you will be soon, you will take my advice, of course, in all such matters, won't you? And you may as well begin by taking it now. I have great hopes, Ethel, that before very long my circumstances will be so much improved that I shall be able to marry you—I hardly know how quickly; perhaps even before next Christmas.

'But meanwhile, darling, I have something to break to you that I dare say will grieve you a little for the moment, though it's for your ultimate good, birdie—for your ultimate good. The Colonial Office people have selected me to go to Jamaica on some confidential Government business, which may keep me there for three months or so. It's a dreadful thing to be away from you so long, Ethel; but if I manage the business successfully—and I shall, I know—I shall get promoted when I come back, well promoted, perhaps to the chief clerkship in the Department; and then we could marry comfortably almost at once.'

'To Jamaica! Oh, Cecil! How awfully far! And suppose you were to get yellow fever or something.'

'But I won't, Ethel; I promise you I won't, and I'll guarantee it with a kiss, birdie; so now, that's settled. And then, consider the promotion! Only three months, probably, and when I come back, we can be actually married. It's a wonderful stroke of luck, and I only heard of it this morning. I couldn't rest till I came and told you.'

Ethel wiped a tear away silently, and only answered 'If you're glad,

Cecil dearest, I'm glad too.'

'Well now, Ethel,' Cecil Mitford went on as gaily as he could, 'that brings me up to the second point. I want you to sell out these wretched New Zealands, so as to take the money with me to invest on good mortgages in Jamaica. My experience in West Indian matters—after three years in the Department—will enable me to lay it out for you at nine *per cent.*—nine *per cent.*, observe, Ethel—on absolute security of landed property. Planters want money to improve their estates, and can't get it at less than that rate. Your three hundred would bring you in twenty-seven pounds, Ethel; twenty-seven pounds is a lot of money!'

What could poor Ethel do? In his plausible, affectionate manner—and all for her own good, too—Cecil talked her over quickly between love and business experience, coaxing kisses and nine *per cent.* interest, endearing names and knowledge of West Indian affairs, till helpless little Ethel willingly promised to give up her poor little three hundred, and even arranged to meet Cecil secretly on Thursday at the Bank of England, about Colonial Office dinner-hour, to effect the transfer on her own account, without saying a single word about it to Aunt Emily or Mr. Cartwright. Cecil's conscience—for he *had* a conscience, though he did his best to stifle it—gave him a bitter twinge every now and then, as one question after another drove him time after time into a fresh bit of deceit; but he tried to smile and smile and be a villain as unconcernedly and lightly as possible.

Once only towards the end of the evening, when everything was settled, and Cecil had talked about his passage, and the important business with which he was intrusted, at full length, a gleam of suspicion seemed to flash for a single second across poor Ethel's deluded little brains. Jamaica—promotion—three hundred pounds—it was all so sudden and so connected; could Cecil himself be trying to deceive her, and using her money for his wild treasure hunt? The doubt was horrible, degrading, unworthy of her or him; and yet somehow for a single moment she could not help half-unconsciously entertaining it.

'Cecil,' she said, hesitating, and looking into the very depths of his truthful blue eyes; 'you're not concealing anything from me, are you? It's not some journey connected with John Cann?'

Cecil coughed and cleared his throat uneasily, but by a great effort he kept his truthful blue eyes still fixed steadily on hers. (He would have given the world if he might have turned them away, but that would have been to throw up the game incontinently.) 'My darling

84

Ethel,' he said evasively, 'how on earth could the Colonial Office have anything to do with John Cann?'

'Answer me Yes or No, Cecil. Do please answer me Yes or No.'

Cecil kept his eyes still fixed immovably on hers, and without a moment's hesitation answered quickly 'No.' It was an awful wrench, and his lips could hardly frame the horrid falsehood, but for Ethel's sake he answered 'No.'

'Then I know I can trust you, Cecil,' she said, laying her head for forgiveness on his shoulder. 'Oh, how wrong it was of me to doubt you for a second!'

Cecil sighed uneasily, and kissed her white forehead without a single word.

'After all,' he thought to himself, as he walked back to his lonely lodgings late that evening, 'I need never tell her anything about it. I can pretend, when I've actually got John Cann's treasure, that I came across the clue accidentally while I was in Jamaica; and I can lay out three hundred of it there in mortgages: and she need never know a single word about my innocent little deception. But indeed, in the pride and delight of so much money, all our own, she'll probably never think at all of her poor little paltry three hundred.'

3

It was an awfully long time, that eighteen days at sea, on the Royal Mail Steamship *Don*, bound for Kingston, Jamaica, with John Cann's secret for ever on one's mind, and nothing to do all day, by way of outlet for one's burning energy, but to look, hour after hour, at the monotonous face of the seething water. But at last the journey was over; and before Cecil Mitford had been twenty-four hours at Date Tree Hall, the chief hotel in Kingston, he had already hired a boat and sailed across the baking hot harbour to Port Royal, to look in the dreary, sandy cemetery for any sign or token of John Cann's grave.

An old grey-haired negro, digging at a fresh grave, had charge of the cemetery, and to him Cecil Mitford at once addressed himself, to find out whether any tombstone about the place bore the name of John Cann. The old man turned the name over carefully in his stolid brains, and then shook his heavy grey head with a decided negative. 'Massa John Cann, sah,' he said dubiously, 'Massa John Cann; it don't nobody buried here by de name ob Massa John Cann. I sartin, sah, be-case I's sexton in dis here cemetry dese fifty year, an' I know de grabe ob ebbery buckra gentleman dat ebber buried here since I fuss came.'

Cecil Mitford tossed his head angrily. 'Since *you* first came, my good man,' he said with deep contempt. 'Since you first came! Why, John Cann was buried here ages and ages before you yourself were ever born or thought of.'

The old negro looked up at him inquiringly. There is nothing a negro hates like contempt; and he answered back with a disdainful tone, 'Den I can find out if him ebber was buried here at all, as well as you, sah. We has register here; we don't ignorant heathen. I has register in de church ob every pusson dat ebber buried in dis cemetry from de berry beginnin—from de year ob de great earthquake itself. What year dis Massa John Cann him die, now? What year him die?'

Cecil pricked up his ears at the mention of the register, and answered eagerly, 'In the year 1669.'

The old negro sat down quietly on a flat tomb, and answered with a smile of malicious triumph, 'Den you is ignorant know-nuffin pusson for a buckra gentleman, for true, sah, if you tink you will find him grabe in dis here cemetry. Don't you nebber read your history book, dat all Port Royal drowned in de great earthquake ob de year 1692? We has register here for ebbery year, from de year 1692 downward; but de grabes, and de cemetery, and de register, from de year 1692 upward, him all swallowed up entirely in de great earthquake, bress de Lord!'

Cecil Mitford felt the earth shivering beneath him at that moment, as verily as the Port Royal folk had felt it shiver in 1692. He clutched at the headstone to keep him from falling, and sat down hazily on the flat tomb, beside the grey-headed old negro, like one unmanned and utterly disheartened. It was all only too true. With his intimate knowledge of John Cann's life, and of West Indian affairs generally, how on earth could he ever have overlooked it? John Cann's grave lay buried five fathoms deep, no doubt, under the blue waters of the Caribbean.

And it was for this that he had madly thrown up his Colonial Office appointment, for this that he had wasted Ethel's money, for this that he had burdened his conscience with a world of lies; all to find in the end that John Cann's secret was hidden under five fathoms of tropical lagoon, among the scattered and water-logged ruins of Old Port Royal. His fortitude forsook him for a single moment, and burying his face in his two hands, there, under the sweltering mid-day heat of that deadly sandbank, he broke down utterly, and sobbed like a child before the very eyes of the now softened old negro sexton.

4

It was not for long, however. Cecil Mitford had at least one strong quality—indomitable energy and perseverance. All was not yet lost: if need were, he would hunt for John Cann's tomb in the very submerged ruins of Old Port Royal. He looked up once more at the puzzled negro, and tried to bear this bitter downfall of all his hopes with manful resignation.

At that very moment, a tall and commanding-looking man, of about sixty, with white hair but erect figure, walked slowly from the cocoa-nut grove on the sand-spit into the dense and tangled precincts of the cemetery. He was a brown man, a *mulatto* apparently, but his look and bearing showed him at once to be a person of education and distinction in his own fashion. The old sexton rose up respectfully as the stranger approached, and said to him in a very different tone from that in which he had addressed Cecil Mitford, 'Marnin, sah; marnin, Mr. Barclay. Dis here buckra gentleman from Englan', him come 'quiring in de cemetry after de grabe of pusson dat dead before de great earthquake. What for him come here like-a-dat on fool's errand, eh, sah? What for him not larn before him come dat Port Royal all gone drowned in de year 1692?'

The new-comer raised his hat slightly to Cecil Mitford, and spoke at once in the grave gentle voice of an educated and cultivated *mulatto*. 'You wanted some antiquarian information about the island, sir; some facts about someone who died before the Port Royal earthquake? You have luckily stumbled across the right man to help you; for I think if anything can be recovered about anybody in Jamaica, I can aid you in recovering it. Whose grave did you want to see?'

Cecil hardly waited to thank the polite stranger, but blurted out at once, 'The grave of John Cann, who died in 1669.'

The stranger smiled quietly. 'What! John Cann, the famous buccaneer?' he said, with evident delight. 'Are you interested in John Cann?'

'I am,' Cecil answered hastily. 'Do you know anything about him?'

'I know all about him,' the tall *mulatto* replied. 'All about him in every way. He was not buried at Port Royal at all. He intended to be, and gave orders to that effect; but his servants had him buried quietly elsewhere, on account of some dispute with the governor of the time being, about some paper which he desired to have placed in his coffin.'

'Where, where?' Cecil Mitford gasped out eagerly, clutching at this fresh straw with all the anxiety of a drowning man.

'At Spanish Town,' the stranger answered calmly. 'I know his grave there well to the present day. If you are interested in Jamaican antiquities, and would like to come over and see it, I shall be happy to show you the tomb. That is my name.' And he handed Cecil Mitford his card, with all the courteous dignity of a born gentleman.

Cecil took the card and read the name on it: 'The Hon. Charles Barclay, Leigh Caymanas, Spanish Town.' How his heart bounded again that minute! Proof was accumulating on proof, and luck on luck! After all, he had tracked down John Cann's grave; and the paper was really there, buried in his coffin. He took the handkerchief from his pocket and wiped his damp brow with a feeling of unspeakable relief. Ethel was saved, and they might still enjoy John Cann's treasure.

Mr. Barclay sat down beside him on the stone slab, and began talking over all he knew about John Cann's life and actions. Cecil affected to be interested in all he said, though really, he could think of one thing only: the treasure, the treasure, the treasure. But he managed also to let Mr. Barclay see how much he too knew about the old buccaneer; and Mr. Barclay, who was a simple-minded learned enthusiast for all that concerned the antiquities of his native island, was so won over by this display of local knowledge on the part of a stranger and an Englishman, that he ended by inviting Cecil over to his house at Spanish Town, to stop as long as he was able. Cecil gladly accepted the invitation, and that very afternoon, with a beating heart, he took his place in the lumbering train that carried him over to the final goal of his Jamaican expedition.

5

In a corner of the Cathedral graveyard at Spanish Town, overhung by a big spreading mango tree, and thickly covered by prickly scrub of *agavé* and cactus, the white-haired old *mulatto* gentleman led Cecil Mitford up to a water-worn and weathered stone, on which a few crumbling letters alone were still visible. Cecil kneeled down on the bare ground, regardless of the sharp cactus spines that stung and tore his flesh, and began clearing the moss and lichen away from the neglected monument. Yes, his host was right! right, right, right, indubitably.

The first two letters were Io, then a blank where others were obliterated, and then came ANN. That stood clearly for Iohn Cann. And below he could slowly make out the words, 'Born at . . . vey Tra . . . Devon . . .' with an illegible date, 'Died at P . . . Royal, May 12, 1669.' Oh, great heavens, yes. John Cann's grave! John Cann's grave! John Cann's grave! Beyond any shadow or suspicion of mistake, John Cann and his precious secret lay buried below that mouldering tombstone.

That very evening Cecil Mitford sought out and found the Spanish Town gravedigger. He was a solemn-looking middle-aged black man, with a keen smart face, not the wrong sort of man, Cecil Mitford felt sure, for such a job as the one he contemplated. Cecil didn't beat about the bush or temporise with him in any way. He went straight to the point, and asked the man outright whether he would undertake to open John Cann's grave, and find a paper that was hidden in the coffin. The gravedigger stared at him, and answered slowly, 'I don't like de job, sah; I don't like de job. Perhaps Massa John Cann's ghost, him come and trouble me for dat: I don't going to do it. What you gib me, sah; how much you gib me?'

Cecil opened his purse and took out of it ten gold sovereigns. 'I will give you that,' he said, 'if you can get me the paper out of John Cann's coffin.'

The negro's eyes glistened, but he answered carelessly, 'I don't tink I can do it. I don't want to open grabe by night, and if I open him by day, de magistrates dem will hab me up for desecration ob interment. But I can do dis for you, sah. If you like to wait till some buckra gentleman die—John Cann grabe among de white man side in de grabeyard—I will dig grabe alongside ob John Cann one day, so let you come yourself in de night and take what you like out ob him coffin. I don't go meddle with coffin myself, to make de John Cann duppy trouble me, and magistrate send me off about me business.'

It was a risky thing to do, certainly, but Cecil Mitford closed with it, and promised the man ten pounds if ever he could recover John Cann's paper. And then he settled down quietly at Leigh Caymanas with his friendly host, waiting with eager, anxious expectation—till some white person should die at Spanish Town.

What an endless aimless time it seemed to wait before anybody could be comfortably buried! Black people died by the score, of course: there was a smallpox epidemic on, and they went to wakes over one another's dead bodies in wretched hovels among the back alleys, and caught the infection and sickened and died as fast as the wildest imagination could wish them; but then, they were buried apart by themselves in the pauper part of the Cathedral cemetery. Still, no white man caught the smallpox, and few *mulattoes*: they had all been vaccinated, and nobody got ill except the poorest negroes. Cecil Mitford waited with almost fiendish eagerness to hear that some prominent white man was dead or dying.

A month, six weeks, two months, went slowly past, and still nobody of consequence in all Spanish Town fell ill or sickened. Talk about tropical diseases! why, the place was abominably, atrociously, outrageously healthy. Cecil Mitford fretted and fumed and worried by himself, wondering whether he would be kept there for ever and ever, waiting till some useless nobody chose to die. The worst of it all was, he could tell nobody his troubles: he had to pretend to look unconcerned and interested, and listen to all old Mr. Barclay's stories about Maroons and buccaneers as if he really enjoyed them.

At last, after Cecil had been two full months at Spanish Town, he heard one morning with grim satisfaction that yellow fever had broken out at Port Antonio. Now, yellow fever, as he knew full well, attacks only white men, or men of white blood: and Cecil felt sure that before long there would be somebody white dead in Spanish Town. Not that he was really wicked or malevolent or even unfeeling at heart; but his wild desire to discover John Cann's treasure had now overridden every better instinct of his nature, and had enslaved him, body and soul, till he could think of nothing in any light save that of its bearing on his one mad imagination. So, he waited a little longer, still more eagerly than before, till yellow fever should come to Spanish Town.

Sure enough, the fever did come in good time, and the very first person who sickened with it was Cecil Mitford. That was a contingency he had never dreamt of, and for the time being it drove John Cann's treasure almost out of his fevered memory. Yet not entirely, even so, for in his delirium he raved of John Cann and his *doubloons* till good old Mr. Barclay, nursing at his bedside like a woman, as a tender-hearted *mulatto* always will nurse any casual young white man, shook his head to himself and muttered gloomily that poor Mr. Mitford had overworked his brain sadly in his minute historical investigations.

For ten days Cecil Mitford hovered fitfully between life and death, and for ten days good old Mr. Barclay waited on him, morning, noon, and night, as devotedly as any mother could wait upon her first-born. At the end of that time he began to mend slowly; and as soon as the crisis was over, he forgot forthwith all about his illness, and thought once more of nothing on earth save only John Cann's treasure. Was anybody else ill of the fever in Spanish Town? Yes, two, but not dangerously. Cecil's face fell at that saving clause, and in his heart, he almost ventured to wish it had been otherwise. He was no murderer, even in thought; but John Cann's treasure! John Cann's treasure! John Cann's treasure! What would not a man venture to do or pray, in order that he might become the possessor of John Cann's treasure?

As Cecil began to mend, a curious thing happened at Leigh Cay-manas, contrary to almost all the previous medical experience of the whole Island. Mr. Barclay, though a full *mulatto*, of half-black blood, suddenly sickened with the yellow fever. He had worn himself out with nursing Cecil, and the virus seemed to have got into his blood in a way that it would never have done under other circumstances. And when the doctor came to see him, he declared at once that the symptoms were very serious. Cecil hated and loathed himself for the thought; and yet, in a horrid, indefinite way he gloated over the pos-sibility of his kind and hospitable friend's dying.

Mr. Barclay had tended him so carefully that he almost loved him; and yet, with John Cann's treasure before his very eyes, in a dim, uncertain, awful fashion, he almost looked forward to his dying. But where would he be buried? that was the question. Not, surely, among the poor black people in the pauper corner. A man of his host's dis-tinction and position would certainly deserve a place among the most exalted white graves—near the body of Governor Modyford, and not far from the tomb of John Cann himself.

Day after day Mr. Barclay sank slowly but surely, and Cecil, weak and hardly convalescent himself, sat watching by his bedside, and nurs-ing him as tenderly as the good brown man had nursed Cecil him-self in his turn a week earlier. The young clerk was no hard-hearted wretch who could see a kind entertainer die without a single passing pang; he felt for the grey old *mulatto* as deeply as he could have felt for his own brother, if he had had one. Every time there was a sign of suffering or feebleness, it went to Cecil's heart like a knife—the very knowledge that on one side of his nature he wished the man to die made him all the more anxious and careful on the other side to do everything he could to save him, if possible, or at least to al-leviate his sufferings. Poor old man! it was horrible to see him lying there, parched with fever and dying by inches; but then—John Cann's treasure! John Cann's treasure! John Cann's treasure! every shade that passed over the good *mulatto's* face brought Cecil Mitford a single step nearer to the final enjoyment of John Cann's treasure.

6

On the evening when the Hon. Charles Barclay died, Cecil Mit-ford went out, for the first time after his terrible illness, to speak a few words in private with the negro sexton. He found the man lounging in the soft dust outside his hut, and ready enough to find a place for the corpse (which would be buried next morning, with the ordinary tropical haste) close beside the spot actually occupied by John Cann's coffin. All the rest, the sexton said with a horrid grin, he would leave to Cecil.

At twelve o'clock of a dark moonless night, Cecil Mitford, still weak and ill, but trembling only from the remains of his fever, set out stealthily from the dead man's low bungalow in the outskirts of Spanish Town, and walked on alone through the unlighted, unpaved streets of the sleeping city to the Cathedral precinct. Not a soul met or passed him on the way through the lonely alleys; not a solitary candle burned anywhere in a single window. He carried only a little dark lantern in his hand, and a very small pick that he had borrowed that same afternoon from the negro sexton. Stumbling along through the unfamiliar lanes, he saw at last the great black mass of the gaunt ungainly Cathedral, standing out dimly against the hardly less black abyss of night that formed the solemn background.

But Cecil Mitford was not awed by place or season; he could think only of one subject, John Cann's treasure. He groped his way easily through scrub and monuments to the far corner of the churchyard; and there, close by a fresh and open grave, he saw the well-remembered, half-effaced letters that marked the mouldering upright slab as John Cann's gravestone. Without a moment's delay, without a touch of hesitation, without a single tinge of womanish weakness, he jumped down boldly into the open grave and turned the light side of his little lantern in the direction of John Cann's undesecrated coffin.

A few strokes of the pick soon loosened the intervening earth sufficiently to let him get at a wooden plank on the nearer side of the coffin. It had mouldered away with damp and age till it was all quite soft and pliable; and he broke through it with his hand alone, and saw lying within a heap of huddled bones, which he knew at once for John Cann's skeleton. Under any other circumstances, such a sight, seen in the dead of night, with all the awesome accessories of time and place, would have chilled and appalled Cecil Mitford's nervous blood; but he thought nothing of it all now; his whole soul was entirely concentrated on a single idea—the search for the missing paper. Leaning over toward the breach he had made into John Cann's grave, he began groping about with his right hand on the floor of the coffin.

After a moment's search his fingers came across a small rusty metal object, clasped, apparently, in the bony hand of the skeleton. He drew it eagerly out; it was a steel snuff-box. Prising open the corroded hinge with his pocket-knife, he found inside a small scrap of dry paper. His fingers trembled as he held it to the dark lantern; oh heavens, success! success! it was, it was—the missing document!

He knew it in a moment by the handwriting and the cypher! He couldn't wait to read it till he went home to the dead man's house; so, he curled himself up cautiously in Charles Barclay's open grave, and proceeded to decipher the crabbed manuscript as well as he was able by the lurid light of the lantern. Yes, yes, it was all right: it told him with minute and unmistakable detail the exact spot in the valley of the Bovey where John Cann's treasure lay securely hidden. Not at John Cann's rocks on the hilltop, as the local legend untruly affirmed— John Cann had not been such an unguarded fool as to whisper to the idle gossips of Bovey the spot where he had really buried his precious *doubloons*—but down in the valley by a bend of the river, at a point that Cecil Mitford had known well from his childhood upward. Hurrah! hurrah! the secret was unearthed at last, and he had nothing more to do than to go home to England and proceed to dig up John Cann's treasure!

So he cautiously replaced the loose earth on the side of the grave, and walked back, this time bold and erect, with his dark lantern openly displayed (for it mattered little now who watched or followed him), to dead Charles Barclay's lonely bungalow. The black servants were crooning and wailing over their master's body, and nobody took much notice of the white visitor. If they had, Cecil Mitford would have cared but little, so long as he carried John Cann's last dying directions safely folded in his leather pocket-book.

Next day, Cecil Mitford stood once more as a chief mourner beside the grave he had sat in that night so strangely by himself: and before the week was over, he had taken his passage for England in the Royal Mail Steamer *Tagus*, and was leaving the cocoa-nut groves of Port Royal well behind him on the port side. Before him lay the open sea, and beyond it, England, Ethel, and John Cann's treasure.

7

It had been a long job after all to arrange fully the needful preliminaries for the actual search after John Cann's buried *doubloons*. First of all, there was Ethel's interest to pay, and a horrid story for Cecil to concoct—all false, of course, worse luck to it—about how he had managed to invest her poor three hundred to the best advantage.

Then there was another story to make good about three months' extra leave from the Colonial Office. Next came the question of buying the land where John Cann's treasure lay hidden, and this was really a matter of very exceptional and peculiar difficulty. The owner—pig-headed fellow!—didn't want to sell, no matter how much he was offered, because the corner contained a clump of trees that made a specially pretty element in the view from his dining-room windows. His dining-room windows, forsooth! What on earth could it matter, when John Cann's treasure was at stake, whether anything at all was visible or otherwise from his miserable dining-room windows? Cecil was positively appalled at the obstinacy and narrow-mindedness of the poor squireen, who could think of nothing at all in the whole world but his own ridiculous antiquated windows.

However, in the end, by making his bid high enough, he was able to induce this obstructive old curmudgeon to part with his triangular little corner of land in the bend of the river. Even so, there was the question of payment: absurd as it seemed, with all John Cann's money almost in his hands, Cecil was obliged to worry and bother and lie and intrigue for weeks together in order to get that paltry little sum in hard cash for the matter of payment. Still, he raised it in the end; raised it by inducing Ethel to sell out the remainder of her poor small fortune, and cajoling Aunt Emily into putting her name to a bill of sale for her few worthless bits of old-fashioned furniture. At last, after many delays and vexatious troubles, Cecil found himself the actual possessor of the corner of land wherein lay buried John Cann's treasure.

The very first day that Cecil Mitford could call that coveted piece of ground his own, he could not restrain his eagerness (though he knew it was imprudent in a land where the unjust law of treasure-trove prevails), but he must then and there begin covertly digging under the shadow of the three big willow trees in the bend of the river. He had eyed and measured the bearings so carefully already that he knew the very spot to a nail's-breadth where John Cann's treasure was actually hidden. He set to work digging with a little pick as confidently as if he had already seen the *doubloons* lying there in the strong box that he knew enclosed them. Four feet deep he dug, as John Cann's instructions told him; and then, true to the inch, his pick struck against a solid oaken box, well secured with clamps of iron.

Cecil cleared all the dirt away from the top, carefully, not hurriedly, and tried with all his might to lift the box out, but all in vain. It was far too heavy, of course, for one man's arms to raise: all that weight of gold and silver must be ever so much more than a single pair of hands could possibly manage. He must try to open the lid alone, so as to take the gold out, a bit at a time, and carry it away with him now and again, as he was able, covering the place up carefully in between, for fear of the Treasury and the Lord of the Manor. How abominably unjust it seemed to him at that moment—the legal claim of those two indolent hostile powers! to think that after he, Cecil Mitford, had borne the brunt of the labour in adventurously hunting up the whole trail of John Cann's secret, two idle irresponsible participators should come in at the end, if they could, to profit entirely by *his* ingenuity and *his* exertions!

At last, by a great effort, he forced the rusty lock open, and looked eagerly into the strong oak chest. How his heart beat with slow, deep throbs at that supreme moment, not with suspense, for he *knew* he should find the money, but with the final realisation of a great hope long deferred! Yes, there it lay, in very truth, all before him—great shining coins of old Spanish gold—gold, gold, gold, arranged in long rows, one coin after another, over the whole surface of the broad oak box. He had found it, he had found it, he had really found it! After so much toilsome hunting, after so much vain endeavour, after so many heart-breaking disappointments, John Cann's treasure in very truth lay open there actually before him!

For a few minutes, eager and frightened as he was, Cecil Mitford did not dare even to touch the precious pieces. In the greatness of his joy, in the fierce rush of his overpowering emotions, he had no time to think of mere base everyday gold and silver. It was the future and the ideal that he beheld, not the piled-up heaps of filthy lucre. Ethel was his, wealth was his, honour was his! He would be a rich man and a great man now and henceforth for ever! Oh, how he hugged himself in his heart on the wise successful fraud by which he had in-duced Ethel to advance him the few wretched hundreds he needed for his ever-memorable Jamaican journey! How he praised to himself his own courage, and ingenuity, and determination, and inexhaustible patience! How he laughed down that foolish conscience of his that would fain have dissuaded him from his master-stroke of genius.

He deserved it all, he deserved it all! Other men would have flinched before the risk and expense of the voyage to Jamaica, would have given up the scent for a fool's errand in the cemetery at Port Royal, would have shrunk from ransacking John Cann's grave at dead of night in the Cathedral precincts at Spanish Town, would have feared to buy the high-priced corner of land at Bovey Tracy on a pure imaginative speculation. But he, Cecil Mitford, had had the boldness and the cleverness to do it every bit, and now, wisdom was justified of all her children. He sat for five minutes in profound meditation on the edge of the little pit he had dug, gloating dreamily over the broad gold pieces, and inwardly admiring his own bravery and foresight and indomitable resolution. What a magnificent man he really was—a worthy successor of those great freebooting, buccaneering, filibustering Devonians of the grand Elizabethan era! To think that the worky-day modern world should ever have tried to doom him, Cecil Mitford, with his splendid enterprise and glorious potentialities, to a hundred and eighty a year and a routine clerkship at the Colonial Office!

After a while, however, mere numerical cupidity began to get the better of this heroic mood, and Cecil Mitford turned somewhat languidly to the vulgar task of counting the rows of *doubloons*. He counted up the foremost row carefully, and then for the first time perceived, to his intense surprise, that the row behind was not gold, but mere silver Mexican pistoles. He rubbed his eyes and looked again, but the fact was unmistakable; there was only one row of yellow gold in the top layer, and all the rest was merely bright and glittering silver. Strange that John Cann should have put coins of such small value near the top of his box: the rest of the gold must certainly be in successive layers down further. He lifted up the big gold *doubloons* in the first row, and then, to his blank horror and amazement, came to—not more gold, not more silver, but—but—but—ay, incredible as it seemed, appalling, horrifying—a wooden bottom!

Had John Cann, in his care and anxiety, put a layer of solid oak between each layer of gold and silver? Hardly that, the oak was too thick. In a moment Cecil Mitford had taken out all the coins of the first tier, and laid bare the oaken bottom. A few blows of the pick loosened the earth around, and then, oh horror, oh ghastly disappointment, oh unspeakable heart-sickening revelation, the whole box came out entire. It was only two inches deep altogether, including the cover—it was, in fact, a mere shallow tray or saucer, something like the sort of thin wooden boxes in which sets of dessert-knives or fish-knives are usually sold for wedding presents!

For the space of three seconds Cecil Mitford could not believe his eyes, and then, with a sudden flash of awful vividness, the whole terrible truth flashed at once across his staggering brain. He had found John Cann's treasure indeed—the John Cann's treasure of base actual reality; but the John Cann's treasure of his fervid imagination, the John Cann's treasure he had dreamt of from his boyhood upward, the John Cann's treasure he had risked all to find and to win, did not exist, could not exist, and never had existed at all anywhere! It was all a horrible, incredible, unthinkable delusion! The hideous fictions he had told would everyone be now discovered; Ethel would be ruined; Aunt Emily would be ruined; and they would both know him, not only for a fool, a dreamer, and a visionary, but also for a gambler, a thief, and a liar.

In his black despair he jumped down into the shallow hole once more, and began a second time to count slowly over the accursed dollars. The whole miserable sum—the untold wealth of John Cann's treasure—would amount altogether to about two hundred and twenty pounds of modern sterling English money. Cecil Mitford tore his hair as he counted it in impotent self-punishment; two hundred and twenty pounds, and he had expected at least as many thousands! He saw it all in a moment. His wild fancy had mistaken the poor outcast hunted-down pirate for a sort of ideal criminal millionaire; he had erected the ignorant, persecuted John Cann of real life, who fled from the king's justice to a nest of chartered outlaws in Jamaica, into a great successful naval commander, like the Drake or Hawkins of actual history.

The whole truth about the wretched solitary old robber burst in upon him now with startling vividness; he saw him hugging his paltry two hundred pounds to his miserly old bosom, crossing the sea with it stealthily from Jamaica, burying it secretly in a hole in the ground at Bovey, quarrelling about it with his peasant relations in England, as the poor will often quarrel about mere trifles of money, and dying at last with the secret of that wretched sum hidden in the snuff-box that he clutched with fierce energy even in his lifeless skeleton fingers. It was all clear, horribly, irretrievably, unmistakably clear to him now; and the John Cann that he had once followed through so many chances and changes had faded away at once into absolute nothingness, now and for ever!

If Cecil Mitford had known a little less about John Cann's life and exploits, he might still perhaps have buoyed himself up with the vain hope that all the treasure was not yet unearthed—that there were more boxes still buried in the ground, more *doubloons* still hidden further down in the unexplored bosom of the little three-cornered field. But the words of John Cann's own dying directions were too explicit and clear to admit of any such gloss or false interpretation. 'In a strong oaken chest, bound round with iron, and buried at four feet of depth in the south-western angle of the Home Croft, at Bovey,' said the document, plainly: there was no possibility of making two out of it in any way. Indeed, in that single minute, Cecil Mitford's mind had undergone a total revolution, and he saw the John Cann myth for the first time in his life now in its true colours.

The bubble had burst, the halo had vanished, the phantom had faded away, and the miserable squalid miserly reality stood before him with all its vulgar nakedness in their place. The whole panorama of John Cann's life, as he knew it intimately in all its details, passed before his mind's-eye like a vivid picture, no longer in the brilliant hues of boyish romance, but in the dingy sordid tones of sober fact. He had given up all that was worth having in this world for the sake of a poor gipsy pirate's penny-saving hoard.

A weaker man would have swallowed the disappointment or kept the delusion still to his dying day. Cecil Mitford was made of stronger mould. The ideal John Cann's treasure had taken possession of him, body and soul; and now that John Cann's treasure had faded into utter nonentity—a paltry two hundred pounds—the whole solid earth had failed beneath his feet, and nothing was left before him but a mighty blank. A mighty blank. Blank, blank, blank. Cecil Mitford sat there on the edge of the pit, with his legs dangling over into the hollow where John Cann's treasure had never been, gazing blankly out into a blank sky, with staring blank eyeballs that looked straight ahead into infinite space and saw utterly nothing.

How long he sat there no one knows; but late at night, when the people at the Red Lion began to miss their guest, and turned out in a body to hunt for him in the corner field, they found him sitting still on the edge of the pit he had dug for the grave of his own hopes, and gazing still with listless eyes into blank vacancy. A box of loose coin lay idly scattered on the ground beside him. The poor gentleman had been struck crazy, they whispered to one another; and so indeed he had: not raving mad with acute insanity, but blankly, hopelessly, and helplessly imbecile. With the loss of John Cann's treasure the whole universe had faded out for him into abject nihilism. They carried him home to the inn between them on their arms, and put him to bed carefully in the old bedroom, as one might put a new-born baby.

The Lord of the Manor, when he came to hear the whole pitiful story, would have nothing to do with the wretched *doubloons*; the curse of blood was upon them, he said, and worse than that; so the

Treasury, which has no sentiments and no conscience, came in at the end for what little there was of John Cann's unholy treasure.

8

In the County Pauper Lunatic Asylum for Devon there was one quiet impassive patient, who was always pointed out to horror-loving visitors, because he had once been a gentleman, and had a strange romance hanging to him still, even in that dreary refuge of the destitute insane. The lady whom he had loved and robbed—all for her own good—had followed him down from London to Devonshire; and she and her aunt kept a small school, after some struggling fashion, in the town close by, where many kind-hearted squires of the neighbourhood sent their little girls, while they were still very little, for the sake of charity, and for pity of the sad, sad story.

One day a week there was a whole holiday—Wednesday it was—for that was visiting-day at the County Asylum; and then Ethel Sutherland, dressed in deep mourning, walked round with her aunt to the gloomy gateway at ten o'clock, and sat as long as she was allowed with the faded image of Cecil Mitford, holding his listless hand clasped hard in her pale white fingers, and looking with sad, eager anxious eyes for any gleam of passing recognition in his. Alas! the gleam never came (perhaps it was better so); Cecil Mitford looked always straight before him at the blank whitewashed walls, and saw nothing, heard nothing, thought of nothing, from week's end to week's end.

Ethel had forgiven him all; what will not a loving woman forgive? Nay, more, had found excuses and palliations for him which quite glossed over his crime and his folly. He must have been losing his reason long before he ever went to Jamaica, she said; for in his right mind he would never have tried to deceive her or himself in the way he had done. Did he not fancy he was sent out by the Colonial Office, when he had really gone without leave or mission? And did he not persuade her to give up her money to him for investment, and after all never invest it? What greater proofs of insanity could you have than those? And then that dreadful fever at Spanish Town, and the shock of losing his kind entertainer, worn out with nursing him, had quite completed the downfall of his reason.

So, Ethel Sutherland, in her pure beautiful woman's soul, went on believing, as steadfastly as ever, in the faith and the goodness of that Cecil Mitford that had never been. *His* ideal had faded out before the first touch of disillusioning fact; *hers* persisted still, in spite of all the rudest assaults that the plainest facts could make upon it. Thank Heaven for that wonderful idealising power of a good woman, which enables her to walk unsullied through this sordid world, unknowing and unseeing.

At last one night, one terrible windy night in December, Ethel Sutherland was wakened from her sleep in the quiet little school-house by a fearful glare falling fiercely upon her bedroom window. She jumped up hastily and rushed to the little casement to look out towards the place whence the glare came. One thought alone rose instinctively in her white little mind—Could it be at Cecil's Asylum? Oh, horror, yes; the whole building was in flames, and if Cecil were taken—even poor mad imbecile Cecil—what, what on earth would then be left her?

Huddling on a few things hastily, anyhow, Ethel rushed out wildly into the street, and ran with incredible speed where all the crowd of the town was running together, towards the blazing Asylum. The mob knew her at once, and recognised her sad claim; they made a little lane down the surging mass for her to pass through, till she stood beside the very firemen at the base of the gateway. It was an awful sight—poor mad wretches raving and imploring at the windows, while the fire-men plied their hose and brought their escapes to bear as best they were able on one menaced tier after another. But Ethel saw or heard nothing, save in one third-floor window of the right wing, where Cecil Mitford stood, no longer speechless and imbecile, but calling loudly for help, and flinging his eager arms wildly about him. The shock had brought him back his reason, for the moment at least: oh, thank God, thank God, he saw her, he saw her!

With a sudden wild cry Ethel burst from the firemen who tried to hold her back, leaped into the burning building and tore up the blazing stairs, blinded and scorched, but by some miracle not quite suffocated, till she reached the stone landing on the third story. Turn-ing along the well-known corridor, now filled with black wreaths of stifling smoke, she reached at last Cecil's ward, and flung herself madly, wildly into his circling arms. For a moment they both forgot the awful death that girt them round on every side, and Cecil, rising one second superior to himself, cried only, 'Ethel, Ethel, Ethel, I love you; forgive me!' Ethel pressed his hand in hers gently, and answered in an agony of joy, 'There is nothing to forgive, Cecil; I can die happy now, now that I have once more heard you say you love me, you love me.'

Hand in hand they turned back towards the blazing staircase, and reached the window at the end where the firemen were now bringing their escape-ladder to bear on the third story. The men below beckoned them to come near and climb out on to the ladder, but just at that moment something behind seemed incomprehensibly to fascinate and delay Cecil, so that he would not move a step nearer, though Ethel led him on with all her might. She looked back to see what could be the reason, and beheld the floor behind them rent by the flames, and a great gap spreading downward to the treasurer's room. On the tiled floor a few dozen pence and shillings and other coins lay, white with heat, among the glowing rubbish; and the whole mass, glittering like gold in the fierce glare, seemed some fiery cave filled to the brim with fabulous wealth. Cecil's eye was riveted upon the yawning gap, and the corners of his mouth twitched horribly as he gazed with intense interest upon the red cinders and white-hot coin beneath him.

Instinctively Ethel felt at once that all was lost, and that the old mania was once more upon him. Clasping her arm tight round his waist, while the firemen below shouted to her to leave him and come down as she valued her life, she made one desperate effort to drag him by main force to the head of the ladder. But Cecil, strong man that he was, threw her weak little arm impetuously away, as he might have thrown a two-year-old baby's, and cried to her in a voice trembling with excitement, 'See, see, Ethel, at last, at last; there it is, there it is in good earnest. John Cann's Treasure!'

Ethel seized his arm imploringly once more. 'This way, darling,' she cried, in a voice choked by sobs and half stifled with the smoke. 'This way to the ladder.'

But Cecil broke from her fiercely, with a wild light in his big blue eyes, and shouting aloud, 'The treasure, the treasure!' leaped with awful energy into the very centre of the seething fiery abyss. Ethel fell, fainting with terror and choked by the flames, on to the burning floor of the third story. The firemen, watching from below, declared next day that that crazy madman must have died stifled before he touched the heap of white-hot ruins in the central shell, and the poor lady was insensible or dead with asphyxia full ten minutes before the flames swept past the spot where her lifeless body was lying immovable.

Pallinghurst Barrow

1

Rudolph Reeve sat by himself on the Old Long Barrow on Pallinghurst Common. It was a September evening and the sun was setting. The west was all aglow with a mysterious red light, very strange and lurid—a light that reflected itself in glowing purple on the dark brown heather and the dying bracken. Rudolph Reeve was a journalist and a man of science; but he had a poet's soul for all that, in spite of his avocations, neither of which is usually thought to tend towards the spontaneous development of a poetic temperament.

He sat there long, watching the livid hues that incarnadined the sky—redder and fiercer than anything he ever remembered to have seen since the famous year of the Krakatoa sunsets—though he knew it was getting late, and he ought to have gone back long since to the manor-house to dress for dinner. Mrs. Bouverie-Barton, his hostess, the famous Woman's Rights woman, was always such a stickler for punctuality and dispatch, and all the other unfeminine virtues! But, in spite of Mrs. Bouverie-Barton, Rudolph Reeve sat on. There was something about that sunset and the lights on the bracken—something weird and unearthly—that positively fascinated him.

The view over the common, which stands high and exposed, a veritable waste of heath and gorse. is strikingly wide and expansive. Pallinghurst Ring, or the "Old Long Barrow," a well-known landmark, familiar by that name from time immemorial to all the countryside, crowns its actual summit, and commands from its top the surrounding hills far into the shadowy heart of Hampshire. On its terraced slope Rudolph sat and gazed out, with all the artistic pleasure of a poet or a painter (for he was a little of both) in the exquisite flush of the dying reflections from the dying sun upon the dying heather. He sat and wondered to himself why death is always so much more beautiful, so much more poetical, so much calmer than life—and why you invariably enjoy things so very much better when you know you ought to be dressing for dinner.

He was just going to rise, however, dreading the lasting wrath of Mrs. Bouverie-Barton, when of a sudden a very weird yet definite feeling caused him for one moment to pause and hesitate. Why he felt it he knew not; but even as he sat there on the grassy tumulus, covered close with short sward of subterranean clover, that curious, cunning plant that buries its own seeds by automatic action, he was aware, through no external sense, but by pure internal consciousness, of something or other living and moving within the barrow. He shut his eyes and listened. No; fancy, pure fancy!

Not a sound broke the stillness of early evening, save the drone of insects—those dying insects, now beginning to fail fast before the first chill breath of approaching autumn, Rudolph opened his eyes again and looked down on the ground. In the little boggy hollow by his feet innumerable plants of sundew spread their murderous rosettes of sticky red leaves, all bedewed with viscid gum, to catch and roll round the struggling flies that wrenched their tiny limbs in vain efforts to free themselves. But that was all. Nothing else was astir.

In spite of sight and sound, however, he was still deeply thrilled by this strange consciousness as of something living and moving in the barrow underneath; something living and moving—or was it moving and dead? Something crawling and creeping, as the long arms of the sundews crawled and crept around the helpless flies, whose juices they sucked out. A weird and awful feeling, yet strangely fascinating! He hated the vulgar necessity for going back to dinner. Why do people dine at all? So material! so commonplace! And the universe all teeming with strange secrets to unfold! He knew not why, but a fierce desire possessed his soul to stop and give way to this overpowering sense of the mysterious and the marvellous in the dark depths of the barrow.

With an effort he roused himself, and put on his hat, which he had been holding in his hand, for his forehead was burning. The sun had now long set, and Mrs. Bouverie-Barton dined at 7.30 punctually. He must rise and go home. Something unknown pulled him down to detain him. Once more he paused and hesitated. He was not a superstitious man, yet it seemed to him as if many strange shapes stood by unseen, and watched with great eagerness to see whether he would rise and go away, or yield to the temptation of stopping and indulging his curious fancy. Strange!—he saw and heard absolutely nobody and nothing; yet he dimly realised that unseen figures were watching him close with bated breath, and anxiously observing his every movement, as if intent to know whether he would rise and move on, or remain to investigate this causeless sensation.

For a minute or two he stood irresolute; and all the time he so stood the unseen bystanders held their breath and looked on in an agony of expectation, he could feel their outstretched necks; he could picture their strained attention. At last he broke away. "This is non-sense," he said aloud to himself, and turned slowly homeward. As he did so, a deep sigh, as of suspense relieved, but relieved in the wrong direction, seemed to rise—unheard, impalpable, spiritual—from the invisible crowd that gathered around him immaterial. Clutched hands seemed to stretch after him and try to pull him back. An unreal throng of angry and disappointed creatures seemed to follow him over the moor, uttering speechless imprecations on his head, in some unknown tongue—ineffable, inaudible. This horrid sense of being followed by unearthly foes took absolute possession of Rudolph's mind.

It might have been merely the lurid redness of the afterglow, or the loneliness of the moor, or the necessity for being back not one minute late for Mrs. Bouverie-Barton's dinner-hour; but, at any rate, he lost all self-control for the moment, and ran—ran wildly, at the very top of his speed, all the way from the barrow to the door of the manor-house garden. There he stopped and looked round with a painful sense of his own stupid cowardice. This was positively childish: he had seen noth-ing, heard nothing, had nothing definite to frighten him; yet he had run from his own mental shadow, like the veriest schoolgirl, and was trembling still from the profundity of his sense that somebody unseen was pursuing and following him. "What a precious fool I am," he said to himself, half angrily, "to be so terrified at nothing! I'll go round there by-and-by, just to recover my self-respect, and to show, at least, I'm not really frightened."

And even as he said it he was internally aware that his baffled foes, standing grinning their disappointment with gnashed teeth at the garden gate, gave a chuckle of surprise, delight, and satisfaction at his altered intention.

2

There's nothing like light for dispelling superstitions terrors. Pal-linghurst Manor-house was fortunately supplied with electric light; for Mrs. Bouverie-Barton was nothing if not intensely modern. Long before Rudolph had finished dressing for dinner, he was smiling once more to himself at his foolish conduct. Never in his life before—at least, since he was twenty—had he done such a thing; and he knew why he'd done it now.

It was a nervous breakdown. He had been overworking his brain in town with those elaborate calculations for his *Fortnightly* article on "The Present State of Chinese Finances"; and Sir Arthur Boyd, the famous specialist on diseases of the nervous system, had earned three honest guineas cheap by recommending him "a week or two's rest and change in the country." That was why he had accepted Mrs. Bouverie-Barton's invitation to form part of her brilliant autumn party at Pallinghurst Manor; and that was also doubtless why he had been so absurdly frightened at nothing at all just now on the common. Memorandum: Never to overwork his brain in future; it doesn't pay. And yet, in these days, how earn bread and cheese at literature without overworking it?

He went down to dinner, however, in very good spirits. His hostess was kind; she permitted him to take in that pretty American. Conversation with the soup turned at once on the sunset. Conversation with the soup is always on the lowest and most casual plane; it improves with the fish, and reaches its culmination with the sweets and the cheese; after which it declines again to the fruity level. "You were on the barrow about seven, Mr. Reeve," Mrs. Bouverie-Barton observed severely, when he spoke of the after-glow. "You watched that sunset close. How fast you must have walked home! I was almost half afraid you were going to be late for dinner."

Rudolph coloured up slightly; 'twas a girlish trick, unworthy of a journalist; but still he had it. "Oh dear, no, Mrs. Bouverie-Barton," he answered gravely. "I may be foolish, but not, I hope, criminal. I know better than to do anything so weak and wicked as that at Pallinghurst Manor. I *do* walk rather fast, and the sunset—well, the sunset was just too lovely."

"Elegant," the pretty American interposed, in her language.

"It always is, this night every year," little Joyce said quietly, with the air of one who retails a well-known scientific fact. "It's the night, you know, when the light burns bright on the Old Long Barrow."

Joyce was Mrs. Bouverie-Barton's only child—a frail and pretty little creature, just twelve years old, very light and fairylike, but with a strange cowed look which, nevertheless, somehow curiously became her.

"What nonsense you talk, my child!" her mother exclaimed, darting a look at Joyce which made her relapse forthwith into instant silence. "I'm ashamed of her, Mr. Reeve; they pick up such nonsense as this from their nurses." For Mrs. Bouverie-Barton was modern, and disbelieved in everything. 'Tis a simple creed; one clause concludes it.

But the child's words, though lightly whispered, had caught the quick ear of Archie Cameron, the distinguished electrician, he made a spring upon them at once; for the merest suspicion of the supernatural was to Cameron irresistible. "What's that, Joyce?" he cried, leaning forward across the table. "No, Mrs. Bouverie-Barton, I really *must* hear it. What day is this today, and what's that you just said about the sunset and the light on the Old Long Barrow?"

Joyce glanced pleadingly at her mother, and then again at Cameron. A very faint nod gave her grudging leave to proceed with her tale, under maternal disapprobation; for Mrs. Bouverie-Barton didn't carry her belief in Woman's Rights quite so far as to apply them to the case of her own daughter. We must draw a line somewhere. Joyce hesitated and began. "Well, this is the night, you know," she said, "when the sun turns, or stands still, or crosses the tropic, or goes back again, or something."

Mrs. Bouverie-Barton gave a dry little cough. "The autumnal equinox," she interposed severely, "at which, of course, the sun does nothing of the sort you suppose. We shall have to have your astronomy looked after, Joyce; such ignorance is exhaustive. But go on with your myth, please, and get it over quickly."

"The autumnal equinox; that's just it," Joyce went on, unabashed. "I remember that's the word, for old Rachel, the gipsy, told me so. Well, on this day every year, a sort of glow comes up on the moor; oh! I know it does, mother, for I've seen it myself; and the rhyme about it goes—

Every year on Michael's night
Pallinghurst Barrow burneth bright.'

Only the gipsy told me it was Baal's night before it was St. Michael's; and it was somebody else's night whose name I forget, before it was Baal's. And the somebody was a god to whom you must never sacrifice anything with iron, but always with flint or with a stone hatchet."

Cameron leaned back in his chair and surveyed the child critically. "Now, this is interesting." he said "profoundly interesting. For here we get, what is always so much wanted, first-hand evidence. And you're quite sure, Joyce, you've really seen it?"

"Oh! Mr. Cameron, how can you?" Mrs. Bouverie-Barton cried, quite pettishly; for even advanced ladies are still feminine enough at times to be distinctly pettish. "I take the greatest trouble to keep all such rubbish out of Joyce's way; and then you men of science come down here and talk like this to her, and undo all the good I've taken months in doing."

"Well, whether Joyce has ever seen it not," Rudolph Reeve said gravely, "I can answer for it myself that I saw a very curious light on the Long Barrow tonight; and, furthermore, I felt a most peculiar sensation."

"What was that?" Cameron asked, bending over towards him eagerly. For all the world knows that Cameron, though a disbeliever in most things (except the Brush light), still retains a quaint tinge of Highland Scotch belief in a good ghost story,

"Why, as I was sitting on the barrow," Rudolph began, "just after sunset, I was dimly conscious of something stirring inside, not visible or audible, but—"

"Oh, I know, I know!" Joyce put in, leaning forward, with her eyes staring curiously; "a sort of a feeling that there was somebody somewhere, very faint and dim, though you couldn't see or hear them; they tried to pull you down, clutching at you like this: and when you ran away, frightened, they seemed to follow you and jeer at you. Great gibbering creatures! Oh, I know what all that is! I've been there, and felt it."

"Joyce!" Mrs. Bouverie-Barton put in, with a warning frown, "what nonsense you talk! You're really too ridiculous. How can you suppose Mr. Reeve ran away—a man of science like him—from an imaginary terror?"

"Well, I won't quite say I ran away," Rudolph answered, somewhat sheepishly. "We never do admit these things, I suppose, after twenty. But I certainly did hurry home at the very top of my speed—not to be late for dinner, you know, Mrs. Bouverie-Barton; and I *will* admit, Joyce, between you and me only, I was conscious by the way of something very much like your grinning followers behind me."

Mrs. Bouverie-Barton darted him another look of intense displeasure. "I think," she said, in that chilly voice that has iced whole committees, "at a table like this, and with such thinkers around, we might surely find something rather better to discuss than such worn-out superstitions. Professor Spence, did you light upon any fresh palaeoliths in the gravel-pit this morning?"

<h1 style="text-align:center">3</h1>

In the drawing-room, a little later, a small group collected by the corner bay, remotest from Mrs. Bouverie-Barton's own presidential chair, to hear Rudolph and Joyce compare experiences on the light above the barrow. When the two dreamers of dreams and seers of visions had finished, Mrs. Bruce, the esoteric Buddhist and hostess of Mahatmas (they often dropped in on her, it was said, quite informally, for afternoon tea), opened the flood-gates of her torrent speech with triumphant vehemence.

"This is just what I should have expected," she said, looking round for a sceptic, that she might turn and rend him. "Novalis was right. Children are early men. They are freshest from the truth. They come straight to us from the Infinite. Little souls just let loose from the free expanse of God's sky see more than we adults do—at least, except a few of us. We ourselves, what are we but accumulated layers of phantasmata? Spirit-light rarely breaks in upon our grimed charnel of flesh. The dust of years overlies us. But the child, bursting new upon the dim world of Karma, trails clouds of glory from the beatific vision. So, Wordsworth held; so the Masters of Tibet taught us, long ages before Wordsworth."

"It's curious," Professor Spence put in, with a scientific smile, restrained at the corners, "that all this should have happened to Joyce and to our friend Reeve at a long barrow. For you've seen MacRitchie's last work, I suppose? No? Well, he's shown conclusively that long barrows, which are the graves of the small, squat people who preceded the inroad of Aryan invaders, are the real originals of all the fairy hills and subterranean palaces of popular legend. You know the old story of how Childe Roland to the dark tower came, of course, Cameron?

"Well, that dark tower was nothing more or less than a long barrow; perhaps Pallinghurst Barrow itself, perhaps some other; and Childe Roland went into it to rescue his sister, Burd Ellen, who had been stolen by the fairy king, after the fashion of his kind, for a human sacrifice. The Picts, you recollect, were a deeply religious people, who believed in human sacrifice. They felt they derived from it high spiritual benefit. And the queerest part of it all is that in order to see the fairies you must go round the barrow *widershins*—that is to say, Miss Quackenboss, as Cameron will explain to you, the opposite way from the way of the sun—on this very night of all the year, Michaelmas Eve, which was the accepted old date of the autumnal equinox."

"All long barrows have a chamber of great stones in the centre, I believe," Cameron suggested tentatively.

"Yes, all or nearly all; megalithic, you know; unwrought; and that chamber's the subterranean palace, lit up with the fairy light that's so constantly found in old stories of the dead, and which Joyce and you, alone among moderns, have been permitted to see. Reeve."

"It's a very odd fact," Dr. Porter, the materialist, interposed musingly, "that the only ghosts people ever see are the ghosts of a generation very, very close to them. One hears of lots of ghosts in eighteenth-century costumes, because everybody has a clear idea of wigs and small-clothes from pictures and fancy dresses. One hears of far fewer in Elizabethan dress, because the class most given to beholding ghosts are seldom acquainted with ruffs and farthingales; and one meets with none at all in Anglo-Saxon or Ancient British or Roman costumes, because those are only known to a comparatively small class of learned people; and ghosts, as a rule, avoid the learned except you. Mrs. Bruce—as they would avoid prussic acid.

"Millions of ghosts of remote antiquity must swarm about the world, though, after a hundred years or thereabouts, they retire into obscurity and cease to annoy people with their nasty cold shivers. But the queer thing about these long-barrow ghosts is that they must be the spirits of men and women who died thousands and thousands of years ago, which is exceptional longevity for a spiritual being; don't you think so, Cameron?"

"Europe must be chock-full of them!" the pretty American assented, smiling; "though America hasn't had time, so far, to collect any considerable population of spirits."

But Mrs. Bruce was up in arms at once against such covert levity, and took the field in full force for her beloved spectres. "No, no," she said, "Mr. Porter, there you mistake your subject. You should read what I have written in *The Mirror of Trismegistus*. Man is the focus of the glass of his own senses. There are other landscapes in the fifth and sixth dimensions of space than the one presented to him. As Carlyle said truly, each eye sees in all things just what each eye brings with it the power of seeing. And this is true spiritually as well as physically. To Newton and Newton's dog Diamond what a different universe! One saw the great vision of universal gravitation, the other saw—a little mouse under a chair, as the wise old nursery rhyme so philosophically puts it. Nursery rhymes summarise for us the gain of centuries. Nothing was ever destroyed, nothing was ever changed, and nothing now is over created.

All the spirits of all that is, or was, or over will be, people the universe everywhere, unseen, around us; and each of us sees of them those only he himself is adapted to seeing. The rustic or the clown meets no ghosts of any sort save the ghosts of the persons he knows about otherwise; if a man like yourself saw a ghost at all—which isn't likely—for you starve your spiritual side by blindly shutting your eyes to one whole aspect of nature—you'd be just as likely to see the ghost of a Stone Age chief as the ghost of a Georgian or Elizabethan exquisite."

"Did I catch the word 'ghost'?" Mrs. Bouverie-Barton put in, coming up unexpectedly with her angry glower. "Joyce, my child, go to bed. This is no talk for you. And don't go chilling yourself by standing at the window in your nightdress, looking out on the common to search for the light on the Old Long Barrow, which is all pure moonshine. You nearly caught your death of cold last year with that nonsense. It's always so. These superstitions never do any good to anyone."

And, indeed, Rudolph felt a faint glow of shame himself at having discussed such themes in the hearing of that nervous and high-strung little creature.

4

In the course of the evening, Rudolph's head began to ache, as, to say the truth, it often did; for was he not an author? and sufferance is the badge of all our tribe. His head generally ached: the intervals he employed upon magazine articles. He knew that headache well; it was the worst neuralgic kind—the wet-towel variety—the sort that keeps you tossing the whole night long without hope of respite. About eleven o'clock, when the men went into the smoking-room, the pain became unendurable. He called Dr. Porter aside. "Can't you give me anything to relieve it?" he asked piteously, alter describing his symptoms.

"Oh, certainly," the doctor answered, with that brisk medical confidence we all know so well. "I'll bring you up a draught that will put that all right in less than half an hour. What Mrs. Bruce calls Soma— the fine old crusted remedy of our Aryan ancestor; there's nothing like it for cases of nervous inanition."

Rudolph went up to his room, and the doctor followed him a few minutes later with a very small phial of a very thick green viscid liquid. He poured ten drops carefully into a measured medicine-glass, and filled it up with water. It amalgamated badly. "Drink that off," he said, with the magisterial air of the cunning leech. And Rudolph drank it.

"I'll leave you the bottle," the doctor went on, laying it down on the dressing-table, "only use it with caution. Ten drops in two hours if the pain continues. Not more than ten, recollect. It's a powerful narcotic—I dare say you know its name: it's Cannabis Indica."

Rudolph thanked him inarticulately, and flung himself on the bed without undressing. He had brought up a book with him—that delicious volume, Joseph Jacobs's *English Fairy Tales*—and he tried in some vague way to read the story of Childe Roland, to which Professor Spence had directed his attention. But his head ached so much he could hardly read it; he only gathered with difficulty that Childe Roland had been instructed by witch or warlock to come to a green hill surrounded with terrace-rings—like Pallinghurst Barrow—to walk round it thrice, widershins, saying each time—

Open door! open door!
And let me come in,

and when the door opened to enter unabashed the fairy king's palace. And the third time the door did open, and Childe Roland entered a court, all lighted with a fairy light or gloaming; and then he went through a long passage, till he came at last to two wide stone doors; and beyond them lay a hall—stately, glorious, magnificent—where Burd Ellen sat combing her golden hair with a comb of amber. And the moment she saw her brother, up she stood, and she said—

Woe! worth the day, ye luckless fool,
Or ever that ye were born;
For come the King of Elfland in
Your fortune is forlorn.

When Rudolph had read so far, his head ached so much, he could read no further; so, he laid down the book, and reflected once more in some half-conscious mood on Mrs. Bruce's theory that each man could see only the ghosts he expected. That seemed reasonable enough, for according to our faith is it unto us always. If so, then these ancient and savage ghosts of the dim old Stone Age, before bronze or iron, must still haunt the grassy barrows under the waving pines, where legend declared they were long since buried; and the mystic light over Pallinghurst moor must be the local evidence and symbol of their presence.

How long he lay there he hardly quite know; but the clock struck twice, and his head was aching so fiercely now that he helped himself plentifully to a second dose of the thick green mixture. His hand shook too much to be Puritanical to a drop or two. For a while it relieved him; then the pain grew worse again. Dreamily he moved over to the big north oriel to cool his brow with the fresh night air. The window stood open.

As he gazed out a curious sight met his eye. At another oriel in the wing, which ran in an L-shaped bend from the part of the house where he had been put, he saw a child's white face gaze appealingly across to him. It was Joyce, in her white nightdress, peering with all her might, in spite of her mother's prohibition, on the mystic common. For a second she started. Her eyes met his. Slowly she raised one pale forefinger and pointed. Her lips opened to frame an inaudible word; but he read it by sight. "Look!" she said simply, Rudolph looked where she pointed,

A faint blue light hung lambent over the Old Long Barrow. It was ghostly and vague, like matches rubbed on the palm. It seemed to rouse and call him.

He glanced towards Joyce. She waved her hand to the barrow. Her lips said "Go." Rudolph was now in that strange semi-mesmeric state of self-induced hypnotism when a command, of whatever sort or by whomsoever given, seems to compel obedience. Trembling he rose, and taking his bedroom candle in his hand, descended the stair noiselessly. Then, walking on tiptoe across the tile-paved hall, he reached his hat from the rack, and opening the front door stole out into the garden.

The Soma had steadied his nerves and supplied him with false courage; but even in spite of it he felt a weird and creepy sense of mystery and the supernatural. Indeed, he would have turned back even now, had he not chanced to look up and see Joyce's pale face still pressed close against the window and Joyce's white hand still motioning him mutely onward. He looked once more in the direction where she pointed. The spectral light now burnt clearer and bluer, and more unearthly than ever, and the illimitable moor seemed haunted from end to end by innumerable invisible and uncanny creatures.

Rudolph groped his way on. His goal was the barrow. As he went, speechless voices seemed to whisper unknown tongues encouragingly in his ear; horrible shapes of elder creeds appeared to crowd round him and tempt him with beckoning fingers to follow them. Alone, erect, across the darkling waste, stumbling now and again over roots of gorse and heather, but steadied, as it seemed, by invisible hands, he staggered slowly forward, till at last, with aching head and trembling feet, he stood beside the immemorial grave of the savage chieftain. Away over in the east the white moon was just rising.

After a moment's pause, he began to walk round the tumulus. But something clogged and impeded him. His feet wouldn't obey his will; they seemed to move of themselves in the opposite direction. Then all at once he remembered he had been trying to go the way of the sun, instead of widershins. Steadying himself, and opening his eyes, he walked in the converse sense. All at once his feet moved easily, and the invisible attendants chuckled to themselves so loud that he could almost hear them. After the third round his lips parted, and he murmured the mystic words: "Open door! open door! Let me come in." Then his head throbbed worse than over with exertion and giddiness, and for two or three minutes more he was unconscious of anything.

When he opened his eyes again a very different sight displayed itself before him. Instantly he was aware that the age had gone back upon its steps ten thousand years, as the sun went back upon the dial of Ahaz; he stood face to face with a remote antiquity. Planes of existence faded; new sights floated over him; new worlds were penetrated; new ideas, yet very old, undulated centrically towards him from the universal flat of time and space and matter and motion. He was projected into another sphere and saw by fresh senses. Everything was changed, and he himself changed with it.

The blue light over the barrow now shone clear as day, though infinitely more mysterious. A passage lay open through the grassy slope into a rude stone corridor. Though his curiosity by this time was thoroughly aroused, Rudolph shrank with a terrible shrinking from his own impulse to enter this grim black hole, which led at once, by an oblique descent, into the bowels of the earth. But he couldn't help himself. For, O God! looking round him, he saw, to his infinite terror, alarm, and awe, a ghostly throng of naked and hideous savages.

They were spirits, yet savages. Eagerly they jostled and hustled him, and crowded round him in wild groups, exactly as they had done to the spiritual sense a little earlier in the evening, when he couldn't see them. But now he saw them clearly with the outer eye; saw them as grinning and hateful barbarian shadows, neither black nor white, but tawny-skinned and low-browed; their tangled hair falling unkempt in matted lucks about their receding foreheads; their jaws large and fierce; their eyebrows shaggy and protruding like a gorilla's; their loins just girt with a few scraps of torn skin; their whole mien inexpressibly repulsive and bloodthirsty.

They were savages, yet they were ghosts. The two most terrible and dreaded foes of civilized experience seemed combined at once in them. Rudolph Reeve crouched powerless in their intangible hands; for they seized him roughly with incorporeal fingers, and pushed him bodily into the presence of their sleeping chieftain. As they did so they raised loud peals of discordant laughter. It was hollow, but it was piercing. In that hateful sound the triumphant whoop of the Red Indian and the weird mockery of the ghost were strangely mingled into some appalling harmony.

Rudolph allowed them to push him in; they were too many to resist; and the Soma had sucked all strength out of his muscles. The women were the worst: ghastly hags of old, witches with pendent breasts and bloodshot eyes, they whirled round him in triumph, and shouted aloud in a tongue he had never before heard, though he understood it instinctively, "A victim! A victim! We hold him! We have him!"

Even in the agonised horror of that awful moment Rudolph knew why he understood those words, unheard till then. They were the first language of our race—the natural and instinctive mother-tongue of humanity.

They haled him forward by main force to the central chamber, with hands and arms and ghostly shreds of buffalo-hide. Their wrists compelled him as the magnet compels the iron bar. He entered the palace. A dim phosphorescent light, like the light of a churchyard or of decaying paganism, seemed to illumine it faintly. Things loomed dark before him; but his eyes almost instantly adapted themselves to the gloom, as the eyes of the dead on the first night in the grave adapt themselves by inner force to the strangeness of their surroundings.

The royal hall was built up of cyclopean stones, each as big as the head of some colossal Sesostris. They were of ice-worn granite and a dusky-grey sandstone, rudely piled on one another, and carved in relief with representations of serpents, concentric lines, interlacing zigzags, and the mystic swastika. But all these things Rudolph only saw vaguely, if he saw them at all; his attention was too much concentrated on devouring fear and the horror of his situation.

In the very centre a skeleton sat crouching on the floor in some loose, huddled fashion. Its legs were doubled up, its hands clasped round its knees, its grinning teeth had long been blackened by time or by the indurated blood of human victims. The ghosts approached it with strange reverence, in impish postures.

"See! We bring you a slave, great king!" they cried in the same barbaric tongue—all clicks and gutturals. "For this is the holy night of your father, the Sun, when he turns him about on his yearly course through the stars and goes south to leave us. We bring you a slave to renew your youth. Rise! Drink his hot blood! Rise! Kill and eat him!"

The grinning skeleton turned its head and regarded Rudolph from its eyeless orbs with a vacant glance of hungry satisfaction. The sight of human meat seemed to create a soul beneath the ribs of death in some incredible fashion. Even as Rudolph, held fast by the immaterial hands of his ghastly captors, looked and trembled for his fate, too terrified to cry out or even to move and struggle, he beheld the hideous thing rise and assume a shadowy shape, all pallid blue light, like the shapes of his jailers.

Bit by bit, as he gazed, the skeleton seemed to disappear, or rather to fade into some unsubstantial form, which was nevertheless more human, more corporeal, more horrible than the dry bones it had come from. Naked and yellow like the rest, it wore round its dim waist just an apron of dry grass, or, what seemed to be such, while over its shoulders hung the ghost of a bearskin mantle. As it rose, the other spectres knocked their foreheads low on the ground before it, and grovelled with their long locks in the ageless dust, and uttered elfin cries of inarticulate homage.

The great chief turned, grinning, to one of his spectral henchmen. "Give a knife!" he said curtly, for all that these strange shades uttered was snapped out in short, sharp sentences, and in a monosyllabic tongue, like the bark of jackals or the laugh of the striped hyena among the graves at midnight.

The attendant, bowing low once more, handed his liege a flint flake, very keen-edged, but jagged, a rude and horrible instrument of barbaric manufacture. But what terrified Rudolph most was the fact that this flake was no ghostly weapon, no immaterial shred, but a fragment of real stone, capable of inflicting a deadly gash or long torn wound. Hundreds of such fragments, indeed, lay loose on the concreted floor of the chamber, some of them roughly chipped, others ground and polished. Rudolph had seen such things in museums many times before; with a sudden rush of horror, he recognised now for the first time in his life with what object the savages of that far-off day had buried them with their dead in the chambered barrows.

With a violent effort he wetted his parched lips with his tongue, and cried out thrice in his agony the one word "Mercy!"

At that sound the savage king burst into a loud and fiendish laugh. It was a hideous laugh, halfway between a wild beast's and a murderous maniac's: it echoed through the long hall like the laughter of devils when they succeed in leading a fair woman's soul to eternal perdition. "What does he say?" the king cried, in the same transparently natural words, whose import Rudolph could understand at once. "How like birds they talk, these white-faced men, whom we got for our only victims since the years grow foolish! 'Mu-mu-mu-moo!' they say; 'Mu-mu-mu-moo!' more like frogs than men and women!"

Then it came over Rudolph instinctively, through the maze of his terror, that he could understand the lower tongue of these elfish visions because he and his ancestors had once passed through it; but they could not understand his, because it was too high and too deep for them. He had little time for thought, however. Fear bounded his horizon. The ghosts crowded round him, gibbering louder than before. With wild cries and heathen screams, they began to dance about their victim. Two advanced with measured steps and tied his hands and feet with a ghostly cord. It cut into the flesh like the stab of a great sorrow.

They bound him to a stake which Rudolph felt conscious was no earthly and material wood, but a piece of intangible shadow; yet he could no more escape from it than from the iron chain of an earthly prison. On each side the stake two savage hags, long-haired, ill-favoured, inexpressibly cruel-looking, set two small plants of Enchanter's Nightshade. Then a fierce orgiastic shout went up to the low roof from all the assembled people. Rushing forward together, they covered his body with what, seemed to be oil and butter; they hung grave-flowers round his neck; they quarrelled among themselves with clamorous cries for hairs and rags torn from his head and clothing. The women, in particular, whirled round him with frantic Bacchanalian gestures, crying aloud as they circled, "O great chief! O my king! we offer you this victim; we offer you new blood to prolong your life. Give us in return sound sleep, dry graves, sweet dreams, fair seasons!"

They cut themselves with flint knives. Ghostly ichor streamed copious.

The king meanwhile kept close guard over his victim, whom he watched with hungry eyes of hideous cannibal longing. Then, at a given signal, the crowd of ghosts stood suddenly still. There was an awesome pause. The men gathered outside, the women crouched low in a ring close lip to him. Dimly at that moment Rudolph noticed almost without noticing it that each of them had a wound on the side of his own skull; and he understood why: they had themselves been sacrificed in the dim long ago to hear their king company to the world of spirits.

Even as he thought that thought, the men and women with a loud whoop raised hands aloft in unison. Each grasped a sharp flake, which he brandished savagely. The king gave the signal by rushing at him with a jagged and saw-like knife. It descended on Rudolph's head. At the same moment, the others rushed forward, crying aloud in their own tongue, "Carve the flesh from his bones! Slay him! hack him to pieces!"

Rudolph bent his head to avoid the blows. He cowered in abject terror. Oh! what fear would any Christian ghost have inspired by the side of these incorporeal pagan savages! Ah! mercy! mercy! They would tear him limb from limb! They would rend him in pieces!

At that instant he raised his eyes, and, as by a miracle of fate, saw another shadowy form floating vague before him. It was the form of a man in sixteenth-century costume, very dim and uncertain. It might have been a ghost—it might have been a vision—but it raised its shadowy hand and pointed towards the door, Rudolph saw it was unguarded. The savages were now upon him, their ghostly breath blew chill on his cheek. "Show them iron!" cried the shadow in an English voice. Rudolph struck out with both elbows and made a fierce effort for freedom. It was with difficulty he roused himself, but at last he succeeded, he drew his pocket-knife and opened it. At sight of the cold steel, which no ghost or troll or imp can endure to behold, the savages fell back, muttering.

But 'twas only for a moment. Next instant, with a howl of vengeance even louder than before, they crowded round him and tried to intercept him. He shook them off with wild energy, though they jostled and hustled him, and struck him again and again with their sharp flint edges. Blood was flowing freely now from his hands and arms—red blood of this world; but still he fought his way out by main force with his sharp steel blade towards the door and the moonlight. The nearer he got to the exit, the thicker and closer the ghosts pressed around, as if conscious that their power was bounded by their own threshold. They avoided the knife, meanwhile, with superstitious terror. Rudolph elbowed them fiercely aside, and lunging at them now and again, made his way to the door.

With one supreme effort he tore himself madly out, and stood once more on the open heath, shivering like a greyhound. The ghosts gathered grinning by the open vestibule, their fierce teeth, like a wild beast's, confessing their impotent anger. But Rudolph started to run, all wearied as he was, and ran a few hundred yards before he fell and fainted. He dropped on a clump of white heather by a sandy ridge, and lay there unconscious till well on into the morning.

5

When the people from the Manor-house picked him up next day, he was hot and cold, terribly pale from fear, and mumbling incoherently. Dr. Porter had him put to bed without a moment's delay. "Poor fellow!" he said, leaning over him, "he's had a very narrow escape indeed of a bad brain fever. I oughtn't to have exhibited Cannabis in his excited condition; or, at any rate, if I did, I ought, at least, to have watched its effect more closely. He must be kept very quiet now, and on no account whatever, nurse, must either Mrs. Bruce or Mrs. Bouverie-Barton be allowed to come near him."

But late in the afternoon Rudolph sent for Joyce.

The child came creeping in with an ashen face. "Well?" she murmured, soft and low, taking her seat by the bedside; "so the King of the Barrow very nearly had you!"

"Yes," Rudolph answered, relieved to find there was somebody to whom he could talk freely of his terrible adventure. "He nearly had me. But how did you come to know it?"

"About two by the clock," the child replied, with white lips of terror, "I saw the fires on the moor burn brighter and bluer: and then I remembered the words of a terrible old rhyme the gipsy woman taught me—

Pallinghurst Barrow—Pallinghurst Burrow!
Every year one heart thou'lt lharrow!
Pallinghurst King—Pallinghurst King!
A bloody man is thy ghostly king.
Men's bones he breaks, and sucks their marrow,
In Pallinghurst Ring on Pallinghurst Barrow;

...and just as I thought it, I saw the lights burn terribly bright and clear for a second, and I shuddered for horror. Then they died down low at once, and there was moaning on the moor, cries of despair, as from a great crowd cheated, and at that I knew that you were not to be the Ghost-king's victim."

My New Year's Eve among the Mummies

January 1880

I have been a wanderer and a vagabond on the face of the earth for a good many years now, and I have certainly had some odd adventures in my time; but I can assure you, I never spent twenty-four queerer hours than those which I passed some twelve months since in the great unopened Pyramid of Abu Yilla.

The way I got there was itself a very strange one. I had come to Egypt for a winter tour with the Fitz-Simkinses, to whose daughter Editha I was at that precise moment engaged. You will probably remember that old Fitz-Simkins belonged originally to the wealthy firm of Simkinson and Stokoe, worshipful vintners; but when the senior partner retired from the business and got his knighthood, the College of Heralds opportunely discovered that his ancestors had changed their fine old Norman name for its English equivalent some time about the reign of King Richard I; and they immediately authorised the old gentleman to resume the patronymic and the armorial bearings of his distinguished forefathers. It's really quite astonishing how often these curious coincidences crop up at the College of Heralds.

Of course it was a great catch for a landless and briefless barrister like myself—dependent on a small fortune in South American securities, and my precarious earnings as a writer of burlesque—to secure such a valuable prospective property as Editha Fitz-Simkins. To be sure, the girl was undeniably plain; but I have known plainer girls than she was, whom forty thousand pounds converted into My Ladies: and if Editha hadn't really fallen over head and ears in love with me, I suppose old Fitz-Simkins would never have consented to such a match. As it was, however, we had flirted so openly and so desperately during the Scarborough season, that it would have been difficult for Sir Peter to break it off: and so I had come to Egypt on a tour of insurance to secure my prize, following in the wake of my future mother-in-law, whose lungs were supposed to require a genial climate though in my private opinion they were really as creditable a pair of pulmonary appendages as ever drew breath.

Nevertheless, the course of true love did not run so smoothly as might have been expected. Editha found me less ardent than a devoted squire should be; and on the very last night of the old year she got up a regulation lovers' quarrel, because I had sneaked away from the boat that afternoon under the guidance of our *dragoman*, to witness the seductive performances of some fair Ghawzi, the dancing girls of a neighbouring town. How she found it out heaven only knows, for I gave that rascal Dimitri five *piastres* to hold his tongue: but she did find it out somehow, and chose to regard it as an offence of the first magnitude: a mortal sin only to be expiated by three days of penance and humiliation.

I went to bed that night, in my hammock on deck, with feelings far from satisfactory. We were moored against the bank at Abu Yilla, the most pestiferous hole between the cataracts and the Delta. The mosquitoes were worse than the ordinary mosquitoes of Egypt, and that is saying a great deal. The heat was oppressive even at night, and the malaria from the lotus beds rose like a palpable mist before my eyes. Above all, I was getting doubtful whether Editha Fitz-Simkins might not after all slip between my fingers. I felt wretched and feverish: and yet I had delightful interlusive recollections, in between, of that lovely little Ghziyah, who danced that exquisite, marvellous, entrancing, delicious, and awfully oriental dance that I saw in the afternoon.

By Jove, she was a beautiful creature. Eyes like two full moons; hair like Milton's Penseroso; movements like a poem of Swinburne's set to action. If Editha was only a faint picture of that girl now! Upon my word, I was falling in love with a Ghziyah!

Then the mosquitoes came again. *Buzz—buzz—buzz*. I make a lunge at the loudest and biggest, a sort of *prima donna* in their infernal opera. I kill the *prima donna*, but ten more shrill performers come in its place. The frogs croak dismally in the reedy shallows. The night grows hotter and hotter still. At last, I can stand it no longer. I rise up, dress myself lightly, and jump ashore to find some way of passing the time.

Yonder, across the flat, lies the great unopened Pyramid of Abu Yilla. We are going tomorrow to climb to the top; but I will take a turn to reconnoitre in that direction now. I walk across the moonlit fields, my soul still divided between Editha and the Ghziyah, and approach the solemn mass of huge, antiquated granite blocks standing out so grimly against the pale horizon. I feel half awake, half asleep, and altogether feverish: but I poke about the base in an aimless sort of way, with a vague idea that I may perhaps discover by chance the secret of its sealed entrance, which has ere now baffled so many pertinacious explorers and learned Egyptologists.

As I walk along the base, I remember old Herodotus's story, like a page from the *Arabian Nights*, of how King Rhampsinitus built himself a treasury, wherein one stone turned on a pivot like a door; and how the builder availed himself of this his cunning device to steal gold from the king's storehouse. Suppose the entrance to the unopened Pyramid should be by such a door. It would be curious if I should chance to light upon the very spot.

I stood in the broad moonlight, near the north-east angle of the great pile, at the twelfth stone from the corner. A random fancy struck me, that I might turn this stone by pushing it inward on the left side. I leant against it with all my weight, and tried to move it on the imaginary pivot. Did it give way a fraction of an inch? No, it must have been mere fancy. Let me try again. Surely it is yielding! Gracious Osiris, it has moved an inch or more! My heart beats fast, either with fever or excitement, and I try a third time. The rust of centuries on the pivot wears slowly off, and the stone turned ponderously round, giving access to a low dark passage.

It must have been madness which led me to enter the forgotten corridor, alone, without torch or match, at that hour of the evening; but at any rate I entered. The passage was tall enough for a man to walk erect, and I could feel, as I groped slowly along, that the wall was composed of smooth polished granite, while the floor sloped away downward with a slight but regular descent. I walked with trembling heart and faltering feet for some forty or fifty yards down the mysterious vestibule: and then I felt myself brought suddenly to a standstill by a block of stone placed right across the pathway. I had had nearly enough for one evening, and I was preparing to return to the boat, agog with my new discovery, when my attention was suddenly arrested by an incredible, a perfectly miraculous fact.

The block of stone which barred the passage was faintly visible as a square, by means of a struggling belt of light streaming through the seams. There must be a lamp or other flame burning within. What if this were a door like the outer one, leading into a chamber perhaps inhabited by some dangerous band of outcasts? The light was a sure evidence of human occupation: and yet the outer door swung rustily on its pivot as though it had never been opened for ages. I paused a moment in fear before I ventured to try the stone: and then, urged on once more by some insane impulse, I turned the massive block with all my might to the left. It gave way slowly like its neighbour, and finally opened into the central hall.

Never as long as I live shall I forget the ecstasy of terror, astonishment, and blank dismay which seized upon me when I stepped into that seemingly enchanted chamber. A blaze of light first burst upon my eyes, from jets of gas arranged in regular rows tier above tier, upon the columns and walls of the vast apartment. Huge pillars, richly painted with red, yellow, blue and green decorations, stretched in endless succession down the dazzling aisles. A floor of polished syenite reflected the splendour of the lamps, and afforded a base for red granite sphinxes and dark purple images in porphyry of the cat-faced goddess Pasht, whose form I knew so well at the Louvre and the British Museum. But I had no eyes for any of these lesser marvels, being wholly absorbed in the greatest marvel of all: for there, in royal state and with mitred head, a living Egyptian king, surrounded by his coiffured court, was banqueting in the flesh upon a real throne, before a table laden with Memphian delicacies!

I stood transfixed with awe and amazement, my tongue and my feet alike forgetting their office, and my brain whirling round and round, as I remember it used to whirl when my health broke down utterly at Cambridge after the Classical Tripos. I gazed fixedly at the strange picture before me, taking in all its details in a confused way, yet quite incapable of understanding or realising any part of its true import. I saw the king in the centre of the hall, raised on a throne of granite inlaid with gold and ivory; his head crowned with the peaked cap of Rameses, and his curled hair flowing down his shoulders in a set and formal frizz. I saw priests and warriors on either side, dressed in the costumes which I had often carefully noted in our great collections; while bronze-skinned maids, with light garments round their waists, and limbs displayed in graceful picturesqueness, waited upon them, half nude, as in the wall paintings which we had lately examined at Karnak and Syene.

I saw the ladies, clothed from head to foot in dyed linen garments, sitting apart in the background, banqueting by themselves at a separate table; while dancing girls, like older representatives of my yesternoon friends, the Ghawzi, tumbled before them in strange attitudes, to the music of four-stringed harps and long straight pipes. In short, I beheld as in a dream the whole drama of everyday Egyptian royal life, playing itself out anew under my eyes, in its real original properties and personages.

Gradually, as I looked, I became aware that my hosts were no less surprised at the appearance of their anachronistic guest than was the guest himself at the strange living panorama which met his eyes. In a moment music and dancing ceased; the banquet paused in its course, and the king and his nobles stood up in undisguised astonishment to survey the strange intruder.

Some minutes passed before any one moved forward on either side. At last a young girl of royal appearance, yet strangely resembling the Ghziyah of Abu Yilla, and recalling in part the laughing maiden in the foreground of Mr Long's great canvas at the previous Academy, stepped out before the throng.

'May I ask you,' she said in Ancient Egyptian, 'who you are, and why you come hither to disturb us?'

I was never aware before that I spoke or understood the language of the hieroglyphics: yet I found I had not the slightest difficulty in comprehending or answering her question. To say the truth, Ancient Egyptian, though an extremely tough tongue to decipher in its written form, becomes as easy as love-making when spoken by a pair of lips like that Pharaonic princess's. It is really very much the same as English, pronounced in a rapid and somewhat indefinite whisper, and with all the vowels left out.

'I beg ten thousand pardons for my intrusion,' I answered apologetically: 'but I did not know that this Pyramid was inhabited, or I should not have entered your residence so rudely. As for the points you wish to know, I am an English tourist, and you will find my name upon this card;' saying which I handed her one from the case which I had fortunately put into my pocket, with conciliatory politeness. The princess examined it closely, but evidently did not understand its import.

'In return,' I continued, 'may I ask you in what august presence I now find myself by accident?'

A court official stood forth from the throng, and answered in a set heraldic tone: 'In the presence of the illustrious monarch, Brother of the Sun, Thothmes the Twenty-Seventh, king of the Eighteenth

Dynasty.'

'Salute the Lord of the World,' put in another official in the same regulation drone.

I bowed low to his Majesty, and stepped out into the hall. Apparently my obeisance did not come up to Egyptian standards of courtesy, for a suppressed titter broke audibly from the ranks of bronze-skinned waiting-women. But the king graciously smiled at my attempt, and turning to the nearest nobleman, observed in a voice of great sweetness and self-contained majesty: 'This stranger, Ombos, is certainly a very curious person. His appearance does not at all resemble that of an Ethiopian or other savage, nor does he look like the pale-faced sailors who come to us from the Achaian land beyond the sea. His features, to be sure, are not very different from theirs; but his extraordinary and singularly inartistic dress shows him to belong to some other barbaric race.'

I glanced down at my waistcoat, and saw that I was wearing my tourist's check suit, of grey and mud colour, with which a Bond Street tailor had supplied me just before leaving town, as the latest thing out in fancy tweeds. Evidently these Egyptians must have a very curious standard of taste not to admire our pretty and graceful style of male attire.

'If the dust beneath your Majesty's feet may venture upon a suggestion,' put in the officer whom the king had addressed, 'I would hint that this young man is probably a stray visitor from the utterly uncivilized lands of the North. The headgear which he carries in his hand obviously betrays an Arctic habitat.'

I had instinctively taken off my round felt hat in the first moment of surprise, when I found myself in the midst of this strange throng, and I was standing now in a somewhat embarrassed posture, holding it awkwardly before me like a shield to protect my chest.

'Let the stranger cover himself,' said the king.

'Barbarian intruder, cover yourself,' cried the herald. I noticed throughout that the king never directly addressed anybody save the higher officials around him.

I put on my hat as desired. 'A most uncomfortable and silly form of tiara indeed,' said the great Thothmes.

'Very unlike your noble and awe-spiring mitre, Lion of Egypt,' answered Ombos.

'Ask the stranger his name,' the king continued.

It was useless to offer another card, so I mentioned it in a clear voice.

'An uncouth and almost unpronounceable designation truly,' commented His Majesty to the Grand Chamberlain beside him. 'These savages speak strange languages, widely different from the flowing tongue of Memnon and Sesostris.'

The chamberlain bowed his assent with three low genuflexions. I began to feel a little abashed at these personal remarks, and I almost think (though I shouldn't like it to be mentioned in the Temple) that a blush rose to my cheek.

The beautiful princess, who had been standing near me meanwhile in an attitude of statuesque repose, now appeared anxious to change the current of the conversation. 'Dear father,' she said with a respectful inclination, 'surely the stranger, barbarian though he be, cannot relish such pointed allusions to his person and costume. We must let him feel the grace and delicacy of Egyptian refinement. Then he may perhaps carry back with him some faint echo of its cultured beauty to his northern wilds.'

'Nonsense, Hatasou,' replied Thothmes XXVII testily. 'Savages have no feelings, and they are as incapable of appreciating Egyptian sensibility as the chattering crow is incapable of attaining the dignified reserve of the sacred crocodile.'

'Your Majesty is mistaken,' I said, recovering my self-possession gradually and realising my position as a freeborn Englishman before the court of a foreign despot—though I must allow that I felt rather less confident than usual, owing to the fact that we were not represented in the Pyramid by a British Consul—'I am an English tourist, a visitor from a modern land whose civilization far surpasses the rude culture of early Egypt; and I am accustomed to respectful treatment from all other nationalities, as becomes a citizen of the First Naval Power in the World.'

My answer created a profound impression. 'He has spoken to the Brother of the Sun,' cried Ombos in evident perturbation. 'He must be of the Blood Royal in his own tribe, or he would never have dared to do so!'

'Otherwise,' added a person whose dress I recognised as that of a priest, 'he must be offered up in expiation to Amon-Ra immediately.'

As a rule I am a decent truthful person, but under these alarming circumstances I ventured to tell a slight fib with an air of nonchalant boldness. 'I am a younger brother of our reigning king,' I said without a moment's hesitation; for there was nobody present to gainsay me, and I tried to salve my conscience by reflecting that at any rate I was only claiming consanguinity with an imaginary personage.

'In that case,' said King Thothmes, with more geniality in his tone, 'there can be no impropriety in my addressing you personally. Will you take a place at our table next to myself, and we can converse together without interrupting a banquet which must be brief enough in any circumstances? Hatasou, my dear, you may seat yourself next to the barbarian prince.'

I felt a visible swelling to the proper dimensions of a Royal Highness as I sat down by the king's right hand. The nobles resumed their places, the bronze-skinned waitresses left off standing like soldiers in a row and staring straight at my humble self, the goblets went round once more, and a comely maid soon brought me meat, bread, fruits and date wine.

All this time I was naturally burning with curiosity to inquire who my strange host might be, and how they had preserved their existence for so many centuries in this undiscovered hall; but I was obliged to wait until I had satisfied his Majesty of my own nationality, the means by which I had entered the Pyramid, the general state of affairs throughout the world at the present moment, and fifty thousand other matters of a similar sort. Thothmes utterly refused to believe my reiterated assertion that our existing civilization was far superior to the Egyptian; 'because,' he said, 'I see from your dress that your nation is utterly devoid of taste or invention;' but he listened with great interest to my account of modern society, the steam-engine, the Permissive Prohibitory Bill, the telegraph, the House of Commons, Home Rule, and other blessings of our advanced era, as well as to a brief resume of European history from the rise of the Greek culture to the Russo-Turkish war. At last his questions were nearly exhausted, and I got a chance of making a few counter inquiries on my own account.

'And now,' I said, turning to the charming Hatasou, whom I thought a more pleasing informant than her august papa, 'I should like to know who you are.'

'What, don't you know?' she cried with unaffected surprise. 'Why, we're mummies.'

She made this astonishing statement with just the same quiet unconsciousness as if she had said, 'we're French,' or 'we're Americans.' I glanced round the walls, and observed behind the columns, what I had not noticed till then—a large number of empty mummy-cases, with their lids placed carelessly by their sides.

'But what are you doing here?' I asked in a bewildered way.

'Is it possible,' said Hatasou, 'that you don't really know the object of embalming? Though your manners show you to be an agreeable and well-bred young man, you must excuse my saying that you are shockingly ignorant. We are made into mummies in order to preserve our immortality. Once in every thousand years we wake up for twenty-four hours, recover our flesh and blood, and banquet once more upon the mummied dishes and other good things laid by for us in the Pyramid. Today is the first day of a millennium, and so we have waked up for the sixth time since we were first embalmed.'

'The sixth time?' I inquired incredulously. 'Then you must have been dead six thousand years.'

'Exactly so.'

'But the world has not yet existed so long,' I cried, in a fervour of orthodox horror.

'Excuse me, barbarian prince. This is the first day of the three hundred and twenty-seven thousandth millennium.'

My orthodoxy received a severe shock. However, I had been accustomed to geological calculations, and was somewhat inclined to accept the antiquity of man; so I swallowed the statement without more ado. Besides, if such a charming girl as Hatasou had asked me at that moment to turn Mohammedan, or to worship Oysteries, I believe I should incontinently have done so.

'You wake up only for a single day and night, then?' I said.

'Only for a single day and night. After that, we go to sleep for another millennium.'

'Unless you are meanwhile burned as fuel on the Cairo Railway,' I added mentally. 'But how,' I continued aloud, 'do you get these lights?'

'The Pyramid is built above a spring of inflammable gas. We have a reservoir in one of the side chambers in which it collects during the thousand years. As soon as we awake, we turn it on at once from the tap, and light it with a lucifer match.'

'Upon my word,' I interposed, 'I had no notion you Ancient Egyptians were acquainted with the use of matches.'

'Very likely not. "There are more things in heaven and earth, Cephrenes, than are dreamt of in your philosophy," as the bard of Philae puts it.'

Further inquiries brought out all the secrets of that strange tomb-house, and kept me fully interested till the close of the banquet. Then the chief priest solemnly rose, offered a small fragment of meat to a deified crocodile, who sat in a meditative manner by the side of his deserted mummy-case, and declared the feast concluded for the night. All rose from their places, wandered away into the long corridors or side-aisles, and formed little groups of talkers under the brilliant gas-lamps.

For my part, I strolled off with Hatasou down the least illuminated of the colonnades, and took my seat beside a marble fountain, where several fish (gods of great sanctity, Hatasou assured me) were disport-ing themselves in a porphyry basin. How long we sat there I can-not tell, but I know that we talked a good deal about fish, and gods, and Egyptian habits, and Egyptian philosophy, and, above all, Egyptian love-making. The last-named subject we found very interesting, and when once we got fully started upon it, no diversion afterwards oc-curred to break the even tenour of the conversation. Hatasou was a lovely figure, tall, queenly, with smooth dark arms and neck of pol-ished bronze: her big black eyes full of tenderness, and her long hair bound up into a bright Egyptian headdress, that harmonized to a tone with her complexion and her robe. The more we talked, the more desperately did I fall in love, and the more utterly oblivious did I become of my duty to Editha Fitz-Simkins. The mere ugly daughter of a rich and vulgar brand-new knight, forsooth, to show off her airs before me, when here was a princess of the Blood Royal of Egypt, obviously sensible to the attentions which I was paying her, and not unwilling to receive them with a coy and modest grace.

Well, I went on saying pretty things to Hatasou, and Hatasou went on deprecating them in a pretty little way, as who should say, 'I don't mean what I pretend to mean one bit;' until at last I may confess that we were both evidently as far gone in the disease of the heart called love as it is possible for two young people on first acquaintance to become. Therefore, when Hatasou pulled forth her watch—another piece of mechanism with which antiquaries used never to credit the Egyptian people—and declared that she had only three more hours to live, at least for the next thousand years, I fairly broke down, took out my handkerchief, and began to sob like a child of five years old.

Hatasou was deeply moved. Decorum forbade that she should console me with too much empressement; but she ventured to re-move the handkerchief gently from my face, and suggested that there was yet one course open by which we might enjoy a little more of one another's society. 'Suppose,' she said quietly, 'you were to become a mummy. You would then wake up, as we do, every thousand years;

and after you have tried it once, you will find it just as natural to sleep for a millennium as for eight hours. Of course,' she added with a slight blush, 'during the next three or four solar cycles there would be plenty of time to conclude any other arrangements you might possibly contemplate, before the occurrence of another glacial epoch.'

This mode of regarding time was certainly novel and somewhat bewildering to people who ordinarily reckon its lapse by weeks and months; and I had a vague consciousness that my relations with Editha imposed upon me a moral necessity of returning to the outer world, instead of becoming a millennial mummy. Besides, there was the awkward chance of being converted into fuel and dissipated into space before the arrival of the next waking day. But I took one look at Hatasou, whose eyes were filling in turn with sympathetic tears, and that look decided me. I flung Editha, life, and duty to the dogs, and resolved at once to become a mummy.

There was no time to be lost. Only three hours remained to us, and the process of embalming, even in the most hasty manner, would take up fully two. We rushed off to the chief priest, who had charge of the particular department in question. He at once acceded to my wishes, and briefly explained the mode in which they usually treated the corpse.

That word suddenly aroused me. 'The corpse!' I cried; 'but I am alive. You can't embalm me living.'

'We can,' replied the priest, 'under chloroform.'

'Chloroform!' I echoed, growing more and more astonished: 'I had no idea you Egyptians knew anything about it.'

'Ignorant barbarian!' he answered with a curl of the lip; 'you imagine yourself much wiser than the teachers of the world. If you were versed in all the wisdom of the Egyptians, you would know that chloroform is one of our simplest and commonest anaesthetics.'

I put myself at once under the hands of the priest. He brought out the chloroform, and placed it beneath my nostrils, as I lay on a soft couch under the central court. Hatasou held my hand in hers, and watched my breathing with an anxious eye. I saw the priest leaning over me, with a clouded phial in his hand, and I experienced a vague sensation of smelling myrrh and spikenard. Next, I lost myself for a few moments, and when I again recovered my senses in a temporary break, the priest was holding a small greenstone knife, dabbled with blood, and I felt that a gash had been made across my breast. Then they applied the chloroform once more; I felt Hatasou give my hand a gentle squeeze; the whole panorama faded finally from my view; and I went to sleep for a seemingly endless time.

When I awoke again, my first impression led me to believe that the thousand years were over, and that I had come to life once more to feast with Hatasou and Thothmes in the Pyramid of Abu Yilla. But second thoughts, combined with closer observation of the surroundings, convinced me that I was really lying in a bedroom of Shepheard's Hotel at Cairo. An hospital nurse leant over me, instead of a chief priest; and I noticed no tokens of Editha Fitz-Simkins's presence. But when I endeavoured to make inquiries upon the subject of my whereabouts, I was peremptorily informed that I mustn't speak, as I was only just recovering from a severe fever, and might endanger my life by talking.

Some weeks later I learned the sequel of my night's adventure. The Fitz-Simkinses, missing me from the boat in the morning, at first imagined that I might have gone ashore for an early stroll. But after breakfast time, lunch time, and dinner time had gone past, they began to grow alarmed, and sent to look for me in all directions. One of their scouts, happening to pass the Pyramid, noticed that one of the stones near the north-east angle had been displaced, so as to give access to a dark passage, hitherto unknown. Calling several of his friends, for he was afraid to venture in alone, he passed down the corridor, and through a second gateway into the central hall. There the Fellahin found me, lying on the ground, bleeding profusely from a wound on the breast, and in an advanced stage of malarious fever. They brought me back to the boat, and the Fitz-Simkinses conveyed me at once to Cairo, for medical attendance and proper nursing.

Editha was at first convinced that I had attempted to commit suicide because I could not endure having caused her pain, and she accordingly resolved to tend me with the utmost care through my illness. But she found that my delirious remarks, besides bearing frequent reference to a princess, with whom I appeared to have been on unexpectedly intimate terms, also related very largely to our *casus belli* itself, the dancing girls of Abu Yilla.

Even this trial she might have borne, setting down the moral degeneracy which led me to patronize so degrading an exhibition as a first symptom of my approaching malady: but certain unfortunate observations, containing pointed and by no means flattering allusions to her personal appearance—which I contrasted, much to her disadvantage, with that of the unknown princess—these, I say, were things which she could not forgive; and she left Cairo abruptly with her parents for the Riviera, leaving behind a stinging note, in which she denounced my perfidy and empty-heartedness with all the flowers of feminine eloquence. From that day to this I have never seen her.

When I returned to London and proposed to lay this account before the Society of Antiquaries, all my friends dissuaded me on the grounds of its apparent incredibility. They declare that I must have gone to the Pyramid already in a state of delirium, discovered the entrance by accident, and sunk exhausted when I reached the inner chamber. In answer, I would point out three facts. In the first place, I undoubtedly found my way into the unknown passage—for which achievement I afterwards received the gold medal of the Societe Khediviale, and of which I retain a clear recollection, differing in no way from my recollection of the subsequent events.

In the second place, I had in my pocket, when found, a ring of Hatasou's, which I drew from her finger just before I took the chloroform, and put into my pocket as a keepsake. And in the third place, I had on my breast the wound which I saw the priest inflict with a knife of greenstone, and the scar may be seen on the spot to the present day. The absurd hypothesis of my medical friends, that I was wounded by falling against a sharp edge of rock, I must at once reject as unworthy of a moment's consideration.

My own theory is either that the priest had not time to complete the operation, or else that the arrival of the Fitz-Simkins' scouts frightened back the mummies to their cases an hour or so too soon. At any rate, there they all were, ranged around the walls undisturbed, the moment the Fellahin entered.

Unfortunately, the truth of my account cannot be tested for another thousand years. But as a copy of this book will be preserved for the benefit of posterity in the British Museum, I hereby solemnly call upon Collective Humanity to try the veracity of this history by sending a deputation of archaeologists to the Pyramid of Abu Yilla, on the last day of December, Two thousand eight hundred and seventy-seven. If they do not then find Thothmes and Hatasou feasting in the central hall exactly as I have described, I shall willingly admit that the story of my New Year's Eve among the Mummies is a vain hallucination, unworthy of credence at the hands of the scientific world.

The Miraculous Explorer

I never knew a stranger or more mysterious man than Dr. Emil Ritter. He was a sphinx incarnate. From the first moment I met him he exercised over my mind a singular fascination. Tall, dark, and supple, he moved through a room with a cat-like tread, which was yet so refined that instead of being stealthy it simply impressed one with a general sense of delicate noiselessness. He stepped as if on ether. His eyes were large, and pathetic like a gazelle's; his long lank hair was straight, black, and wiry. The very first evening I spent in his company was at a friend's in South Kensington. I was then a junior assistant in the Egyptian department at the British Museum.

"Oh, Mr. Harvey, you'll be delighted to meet one person who's coming here tonight," my hostess said with a smile as I shook hands with her on entering.

"Indeed;" I answered, "a pretty girl?"

"A pretty girl! What a notion! No, no. Dr. Emil Ritter."

And I *was* delighted, for everyone just then was talking of Ritter's extraordinary excavations at Tel-el-Magada. "I hope he speaks English," I answered dubiously, for my German is practically a vanishing quantity."

"English? as well as you do. And everything else too—French, Spanish, Italian, and above all Arabic."

When the great man arrived, I could have taken him at first sight for an Egyptian or an Arab. His skin, naturally dark, had been still further bronzed by some years of exposure to the sun of the desert. He had all the Oriental gravity and dignity: but those pathetic eyes flashed now and again with an eager fire which was wholly western. In spite of his name, indeed, as I soon found out, he was not German but American, though his education at Berlin had made him quite at home in the land of his ancestors. In less than three minutes we were deep in Egypt, like two of a trade, discussing the chronology of the Eleventh Dynasty.

It was all very sudden, but the man inspired me. As he talked, he let in new floods of light on many obscure corners of Egyptian religion, or law, or custom. Talk of our Museum authorities! I had never met anybody in my life before half so deeply versed in all the wisdom of the Egyptians. To him, the monuments were no mere dry bones; he seemed to breathe into them the breath of life. Thebes and Memphis at his word appeared to rise and live again. I liked him immensely. An enthusiast from the beginning for the Upper and Lower Kingdoms, I was carried away at once by the fire of his eloquence and the profundity of his learning. Ritter, too, if I may venture to say so, was almost as much impressed by me as I by him. He took to me instantly. Like magnet to magnet, we leapt at one another.

"Throw up your appointment," he said at last, "and come out to Egypt with me!"

I was only twenty-four: it was giving up a certainty for unknown contingencies—no future, no pension. But the proposal flattered me. The man was so great. "I will," I said. "How soon do you start?"

"On Friday,"

"I will be with you."

So, to Egypt I went, and I have never regretted it.

After a day or two at Cairo, the Ghizeh Museum, the tombs of Sakkarah, the Sphinx, the Pyramids, we took the postal boat to the scene of his excavations. A week at Thebes filled me fuller than ever with intense admiration for my new companion. He was wonderful, wonderful! As we roamed through the massy colonnades of Karnak, he explained to me so well the hidden meaning of every petty detail, every knop and lotus, not like a dry pedant, but with the eye and the brain of a sculptor and an architect. Difficulties that seemed to my mind insuperable he dissipated at a glance.

How did they raise the vast blocks of the architrave to so dizzy a height—solid tons of sandstone? Why, nothing easier—and a diagram lightly traced with his stick in the dust made it plain as a pike-staff. What was the sense of this or that new word in a freshly discovered inscription? Oh, of course, don't you see? it comes from the root of so-and-so, and means a first charge on the date-trees of a district. He jumped at everything as if by intuition. It was genius at work. Exploration with him was pure knack, not science.

When we passed on to our proper task at Tel-el-Magada, my surprise and admiration deepened daily. Ritter excavated by instinct. "Dig here!" he said to his men—and lo! the foundations of a granite temple:"Dig there!" and lo! the buried hoard of some forgotten monarch. His power over his workmen was something almost magical. Daily, as I lived with him, the sense of his weirdness, of some mystic and supernatural force about the man, quickened and strengthened within me. Yet he ate tinned meats like the most ordinary mortal, and had a special weakness for a cup of strong tea at half-past four on the verge of the desert.

So, the winter wore away. One afternoon in early spring, when the sun was beginning to stand well overhead, I walked with him on a narrow, dusty path that led between two fields of waving *doorah*. A *khamseen* was blowing. Suddenly, at one point in our walk, he stopped dead short, and seemed to be making a mental calculation. All at once he moved a few feet aside among the standing stalks and called to the *fellah* who was weeding between them. "I want to dig here," he said, tracing lines with his stick on the ground among the crop. "What will you charge me for doing it?"

The *fellah* named a sum with a promptitude and certainty which nobody but Ritter could have extracted from an Egyptian. They knew his plan—one price, money down, and not a *piastre* for *backshish*. In less than an hour our men were at work, and at the end of ten days they had come upon a tomb containing the finest and most valuable set of enamelled gold jewellery ever found in the country. It is now in the Imperial Museum at St. Petersburg.

That evening we sat together in our tent on the desert slope, overlooking the cultivated plain of Magada. The sun was setting; strange rosy lights flushed the dry summits of the eternal hills, whose arid range bounds the view to eastward. It was that weird pink light which one never sees on earth save on the mouldering sandstone of Upper Egypt. Ritter's eyes looked away with a vague gaze on infinity. He was silent and moody, more mysterious than ever. We sat there long by the tent door, looking out without a word on that marvellous sunset. At last I broke the stillness with a sudden question. "How on earth did you know, Ritter, those jewels were buried there?"

The keen eyes came back to earth with a flash, and looked me through and through in the gloaming for a moment. "Dare I trust you?" he asked. "If I tell you, will you betray me?"

"Betray you! Why, Ritter, I'd lay down my life for you!"

He looked me through and through once more as if in doubt;

then he made up his mind. "I'll tell you," he answered very slowly and calmly. "*I put them there.*"

For a second I paused. Much as I loved and admired him, a violent revulsion of horror came over me. "You put them there!" I cried, drawing back and biting my lip. "Oh, Ritter, Ritter, you don't mean to tell me you're a fraud and a humbug!"

He clapped his hand to his head. "Great Heavens," he answered, "that you, too, should misunderstand me! Oh, Khem! Oh, Nephthys! I put them there myself, not this year or last, but five thousand years ago!"

"My friend," I said, "are you mad?"

He rose and faced me. His dark complexion gleamed ruddy in the last reflected rays of the sun. He looked the very image of the painted Egyptians on the walls of the Tombs of the Kings at Thebes. "No, no," he said impatiently. "Don't you know what I am? Don't you guess how I come to have learned so much about ancient Egypt, Its people, and its language? Look at me, Harvey! Can't you see for yourself I am a reincarnation?"

And indeed, he looked it.

I seized his hand. "Why, Ritter," I cried, "how burning hot you are!"

"Yes, hot, very hot," he said slowly, in a voice like a dream. "I'll go and lie down. I think I have fever."

For a week he lay ill in the tent on the desert. In his delirium he raved prayers to Pasht and Amun-Ra, to Thoth and Osiris. On the eighth day he died. We buried him near the little mosque of Magada. He sleeps in the beloved soil of Egypt.

Was it the fever coming on? Was it a foretaste of his delirium? I cannot say; but of this I feel sure: he believed it himself that night when he said it. And ever since, when I think of his incredible instinct of discovery, sceptic as I am, I feel more than half inclined to agree with him.

Kalee's Shrine

Prologue

IN INDIA

White-robed and dusky-faced, the *ayah* hurried with trembling: footsteps along the narrow path that threaded tortuously the tangled underbrush of that arid thicket. Her feet and ankles were bare to the knee, and the fine grey dust that covered them deep with its clinging powder bore witness eloquently to the distance she had already carried her precious burden—a pretty, sleeping, two-year-old baby. It was not her own, but a white man's daughter; and the white man was a great English sahib. At every rustle of the bushes in the jungle by her side, the woman shrank back with terrible earnestness—shrank, and pressed the sleeping baby tight to her bosom; for tigers lurked among the tangled brake, and the cobra might at any moment cross her path with his deadly hood erect and hissing.

But still she hurried on alone and breathless, that one solitary Hindu figure, tall and graceful in her snowy robes, with the unconscious white child strained against her breast, and her heart leaping wildly as at every step the bangles clanked together on her brown ankles. The fierce hot sun poured down upon her head mercilessly from above, and the little green lizards darted away with lithe and sinuous motion at the fall of her naked dusky foot upon the staring grey line of the path behind them.

The woman was flying, though no one pursued her; flying with the stealthy, noiseless Indian tread, and looking back furtively over her dark shoulder with eager fear every now and again, to listen for the hoofs of approaching horses. But no one came; no one followed her: and she wound her way silently, alone, through the jungle, with the instinct of the serpent, and the light, unwearied, gliding motion of the

Hindu race. The sun had reached the summit of the heaven now, and the *sahibs* at home would soon be thinking it time for *tiffin*.

She had risked all upon one desperate throw. If only she could return in time to escape detection!

Presently a little clearing in the thicket appeared, and the grimy path ended at last in front of a tiny, shabby, brick-built temple. Around it, the cleared area lay thick in dust, and the garish Indian sun glared hotter than ever on the crumbling plaster of that neglected shrine—the shrine of a hated and proscribed worship.

An old man crouched in the dust before the door. He was a squalid old man, wrinkled and discoloured with age and filth; his matted white locks straggled wildly about his black forehead, and his lean ribs showed in visible outline through the dark skin that seemed to hang loose in folds around them. A few foul rags just covered his loins, and the rags and the man seemed almost to have grown together into one huddled mass by long companionship and ascetic filthiness. He did not lift his eyes as the woman approached, but went on staring vacantly at the temple before him, and repeating, in a low monotonous sing-song, the burden of a ghastly Hindu hymn to the terrible Kalee:

Oh, thou that delightest in fresh warm blood, in red blood,
in the slaughter of thine enemies; girt round with skulls!
we offer up to thee the heart of the victim.

An outcast dog that lay by the ascetic's side was munching away at an oddly-shaped bone. It was round and smooth, and bare at the top; on the sides some fragments of long black hair still clung to the horrid object. The dog pawed it and gnawed it with his teeth, and the shallow scalp, rolled in the dust, yet showed raw and hideous where his fangs had bared it. A vulture perched on top of the shrine; his beak was red, and his eyes closed stupidly in the broad sunshine.

The woman placed herself full in front of the beggar-priest, and with an imperious gesture of her soft round hand and arm, beckoned his attention. The old man slowly rose at her bidding, shook off the dust from his back and shoulders, and stood, a tottering mass of bones and rags, a gaunt outline of fleshless humanity, bowed double almost to the ground, before her.

"Well?" he asked inquiringly, in a shrill quaver. "What do you wish? Why have you come? What brings you here today, to the shrine of Kalee?"

The woman trembled, and drew back with awe at the uttered

140

sound of that unspeakable name.

"See! see!" she cried, holding out the child at both arms' length and quivering as she spoke. "I have brought you an offering—a votary for Kalee."

The old man peered at the child incredulously. His eyes were bleared and dim with sleeplessness.

"But this is an English baby," he said at last, after a long pause. "What is the use of bringing it here to us? The child will serve the gods of the Christians. Kalee needs no half-hearted votaries. The Black One is a jealous goddess indeed, visiting the neglect of the fathers on the children; and those who serve her must serve none other."

The woman gazed at him with wistful eyes. They were beautiful eyes—large, and soft, and dark, and tender,

"Girjee," she said slowly, "it is not true, I know the child can be dedicated to Kalee. Listen to me, and I will tell you why I wish to make her over to the greatest of the goddesses. She shall not serve the gods of the Christians. She is my child. I love her! I love her!"

The *fakir* smiled a horrible, lean, hungry smile, "Then give her over willingly as a sacrifice to Kalee," he answered dryly.

The dog ceased from gnawing at the skull, and looked up in haste into the woman's eyes with eager expectation. The vulture shifted his perch uneasily.

"Not that! not that" she cried, drawing back the child to her bosom in terror. "I give her to Kalee—freely, willingly—but as a worshipper, a votary, not as a sacrifice."

The *fakir* smiled with grim delight once more. "Kalee will have victims and not votaries," he answered in his feeble, tremulous, senile quiver. "Give her, above all, the blood of her enemies. One sacrifice is worth many novices."

The *ayah* bowed down her face to the child's. "Kalee is great," she cried, kissing it hard; "but I love the baby. She is very dear to me. I have nursed her at these breasts. She is like my own daughter. I love her better than I love Jumnee. See these dimples: she is smiling now. Kalee protect her! I love her! I love her!"

The dog returned to his bone, disappointed, once more, and licked the raw scalp all over afresh, cheated of his hope of another meal. The vulture blinked his eyes sleepily.

"Girjee," the woman went on again, with trembling lips, "this is why I want to make her over to Kalee. They will take her away across the great black water, away to England, to the land of the Christians, far off from her foster-mother altogether. Today the *sahib* said to his wife, 'Olga shall go soon to England.' I heard. I said to myself in my heart, 'They will rob me of my child, and she will love me no longer, and forget her foster-mother.' But if I make her over today to Kalee, though they teach her to love the gods of the Christians, the cold white gods that stand on pedestals in the public places, she will only be theirs during the waking hours of the white daytime; at night, in the black darkness, she will be mine—mine and Kalee's! Is it not so, brother?"

"It is so, Gungia. You have heard rightly. If a child be dedicated to one of our gods or goddesses of India, though she serve her own gods faithfully during the day, in her sleep she will be theirs forever and ever. If you give the *sahib's* baby to Kalee, Kalee will watch over her in the dead of night, and be a bond of union between her and her foster-mother for all the incarnations."

"Then take her, Girjee! Make her over to Kalee!"

The old man squatted on the doorstep of the temple. "Do you know the penalty?" he asked; "the token of Kalee? The child made over to the great goddess, can never again close her eyelids in slumber. All night long she lies with her soul spellbound, but her eyes staring wide open and fixed upon Kalee. The *sahibs* will see it: they will notice her eyes: they will know that the child has been given to the Black One."

"No matter," the woman cried eagerly: "they shall not rob me altogether of my pet, my darling. Though the great black water roll between us, she shall know me and love me in her sleep always."

Girjee rose once more from his seat, and, stretching out his gaunt and haggard arms, took the unconscious baby in his lean long fingers. At his touch the child awoke, and began to cry. The man dipped one skinny forefinger in the double gourd that hung by a string at his lank thigh, and touched little Olga's lip for a moment gently with some sweet white mixture. In a few minutes the child was asleep once more, and Girjee and the *ayah* turned solemnly to the brick-built temple.

The lintels were smeared with some reddish-brown colouring matter that bore a suspicious resemblance to stale blood. Within, a little bronze figure held up a row of seven small lamps, all alight, burning perpetually before the altar of Kalee. In the central shrine, a tiny black image of the awful goddess herself held the only niche; for Kalee, as the priest had said, is a jealous deity. Her lips were stained with fresh red blood. Kalee that day had drunk of her victim.

The priest motioned the *ayah* silently to his left. She stood beside him, her full round arms crossed reverently upon her half-open bosom: a beautiful woman, in the purest type of Hindu beauty. The *fakir*, lean and skinny and wrinkled, took his place in his rags beside her, before the shrine of Kalee. The white child slumbered all unconscious in his hands. He laid her down in silence tenderly on the altar.

For a moment there was an awful hushed stillness. The priest bent his head slowly to the ground: the *ayah* allowed her own to fall in muttered prayer upon her bosom. Both with mute lips murmured beneath their breath the short litany of the great goddess Kalee.

Then the priest, taking Olga once more in his arms, cried aloud in a chanting monotone:

Oh, Kalee, goddess of the Thugs, whose lips may only be steeped in human slaughter;
Oh, Kalee, goddess of the Thugs, who delightest in the hot red blood of the victim;
Oh, Kalee, goddess of the Thugs, who tearest the babe from the bosom of its mother;
Oh, thou Black One, thou fierce, thou terrible; oh, thou bloody toothed; mighty and unspeakable;
Dark as the night; of misshapen eyes; crowned with the trident; riding on a tiger;
Horrible of horribles; Kalee the pitiless, whose fangs are red with the flesh of thy victims;
Take, we beseech thee, this child for thine own, and save her forever from the gods of the English,
That she may worship Kalee her whole life long, and bring sacrifice to the Black One in her sleeping hours.
Though through the bright day. and while the sun shines she worship the cold white gods of the Christians
Yet in the dark night, and when the shadows fall, may her eyes be ever open for Kalee:
Open for Kalee. goddess of the Thugs, whose lips are steeped in human slaughter;
Who delights in the warm red blood of the victim, and tears the babe from the bosom of its mother.

As he spoke, he swayed his lean body to and fro with horrible writhings, and dipping his right hand in a bowl on the shrine, traced a trident with his skinny forefinger on the soft skin of the child's white forehead. The trident came out a deep scarlet. There was blood in the bowl: the fresh blood of a human victim.

The woman quivered at the awful sound and sight; but the lean priest smiled ecstatically. His blear eyes looked away vaguely into the dim distance. He saw but Kalee. He was lost in the worship of his hideous goddess.

There was silence again. Presently the man took from the altar once more a small dark object. It was a piece of flint, sharp and clear-cut. Girjee felt its thin edge carefully with his skinny finger.

"Keen, keen," he cried, "like tempered steel, the black dagger of the unspeakably Kalee!"

The *ayah* started, and laid her round hand eagerly upon his haggard arm.

"You will not hurt her!" she cried in terror.

Girjee pushed her back with a gesture of scorn. "Kalee must needs be worshipped with blood," he said. "The child is at rest: she knows not and feels not. Her body—her body only is here: her soul is away in the air with Kalee."

At the word he brought down the flint with dexterous gentleness at a particular spot, first on the right, then on the left temple. The child winced, and puckered its little forehead in its sleep, but did not wake. A small round drop of blood oozed slowly from the tiny severed vessel on either side. The priest dipped his finger solemnly in each, and smeared the blood on the lips of the goddess. He smeared it with deft sleight of hand, so as to produce a faint upward laughing curl at the corners of the black image's mouth.

"See!" he cried to the trembling *ayah*, "Kalee is pleased to accept the offering. The Black One smiles. She smiles on her votary."

The woman bowed her head in awe-struck assent. "Kalee is great," she murmured. "All praise to Kalee, the swarthy fury, of a hideous countenance, dripping with gore, crowned with venomous snakes, hung round with a garland of skulls at her girdle! Kalee is great! Kalee is fierce! Kalee is terrible! Victory to Kalee!"

Girjee held up the child before the image for a second.

"Olga," he said aloud, for he had caught at the name:

"I give you to Kalee. You are Kalee's now, henceforth and for ever. Though your waking hours belong to your own gods, in the hours of your sleep you shall serve Kalee. Remember that Kalee delights in slaughter. Other gods are merciful and kindly and compassionate; but Kalee, the Black One, thirsts ever for the living blood of her victims."

144

He hung a little silver image by a thread round her neck.

This is the badge that you belong to Kalee. Steep her lips in English blood, beyond the great black water, and Kalee will love you as her faithful votary. Milk and rice and oil we offer in propitiation to the other deities; but blood, blood alone, is the fitting food and proper drink for the thirsty lips and soul of Kalee.

He struck the altar thrice with his open palm. A tame snake glided noiselessly, at the well-known summons, from beneath the shrine. Girjee held it gently in his hand, and placed its speckled head against the baby's white forehead. The snake, protruding its forked tongue with rapid vibrations, licked the fresh blood greedily from the trident he had smeared there. When he gave the child back to the *ayah's* arms not a trace was left upon her face or forehead of that mystical ceremony. The woman turned and hurried from the door, crying out as she fled back, "Kalee, Kalee!"

And Olga Trevelyan was ever thenceforth the votary of Kalee.

CHAPTER 1
Persons and Places

Thorborough-on-Sea ranks as the most paradoxically pleasant of all our minor English watering, places. Paradoxically pleasant I say. because in its exterior appearance there is really nothing on earth visible to make it seem so. A drained marsh stretches to the north of it: a drained marsh extends to the south of it: and a drained marsh merges on the west of ii into low wild flats of bracken-covered common. To the east, of course, lies the German Ocean. The town itself—if town it can be called that town is none, but a mere long line of old-fashioned lodging-houses—occupies a petty stunted islet of dry land in the midst of so much unpicturesque marshiness. Nothing in Thorborough commands one's love. And yet everybody who has once been there, still would go; he knows not why and asks not wherefore.

The whole borough like the chameleon of popular natural history, lives on air: for the air of Thorborough is most undeniable. To say it is bracing: is to say too little. It exhilarates the heart of man (and woman) like the best Sillery. People say to one another, with an apologetic smile, "Oh yes, of course, it's very ugly; but the air, you know—the air is really all that one comes for." Whenever a place has absolutely nothing else on earth to recommend it, you may look upon it as a foregone conclusion that it will infallibly plume itself on the purity of its atmosphere.

The little River Thore that drains the surrounding marshes, by the aid of windmills at the side sluices runs into the sea at Thorborough Haven. There lie the fishing-smacks that keep the good folk of the town alive in winter, when they have no visitors to exploit (as men exploit a silver mine), and no lodgers to drain of their gold, as in the summer months: and there the longshoremen ply their mysterious trade of picking up an honest livelihood, in the offseason, by standing all daylong with their hands in their pockets, and a short black clay stuck idly between their teeth for mute companionship. Around that mud-blocked Haven centres the slumberous life of Thorborough, knowing but two alternative phases: in summer, pleasure-boats; in winter, bloaters. An ancient and a fish-like smell pervades the quay, where superannuated mariners lean upon the old cannon, half-buried in the ground as posts, and survey mankind from their coigns of vantage in that broad spirit of generous impartiality begotten of long contact with danger and vicissitude.

Nobody (who is anybody) ever goes to Thorborough-on-Sea without getting to know Mrs. Hilary Tristram. Society at Thorborough sums itself up in her pleasant, cultivated, and hospitable person. Her house stands near the upper end of the Shell Path—the sole marine parade of Thorborough—embowered by the only trees the place can boast, much blown on one side by the stern east winds of March and April. In the season, which lasts for six feverish weeks of August and September, Mrs. Hilary Tristram's expensive house teems with visitors. She descends upon Thorborough then from town, accompanied by a brilliant horde of followers—old men and matrons, young men and maidens—and pervades the place, as long as she remains, with ubiquitous detachments of herself and her company.

"Olga," said Mrs. Hilary Tristram, at one of her biggest garden-parties, "allow me to introduce you to Mr. Alan Tennant. Mr. Tennant, this is my friend Miss Trevelyan. You've heard of her father of course—Sir Everard Trevelyan—Commissioner of British Bhootan, and the eminent botanist? Ah! I thought so; I knew you'd remember him; you take such an interest in everything scientific."

Olga Trevelyan bowed slightly to the handsome young man her hostess had introduced to her. She was a beautiful girl, lithe and stately; a daughter of the gods, divinely tall and most divinely dark, with large soft eyes, and a lavish wealth of silky-black hair that blew lightly about

146

her high white forehead. Something strange in those big brown eyes struck Alan Tennant at once as very unusual—a sort of falling droop of the lids and lashes that he had but once before observed in anyone. For reasons of his own Alan Tennant was profoundly interested in eyes and eyelashes.

"Do you live in Thorborough?" Olga asked, simply, raising the long lashes as she spoke with a sort of curious effort, and speaking in a sweetly musical voice; "or are you only a summer visitor down here, like all the rest of us?"

"A visitor," Alan Tennant answered, with a pleasant smile: "a bird of passage. I come, like everybody else, from the big ant-hill. A London doctor, in fact, out for my holiday. We work hard, you know, through the London season, and we're glad enough to get away now and then for a breath of fresh air and a little respite. We don't quite fulfil the apostolic precept, I'm afraid: we're often weary with well-doing."

"Ah! but it *is* well-doing, you know," Olga said, timidly. "It's almost the only profession, of course, where a man can be quite certain he's really and truly doing good. That must be a great consolation to you, after all, among the endless discomforts of a doctor's life."

"Mr. Tennant hasn't many discomforts," a pretty little girl at her side interrupted briskly. "Have you, Mr. Tennant.? He doesn't have to run about at night and visit patients. Don't you recollect his name, Olga? He's the great oculist, you know; the famous oculist. He only has to sit at home in his own house, with a most imposing butler to open the door, and wait for people to pour in upon him and be cured immediately."

Olga's face coloured up slightly. "I beg your pardon," she said, with still more marked timidity. "I—I suppose it's very stupid of me not to know it; but one can't know *all* Mrs. Tristram's friends, can one, Norah? She seems to me to know half London."

"And the other half isn't worth knowing," Norah Bickersteth answered lightly.

The young doctor smiled once more. "Miss Bickersteth overrates my humble merits," he said with a careless disclaimer. "I can't pretend to be so very famous that not to know me argues oneself unknown. To recognise all Mrs. Tristram's acquaintances would be to pose as a walking edition of *Men of the Time*, with a bowing knowledge of all the bishops, judges, and painters in England. Nobody else ever expects to keep pace in that matter with your aunt, Miss Bickersteth."

Just as he spoke, the hostess herself came up once more, and, with an apologetic smile to Alan Tennant, turned gently to Olga Trevelyan.

147

"My dear," she said, "I'm going to carry you off again, to introduce you to Lady Mackinnon. Sir Donald knows your papa in India, and they're both of them just dying to make your acquaintance. Mr. Tennant, I see you're in my niece's hands: take care Mr. Tennant is introduced to everybody, Norah. This way, Olga, my dear: that's Lady Mackinnon, the dear ugly old lady on the chair over yonder, in the speckly dress and impossible bonnet."

"An Indian girl?" Alan Tennant asked interrogatively as she turned away.

"Yes, an Indian girl," Norah Bickersteth answered with a smile. "A great favourite of auntie's. Isn't she beautiful, Mr. Tennant? Isn't she delicious? Isn't she charming?"

"She *is* beautiful," the young man replied frankly. "Delicious and charming are epithets of maturer knowledge; but I can safely say at first sight, I don't know that I ever before saw anybody quite so beautiful."

"I'm so glad you think so. She's just a darling. We were at school together, you know, Olga and I, and I positively love her."

"You have every excuse," the young doctor answered pensively, glancing after Olga as she moved with lithe and graceful motion through the crowd on the terrace. "What exquisite eyes! It may, perhaps, be a professional instinct; but I think, Miss Bickersteth, a pair of lovely eyes really move me more than anything else in human beauty."

"Aren't they lovely! So soft and big!" And Norah Bickersteth lifted her own laughing little blue ones to the young doctor's face. "They seem to have some strange fascination about them that I never saw in anybody else's!"

A military bachelor of sixty would promptly have responded, "That's because you've never seen your own;" but Alan Tennant was younger and wiser: he merely said, "Exactly, Miss Bickersteth; I quite agree with you."

"There's one very odd thing about them, too," Norah Bickersteth went on carelessly. "Isn't it funny? Olga always sleeps with her eyes open; she never shuts them day or night. You can't imagine anything so queer as it looks to see her sleeping with her eyes staring right up at the ceiling."

The young doctor pricked up his ears. "Dear me!" he said. "Are you sure of that? I noticed the lids had a very curious, unusual appearance. There seems to be a sort of falling droop about them, as though they half-closed of themselves, and were hardly under full control of

148

the muscles."

"Oh! I'm quite sure it's so, Mr. Tennant; I've seen it often. Olga and I sleep together, and you can never know whether she's awake or asleep until you've touched her, or roused her, or spoken to her, or something. She lies with her eyes wide open, and her eyeballs staring out blankly at nothing, as if she were looking at some invisible person ever so far away in the dim distance."

"She comes from India," Alan Tennant repeated stroking his moustache with meditative fingers. "Odd; very odd: most odd, certainly. I had once just such a case before—and that was from India too—but he was a native: a terrible-looking old man, with bushy eyebrows, who came over in the retinue of the *Maharajah* of somewhere-or-other unpronounceable. They said he had been a Thug in his youth. I could easily believe it: a fearful old wretch, with white moustaches and beard and whiskers, and a wicked leer about his bad old eyes, like a born murderer's."

"A Thug!" Norah said, shuddering slightly. "That's one of the dreadful strangling and murdering sect, isn't it?"

"Yes; a homicidal caste or sect or tribe, I think, who worship nobody but the goddess Kalee, I fancy they call her. They used to catch travellers by the roadside, strangle them and rob them, and offer their blood up in a bowl on the altar of their goddess. A very neat thing indeed in the way of religions! However, I believe that's all put down long ago now. Old Sir Donald Mackinnon there stamped the very last of it out; he tells the story himself at great length—something about some little forgotten jungle temple, and some awful creature of a mendicant priest—a hungry, half-starved, murderous ascetic, to whom the last of the Thugs used to bring the blood of their human victims.

"Capital title for a novel that—*The Last of the Thugs.* Don't mention the subject to Sir Donald, though, or he won't let you off under three hours and the minutest details. Nothing on earth would induce him to forego a single item of all the horrors; he perfectly revels in human gore, as if he had caught it from the Thugs in person."

"Horrid old man! How very dreadful of him! But this Thug patient of yours—did he keep his eyes always open too, just like Olga Trevelyan?"

"Well, so they said; and, by Jove! when I came to examine him, it was certainly true. I found two tiny scars, one on each temple, most cleverly cut; the operator had severed a particular nerve which governs the opening and closing of the eyelids. No European surgeon could have done it more admirably. I made inquiries about it, but could learn nothing from the man himself; he was very reticent on the subject—afraid I should suspect him of complicity with Thuggee, as the Anglo-Indians call it, and perhaps get him hanged, as he richly deserved to be. However, I found out by asking elsewhere that this was a regular custom of the Thugs.

"Whenever any child was dedicated to Kalee, as was the case with every well-conducted Thug baby the priest used to make a little incision on each side of the forehead, and offer a drop of its blood as a sacrifice to the goddess. At least, so he told the pious parents; but in reality, and that's just the trick of it, he very cleverly cut the nerve that moves the erector muscles of the eyelid; and after that, the child could never close its eyes or open them wide, except with a distinct and unpleasant effort."

"Why, that's just what's the matter with dear Olga! the girl answered quickly. "She can only shut her eyes if she tries to on purpose."

"Ah! I dare say," the young doctor went on in an unconcerned tone. "In her case, no doubt there's been some slight unintentional injury to the nerves, probably from disease, or perhaps congenital, and the eyelids refuse to obey the will except with a strong and deliberate effort. But these Thugs, of course did it on purpose; it was a way of showing the power of the goddess. The priest tells them, if once a child is dedicated to Kalee, it will sleep for ever after with its eyes open. Kalee, it seems, is the goddess of blackness and darkness as well as of murder—murder being presumably a dark deed—and so the votary of Kalee never shuts his eyes, but looks out for ever on the night and the goddess. A very interesting and poetical superstition!"

"And did you cure your Thug patient?"

"Oh! of course; cured him easily. Merely a question of cutting through another nerve—an inhibitory, they call it,—and the thing at once recovers its normal habit. In a case like the Thug's, I mean, that is to say: your friend Miss Trevelyan probably owes her peculiarity to disease, and that would be a far more difficult matter to tackle. I shall watch her closely now—only don't tell her so. She's very beautiful (which is always interesting), and this gives me a professional interest in her as well. But I shall watch her all the better if she doesn't know about it. I notice that young ladies, when they know you're watching them, fail to exhibit that regularity of demeanour and unconsciousness of action which is indispensable to the medical mind."

Norah laughed. "I should think not," she said gayly. "How on earth can you expect us to be light and natural if we know you've got your searching eyes fixed firmly upon us for a scientific purpose?

Alan Tennant certainly kept his searching eyes firmly fixed upon Olga Trevelyan all that afternoon. Wherever she moved, his keen gaze followed her. And he was vaguely aware in his own mind that his interest was something more than merely professional. He had achieved fame with extraordinary rapidity; but after all, a man can't live on fame alone; he requires some emotion a little more human to cheer and sustain him. At twenty-nine, men are still very human. And at twenty-one, women, for their part, are very attractive. Those were just the respective ages of Alan Tennant and Olga Trevelyan.

Once more in the course of the afternoon he had a few minutes' passing conversation with Olga. Norah Bickersteth took them round together, not perhaps quite by accident, to look at the ferns and bananas in the big conservatory. Olga's voice was sweet and low, and she spoke with a grave yet delightful earnestness that mightily took the fancy of the young doctor.

"With a woman like that," he thought seriously to himself, "a man might do some good in the world in his generation." He picked a superfluous blossom or two from the conservatory pots, without asking for leave, and fastened them together with a spray of maidenhair into two tiny dress-bouquets—red and white for Olga, yellow and blue for Norah. Then he handed them over to the two girls with not ungraceful old-fashioned politeness. Norah took her little bunch *coquettishly*, and stuck it at once between the opening of her bodice.

"I shall tell everybody," she said with her laughing voice, "that these were given me by the great Mr. Tennant."

But Olga held hers pensively in her hand, and hardly seemed to know whether or not she ought to wear them. Later in the day he saw she had pinned them daintily in her bosom, and he went away feeling the happier for it. To such absurd little flutters and tremors of that central vascular organ, the heart, is even the scientific breast at twenty-nine a willing victim.

CHAPTER 2

Kalee in Suffolk

It was a wild and awful night, some evenings later, on the shore at Thorborough. The east wind was dashing the breakers fiercely upon the beach, a mere narrow barrier of cast-up shingle, that ill-protected the long line of parade and lodging-houses in its rear from the fury of their onslaught. Sailors and coastguardsmen were gathered in little knots upon the Shell Path, eagerly watching the fishing, smacks that fought bravely for life against the teeth of the gale in their fierce endeavour to make the mouth of the tiny harbour. With scarcely a rag of sail up, in the face of that terrific tempest, one after another rode aloft upon the surf of the bar, and sank again invisible in the intervening troughs. One after another, dexterously steered by strong hands and stout hearts through spray and billows, made its way at last, groaning and creaking, into the haven of safety.

The wind howled ominously through the slender rigging, and shrieked around the corners of the Thorborough houses. Anxious women watching from the beach, wrung their hands in terror and suspense as each well-known hull, driving half-helplessly ahead before the force of the gale, approached the long white battling breakers of the bar, and tossed about like a cockboat on that yeasty turmoil of wandering waters. Strong men held their breath and strained their eyes to watch the fate of each in turn as it fought for life with terrible earnestness in that desperate struggle against the maddened elements.

But inside Mrs. Hilary Tristram's house on the North Parade, nobody noticed the storm or its fury. Now and again, to be sure, the groaning of the wind, as it tore round the gables and shook the beams to their very foundations, disturbed a little the tone of the grand piano. But who thinks of wind or sea in a well-lighted room, full of guests and music, at ten in the evening? By two o'clock, to be sure, it is very different: then, when one lies awake alone in bed, the deep roar of the breakers as they crash upon the beach, and the wild cries of the wind as it rages among the chimney-stacks, absorb and engross and appal one's spirit. But, earlier in the evening, lights and company make all the difference.

While the fisherwomen outside, but ten yards off, were wringing their hands, and straining; their eyeballs to catch the dim outline of the tossing hulls by the faint glimmer of the long August twilight, Olga Trevelyan, in the drawing-room within, was singing a pretty English song; while Alan Tennant, leaning over the piano, was pretending sedulously to turn the music, which he could only read by the aid of Olga's nod. Alan Tennant was always handsome, but in evening clothes he looked handsomer than ever; and the graceful attitudes into which he seemed naturally to throw himself added not a little to his manly beauty.

"How warm and cosy you all look in here!" the latest comer cried cheerily, as he entered the room to fetch his sister, a Thorborough native. "It's an awful night outside with a vengeance, I can tell you. I never remember anything at Thorborough like it. You'd better sit up all night, I should say, Mrs. Tristram, and be prepared with an ark to carry off your goods and chattels, in case of the deluge; for the sea's dashing over the Shell Path like a young Niagara, and I expect half Thorborough'll be washed away to the bottom of the ocean by tomorrow morning, Future generations of fishermen will earn a precarious livelihood by pointing out to future generations of London tourists on calm mornings the foundations of Mrs. Hilary Tristram's celebrated marine villa, under five fathoms of the North Sea."

"Is it really so very rough?" Olga asked in surprise, rising hastily from her seat at the piano. "You don't mean to say there's any danger, is there?"

"Well, not exactly danger," the visitor answered, with a careless wave of the hand: "that is to say, at present, you know. I dare say Thorborough'll weather the gale somehow till morning. You're pretty safe up at the north part here, though down below, at the poor end of the town, some cottages may really go squash before long. But the fisher people are in an awful way: the smacks are half of them out there still. What was that you were singing as I came in—wasn't it 'The harbour bar is moaning'?"

Olga blushed a deep crimson, and clasped her hands nervously as she answered, in a half-penitent voice, "Yes, it was: 'The Three Fishers.' I'm sorry I sang it. How terrible to think that while I've been singing about it so carelessly in here, the poor souls outside have been really living it and feeling it in grim earnest! Why, just listen now to the shrieking of the wind! How could we ever come to overlook it? I shall never forgive myself as long as I live for singing that song while the men have been working and the women weeping in stern reality so close beside me!"

"Only ten yards off," the young man of the town answered casually.

"Life is always very full of misery," Alan Tennant put in, endeavouring to relieve the poor girl's evidently genuine distress. "Nobody knows that better than we doctors do. We're accustomed, unhappily, to coming away from some bed of pain and going right off, with a smiling face and a flower in our buttonhole, into somebody's drawing-room, just as if we really thought life was all champagne and Italian opera. It's well for most of us that we don't always realize the full extent of the misery around us: if we did, we should never be happy at all, and the world would be only a loser in the end by the destruction of so much innocent merriment. I don't think you have anything to reproach yourself with tonight, Miss Trevelyan."

"It wasn't a comic song, anyhow," the native ventured to suggest good-humouredly. "Very appropriate to the situation, I should have said, for my part."

"Ah, but when the misery comes so very near one!" Olga cried earnestly. "When one seems even to insult it to its face by one's untimely happiness! See—the blinds are up over yonder: the poor people on the Shell Path can look in upon us, all chatting and laughing and enjoying ourselves in here, with the red shades on the lamps and the bright dresses on the women; while they must be watching in fear and wretchedness and despair out there, wringing their hands and wiping their eyes, and praying for their sons and their fathers and their brothers! Oh, it's too awful! I can't bear to think of it! How terribly cruel and wicked we must seem to them! The least we can do is to shut out the light."

And as she spoke, she moved gently to the window, and began pulling down the blinds that, with seaside freedom, has been left undrawn for the whole evening.

"You *did* look awfully jolly in here, certainly," the native murmured, with the air of a man who makes a candid admission. "It must really have seemed just a little bit heartless."

Olga answered never a word. She was clearly too much distressed at the incongruity of their occupations to care for any more conversation.

"I think, Mr, Tennant," she said in a low voice, "I shall just go up to my own room. I can look out there upon the poor people on the beach outside. I wonder, whether any of the sailors are lost? I shall never forgive myself: never, never!"

She touched his hand lightly with her own, and then glided unobtrusively, with a slight bow, from the room. Alan noticed that she singled him out, as it were, from the whole company for the sole honour of a farewell that evening. He noticed it, and felt once more that peculiar tremor—due, as he imagined, to a withdrawal of inhibitory nervous action from the muscles of the heart. (What a blessed thing it is to be a man of science!)

But then, the next moment he chilled himself by reflecting, on the other hand, that he was the only person in the whole room with whom she was just then and there engaged in conversation, and that she was evidently very anxious to quit the company as unostentatiously and quietly as possible. Anyhow, she was a very tender-hearted girl, and her conscience was reproaching her far too bitterly for a mere act of unconscious thoughtlessness, which she had amply shared with all the rest of the party. Alan liked her all the better for that, however. Earnest men are always attracted by earnestness in women much more than by flippancy.

He went back soon to his hotel, and Mrs. Tristram's party broke up for the night. At the hotel, which lay at the south end of the town, Alan Tennant called for a brandy and soda, lit his cigar, and sat up reading a sensational novel of Gaboriau's late into the evening. He wanted to see if the smacks all got in safely; and from time to time he rose from his chair, leaned out of his window with his elbows on the frame, and inquired from the little knot of men below how the fishermen were faring through that terrible weather.

Human nature is very complex. Alan Tennant reflected somewhat remorsefully to himself that his main interest in the fishermen's fate was not for the sake of their wives and children (whom he did not know), but for the sake of Olga Trevelyan's tender conscience. "What would you have?" he thought to himself, puffing away reflectively at his big cigar. He had never seen the worthy fisher-folk. He *had* seen Olga Trevelyan. The smallest headache or heartache of those whom you know—and love—he thought it deliberately—is ten thousand times worse to you, rightly or wrongly, than the bitterest griefs of the vast unknown and unnumbered multitude. A child's cut finger affects his mother more than a famine in China or an earthquake in Peru. It must needs be so. How can you help it? The man you do not know is an abstract idea to you; and you can't possibly sympathize to any profound extent with a mere abstraction.

By-and-by, a stir and noise on the beach below roused Alan dreamily from the terrors of Gaboriau. Something more real and serious was evidently afloat. Lights appeared on the foreshore beneath, and men were running eagerly about before him.

Alan put his head out of the window and called once more: "What's up now? Anything wrong? Smack in danger?"

"No, sir," the coastguardsman answered with a loud shout, in a lull of the wind; "smacks are all in, the Lord be praised! Vessel in distress off the bar there. Seemingly collier. We're putting out lifeboat."

Alan rose and looked at his watch. Gaboriau had proved too wickedly enticing. The novel was a thrilling one. It was two in the morning.

He seized his hat and a light dust-coat, and hurried down to the front door. It stood open still: one or two of the guests were on their way to see the launch of the Thorborough lifeboat.

The boat was safely pushed through the surf, and began to make its way with toilsome lunges among the big billows. It was a moonlight night, in spite of the storm, and Alan could see the whole scene from where he stood, distinctly. A crowd was gathering opposite Mrs. Hilary Tristram's. The vessel lay there, a black hulk, driving helplessly before the gusts of that awful storm. Alan Tennant followed the rest of the world to the scene of action. Only, for some reason best known to himself, he walked, not by the beach, but along the Shell Path, till he came to Mrs. Hilary Tristram's.

As he passed the house he looked up. All the windows were dark save one with a balcony. There a candle burnt upon a table, and a huddled figure in a soft white wrap lay with its face buried in its arms inside the window. Whoever it was, he or she had evidently fallen asleep without undressing, perhaps after long watching at the window. Alan's heart beat fast and high. He wondered if that room was Olga Trevelyan's.

His hand fell for a moment to his side. The last time he had worn the dust-coat was to the theatre in London. His opera-glasses were still in his pocket. He took them out and focussed them on the vessel.

It was an awful sight. The bare black hull drifted, drifted, drifted hopelessly among the huge white breakers that roared and shivered and careered around her. She was a collier, no doubt, a heavily-laden collier, loaded down to the very verge of Plimsoll's line, and a rackety, unseaworthy tub at that a coffin-ship of the worst type in fact, if ever there was one. Her masts and rigging were all long since torn away, and a bit of loose canvas, hastily fastened to the broken stump of the mainmast, alone carried her on before the raging tempest. One dark figure stood beside the stump; another, dimmer and harder to make out, still grasped the tiller. The rest were gone: all washed overboard.

Presently the moonlight fell fuller upon her Alan then saw by the shimmer of the rays that the shape by the stump was a tall man; but the other huddled up in frantic terror at the helm, was the figure of a woman.

The lifeboat tugged and urged her course in vain. The storm was too fierce for her to make any definite headway against its overwhelming force. The man on the wreck beckoned them frantically on Accustomed as he was to sights of pain, this sight of terror made Alan Tennant's blood curdle in his veins, and his breath seemed to fail heavily in his nostrils.

Next moment a huge breaker dashed over the hull. When the foam cleared away, and the black wreck reappeared for a second against the grey horizon on the crest of a wave, the man was gone. The woman alone, drenched and dripping, clung madly and desperately to the unbroken tiller. It was clear she was lashed there. They might yet save her.

The lifeboat drew a little nearer. Stroke after stroke, she gained upon the wreck. It was a neck-and-neck race, now, between death and the deliverers. Every heart within that watching crowd on shore stood still and waited as the light craft almost touched the broadside of the sinking vessel. Then a terrible billow burst upon her once more; the lifeboat bounded away like a cork on the surface; and the wreck, foundering before their very eyes, sank to the bottom in a great round eddy.

As it sank the woman threw up her bare brown arms toward heaven in unspeakable horror. Every eye saw her for a second silhouetted black and awful against the moonlit sky: the next instant she was gone forever. Not a sound rose above the roaring of the sea; but Alan Tennant, watching with his glass, seemed actually to behold in the expression of her face her wild death-scream of unutterable agony.

At that moment a strange noise burst suddenly and incongruously upon his startled ears—a noise audibles even in the midst of that terrible turmoil: the loud and joyous laugh of a woman. It was no hysterical outburst of emotion at the ghastly sight: it was no uncontrollable explosion of feeling: it was simple laughter, merry and triumphant—the ecstatic *paean* of a victorious player. The laughter seemed to mock the agonised death-throes of the drowning woman. There was something positively fiendish and inhuman in the reckless glee of that inopportune merriment.

What ghoul could thus insult the most frantic terror of dying humanity? What devilish joy could thus brutally obtrude itself upon the wrought-up feelings of those awestruck spectators?

Alan Tennant turned to look. On the lighted balcony of Mrs. Hilary Tristram's house the window had been flung carelessly open, and a young girl, in evening dress, a woollen wrap cast lightly round her shoulders, and a faded bouquet of red and white flowers held tight in her right hand, stood gazing out with big luminous eyes straight upon the bloodcurdling scene before her. The girl was tall, and graceful, and beautiful: but in her proud face, lighted up by the solitary candle, appeared no tinge of sympathy or suspense or terror. She looked with calm eyes at the spot where the wreck had just foundered so awfully, and she laughed like a maniac at the horrible catastrophe; laughed, and laughed, and laughed again, with inextinguishable merriment, as though the sight of the drowning woman were to her unnatural soul the most amusing and delightful episode in all creation.

Alan Tennant stood there spellbound. The girl in evening dress was Olga Trevelyan!

CHAPTER 3

Second Thoughts

For a minute or two he could neither move nor speak: the jar of that horrid unearthly laughter bursting upon him at so solemn a juncture had too wholly unmanned him for word or motion. His head swam. He merely steadied himself feebly with his hand on the broken windlass that stood, gaunt and rusty, upon the bare Leach, and gazed up, horror-struck, at the balcony window.

Then, slowly, his senses came to him again, and his professional instinct got the better once more of his half-superstitious awe and amazement. Gaboriau and the terrible scene before him combined must have conspired to deprive him for a moment of his wonted calmness. The weird sight had temporarily overcome him: but now, with a sudden effort of will, he faced and explained to himself the whole mystery. Olga, his beautiful, tender Olga—(he would call her so still!)—could never knowingly have laughed like that at so awful an episode. He remembered at once what Norah had told him. Olga slept always with her eyes open. Clearly—clearly she was asleep now! That must be the explanation of her seeming callousness. Callousness? Nay, rather, if she were really awake, devilish exultation at a fellow-creature's dying agony.

He cast his eyes nervously towards the beach. Had any of the crowd observed or overheard his beautiful Olga? Thank heaven! No, not a soul of them anywhere! They were all too absorbed with the incident of the wreck to think of watching Mrs. Tristram's windows. They were eagerly following the half-overpowered lifeboat in its despairing struggle to return shoreward from its vain and fruitless errand of mercy. No eye or ear on earth save his own had noted in any way that appalling interlude of unconscious laughter. No living soul but himself knew anything about it; and he—he could never misunderstand or distrust in any way his beautiful Olga.

He hated himself for having, even for one second, seemed to doubt her.

For like a flash of lightning, at that supreme moment, the truth had forced itself with startling vividness upon Alan Tennant's wavering soul, that he was profoundly in love with Olga Trevelyan.

He knew he loved her. He was certain he loved her. The very force and intensity of his momentary revulsion, when for one brief space of time he imagined the laughter was really wrung from her by that awful sight, in itself revealed to him the depth and reality of his new-born passion. It was long past midnight, and in those deepest hours of the waning night the heart of man knows itself with more profound intensity than ever elsewhere. Alan Tennant knew now without a shadow of doubt that he was desperately in love with Olga Trevelyan.

He grasped his opera-glass feverishly in his hand. The last time he used it was at the theatre in London. And the opera that night—ha—it was *La Sonnambula!* The coincident gave him a pregnant hint at once. Olga Trevelyan must clearly be a somnambulist!

He levelled the glass at the window once more. Olga stood gazing out tranquilly still, with sparkling eyes, directed now at him, and now at the spot where the ship had just foundered. Already Alan had almost forgotten the terror of the wreck. His whole interest and anxiety centred now on this deadly mystery of Olga's proceedings.

"My darling!" he murmured to himself, half below his breath. "My darling! My darling! She shouldn't expose herself at night like that, even in August! The cold will hurt her: it will chill her blood. Shall I call them up, and tell them to wake her?"

A dark figure stood unseen behind him: hidden from his sight by the windlass on the beach. The dark figure was watching too—watching them both with a strange and half-superstitious eagerness. It was Sir Donald Mackinnon, the retired Anglo-Indian, who had brought down his yacht, and leased the Manor House at Thorborough for the season. A weird fancy seemed to chain him to the spot. He cast his eyes from Alan to Olga, and from Olga to Alan, in alternate scrutiny.

Alan gazed still at the balcony window, in doubt what action he should take to recall her once more to her senses.

Just at that moment, a white shape, dimly seen in the room behind, glided with noiseless feet across the floor, and putting forth a soft fair hand, with a bangle gleaming on the wrist, caught Olga's arm just below the shoulder, and pulled her gently from the open balcony. A curtain screened the shape from fuller view, but Alan Tennant knew intuitively that it was Norah Bickersteth.

With a sudden cry, Olga started in alarm and flung up her hands—

flung them up, as Alan noticed half-unconsciously in the haste of the moment, exactly as the woman lashed to the wreck had flung up hers to the heavens above in her last death-throes.

Sir Donald Mackinnon, unseen behind, noted the coincidence as eagerly as Alan did.

There was an instantaneous flurry and excitement in the house, a ringing of bells and lighting of candles, as Alan judged by the glare at the upper windows; and then the front door opened suddenly, and a man-servant, half-dressed and loosely muffled round the throat, came out in haste, as if sent at full speed in search of a doctor.

"Anything the matter?" Alan cried, coming up to him hurriedly.

"Miss Trevelyan's took ill, sir," the man answered with a start. "Had a fit or something. I'm going for Dr. Hazleby."

"Go quickly," Alan said with an eager heart. "But it'll be some time before you can get him up: he sleeps soundly. I'm a medical man myself. In such an emergency, I think it would be no breach of etiquette if I were to watch Miss Trevelyan until he comes to see her. Every minute's precious in cases like this. I'll go into the house at once and see her."

He walked to the door and rang the bell. Mrs. Hilary Tristram herself (in a becoming dressing-gown and mob-cap—nobody ever took Mrs. Hilary Tristram at a disadvantage) opened the door for him in much agitation.

"Oh, Mr. Tennant," she cried, "I'm so glad you've come. What late hours you must keep, to be sure! Naughty man: ruining your constitution. Poor Olga's had *such* a dreadful turn! She was sleeping in Norah's room, as usual; and when they went up to bed; you know, Olga *would* sit up and watch the waves—she's *so* sentimental! And she said perhaps the fishermen would be drowned. Poor souls! but then, I suppose they're used to it. Been accustomed to drowning all their lives, of course; though I know it's only once fatal. Well, Norah went to bed, like a sensible girl, and fell asleep: but Olga sat up, watching by the window, and by-and-by, as might naturally be expected, she dozed off, with her arms on the table.

"In time, it seems, she got up, still fast asleep—I'd no idea the poor child was a somnambulist—and opened the window, and stepped on to the balcony. There she stood, catching her death of cold, heaven knows how long, till Norah happened to wake with a start, and found her laughing, positively laughing—in her sleep, you understand—at the top of her voice too! Nora crept out and touched her with her hand, and the poor child she just sprang back, and screamed and fainted. I've sent for Dr. Hazleby, who lives quite near; but, meanwhile, perhaps you'd like to go up yourself and see her."

Alan followed her, without a word, into the room where Olga was lying on a sofa, still dressed in her evening dress, and grasping in her hand—his heart beat fast—the little bouquet he himself had given her!

She was very white and cold and pallid. He felt her pulse: it beat feebly. Clearly, she had just passed through some nervous crisis, which had left her weak, and weary, and flaccid. He had seen a good deal of hospital practice before an almost accidental success in a critical operation had brought him name and fame as an oculist; and he recognised at once, from Olga's condition, that the crisis must have been a very severe one.

Her face was turned to the sofa-back as she lay. Alan took her head gently and reverently in his hands, and turned it towards him. As he did so he gave a little involuntary start: the eyes were staring wide and open.

He knew it before. He fully expected it. And yet the sight of that vacant stare—not fixed on anything near or earthly, but gazing intent, with rigid pupils, as on some terrible object at an infinite distance—alarmed and appalled him in some mysterious manner.

"Olga! Olga!" he half whispered in his dismay. Then, recollecting himself hastily, he said aloud, "Miss Trevelyan! Miss Trevelyan!"

Olga lay as motionless as a corpse, and never turned or seem to hear him.

The young man leaned over her closely and watched her face. Round her neck a little silver image hung by a silken thread; Indian work; he scarcely noticed it. The corners of her mouth were pinched and firm. The nostrils, still distended a little, showed signs by their tremor of recent violent passion. The eyelids hardly quivered perceptibly. The pupils were dilated and very brilliant.

What made the eyelids keep unclosed? The young doctor examined them narrowly. Defective nourishment, or some accidental lesion of the nerve supplied to the elevator muscle. From what cause? . . . Great heaven! how he started! . . . Close to the corner of either temple his quick eye detected at once a tiny scar—a very tiny scar—a long-healed cicatrix, almost invisible. Those two small marks must have been produced when Olga herself was quite a baby.

The line remained, scored deep in the skin, exactly like the scar of vaccination. They were not accidental: that much was certain. No accident on earth could possibly have severed both nerves alike on either side with such admirable dexterity. They had been cut on purpose; and not with a knife either. Alan Tennant's quick, experienced senses recognised in a second the distinctive broad-cut scar of a piece of glass or a stone implement. Steel and the metals generally cut deeper and clearer, with a fainter cicatrix.

Precisely the same scars, and in precisely the same spot, as in the case of his one Thug patient! How very strange, how more than strange, that Olga Trevelyan too, like the Thug himself, should have come from India!

However, this was no time for idle speculation. Olga was ill. Olga was in danger. Too hasty an awakening from the somnambulist state had been followed, as usual, by collapse and possible utter prostration. Unless restoratives were applied at once, the action of the heart might cease altogether.

"You ought not to have waked her," he said, gently, to Norah. "In future take care, when you see her like that, you never wake her; or at least, only very gradually, if absolutely indispensable. The sudden recall to intermittent consciousness might easily prove fatal. Brandy at once, please; brandy and *sal-volatile*."

They brought them in haste, and Alan poured a glassful quickly down the poor girl's throat. After a little while she revived somewhat, and feebly held up the faded flowers.

"Oh, Norah!" she murmured, half below her breath, her eyes meanwhile coming back to earth with a gradual return from the abysses of infinity; "I've had such a terrible, terrible dream. . . . A ghastly dream! . . . but I am sure I don't know what on earth it was about. . . . I was laughing, laughing, laughing so hard. . . . I can't remember most of my dream, but just the end. I thought—" and she looked at the flowers dreamily; "I thought I saw Mr. Alan Tennant."

Alan's heart leaped up in his breast. It was too terrible . . . or too delightful. Had she really seen him with her staring, wide eyes? Then if so, she must have seen, too, that awful episode. Or had she merely been dreaming a maiden's dream about him? Then if so, at that his very heart within him was reverently silent.

He dropped the hand whose pulse he was slowly counting, and glided from the room, unseen by Olga. He could never let her know he had possibly surprised even so much (if anything) of her heart's vague imaginings. It would be cruel and unfair to her—a mean advantage. He beckoned Norah and Mrs. Tristram silently from the room. They left Olga for the minute in charge of the servants.

"I'll go below till Dr. Hazleby comes," he said, "in case I should be needed. Meanwhile, go on giving her the brandy frequently. But don't let her know I've seen her at all. Poor child! it might make her feel awkward with me afterward."

Norah smiled a knowing little smile. "Very well," she said, with a meaning look. "We can keep our own counsel, you may be sure, Mr. Tennant. . . . But how strange you should happen to be so near at hand just at the very moment when dear Olga wanted you! Quite in the Romeo and Juliet style, you know. A serenade by midnight—without the music. It strikes me, Mr. Tennant, you must have been taking a moonlight stroll very late right under Olga's window too, for a wonder!"

Alan drew himself up shortly. "I was out," he said "watching the lifeboat, which had just put off to assist a wreck. The wreck went down exactly opposite your aunt's windows. It was a terrible sight, indeed, Miss Bickersteth; the most terrible, save one, I ever beheld in all my life. . . . Miss Trevelyan is in a very excited and nervous condition. She's a young lady whose nerves should not be overwrought. If possible, keep the facts about the wreck from her. In her present state, I'm afraid they might do her serious injury."

"He's very much in love," Norah whispered to her aunt as they went back to the sick-room again. "He doesn't like to be teased about her. When a man doesn't like to be teased about a pretty girl, you may be fairly sure there's something serious in it."

Alan slipped down to the dimly-lighted drawing-room, and waiting there patiently till Dr. Hazleby arrived, briefly explained what he had seen and heard, and waited for his final verdict. In a few minutes Dr. Hazleby came down again, with his heavy tread resounding on the staircase, and reported the patient as distinctly better.

"She doesn't know you've seen her, I gather," he said brusquely.

"No," Alan answered with some hesitation. "I hope you didn't mention it?"

"I didn't," the country doctor replied, taking up his hat. "And as I was walking down the stairs, I heard her say to Mrs. Tristram—admirable woman, Mrs. Tristram—'For heaven's sake, don't mention a word of all this to Mr. Tennant.' So, you see, my dear sir, you mustn't be supposed to know anything about it. Don't tell the young lady you saw her at all. She's a poor, nervous, weak-minded creature!"

There's nothing on earth more exasperating to a well-balanced masculine mind than the commonplace way in which other people discuss the characteristics of the admirable girl you yourself are profoundly in love with! They positively talk about her for all the world just the same as if she were any other fellow's ordinary sweetheart!

Dream Faces

It may be accepted as a general rule in life that everything always looks very different the next morning. As Alan Tennant sat by himself at his ten o'clock breakfast in the comfortable coffee-room of the Royal Alexandra (formerly the old White Lion) he reflected with his own mind that after all he too, as well as his patient, had been in a horribly overwrought condition the previous evening. Gaboriau, and brandy and soda, and three cigars, and the small hours of the night, and a violent storm, all piled one on top of the other, had evidently combined to make him that evening most absurdly and stupidly morbid and hysterical.

But in his sober moments, a man of science ought not to give way to such weak romanticism. After all, what did the evening's horrors really amount to? There had been a wreck; and wrecks, at least, are unhappily common objects of the seashore in this favoured country. Then, in addition, Miss Trevelyan had had a slight turn of somnambulism. A turn of somnambulism, even if interfered with, is not a very serious or mysterious affair. Finally, as to his ideas about Miss Trevelyan herself, why

But no. That is a point on which even the man of science (especially at twenty-nine years of age) is by common consent allowed to be romantic. Alan Tennant said it outright to himself once more by broad daylight. He was in love with Olga Trevelyan.

All through his breakfast he was longing to know how she had borne last evening's shock. Had she really seen the episode of the wreck, and tortured it somehow into something utterly different in her dreaming consciousness? Would she vaguely remember it now she had come to herself again? Would somebody incautiously blurt out all about it, and so recall it with a terrible rush to her half-oblivious memory? He hoped not! He trusted not!

But people are always so very imprudent. And in a little place like Thorborough, too, a wreck would surely be the talk of the town for the next fortnight. He wished he could manage to get her well out of it! The incident was one that might haunt and dog a sensitive nature like hers for months together! At the risk of being thought too obtrusively solicitous, he had scribbled off a hasty pencil-note early in the morning to Mrs. Tristram:

"For heaven's sake, whatever you do, try to keep the news of the wreck from her."

Then, remembering himself, with a *"Pshaw"* and a smile, he changed the last word carefully into "Miss Trevelyan," just as if he really thought there was only one *her* in the whole universe!

After breakfast he lighted his cigar—tobacco was Alan Tennant's one weakness—and strolled round to inquire about-well, about Olga. Why not frankly, in his own mind, say Olga? When a man is just beginning to fall in love, he feels himself quite a daring person if he ventures to call the object of his choice by her Christian name in his unspoken thoughts even. He could only inquire about her: he mustn't ask to look at her. She wasn't his patient, but Dr. Hazleby's; and medical etiquette, that vast organised professional tradesunionism, effectually prevented him from asking to see her. But he could at least inquire. No harm in inquiring.

Mrs. Tristram met him in the garden as he entered. Olga was very much better this morning, thank you; in fact, apparently, quite herself again. Dear child, she had just had a horrid fit of walking in her sleep, and been alarmed and frightened at her sudden waking; but this morning, after a night's rest and a good breakfast, she seemed as if nothing at all was the matter with her. Mrs. Tristram had sent her out with the girls and young men to stroll along the beach—looking for amber. She thought it would take their minds off last night's troubles. Amber was always thrown up upon the beach between Thorborough and Yarford after stormy weather. The big lump with the two large flies in it on the drawing-room whatnot had been picked up after the great storm last November. The girls all wanted to go out amber-hunting. It was so amusing. Would Mr. Tennant walk that way and meet them?

A vague dread smote upon Alan's mind. They were sure to come upon some planks of the wreck then. The beach was certain to be covered with fragments. If so, it would be impossible any longer to conceal the truth from Olga.

He hurried off eagerly along the beach towards Yarford, walking on the narrow strip of sand for greater expedition, and scanning the shore for any indication of Mrs. Tristram's party.

Half a mile from Yarford Gap, he saw them in front of him, all closely intent, upon the edge of the beach at the point where the wet and matted seaweed had been tossed and left by the storm in its frenzy.

As he came up, Norah bowed to him with an arch little smile, as who should say, "I know your secret." Olga, prettier than ever in her blushes and her morning print, gave him her hand with a dainty reserve that thrilled straight to the young man's heart from the tips of her fingers. She was looking perfectly well and even rosy; and she held out a small round lump of rough amber with a smile of triumph, saying as she did so, "You see, Mr. Tennant, I'm the only one, so far, whom the gods have favoured."

What was there about that pretty smile that struck a cold chill for a second to Alan's heart? He hardly even knew himself: and yet, in some vague back-chamber of consciousness, he remembered to have seen it before—and shuddered. It was a smile of triumph—innocent triumph; but it smote him hard with an awful sense of imperfect recognition.

They walked along, homeward now, and Alan and Olga led the way: the rest, with little smiles and nods of wise observation, allowing them to head the tiny procession.

Olga talked charmingly and prettily. She really was the very sweetest girl Alan Tennant had ever come across. Her mood that morning was a trifle more girlish and less earnest than usual: she watched the big waves still tumbling on the beach with *naïf* delight, and seemed somehow happier and more thoroughly at home than Alan had ever yet seen her.

"All the fishermen got back quite safe at last, you know," she said with a light smile, as she gazed at the huge breakers curling on the foreshore; so, one can admire the high sea with a clear conscience now. I love to watch it foaming like that, when I'm perfectly sure nobody's in any danger from it."

"It is beautiful," Alan said, hurrying her on none the less. "Very beautiful. Just like a bit of Henry Moore. How exquisite the shimmer on their great crests as they curve and flash over on to the barrier of shingle! Do you paint. Miss Trevelyan?"

"Oh, yes. I'm simply just wild about painting. I paint continually. Not sea, though, of course: sea is only for the great artists. Flowers, and cottages, and rustic children, and that sort of thing: the regular amateur subjects, you know."

"The fresh seaweed looks lovely in the sun, too, doesn't it?" Alan went on, carelessly, as they approached a great tangled mass near the high-water line. "Such delicate tints of brown and yellow, glistening wet. There's nothing else in all nature like them."

"Nothing," Olga answered, turning over the matted fronds lightly with her parasol. "Why, Mr. Tennant, what on earth's that? Just look: a woman's dress among the new seaweed!"

Before Alan could utter a word of warning, or divert her attention by some petty stratagem, she had turned up the mass that lay above the dress, and stood rooted to the ground, with eyes of horror wildly staring at the ghastly object that now fronted her on the foreshore.

A faint cry burst from her lips. Then in a moment she was suddenly and ominously silent.

The thing that gazed upon her awfully from the sands was a woman's face: a woman's face, battered and distorted, livid with long tossing and tumbling on the shore, bronzed with the sun, but now pale in death, and terribly ghastly. The body was lashed to a broken spar—the tiller of the coal vessel that went down in the storm before Alan Tennant's eyes the previous evening.

In his tender anxiety, the young man took her unconsciously by the arm, and tried to lead her away perforce from the sickening sight. But Olga could not be moved or distracted. She gazed with one long fixed stare at the face, mutilated and horrible, but still perfectly recognisable. Its eyes lay open, staring back at her own; staring through them, as it were, into dim infinity.

"Miss Trevelyan," Alan cried with a tone of authority, "you must come away: you must come home immediately. This is no fit sight for such as you. Leave us men to do all that is necessary. A wreck took place last night off the coast here at Thorborough, and this poor creature is one of the victims. We did not wish you to know anything about it: but now that you know, you must go home at once: you mustn't terrify yourself by looking at it any longer."

"It isn't that," Olga cried convulsively, finding tongue at last, and clutching at Norah, who had just come up, and was gazing awestruck by her side at the pallid corpse: "it isn't that, but, oh, Norah! darling! . . Mr. Tennant! Mr. Tennant, I know the face. . . . I'm sure I know it. I've seen it somewhere. I recollect it well. Oh, so vividly: with eyes staring open wide like that, and arms flung up—so—piteously to heaven. . . Where could I have seen her? Oh, Norah, Norah! For heaven's sake tell me, where could I have seen her?"

And then, with a sudden burst of recollection, burying her face in her friend's hands, she cried aloud in a voice broken with horror, "It was last night! In my dream, Norah! And I thought—Oh, heaven, I don't know what I thought. . . . But I never, never knew the poor soul was drowning!"

Alan Tennant took one arm tenderly. "Lift her up," he said to Norah's brother, young Harry Bickersteth. They lifted her up between them in their arms, and carried her, a listless, half-fainting burden, as far as the first bench on the walk outside the town. There Alan laid her gently down, and sent Harry for a fly to the Royal Alexandra to drive her back to Mrs. Tristram's.

"She must have perfect quiet." he said in a tone of command to Norah. "This double shock is a terrible strain on so excitable a nature. Take her home and send for Dr. Hazleby. I must go back now and see after the body."

Chapter 5
A Soap Bubble

At twenty-one, nature is happily very elastic. Three weeks of quiet at Mrs. Hilary Tristram's seemed quite to restore Olga's shattered nerves: and Norah Bickersteth was certainly the very best nurse and companion in the world at such a time for such a patient. Norah's gayety was beyond eclipse: and her lively talk and innocent merriment proved better for Olga than a thousand doctors. Indeed, one doctor, if unmarried and handsome, is often worth a great deal more than a full thousand. And Alan Tennant, looking in unprofessionally as often as politeness permitted, noticed with pleasure that Olga's temperament, though very subtle, possessed plastic powers of recuperation.

"What a blessed thing it is to be young," he thought to himself. At twenty-nine, a man considers himself entitled to assume a middle-aged air and tone towards the foibles and follies of early adolescence. And yet twenty-nine itself is not very old. A man of twenty-nine has still a heart, and that heart is still capable at times of a not wholly disagreeable fluttering palpitation.

Mrs. Hilary Tristram noticed, too, that Alan's visits were unnecessarily frequent. Last summer, she said, Mr. Tennant had been a perfect martyr to the royal game of golf: this year, the links were completely neglected, and the only manly amusement for which he seemed to retain the slightest taste was boating on the river. Now boating, as an acute intelligence will immediately perceive, is not a selfish or monopolist pleasure: in a boat, for example, you can carry passengers.

Alan's boat, manned as a rule by himself and Harry Bickersteth, carried three or four inside: and among them were generally Olga and Norah, marshalled by that discreet and amiable chaperon, Mrs. Hilary Tristram. The mysterious game of golf does not readily lend itself to the softer pleasures of female society, or the practice of the innocent art of flirting. A boat, on the contrary, as everybody knows, forms one of the most harmless, even if necessarily space-restricted, meeting-places of the young, the gay, the giddy, and the thoughtless. That perhaps—though it is always rash to speculate on human motives—was the main reason why Alan Tennant had deserted golf and taken instead to an aquatic existence.

Mrs. Hilary Tristram was not unaware that Alan Tennant had "formed an attachment" (such is, I believe, the correct phrase for these earlier stages) towards Olga Trevelyan. On that point, Mrs. Tristram wisely reserved judgment: or, to speak more correctly, assumed the attitude of a benevolent neutral. She would have wished, indeed, it had been dear Norah: Mr. Tennant was such an excellent, well-principled young man: but dear Norah was still very young, and a niece of Mrs. Hilary Tristram's need never fear the lack of fitting matrimonial opportunities in London society. One doubtful question alone remained—would Sir Everard Trevelyan, that stern civil servant, away over in Bhootan or whatever they called it, consider Mrs. Tristram had done right in allowing his daughter to contract an affection (correct phrase again) for the young oculist?

Of course, Mr. Tennant was a very distinguished coming man—extraordinarily distinguished for his age and profession—and sure to rise, and to be knighted and so forth, and really a very excellent catch—in these hard times, you know—for anybody below the rank of an earl's daughter. For it must at once be admitted, to put it bluntly, that a general tightness 'prevails in the marriage market. Husbands are not so abundant as they used to be a few years since, and when found, they are apt, like all other commodities when the demand exceeds the supply, to put a fancy price upon themselves.

They give themselves airs, in short, and think hardly anybody good enough for them. Still, your Indian magnate has often such an exaggerated idea of his own mightiness, that Mrs. Tristram scarcely knew whether Sir Everard would approve of his daughter's marriage with a mere oculist—a common surgeon, you observe, not even physician! So, she prudently abstained from overt recognition of this little affair, for good or for evil. It was not her fault, of course, if Mr. Tennant and dear Olga privately formed a mutual attachment for one another. She, at any rate, had done nothing in any way to throw the young people together or to promote an engagement.

And yet, need it be said that in her heart of hearts (so profound is the love of match-making among women) Mrs. Hilary Tristram would have been vastly disappointed if Alan Tennant had not proposed to

Olga Trevelyan, or, having proposed, had been rejected by her?

At the end of three weeks, Sir Donald and Lady Mackinnon gave a picnic.

Lady Mackinnon's picnics were grandiose and Anglo-Indian. Sir Donald, like a canny Scot that he was, had married money. This money, originally accumulated by his respected father-in-law in the engrossing pursuit of the nimble quotation (as quotation is understood in Capel Court), enabled him to rent the Manor House at Thorborough, and support the dignity of a K. C. S. I. with a becoming degree of social munificence. The picnics attested and enforced that dignity. Sir Donald's steam yacht made its way solemnly up the River Thore to a convenient point, laden with as many young men and maidens as it could conveniently hold; and there, standing aside from the main channel, under the shadow of the low sandstone cliff at Ponton, anchored seriously, with many premonitory puffs and snorts, for the discussion of luncheon.

Everything was done decently and in order. The champagne was unexceptionably iced, and the tablecloth was spread on deck on an improvised table of polished boards and mock-rustic trestles. The lobster blushed ingenuous in the silver dishes, and the salad smiled serenely complacent in a delicate bowl of Persian pottery. In short, the picnic was reduced as nearly to the level of a civilized dinner party as was possible under the circumstances of river yachting: and stewards and footmen did their level best to get rid of that delicious primitive simplicity which is the very breath of life and *raison d'être* of the genuine unsophisticated natural picnic.

Alan and Olga were among the bidden to this particular feast, as well, of course, as the remainder of Mrs. Hilary Tristram's expansive party. Norah was there, looking simply enchanting in a sweet little figured morning dress, and chatting away in her childish gayety to all and sundry about everything and nothing Alan stood talking to her long by the gunwale, peering at the herons fishing in the streams left by the ebbing tide, and listening to her charmingly *naïf* remarks about men and things and the universe generally. At last, a more favoured youth absorbed her conversation, and Alan, strolling forward, came suddenly upon Olga, watching the water almost alone near the yacht's bow.

"What a delightful little person your friend Miss Bickersteth is," he said to her, with a smile. "She's been keeping us all amused over yonder this last half-hour with her funny little speeches."

"Yes, isn't she clever!" Olga cried enthusiastically. And so pretty, too. And so delightfully natural. And such a sweet girl, Mr. Tennant, when you really get to know her. Not a bit spoiled by all the admiration she receives, though she lives so much in such great society! I'm so glad you admire her! She's my dearest friend in all the world. Just look at her now! Did you ever see anybody so perfectly graceful and so perfectly beautiful?"

"She's certainly very pretty," Alan answered, glancing across at her with an admiring eye. "Pretty rather than beautiful, I should say. Those *mignonne* figures are extremely charming, but not exactly what one calls beautiful."

"Oh, but prettiness after all is more than beauty, Mr. Tennant. It implies something. It's a speaking quality. It means they're good and true and sweet and lovable as well as merely pleasing objects for the eye to look at."

Alan nodded. "I'm glad you are so enthusiastic about her," he said warmly. He hated jealousy. It's a great point in a girl's favour when she can be frankly enthusiastic over another girl's beauty.

Olga smiled a pretty little smile. She was pleased that Mr. Tennant admired her friend. Dear little Norah. Nobody on earth—except perhaps Mr. Tennant—was really and truly quite good enough for her.

A flower on an islet of mud in the side stream attracted for a passing moment Olga's attention.

"How curious!" she said, pointing to it with her fan; "I never saw it before. So light and feathery. It's a beautiful thing. I should love to paint it."

"It's peculiar to the Eastern counties," Alan said, at a glance. "I know it well. I've botanised it before now. I'll try to get you a bit one day for painting."

A small circumstance, unnoted at the time, but not uneventful. These small circumstances govern our lives for us.

Sir Donald came up as they stood and talked.

"Insufferable old bore!" Alan said to himself with scant courtesy to his host—pardonable under the circumstances. "Can't he see I want to get a few words by myself with Miss Trevelyan?"

She was "Miss Trevelyan" to him still before others, and in the white daytime: "Olga" only when he rehearsed afresh her slightest movements and speeches to himself at night in his own chamber.

"Fine view," Sir Donald said, pointing with a Inroad sweep of his bronzed hand over the barren flats to east and west of them. "Beautiful prospect! Lovely weather!"

"It *is* beautiful in its way," Alan said, distractedly, gazing at the long flat banks of unrelieved mud on either hand, shining iridescent in the broad sunlight. "There's a vast wealth of undiscovered beauty for the true artist in common mud. It lights up wonderfully now into cloth of gold and Tyrian purple. I saw Wyllie make an exquisite sketch of these very flats when I was boating here last summer. Do you think, Miss Trevelyan, you could ever paint them?"

"No," Olga answered, gazing at the glistening expanse dreamily. "It would take a great colourist to do it full justice. You're quite right. Sir Donald. It's really beautiful."

She turned her face up to him as she spoke, in the full glare of the August sun; and the old Indian, looking gently down at her, smiled with delight like a child for a moment at discovering that so intelligent and discerning a sense had been read by them both into his casual observation. It's so delightful to find you've made a brilliant remark without even yourself either knowing it or meaning it! The old man was pleased and gratified. Next instant, something unusual in Olga's face seemed strangely to attract and rivet his attention. He gazed at her closely, almost rudely, till Olga drew back a little abashed from his wondering stare. Then he gave a sudden backward jerk of his head muttered something inaudible below his moustache to himself, and remained silent for a few seconds.

At last he spoke: "You were born in India, I believe, my dear," he said, not unkindly.

But Olga evidently resented his manner. "I was, Sir Donald," she answered with some curtness.

"H'm," he repeated. "Born in India! Curious! Curious! One hardly understands it. But queer things will turn up sometimes. Queer place, India, Queer events often happen there. I knew your father, when I was in the service, my dear. Very odd thing happened to me once, in a district where your father was then stationed."

"Indeed!" Olga said with quiet dignity. She did not seem anxious to pursue the subject.

"Yes, Mr. Tennant," Sir Donald went on turning round to the young doctor in his anxiety for a listener. "It must have been when this young lady here was in the nursery, I suppose; I came across one of the last remnants of that abominable Thuggee."

"I thought it was all put an end to long ago," Alan said with a suppressed yawn.

"Put an end to? Not a bit of it!" Sir Donald responded. "It lived on spasmodically till very lately. Why, in the Bengal famine of '66, in a temple of Kalee, only 150 miles upcountry from Calcutta, we found a boy with his throat cut; the eyes staring wide open; and the clotted tongue thrust out between the teeth:—a very horrible sight, I promise you. And in your father's district, my dear, in your father's district, when you were a baby almost, I came upon one very serious case of Thuggee.

"I had sat on the Thuggee commission, you know—helped to stamp the whole thing out—and so, of course, I knew all about it. Horrid practice that of the Thugs. They used to catch wayfaring victims, entice them to dine and then to sleep—drugged, no doubt— strangle them with a handkerchief as they slept on the ground, and offer up their blood to their goddess Kalee. But we stamped it out, stamped it out at last, sir, entirely. Beneficent rule of the British Government stamped out Suttee, stamped out infanticide, stamped out Thuggee, stamped out everything."

"Except famine," Alan said, smiling. He was anxious now to divert the conversation; for he could see that Olga, in spite of an affected air of nonchalance, was eagerly drinking in the whole conversation, and he dreaded the effect upon her nervous constitution of so exciting a subject. He took, as he fancied, a sort of paternal interest in her.

"Except famine, to be sure," the old Anglo-Indian answered good-humouredly, refusing to follow the red rag so industriously trailed across the track of conversation. "Of course, we can't expect to put down famine. We're not answerable if the monsoon doesn't burst at the time it ought to do. Well, as I was telling you, I came across the last relic of Thuggee in the very district where this young lady—at the age of four, I suppose—was then residing.

"In the midst of a jungle, a dense jungle, as impassable as a cactus thicket, we found a little dirty squalid temple—Thugs, if you please— all covered with blood, after their nasty fashion: and a lean old wretch of a *fakir* inside, squatting on his haunches, huddled in his rags, and actually taken in the very act of cutting up a dead body. I give you my word of honour for it, my dear young lady, with a flint knife, cutting up and mutilating a dead body."

Sir Donald paused and wiped his glasses significantly. Olga shuddered visibly as he gazed hard at her.

"And what became of the old man?" she asked, more with a strange interest.

"Oh, the old man! Hanged him, of course: hanged him: hanged

him. He was caught red-handed, and we naturally hanged him. Girjee was the old wretch's name, I remember. Died hard with the rope round his neck, cursing us all in the name of Kalee, and predicting all sorts of hideous vengeance in the future against us. Gave your father quite a turn, the old fellow was so perfectly sure Kalee would avenge his execution on Sir Everard himself and his children's children."

"It was very dreadful," Olga said shuddering.

"My dear," the old Indian asked, turning suddenly upon her, "do you happen to speak any Hindustani?"

"I did once," Olga answered, with a faint blush, "but I've forgotten it all ages ago. Only, sometimes in my sleep, a little of it seems still to come back faintly to me."

He looked her hard in the face with a critical gaze. Olga shrank half alarmed from his inquiring eyes.

"H'm?" he said again, glancing casually at her neck. "What's that you've got there? Eh? Tell me! A piece of Indian silver-work, isn't it?"

"Yes," Olga replied, fingering the image nervously. "A present from my old *ayah* at Moozuffernugger. I wear it always, I'm sure I don't know why. I've grown accustomed to it. It's a sort of sentiment."

Just then, to Alan's unspeakable relief, Norah ran up to take her friend aft and consult her on some small point being eagerly debated by a little crowd in Sir Donald's cabin.

"A pretty girl," Sir Donald muttered confidentially to Alan, "but, by Jove, sir, I wouldn't take ten thousand pounds to be the man that marries her!"

"Perhaps not," Alan said shortly. "But happily, you're not called upon to make the effort, and I don't think she'll have much difficulty in getting a husband in due time without offering such an extravagant figure."

"Ah, I dare say the fellow who marries her wouldn't find her out all at once: but he'd soon discover what was the matter after it was too late, I'm thinking, Mr. Tennant."

"Love is blind," Alan said oracularly.

"Aye, but marriage is just like yourself—a great oculist," the old Anglo-Indian retorted laughing.

Alan answered nothing. He merely glanced after Olga's retreating figure with some little trepidation. Everything that in any way disturbed her mind was now to him a subject for sincere regret.

"She looks to me too beautiful and good to have anything on earth but goodness within her," he said at last, half thinking aloud.

Sir Donald started. "Eh," he said: "That's the way the wind blows, is it, then, Mr. Tennant? Take care what you do. You don't mean to say, young man, you're going yourself to marry that wild young lassie there, are you!"

"If I were," Alan answered evasively with quiet dignity, "it is probable I would take the young lady herself before anybody else into my confidence."

He walked aft to join Norah and Olga. As he reached their group, Norah was just remarking something in a slight undertone about their excellent host.

"Oh, yes, he's a dear old man in his own way," she said smilingly; —but like all Highlanders, you know, he's terribly superstitious."

CHAPTER 6

The Hero Emerges

After lunch, the yacht had to wait two hours for the tide to serve before she could make her way back again in safety down the shrunken channel.

The River Thore, which debouches into the sea at Thorborough (good word, debouches: you will find it in the guide-book), is one of those sluggish tidal East Anglian rivers which meander along, with infinite twists and turns, for miles together through two inimitable boundary plains of festering mud-bank. At high tide, the estuary fills from side to side, and looks like a splendid widespread lake: at low water, it rather resembles a vast desert of unutterable slush, with a narrow thread of river trickling slowly down a hollow in its centre. Landing is impossible on either shore: deep banks of slime and ooze intercept your passage in every direction. You can only keep to the mid-channel, and wait till you come to the rare quays where an artificial landing-place has been duly provided by human means for your special convenience.

The afternoon seemed rather tame as they lay at anchor: so the two row-boats of the yacht were put under requisition, and most of the party went off together, rowed by the attendants, down the side streamlets. The big gig, manned by the two sailors, the footmen, and some of the young men, turned off in one direction to put up the herons on the great mud flats: in the smaller boat, Norah and her brother went with a couple of others to explore the water that ran down a tributary channel from the neighbouring paper mills. Olga complained of a little headache—the sun and the water, she said: and she stayed behind. Alan (oddly enough) preferred to stop with her. In a little while, they were left to themselves, not without the guilty connivance, it is to be feared, of Mrs. Hilary Tristram, who engaged Sir Donald and Lady Mackinnon in an elderly gossip all by themselves beside the companion ladder.

Olga and Alan leaned over the gunwale and talked their own talk confidentially alone, leaving the respected seniors to their private resources.

"Yes," Mrs. Hilary Tristram said, with a confessing smile, in answer to some casual remark of Sir Donald's: "I know I am. I admit the impeachment. It's so pleasant to make young people happy. The difficulty is, nowadays, how to do it. There are so many good girls, and nice girls, and pretty girls, and clever girls, all over England, waiting to be married, and never a man anywhere to marry them. Where are the men? All gone abroad—in the army, in the navy, in India, in the Colonies—wood-cutting in Canada, sheep-farming in New Zealand, tea-planting in Assam, sugar-boiling in Jamaica,—doing anything and everything on earth but what they ought to be—making love at their ease to the nice girls here at home in England.

"And the consequence is, the nice girls are left alone by themselves disconsolate. I really wish I could introduce a Universal British Empire Telephonic Matrimonial Agency, to bring the young people everywhere together. But as I can't, I'm reduced to the sad necessity of inviting the miserable remnant of the men to meet the whole host of nice girls at dinners and dances."

"You're a benefactor of humanity," Lady Mackinnon answered with a nod. "Or ought the right words to be benefactress of femininity?"

"I'm not so sure about the young couple by the gunwale over yonder," Sir Donald interrupted, with a mysterious shake of his sagacious head. "I'm not so sure of your benefaction there, do you know, Mrs. Tristram."

"Not so sure of Mr. Tennant, Sir Donald!" Mrs. Tristram cried, bridling up at once and arching her eyebrows suddenly. "Oh, I assure you, he's a most charming young man, and so well principled too." (Ladies of Mrs. Tristram's age, it may be parenthetically observed, invariably attach a profound importance to those mystic entities known as Principles.) "He'd be a most eligible husband for any good girl: I can't allow you to say a single word against my Mr. Tennant."

"It wasn't of *him* I was thinking, thank you," Sir Donald muttered dryly. "It wasn't of him. It was of the young lady."

"What? Olga! My dear Sir Donald, you must really excuse me, but Olga's one of my most particular favourites. The only doubt I had on my mind was whether my Mr. Tennant, nice as he is, was quite nice enough for dear Olga. I hesitated as to whether I ought to permit the young people to be thrown so very much together."

Sir Donald shrugged his shoulders slightly: that was a Celtic-Scotch trick which his Indian experiences had rather strengthened than otherwise.

"It's none of my business, I'm sure, my dear madam," he said short-ly: "but you know I'm a Scotchman, and we Scotch are a trifle eerie. I have a wee bit of the second sight about me, myself; and I don't just like that young lady's eyes. I've seen something like them in India. . No, no: I'm not going to tell you, for you'd only laugh at me: but I know this much, that if I were a young man I'd think twice before I put my fate, for better for worse, into such hands as Miss Olga Trev-elyan's. She's a friend of yours, and I'll say naught against her: but if second sight counts for anything nowadays, I tell you there's mischief brewing ahead for Mr. Alan Tennant."

Mrs. Hilary Tristram traced a circle uneasily with her parasol on the deck.

"I've had the good fortune to be born south of the Tweed, Sir Donald," she said at last, after an awkward pause, "so the second sight doesn't greatly trouble me."

But it did trouble her, for all that. Being a woman, and therefore impressionable, the mere suggestion of misfortune affected her happi-ness. She spent a sleepless night that memorable Wednesday, thinking over in her own soul by herself all possible evils that could ever be supposed to overshadow in the future Olga Trevelyan and Alan Ten-nant. Perhaps Sir Everard would be very angry, and then what a dread-ful fuss she would get into for having encouraged this unfortunate love affair. The more she thought about it, the more nervous she grew. It's an awful thing to undertake the role of earthly providence to two aspiring and grateful young lives!

Never suggest ill omens to a woman. You are raising more ghosts than all your philosophy can ever exorcise.

Meanwhile, Alan and Olga stood by the gunwale, looking over into the deep clear central stream that moved unsullied between its muddy banks, like a good woman in this wicked world of ours. The boat in which Norah and her party had taken their departure was winding its way slowly up a narrow channel, towards the low bridge some two miles beyond the paper mill. Norah's bright crimson parasol, held open behind her head, made a capital mark to track their course by. Even when the boat itself lay half hidden by the tall mud banks, that brilliant patch of sunlit colour sufficed to reveal at once their exact progress up the tributary channel.

"Take my glass," Alan said, handing it to Olga. "One can see the whole course of the stream with it up as far as the paper mill, spread out just like a map from the deck here before us. How it twists and turns as it crawls along! I went up there, wildfowl shooting, I remember, last summer."

"I'm sorry you shoot," Olga said, turning her deep brown eyes full upon him. "I suppose it's very girlish and all that of me, but I hate bloodshed—even an animal's. Members of a great humane profession like yours, whose very mission it is to alleviate pain, ought surely to amuse themselves with something nobler and better than going wildfowl shooting."

"You are right," Alan answered, converted in a moment from the error of his ways by the tender light in those beautiful eyes of hers. "Forgive the past. In future, Miss Trevelyan, I shall never handle a gun again,"

There was a short pause, during which a few distinct words were wafted over towards them from the region of the quarter-deck.

"The Hindus," Sir Donald was saying in a loud voice, so loud that it broke in for a moment on the young people's colloquy, "will never willingly injure any living creature, especially cows, bulls, or oxen. It's part of their religion. A confoundedly queer religion, I always thought it. Odd that the people who won't eat beefsteak or tread upon a cockroach should have invented the custom of burning their widows, practised infanticide, and winked at the abominable atrocities of Thuggee!"

"Sir Donald has really Thugs on the brain, "Olga murmured smiling. "I've never yet once met him that he hasn't gone back over and over again to that same old subject. Where have they got to now, I wonder, Mr. Tennant.? Can you see Norah anywhere?"

"Oh, yes. There's Miss Bickersteth's parasol by the beacon yonder. I've been watching it all the way along the stream ever since they started."

"I'm so glad, Mr. Tennant," Olga said with meaning. "She's a dear little soul, and she's well worth watching."

Alan Tennant felt a faint blush rise to his cheek, but he said nothing. Clearly, Olga was on the wrong tack: but the present moment, with Lady Mackinnon's eyeglass fixed stonily upon them, was not exactly the best opportunity for a candid explanation.

"They're getting to the bridge now," he said carelessly. "It's a nasty bridge, that: too low almost for a boat to get under. The . . . the duck-boat you know—I allude merely to the sins of the past by way of illustration the duck-boat could just manage to escape it, but I don't suppose Miss Bickersteth's craft can possibly clear it. Lend me the glass a moment, please. Thanks. . . . Ah, yes: the water's somewhat lower than usual today. They can just get under. . . . Why, now they're stopping half-way through the bridge. Miss Bickersteth's putting out a line, I fancy. Excuse me. Miss Trevelyan, if I trample again on your tenderest feelings, but I really think—yes, I'm quite sure—she's going to do a little fishing."

Olga laughed. "I'm afraid I'm not quite true there," she said, "to my own principles. You mustn't expect consistency in a woman. I confess I don't somehow feel as if fishing was really quite so bad as shooting. I wouldn't fish myself, of course, because I wouldn't willingly give pain to any living creature; but I don't feel called upon to be angry with dear Norah if she chooses to do it. For one thing, the fish don't seem quite so much alive, you know, as pheasants and partridges. I don't think they can feel anything like so keenly. And then, besides, one doesn't actually shed their blood, you see: they only choke and die, I suppose, poor creatures."

Once more Sir Donald's voice broke through to where they sat.

"Strangled them with a big silk handkerchief they called a *roomal*," he said impressively, "and offered them up as an expiatory sacrifice to their goddess Kalee."

"But what's become of the Thugs themselves now?" Mrs. Tristram ventured languidly to ask with a faint smile. "They can't all be extinct, of course. They must be doing something or other."

"Ah, yes," Sir Donald replied, with a long, sagacious nod of his head. "Beneficent action of the British Government stamped out the Thugs, viewed as a caste, but left the survivors. They're all now otherwise engaged—as professional poisoners!"

"Really, one may have too much of a good thing," Alan remarked, half beneath his breath, in answer to Olga's silent smile of amusement. "Even the Thugs, blood-curdling as they are, pall at last upon the twentieth repetition. And how very characteristic of our British tinkering! We stamp out infanticide—and substitute a famine: we stamp out the Thugs—and get professional poisoners! Will you take the glasses again? What's that upon the stream away above the bridge there? A flight of herons? or wild ducks, is it? Too white for either, I think! See, see, that long pale band upon the face of the stream yonder. It seems to be moving—moving rapidly."

"It's water," Olga answered, scanning it closely with the glass. "Foam on the river. A sort of bore or big wave, like the one they sometimes get on the Severn. Only it seems to go the opposite way, downstream, you know, instead of upwards."

"Give me the glass," Alan cried in haste. "Let me see what it is! . By Jove, I thought so! It's the water coming down—coming down like mad. Oh, what shall we do! What shall we do for them! They've opened the flood gates at the sluice by the paper mill!"

"And Norah!" Olga cried, clasping her hands frantically. "Do they see it? Do they know it? Are they in any danger?"

"If the water catches them there," Alan answered at once, "it'll rise to the level of the bridge above it always does—I know it of old—and they'll every one of them be drowned to a certainty. They won't be able to get their heads above water, because of the bridge, and they'll be crushed in, as it were, between the boat and the timbers."

Olga started back in an agony of fear. "Oh, save her, save her, Mr. Tennant," she cried aloud in her terror.

"Who? what?" Sir Donald exclaimed, roused by her cry. Then, his experienced eye taking in at a glance the danger of the situation, as Alan pointed mutely with his hand to the low bridge and the rushing flood above it, he called aloud to the stoker below, the one other man left on board the yacht, "Quick, quick! The boat! the boat! Down with it immediately. We must put out this moment and warn them of the danger!"

"There isn't another boat aboard her, sir," the stoker answered with a gesture of despair, silently appreciating the difficulty in his turn. "They're both out with the young gentlemen and ladies."

"Shout! Shout! Wave! Call to them! Whistle! Attract their attention!" Sir Donald cried hastily.

"There's no steam on," the stoker answered; "I've let the fire down. We can't whistle!"

They all raised their voices together in a loud halloo. Unhappily the wind was blowing against them. A waving of hands and beckoning of handkerchiefs, long repeated, proved equally ineffectual. Norah, sitting at her ease in the stern, with her parasol still needlessly open, and the low bridge half hiding her from their sight, blocked the view of all the others. They were too intent upon their fishing to look behind them. It seemed as though they must needs be swamped without hope of rescue by the onward rush of the approaching waters, and drowned in the boat, a perfect death-trap, as the projecting timbers must infallibly catch it and hold it tight with the first flood, while the surging waves rose around and filled it.

"Thank God, there's time still," Sir Donald cried aloud, the perspiration standing in great cold beads upon his bronzed forehead. "Though it's coming down fast, it has a long way, a very long way yet to go, and many turns to make, before it reaches them. Perhaps we may still succeed in attracting their attention. Perhaps they'll see it coming themselves. How does the river twist beyond the bridge, William? If there's an open reach ahead, they'll notice the wave, and get well away before it's down upon them. Below the bridge they may get upset, but they can cling for dear life to the boat, anyhow. Do you know how the river runs, Tennant?"

Alan shook his head ominously. "There's a sharp turn, and high mud-banks, just above the bridge," he answered with a shudder. "They can't see it coming, even if they were looking, until it's close upon them: and besides, they're not looking: they're intent upon their fishing."

Mrs. Hilary Tristram burst into tears. "Oh, Norah, Norah!" she cried piteously. "Sir Donald! Mr. Tennant! Save her! Save her!"

"There's only one way!" Olga cried, trembling and pale as death, but quite firmly. "Somebody must swim out at once and warn them. A good swimmer would have time to do it. Can you swim William?"

"Not a stroke. Miss, worse luck, to save my life even."

Alan Tennant answered nothing, but pulled off his boots and coat in silence. He loosened his collar and flung it on the deck. Then he stepped resolutely on to the parapet of the gunwale. "I'm not an expert," he said, simply; "but perhaps I can manage it. It's a race against time, that's all. There may be just margin enough. Anyhow, a medical man's business is to save life at all hazards."

Olga held out her hand for a second, as if she would check him: then drew it back again irresolutely to her side. "Take care of the wave," she cried in trembling accents; "don't let it swamp you. But save Norah! save Norah!" Alan plunged at the word with a header into the stream, and swam with all his might and main across the main channel towards the little river. Tide had turned now, and that was in his favour. He was a powerful man, though not, as he said, an expert swimmer; and swimming just then, all for haste, as if for dear life, with one arm alternately held above the water—the best way for speed—he stemmed the stream with the flow on the very turn, and made rapid way with his vigorous impulses through the deep water. The eyes of the watchers followed him with eager suspense.

It was an awful moment. The bridge and boat and red parasol stood out distinctly in the middle distance. The white wave, with its sea of waters behind, came steadily onward, advancing from up-stream towards those unconscious young folks in the light pleasure boat. And in front, breasting the water with the mad energy of despair, Alan Tennant's head and arms showed ever and *anon* between the half-burying mud-banks of the lesser river. Would he reach them in time?—that was the question. Would he get near enough to shout aloud, and be heard, and warn them? Oh, for a chance of raising their voices and making themselves noticed to call their attention! The wave was advancing, advancing, advancing! He would never reach them! He would never get near enough! It was hopeless I hopeless! The wave was gaining on them!

The wind! The wind! That cruel wind! They could hear Norah's soft and musical laughter borne to their ears distinctly by the breeze, and yet their own loud cries, wafted the opposite way, were utterly unnoticed, unheeded, undreamt of!

At last Olga had a burst of inspiration.

"The gun! The gun!" she cried, pointing an eager finger to the little brass mortar that stood by the tiller.

They had none of them thought of it.

Fortunately, it was loaded for the customary salute. Quick as lightning, the stoker had brought a live coal up on deck from the smouldering furnace, and hastily, tremulously, touched the priming: *Boom!*— the sound reverberated along the water. Down went the red parasol for a single moment, and the four young people in the boat beneath the bridge, startled by the report, looked round in surprise to see Alan's hand earnestly beckoning to them, and his arm raised in solemn warning well above the level of the surrounding water.

He was almost within earshot now, and gathering up all his voice for a supreme effort, he cried aloud in one wild shout, "Jump out on to the bridge, Harry! Floodgates opened!"

It was just in time. The three lads, taking in his meaning with the rapidity of instinct, pulled the boat out without touching the oars, by pushing at the timbers overhead, leaped on to the low wooden roadway of the bridge, and handed out Norah, in trembling haste, on to the place of safety. Even as they did so, and before they had time so much as to secure the boat, the flood burst upon them with a wild sweep from round the corner, raised the water in the channel to the level of the bridge, and bore down the skiff, tossed lightly bottom upward, on to the foaming summit of its mad forefront.

Norah was safe! So much Olga could clearly see from her post on deck: but Alan Tennant? On what an errand was this that she had so hastily sent him? The fierce flood swept madly onward still, gurgling and roaring like a winter torrent. It boiled and seethed and careered in its frenzy. Could he stem its force—he who was no expert swimmer—or would it drown and overwhelm him without chance of respite?

The high mud-bank on either side hid him now from their view in the narrow channel. They could only see the one white ridge of water where the pent-up flood rushed on rejoicing on its mad course seaward.

Olga stood and watched in breathless suspense. Next moment, in the midst of the great white wave, a solitary black object rose bobbing for a second. She saw what it was: Alan Tennant's head. In another instant—oh, agony! oh, horror!—the white wave swept on resistless, and the black object in its midst, sinking from their view, was no longer visible.

Olga clasped her bloodless hands in terrible self-accusation. "Drowned, drowned!" she cried, in a voice of anguish: "Drowned after saving them? And it was I who sent him!"

They strained their eyes eagerly to watch for the reappearance of the head once more, as the white wave emerged at last from the muddy banks of the minor stream, and joined with a burst the main current of the Thore in the central channel. But no head was anywhere to be seen; and what was stranger still, no boat either. Had both been sucked under by the eddying flood, and would they only reappear again in the calm water a hundred yards or so lower down, where the Thore broadened out into a wide estuary?

As Olga strained and watched and wondered with bated breath, a sudden cry from Sir Donald made her turn her eyes further up the little tributary river, where the old Indian was pointing his thin forefinger. With an involuntary sigh of joy, she recognised the reason. Alan had caught the drifting boat, and was clinging to its side, and pushing it up stream as well as he was able against the battling force of the released current!

In a minute or two more, as the first rage of the flood gradually subsided, he had righted the light boat, and was seated in it, and paddling his way (for the oars were gone) with a short foot-rest which had luckily stuck in its rack in spite of the capsizing. Stirring episodes occupy small space. In far less than a quarter of an hour from the time when he jumped overboard off the yacht's deck, Alan Tennant had reached the bridge, and was standing in safety by Norah's side.

Olga's heart, which had stood still within her while she watched and waited, bounded now with a wild tremor of delight. They were saved, saved! Both of them saved! Norah and—and Alan.

In that moment of agony; her heart, too had confessed its own secret to itself. She knew she loved him! She was certain that she loved him!

CHAPTER 7

Heroism Dry

A hero, it may be confidently asserted, is no hero at all in wet clothes. On the contrary, ne is a wretched, dripping, bedraggled creature, suggestive rather of the need for immediate charity than of the praise and honour due to his tried heroism. Alan Tennant, though new to the role in this particular fashion at least (for every doctor is after all by profession a hero in his own way), so instinctively grasped at that obvious element in the theatrical recognition of the heroic character, that he abstained from returning to the yacht as he stood, and displaying himself before Olga's admiring eyes in his wet, torn, and muddy garments. This is as it should be.

On the stage, indeed, the hero who has saved a beautiful lady from imminent drowning appears on deck immediately afterwards in spotless white shirt and blue Nankin trousers, and has his hand warmly grasped by the lady's friends, or is even embraced bodily before an admiring circle by her grateful mother, her cousins, and her aunts. But then the stage hero comes up from the great deep dry and unhurt (even his hair is not put out of curl), as though water ran off him, by some occult arrangement, in the common fashion of the domestic duck.

But in real life, unfortunately, the hero's head emerges from the wave distinctly disarranged; his collar is moist limp, and uncomfortable, and his clothes cling to him with most unpicturesque and unromantic tightness. Alan Tennant judged it best, therefore, to leave to the lads the task of paddling Norah back to her grateful chaperon: while he himself, dripping wet, coatless and hatless, ran back to Thorborough at the top of his speed by the nearest road without waiting for any theatrical reception.

This was certainly not romantic heroism: but it was warmer and safer: and besides, what man cares to appear before the maiden of his choice, even as a hero, draped from head to fool in. damp and dingy mud-bespattered clothing? That evening, however, at half-past seven, the young doctor issued forth once more resplendent from his hotel, in black coat and white necktie, by special invitation to dine at Mrs. Hilary Tristram's, in his new character as Norah's preserver.

A hero in evening clothes, now—look you—why, that of course is quite another matter. When a man is tall and handsome and rejoices in the possession of a black moustache, there must certainly be something very wrong about him somewhere if he doesn't look, on due occasion given, every inch a hero, standing up by the fireplace, in a swallow-tail coat and white necktie.

Olga Trevelyan thought so indeed as she entered the drawing-room earliest of the party, and found Alan already there, looking none the worse in any way for his afternoon's adventure. In fact, if anything, he looked all the better: for every man's appearance is much improved in certain circumstances by a not ungraceful consciousness of having acquitted himself well and manfully under trying conditions.

Olga took his hand tremulously. He saw she had been crying: she had not quite succeeded after many efforts, in obliterating the traces of it from her swollen eyelids. She said nothing, but held his hand nervously in hers for a moment with a sudden access of mute gratitude. She was too deeply moved to know precisely what she was doing. Thinking only of Norah's safety (and his), she held it long, and let it go reluctantly.

"Mr. Tennant," she said at last, in a trembling voice, "we can never, never, never sufficiently thank you. You have given us back our darling Norah. If it hadn't been for you, we should certainly have lost her. I won't try to tell you how much I admire you for it. It was splendidly done—I am glad in my heart I was there to see it."

Alan smiled and made light of it, of course. (It is part of the role of a hero, once more, you know, always to make light of the danger afterwards.) "Oh, it wasn't really a long swim," he answered carelessly. "The only real difficulty was when that nasty wave came bursting over one. I certainly did think then for a minute I should never live through it: and if I hadn't just happened to clutch at the boat as it passed on the crest of the ridge, I fancy I shouldn't have pulled through, either.

But don't think," and here he lowered his voice a moment, "it was all pure devotion to duty, and saving life, and all that sort of thing, I'm not quite sure, Miss Trevelyan, that for anybody else I should ever have had strength to do it."

Olga looked up at him with a delightful smile. "I'm glad to hear it," she said frankly. "Then I suppose tonight, of course, you'll seize the opportunity at once and propose to her. After that she could never refuse you. . . . And you should just hear, Mr. Tennant, all the things she's been saying to me upstairs about you."

For a moment, Alan drew back in surprise. He could hardly understand what Olga meant by it. Then, as her misconception dawned slowly upon him, he took her hand, unresisted, gently in his own, and led her passive for a moment on to the lawn outside, through the open window.

"Miss Trevelyan," he said, very low and soft, "you don't understand me. I'm not sure that for any other woman on earth but you, I should have had strength to do it. But *you* asked me; *you* sent me: and if you had told me that moment to go to the world's end, I would gladly have done it. I will take your advice and seize the opportunity. Olga, Olga, I love you, I love you."

Olga stood away for a second in surprise. Then she lifted her big eyes slowly to his, and said in the same simple straightforward tone as before, "Why, Mr. Tennant,—I thought—I thought—I thought it was Norah."

Alan Tennant gazed at her with eyes of mingled admiration and amusement.

"Norah!" he cried. "Norah! Norah! Oh, no; oh, no; it wasn't Miss Bickersteth. Ask her, ask her: she knows better. She knows I love you. From the very first moment I ever saw you, I felt in my heart I could never love any lesser creature. And you will let me love you? You will let me love you?"

She paused a moment. "But Norah?" she said. "What about Norah?"

"Norah!" Alan cried, in an impassioned voice. "Norah! Norah! Oh, no: I never cared a pin for Norah! Norah knows I am in love with you, and expects me to tell you so! Olga, Olga, you will not refuse me! You will take me! You will take me!"

Her hero looked absolutely heroic then:—and besides, the five minutes just before dinner is a most cramped and awkward time to choose for such an interview. Olga's face flushed crimson for a moment—Mrs. Tristram would be down before she could get him back safe into the drawing-room: and everybody would notice it and read her secret! She paused again while a man might count ten, and looked at him hesitatingly with her beautiful big eyes. Then she laid her hand once more in his for a brief second, and answered in an almost inaudible voice, "Yes, Mr. Tennant." Next instant, he was standing by himself on the grass, and Olga, crimson still and very tremulous, had run in by the front door, and hurried up again to her own bedroom.

They had to wait dinner full ten minutes for her; and when she came down once more, she looked flushed and agitated. But happily, Alan, as the guest of the evening, did not sit beside her. He took down Mrs. Hilary Tristram, and had Norah (the preserved) on his left hand. That was a great comfort to poor Olga. To be sure, it was rather hard, just after such an interview as hers and Alan's, to engage spasmodically in the small talk of society with the young dragoon who took her into dinner: but at any rate it was better than if she had had to talk to Alan. That, under the circumstances, would have been *too* embarrassing.

Of course, neither of them said anything to anybody about the little episode that had happened before dinner. But women have eyes whose keenness wonderfully puzzles us poor purblind men. As the ladies rose to go into the drawing-room, Norah slipped her arm around Olga's waist playfully in the hall, and whispered in her ear, "I'm *so* glad, darling. I knew he would. I was quite certain of it!" And Olga only blushed once more—she was sweet when she blushed—and gave her pretty little friend's hand a silent squeeze with her burning fingers.

Of course, the engagement was "not announced." Engagements of that informal and purely personal sort never are announced, until the consent of the superior authorities has been duly obtained. But they get whispered about unofficially for all that. And when Mrs. Hilary Tristram mentioned in confidence the very next day to Sir Donald Mackinnon that Norah had told her that Olga had as good as admitted that Alan Tennant had made her an offer, Sir Donald twirled his grey moustache and shook his heavy head ominously.

"Young bodies won't be warned," he said with a gloomy look of intense foreboding. "I was afraid of as much when yon lad spoke of her to me yesterday. People may laugh at the second-sight as much as they will, but I told you then—and you see it's coming true already—there was mischief brewing ahead for young Alan Tennant. The girl's a good lass, and a pretty lass, and a clever lass, and she means no evil: but there's a Thing within her, driving her on, that'll lead her into trouble when she least expects it."

Chapter 8
The Storm Gathers

Time wore on. Alan Tennant's holiday was drawing to a close. Six weeks is a long rest for a busy and successful London specialist: and Alan Tennant had made the best of his, for himself and for Olga. A few days before he was to leave Thorborough, Norah Bickersteth happened to meet him on the Shell Path.

"Oh, I'm so glad I've knocked up against you, Mr. Tennant," she said with a sunny smile, holding out her pretty little gloved hand to him. "Auntie gave me a message for you today. You're going up the river with Harry, aren't you?"

"Yes," Alan answered. "We're going in the duck-boat—the *Indian Princess*, you know—just to let Harry have a general view of the prospects of the wild-fowl shooting."

"Well, auntie wants you to come in this evening, after dinner—you'll excuse our saying after dinner, won't you? Sir Donald's going to bring round Mr. Keen—the great mesmerist, you know, and thought-reader, and so forth: he does such wonderful tricks, they say: and auntie wants you to come and see him, because you're so clever, and you'll understand all about it."

Alan smiled. "Oh, yes, I'll come," he said. "Only Mrs. Tristram mustn't expect to find me very much of a believer in thought-reading and so forth. Is Mr. Keen stopping with Sir Donald? Ah, yes, I thought so. Sir Donald's a Highlander, with Highland superstitions well ingrained in him, and a little improved (like good Madeira) by twenty years of India. But Miss Bickersteth, mind, there must be no mesmerizing or thought-reading on any account with Olga." (He had seen a good deal of her since the trip on the yacht, and it had come to be plain "Olga" by this time.)

"She isn't strong, and she's had a great deal of nervous excitement to upset her lately, and she should be kept from anything that will excite her in any way. Tell Mrs. Tristram I shall be delighted to drop in. I mustn't keep you: Harry's waiting for me with the boat down yonder at the Haven. Good morning. Till after dinner." And he lifted his hat and walked away briskly.

That evening, Mrs. Hilary Tristram's informal party was larger than usual. Half the visitors at Thorborough had been invited to drop in for the purpose of seeing the celebrated mesmerist's extraordinary performance. Only Harry Bickersteth and Alan Tennant were still absent: delayed up the river, no doubt, by the turn of the tide, and not to be looked for back again till late in the evening.

"It's very odd Alan doesn't turn up," Olga whispered uneasily in Norah's ear. "Ever since that trouble the other day with you, dear, I hate the river. It's so awfully dangerous. I wish he'd come: it quite frightens me."

"Oh, nonsense, darling," Norah answered with a smile, "Of course I know you're very anxious to see him. That's natural; I should be myself, I'm sure. But he's all right: don't be afraid. They'd come home late, and have dinner together in flannels, at the Royal Alexandra; and then they'd have to dress, you know; and they couldn't be here till a good deal later. Hush, hush: Mr. Keen's going to begin the mesmerism now.'Observe, ladies and gentlemen, there's no deception.'You see he's rolling up his sleeves beforehand, just like a conjurer, in order to let us notice he hasn't got any ghosts or spirits or supernatural agents concealed anywhere in his cuffs or coat-lining. What funny thin hands-so strange and ghost-like."

There was a general hush, and the company drew up in a hasty circle, the ladies seated, the men standing behind their chairs, with a clear space for Mr. Keen and his "subjects" in the centre, where a solitary seat was placed for the person to be mesmerised.

"I will begin," Mr. Keen said, looking round him carelessly at the assembled company with the bland smile of the practised performer, "I will begin first upon this young gentleman." He singled out a boy quickly from the group behind. "I see you're susceptible. Stand forward, please. Take a seat there, will you? Now, look steadily into my eyes, my boy, and think about nothing until I tell you."

The boy took the seat where the mesmerist motioned him, and looked as requested deep into his eyes. After a few minutes, his eyelids dropped, and he began to fall back heavily in the chair.

The performer, with practised ease, put him rapidly through all the usual and well-known tricks by which the mesmerist is wont to show the abeyance of the will and the absolute acquiescence of the "subject" in his every suggestion.

"You're a bird, aren't you?" Mr. Keen asked, addressing him authoritatively.

And the boy, with a nod of the head, began at once to flap his arms, run forward flightily, and behave as if he thought himself really flying.

"What are you?" the mesmerist asked in a coaxing voice.

"A bird," the boy answered with the instantaneous force of complete conviction.

"A bird?" dubiously.

"Well—I think so."

"No, not a bird! A bird! Ridiculous!"

The boy laughed. "No, not a *bird*," he said. "A bird! What nonsense."

"Of course not,"the mesmerist went on confidently."You're a fish, you know. A fish, most decidedly."

The boy laughed once more, a nervous laugh. "A fish," he repeated in a bewildered fashion, and throwing himself on the floor began to move his arms slowly and regularly, as if swimming with fins in a sluggish river.

"The stream runs fast," the mesmerist suggested.

The boy immediately quickened the movement, and seemed to be struggling in the violent effort to make headway against some unseen but overwhelming power.

"Do you believe in it?" Norah whispered in a low undertone to Olga.

"Not a bit," Olga answered, shaking her head.

"The boy's shamming; that's my idea about it. It must be a preconcerted thing between them."

Low as she spoke, the mesmerist overheard her.

"You shall try in your turn, young lady," he said severely, glancing at her with his great cold dull blue eyes—eyes that seemed totally devoid of all life or meaning. "You shall see for yourself before the evening's out whether there's anything in it or nothing."

Olga blushed, and remained silent.

"What's that?" the mesmerist cried to the boy suddenly, striking an attitude of attention and listening in surprise. "Do you hear? Do you hear it?"

The boy jumped up immediately from the floor, and stood looking about him and turning his head, first this way, then that, as if straining his ear for some distant sound or other.

"You *must* hear it," the mesmerist said in a half-angry voice. "It's quite distinct. Listen! What is it?"

"I *hear* it," the boy answered. "I hear it, of course, right enough. But I can't make out exactly what it is, for the life of me, somehow. "

"Bells," the mesmerist suggested with confidence.

"Ah," the boy assented. "So it is. Chimes, by Jingo." And he beat time in a jangling singsong with his hand to the quick lilt of the imaginary music.

"It's the cathedral," the mesmerist cried, seizing his arm suddenly. "Let's go inside. What a glorious anthem! By George, it's splendid! I do love to hear the pealing of the organ."

The boy answered nothing, but stood entranced, listening with all his ears to the unheard sounds, and smiling with a face of glowing delight at the inaudible melody.

"Pah," the mesmerist muttered after a minute's pause: "a false note! The fellow plays badly. Inexcusable, quite. The dean and chapter ought really to keep a better organist."

The boy set his teeth on edge at once and drew up his lips with a pained expression, as we all do instinctively at the sound of a discord in the midst of music.

"If it's acting," Mrs. Tristram whispered low to Olga, "it's consummate acting. Perfectly consummate. I don't think Charlie Meredith has got it in him."

"Let us take another subject," the mesmerist said quietly, making a few rapid passes, and releasing the boy. "Will you try, Miss Bickersteth? Thanks. How very good of you. Everybody will know—with a glance at Olga—"that you at least are above suspicion."

Norah walked out timidly into the centre, and took her place, blushing, on the experimenter's chair. In a few minutes, she too was asleep, and doing at once all the mesmerist's bidding.

"Take this cup," Mr. Keen said, handing the girl a lacquered Japanese bowl from the little whatnot. "There, drink it off, that's a good girl. It's very nasty, but you mustn't mind it. It's to do you good! Dr. Hazleby's orders!"

Norah drained off the imaginary draught, and made a most comical wry face after it. "It's very bitter," she said. "I don't like it. Please don't make me take any more of it, will you, auntie?"

"Oh, no," the mesmerist responded promptly, glancing round with a look of triumph at Olga. "Here, have a cup of coffee to take the taste away." And he handed her back the self-same bowl with a little mocking bow of pretended politeness.

Norah took it and emptied it (in imagination) once more. "It's very nice coffee," she said. "Excellent coffee. I'll take another cup of that coffee, thank you."

"Let Mr. Keen try with you, Olga dear," Mrs. Hilary Tristram suggested gently, turning to her. "Don't wake up Norah yet, Mr. Keen.

Let's have a little comedy of two together."

"Oh, please not," Olga cried, shrinking timidly back from the performer's hands, as he took her fingers gently in his. "I don't know whether—" and then she checked herself with a sudden blush. . . . She didn't know whether Alan would approve of it.

Norah could have said her nay at once had Norah been awake: but Norah sat in the chair, silent, bound body and soul in a deathlike trance by the art of the mesmerist.

Mr. Keen, however, had no intention of letting his sceptical hearer off. "Excuse me, young lady," he said severely. "I heard you remark just now that you didn't believe in it. You will have to believe in it before the evening's out, whether you will or no. Come out into the middle! Follow me! Do as I bid you! Don't disobey. Take a seat there!"

He spoke sternly, in a tone of command. Olga followed him reluctantly, but obedient like a child, and sat down, still blushing and trembling, with a sweet shy air, in the centre of the circle. The man's strong will seemed absolutely indisputable: she couldn't even make the necessary effort of will to disobey it.

Sir Donald's eyes were fixed firmly upon her. She averted her own with a violent struggle, and beckoned hastily to Mrs. Tristram.

"Suppose," she whispered low in her hostess's ear, "suppose he were to ask me—you understand, dear Mrs. Tristram—some awkward question?"

Mrs. Tristram smiled and nodded reassuringly. "Don't be afraid, dear," she answered with a smile. "I'll take care of that. He shall ask you nothing about Mr. Tennant."

Olga threw back her beautiful head, a little reassured, and lifted her eyes, half against her will, and full of misgivings, to meet the mesmerist's as he began his passes.

Sir Donald Mackinnon, watching her closely, noticed soon that a weird change came over her face. She did not close her eyes, indeed, like Norah, but gradually sank back, with her eyelids open, and her pupils dilated, staring hard, as it were, into dim vacancy. Then suddenly, with a rise and fall of her heaving bosom, she seemed to become aware of some unseen Presence. She clasped her hands, bending forward eagerly as one who listens, while her whole slight frame quivered and trembled, like a leaf before the wind, with suppressed emotion. A muttered word hung unspoken on her lips. Sir Donald could hardly catch the sound, but he fancied to himself from the shape of the mouth that the word was "Kalee!"

192

Meanwhile the mesmerist, moving his hands rapidly to and fro before her, redoubled his exertions to close her eyes with the intensest energy. He darted his fingers with strange gestures towards the unclosed lids, and seemed by his grimaces to be struggling hard with some invisible enemy. All was in vain: the eyelids still remained obstinately open: and the performer gasped for breath heavily. Big clammy drops stood on his moistened brow: he was straining every nerve and wearying every muscle in the unequal contest. Do what he would, he could not make this obstinate girl shut her eyes: and the very persistence with which she held them open seemed to put him more and more earnestly upon his mettle.

At last he sank exhausted into a chair. "It's no use," he muttered discontentedly, folding his arms. "I was never so utterly baffled in my life before. The girl's an enigma! She's too self-willed for me! And a mere chit of a child too! I must give it up. She won't be mesmerised."

As he spoke, Olga rose slowly, staggering from her seat, and stood gazing with a wild stare into blank space before her.

The mesmerist observed her eyes in sudden amazement. "Great heavens!" he cried, slowly realizing the true state of the case: "she is asleep! Asleep already! Fast asleep all the time, by Jove, and with her eyes open!"

"She always sleeps so," Mrs. Hilary Tristram whispered softly in his ear. "Mr. Tennant told dear Norah it was due to some slight congenital injury to the nerves of the eyelids."

Sir Donald Mackinnon whistled low. "I thought so," he muttered. "Odd—confoundedly odd, too. Keen, come here; I want to tell you something."

The two men whispered together alone for a second, and then Sir Donald, as by mute assent, standing forth in the middle by the mesmerist's side, spoke out a loud short sentence in Hindustani.

Olga started like a frightened fawn, and bowed her head humbly at the sound. "Great Kalee," she cried, in the same language, but in low and strangely altered accents, "I hear thy behest. I obey the summons."

Not a soul present save Sir Donald and Lady Mackinnon knew the precise import of those terrible words: but the deep earnestness and thrilling conviction with which Olga spoke them made everyone in the drawing-room shudder with horror. A terrible change had come at once over her voice and countenance. It was no longer Olga—their gentle, soft-souled Olga, that spoke; it was the low, suppressed implacable murmur of a human tigress.

Sir Donald uttered another word or two, incomprehensible to the rest of the visitors; and then Olga, moving forward a step or two wildly from her seat, cast her hungry eyes around in doubt upon the assembled company.

She scanned them all, with a searching glance: presently, her great glittering pupils fixed themselves upon Norah, where she sat helpless on the chair in the centre. The mesmerist touched Norah's eyes with his flabby fingers, and they opened at once as if by magic. She gazed at Olga in mute fascination. A violent wave of passionate emotion swept with fierce force over the elder girl's agitated features.

"Must *that* be the sacrifice?" she murmured slowly in English, but with concentrated horror. "Must that be the sacrifice? Hard: hard! But Kalee wills it! It is well! It is well! I obey the goddess!"

She drew from her neck her large silk kerchief—an Indian kerchief, delicately figured, folded round her dress diagonally as a sort of fichu; and proceeded to twist it into a running noose. Then she slowly took three steps forward towards the vacantly smiling Norah.

Sir Donald started in a perfect agony of expectation. "Great powers!" he cried. "The girl is twisting that handkerchief round exactly as if she were noosing a *roomal*."

"What is a *roomal?*" Mrs. Hilary Tristram asked in an awed undertone.

"A *roomal!*" Sir Donald answered with affected carelessness. "Oh, nothing, nothing. Just merely a handkerchief A handkerchief used by the Thugs, you know, to throttle and garrotte their helpless victims. The girl looks as if she meant to try it, too. Just notice her action?"

Olga turned and stared him stoutly in the face.

She stared with a bold and impudent air, and answered in a voice of low effrontery, "This isn't a *roomal*, you see," shaking it out; "it's only a neckerchief—a common neckerchief."

"Leave her alone," Mr. Keen interposed in a low undertone. "Let us see the natural end of the whole little drama. We won't interfere. We'll let her act it out. We'll leave her entirely to her own devices and her own promptings."

Olga turned away once more with a glance over her shoulder, and continued twisting the noose in the handkerchief. Then she stepped yet one pace nearer to the unconscious Norah, who sat now with wide-open eyes, gazing helpless at her friend, as if some snake had fascinated her with its fatal glance. A cold chill ran through the fair girl's slight figure as Olga approached, still coiling the handkerchief in her slender fingers. Norah had no power to stir or speak; but with a paralyzed air she watched and waited, as the fluttering bird watches and waits for the advancing serpent. Next moment, she knew, in her dimly conscious mind, that coiling handkerchief would be around her own neck to strangle her pitilessly. It was not her sweet friend who was creeping slowly upon her; it was some evil spirit, some great black creature, coming nearer, nearer.

And yet, she knew not why, she was not afraid; merely spellbound, fascinated, immovable. She did not cry, or try to cry, as in a hideous nightmare: she waited calmly and awfully for her approaching destiny.

As Olga stood there, irresolute and hesitating, with the handkerchief coiled and noosed like a lasso in her tremulous fingers, a sign from Sir Donald informed the mesmerist that enough of the drama had now been acted. The next step in the play would have been far too hideous for public rehearsal.

Sir Donald was satisfied: his conjecture was correct: the votary of Kalee stood openly confessed and unmasked before him. He motioned to Mr. Keen, and Mr. Keen, with a sigh of regret, placing himself behind Norah's chair, began a series of reversed passes, intended to bring the unconscious Olga back to her own waking personality. At the first pass, the bloodless hands ceased as if by magic from twisting the kerchief. Two or three more sufficed to rouse Olga to her first mesmeric stage, as she stood with her big beautiful eyes staring vacantly into space before her. But there the mesmerist's power failed him. He endeavoured in vain to fully wake her. Pass after pass was tried with no effect.

"I can't do it," he muttered angrily at last. "I worked so hard at putting her into the comatose condition that I can't for the life of me now get her out of it again. I'm faint, faint: I have lost power. I went too far. Brandy, brandy, quick! bring me some brandy!"

He sank upon a couch, with his arms folded listlessly in front of him. They brought the brandy, and he poured himself out a big wineglassful, which he tossed off neat without a moment's hesitation. Then he waited and fanned himself with his handkerchief a little. At last, as the spirit gave him fresh strength, he rose slowly, and once more confronted that immovable statue, standing cold and white with the untwisted handkerchief hanging loosely now from the pallid fingers. A few more passes undid the spell. Olga gave a great start—a short sharp cry—and woke up suddenly with a terrible awakening. Her eyes came back at once to measurable space from the remote distance.

The expression of concentrated determination and ferocity in her fixed features gave way first to one of pure bewilderment and next to another of unspeakable shamefaced horror. She gazed around her in awe for a moment as if barely conscious of her present surroundings: then, with the one word "Kalee" bursting painfully from her blanched lips, she dropped the handkerchief in a frenzy of shame, and darted, conscience-stricken, hastily from the room. Mrs. Tristram made a sign with her hand to one of the elder girls. The girl understood and hurriedly followed her.

The mesmerist, with a smile of self-conscious triumph on his inexpressive face, glanced round for applause at the attentive company. Nobody applauded. It was all too life-like, too vivid, too terrible. The line which separates illusion from fact had been overstepped. The suggested tragedy came too near a real one.

Mr. Keen, baffled of his expected applause, moved over quietly to the still smiling Norah. He waved his hands once or twice before her, and she woke forthwith, breathing hard and deep, in a weary fashion.

"What did you think you felt?" Sir Donald asked, coming mysteriously with a whisper to her side.

"I don't exactly remember," Norah answered with a sigh. "I feel so awfully dreamy still. I don't like it I wish I hadn't allowed Mr. Keen to mesmerise me. But I think I fancied I was somewhere in India, in a sort of jungle—I don't know what—but something or other terrible was going to happen. . . . It wasn't snakes and it wasn't tigers. . . . There was a woman . . . a black woman . . . a tall black woman—with awful eyes—" She broke off suddenly. "Give me a glass of wine," she cried in a pained voice. "I can't bear to think any more about it"

Chapter 9
Lowering Clouds

Sir Donald turned and walked into the garden. His brow was hot, and his fancy fired. He paced the lawn quickly and excitedly. The mesmerist stepped with a dejected air in long strides beside him.

"Keen," the old Indian cried at last, "I don't half like the look of it. This is not all right. I'm superstitious, I know, but I don't care a straw what you call me in that matter. Did you see yourself what the girl was doing? She was noosing that kerchief, regular Thug fashion, to strangle Norah Bickersteth!"

The mesmerist bit his lip reflectively. "Never saw such an unappreciative audience in all my life," he said in a testy voice. They might have given me a round with their hands at least. It's the best bit of mesmerism I ever did in my born days. The girl's acting was simply magnificent!"

"Acting!" Sir Donald echoed contemptuously. "It wasn't acting! It was sheer reality! The lassie's a Thug! She's been dedicated to Kalee!"

Mr. Keen glanced curiously sideways at his companion. Scotchmen have certainly got some queer ideas of their own. Besides, the old fellow had obviously appreciated Mrs. Hilary Tristram's excellent cognac. Drunk or mad, one or the other! The mesmerist marvelled, and said nothing.

Presently Sir Donald spoke again. He clutched his friend's arm in the shadow of the lilac bushes.

"Keen," he said, "I want to tell you something. I knew Everard Trevelyan well in India. He had but two children, this girl Olga, and a boy called Theodore. . . . Now, listen to me, and don't make light of it. It's a deuced odd fact, Keen, but it's true for all that, what I'm going to tell you. As I stood there and watched her just this minute, a picture rose distinctly before my eyes—a picture I'd clean forgotten for years—picture of Everard Trevelyan's bungalow at Moozuffernugger.

"The boy was lying dead in his cot—her little brother two days before she came away from India. There was a mystery about it, never cleared up. Some said the bearer, and some the *ayah*; but anyhow the thing was very remarkable. The child had a dark blue line traced right around his throat, and his eyes and tongue protruded horribly, for all the world as if he'd been suffocated. One would say, a handkerchief tied about his neck. They never discovered how it happened. Nobody could be convicted of it. . . . They never thought of his little sister. . . . Deuced odd, I call it, Keen, don't you, really?"

The mesmerist looked at him with glassy eyes.

"Remarkably odd," he said in a careless voice. "Remarkably. Re-markably."

Sir Donald took another turn and muttered half to himself—it was clear his companion was wholly unsympathetic—"Suspicion never pointed to anyone. *Ayah*, desperately fond of the children, wept like a child when Olga was taken from her. . And yet it's certainly very odd. The girl seemed guileless and simple enough. . . . But who can tell? Kalee's emissaries go forth unconscious in their deep sleep. Depend upon it, there's something in it, there's something in it."

He paced the lawn once more feverishly: then he spoke again: "I remember well when the news was broken to her! She cried as if her little heart would burst. Poor little soul, I can see her this minute! . . . It's very strange. I don't half like the look of it."

The mesmerist turned and stared him in the face. "My dear Mackinnon," he said testily, "you're talking an awful lot of pure rubbish. Mesmerism's a very powerful agency. It brought back forgotten old Indian reminiscences to the girl's mind: stirred the inmost chords and fibres of her most intimate nature: set her even speaking her outlandish lingo, in which you and she can jabber together so glibly. She must have heard some Indian servant, who was about her as a child, talk much of the Thugs, or whatever you call them: and that set her excited fancy working, and made her go off at once on the Thug hallucination. Believe me, you underestimate the power of mesmerism."

Sir Donald only looked up meditatively at the stars. "There are more things in heaven and earth, Horatio;" he muttered in a slow drawl, "than are dreamed of in your philosophy."

Meanwhile, Olga, in her own room, had been joined by Norah, who came up pale and trembling to inquire for her.

"What has made you ill, darling?" the younger girl asked her tenderly, throwing her soft arm in a caressing attitude round her friend's neck.

Olga drew back instinctively from her touch. "Oh, don't put your hand on me, don't come near me, Norah," she cried in alarm. "I don't know what's the matter with me tonight. I don't feel a bit like myself at all. I seem to be so wicked, so terribly wicked. You mustn't touch me!"

"You wicked, darling!" Norah echoed, kissing her. "You're not wicked. You could never be wicked. You're just a saint; that's what I call you Olga."

Olga brushed away a rising tear. "I can't understand it at all, Norah pet," she said dreamily. "For the very first time in all my life, I seemed half conscious in my sleep just now of my own actions. I wish—I wish to goodness they hadn't mesmerised me."

Norah drew back with a sudden look of alarm. "Mesmerised you, Olga?" she cried in much surprise. "You don't mean to say you let them mesmerise you? Why, Mr. Tennant begged me not to allow them. I wouldn't have let them if only I'd been awake myself and known all about it."

"But they did," Olga answered, "and I seemed to be dimly aware all the time I was asleep of what I was doing. And when I awoke—oh, it was too horrible! . . . Norah, Norah, my pet, my darling, don't, don't come near me! I beg of you. I implore you."

"Why, Olga, why?"

"Oh, Norah, darling, as I stood there in the drawing-room, waking yet sleeping—I'm afraid to tell you,—I seemed to be aware of some awful being, bloodthirsty, pitiless, black, invisible, floating in front of me, under whose orders I acted without hope of resistance. I saw her before me with my bodily eyes, and I heard her speak to me in some strange language. I had to obey whatever she told me: I had to obey her, though I hated and detested it. I don't know what it all meant, my darling, but I feel as if I was terribly, terribly wicked. . . And what's worst and most awful of all, Norah, I feel, now with my quickened senses, as if that terrible being had always, always been quite familiar to me."

Norah soothed her neck with one hand, and pressed her fingers tenderly with the other, but answered nothing.

The terrified girl laid her face gently on her friend's shoulder and sobbed away her grief for some moments in silence. Then she raised her head once more and murmured, "And Alan didn't want me to be mesmerised! I've disobeyed Alan without knowing it! Where's Alan? Has he come back yet?"

"No," Norah answered. "Harry and he haven't returned. They'll be back soon. Don't worry, darling. Oh, I wish to goodness you hadn't been mesmerised."

"Not comeback," Olga cried in alarm. "Oh, he's lost! he's lost! Norah! Norah! I saw her smiling, smiling horribly. I remember the smile! It means evil! She always smiles like that, I know, when she sees death or misfortune happen to anyone. It was a ghastly smile—so fiendish and exultant. Oh, Norah, Norah, it makes me faint even to think of her."

"Of whom? of whom?" Norah cried in horror.

"I don't know. I can't say, my darling. I can't remember her right name this minute; but I saw her just now! I saw her! I saw her! . . . He's dead! He's dead! I'm perfectly sure he is! I know that smile! Oh, Norah, Norah, her smile is so deadly!"

She flung herself down at full length on the couch, buried her face between her outstretched palms, and cried to herself long and silently.

At last she lifted her head once more. "And I didn't finish doing what she bid me!" she cried in anguish. "It was very wrong of me! I left off in the midst! I ought to have finished doing what she bid me!"

CHAPTER 10

The Storm Bursts

The party in the drawing-room had broken up rather suddenly. Everybody felt, in a certain dim instinctive fashion, there was something uncanny about this mesmerising business. Sir Donald and Mr. Keen were idly pacing the lawn outside together: Norah and Olga had retired to the obscurity of their own bedroom. Conversation languished. Mrs. Hilary Tristram tried in vain the recuperative effect of a little music. One of the guests sat down to the piano, and touching the keys lightly declared in a loud soprano voice she was "a happy haymaker." Nobody took the slightest notice of the romantic and obviously inopportune declaration. The elder men suggested cards: but the younger (as usual) all disclaimed the most elementary knowledge of the game of whist, and sidled off moodily in little knots into remote corners.

It was clear the harmony of the evening had been quite spoilt. That unfortunate mesmerising had totally upset the delicate nerves of the assembled company. Mrs, Hilary Tristram, best and ablest of hostesses, relinquished the position at last as hopeless. Retreating gracefully, she subsided of herself into an easy-chair, and assumed the attitude of one not wholly indisposed at an early hour to speed the parting guest with a glass of seltzer and a friendly valediction.

The guests for their part soon interpreted the languid attitude of their hostess aright. One after another dropped off rapidly, with mechanical thanks, as they bowed themselves out for a very pleasant and interesting evening. "Deuced slow," the men murmured one to the other, as they lit their cigars from borrowed lights outside the front porch. "That mesmerising rubbish simply spoilt the whole evening. Hard lines on those two poor girls, too, to go trying their constitutions in that stupid fashion! Quite surprised at it, for my part, in a sensible, amiable woman of the world like Mrs. Hilary Tristram."

Before the last guests had muttered their farewells, Norah glided softly into the room once more for a brief moment, and whispered something in her aunt's ear. Mrs. Tristram motioned back Dr. Hazleby to a chair with her hand.

"I want to speak with you," she said in a low voice as he took his seat again. "Norah and Olga may wish to consult you."

Dr. Hazleby sat back and waited for the other guests to go. His conscience smote him for having permitted the mesmerist to "carry this wretched nonsense so far with Miss Trevelyan." In his heart of hearts, he was fain to confess to himself, with a tinge of self-contempt for the avowal, that there was "something in it."

So, there was. More than he imagined. Presently Mrs. Tristram ran upstairs, and soon came down again, looking very agitated.

"Poor dear Olga seems dreadfully hysterical," she said with sigh. "She doesn't look yet as if she'd quite got over that horrid mesmerism. I ought never to have allowed the man to work upon her feelings so. She's talking in a rambling, delirious sort of way, poor dear, about somebody having compelled her against her will to do something or other that she thinks dreadfully wicked. And she says there's someone or other smiling horribly at her. Don't you think Dr. Hazleby, just to quiet her nerves, you ought to give her something?"

Ladies, even learned ladies like Mrs. Tristram, regard medical science as a form of magic, and drugs as a sort of charm or fetish. Their universal remedy for all the ills that female flesh is heir to, from paralysis or heart disease down to fainting or hysteria, is to "give her something." What, is immaterial. Morphia or sal-volatile, strychnine and arsenic or *eau sucrée* tempered with orange flower water: a drug, a drug, in the name of all that's merciful.

Dr. Hazleby went up at once to see the interesting patients. Olga's pupils were very dilated. Her pulse was slow, yet bounding and unnatural. She seemed in a very marked state of exhaustion and excitement.

"Don't you think, young ladies," he said cheerily, "you ought each to have a glass of port wine, just to set you up, now?"

Olga assented readily enough, and the good doctor went down in his clumsy, hearty way, himself, to fetch it. "Wait a bit," he said in a stage aside, as Mrs. Tristram poured it out from the decanter. "I'll just run home and get a wee drop of something stronger—something to quiet the nerves, you know. Miss Trevelyan seems to have something weighing on her mind. Your nephew and Mr. Tennant haven't come in yet from the river, I fancy."

"No," Mrs. Tristram answered. "They went up the river this afternoon in the duck-boat. I'm beginning to get a little nervous about them myself, to tell you the truth, my dear Dr. Hazleby."

"Oh, they'll be all right, ma'am," the doctor replied, with gruff kindliness. "Young men are always getting into scrapes, and frightening their friends, and then turning up again. Depend upon it, that's what's the matter with Miss Trevelyan. She won't sleep a single wink tonight if she doesn't have something to quiet her nerves a bit."

And he ran hastily out of the door, to his own surgery just round the next corner.

When he came back, he brought a little phial loose in his hand, and poured a few drops of a sweet white fluid from it into each of the glasses. It was the same white fluid the *fakir* had taken from his double gourd and smeared on Olga's lips the day she was first dedicated to Kalee!

"What is it?" Mrs. Tristram ventured timidly to ask.

"What is it? Oh, *haschish*."

"And pray what's *haschish*?"

"*Haschish?* Why, *haschish* is Indian hemp. You know the stuff——a common drug. It's a powerful narcotic. The Hindu ascetics use it to produce illusions. I always find it a capital soothing draught for nervous excitement. I've frequently given it with the very best results in similar cases."

He took the glasses up on a little tray. Olga was sitting still on the couch, with her head between her hands, and her bosom heaving and falling visibly. "Has—Harry Bickersteth come back yet?" she asked with eager haste. The doctor nodded a sagacious nod to Mrs. Hilary Tristram.

"I told you so." the nod seemed visibly to say. "She's troubling her head about young Alan Tennant."

"No, they've not come back yet," he answered cheerily, handing her the glass, "but they're expected home now every minute. There's no danger: not the slightest danger. Tide was late, owing to the surf on the bar. They'll be back immediately. Here, drink the port. It's very good for you."

Olga took it and drained it off mechanically. Then she buried her head once more in the sofa cushion.

"Come, come," the doctor said, with kindly insistence. "This won't do, my dear young lady. You must both get to bed now, this very minute. It's high time you two were fast asleep and snoring. Young people need plenty of beauty-sleep. Miss Norah, see that your friend goes to bed at once, and doesn't lie awake crying. And you too. You shall hear about your brother and Mr. Tennant the very first thing when you wake in the morning."

Mrs. Hilary Tristram sat up very late by herself that evening, wondering when her nephew would ever come back, and full of dim unshaped forebodings about him. She wished she hadn't let him go out on the river with Mr. Alan Tennant. What was that Sir Donald had said the day of the picnic about the second sight, and misfortune brewing for the young oculist.? She didn't believe in the second sight; but still, one can't help feeling just a little bit nervous. Duck-boats, she knew, were fearfully unsafe, and the branches of the Thore were always shifty. She sat up alone till long past two, watching and waiting eagerly for

Harry's arrival. But no Harry came at last, and she was fain in the end to take up her candlestick with a sinking heart, and mount the lonely staircase tremulously to her own bedroom.

As she passed by Olga's and Norah's door, she heard the sound of a voice or voices. Those naughty girls hadn't fallen asleep yet! They were still talking. Had they too waited and watched up there for Harry and Alan? . . . She listened awhile on tiptoe at the lintel. Her heart beat fast. A voice was certainly speaking—it was evidently Olga's. She caught the very words. It said in clear and definite accents,

"It was very wrong of me! I left off in the midst! I OUGHT TO HAVE FINISHED DOING WHAT SHE BID ME!"

Mrs. Hilary Tristram went on relieved. They were awake, no doubt, but talking about some quite indifferent matters. Some little dereliction of everyday duty. Olga's voice was perfectly wakeful. What a pity the draught had had so little effect upon her.

But if Mrs. Tristram could have looked that moment through the panels of the door, she would have seen Norah lying fascinated in her own bed, and Olga, with wide-staring eyes fixed wildly upon her, standing in her delicate white-frilled night-dress by the rustling curtains, and coiling in her bloodless trembling fingers that big silk handkerchief—the Indian *roomal!*

CHAPTER 11
After the Tempest

Next morning, Olga remembered in a dim way that she had slept very, very soundly: and she awoke with that painful weary feeling in the muscles of the throat and neck which often follows a strong dose of any powerful narcotic. She was sure Dr. Hazleby had given her something to make her doze off: and as she glanced askance at Norah, still sleeping heavily on her own bed—there were two in the room— she felt certain that Norah too had drunk something other than wine in the draught the doctor had so carelessly handed her.

She looked in the glass, and saw there were deep dark rings round her big eyes. Alan would think her quite plain today. . . . Had Alan come back? . . . The thought, recurring slowly, as in a dream, made all her fears revive again. She felt the drug hadn't worn itself out yet, or she would have remembered him sooner! She dressed quickly without waking Norah.

"Poor darling, "she thought; "she was tired too. Let her sleep her sleep out. It will do her good. She isn't as anxious to know about her brother, of course, as I am to hear about dear, dear Alan."

She went downstairs looking pale and haggard.

Mrs. Tristram rose to kiss her as she entered the breakfast-room.

"My dear," she said, "you're not well this morning. That horrid mesmerism did you no good. I shall never allow you again, as long as I live, to play such tricks with your constitution."

"Oh, I shall be all right soon, thanks," Olga answered distractedly, sitting down to the table and turning over the envelope of a letter on her plate with careless fingers. "It tired me rather—that was all. . . . Have Harry Bickersteth and Mr. Tennant come back home yet?"

"No," Mrs. Tristram replied gravely. "But I'm not frightened, dear. . . . At least, not very. If anything serious had happened, we'd surely have heard it long before this time. The fishermen would have told us. Boys will be boys, and will get into mischief. They've gone up the river and got too far or something, and had to stop the night no doubt at Ponton. We shall have a telegram, I fancy, before we've finished breakfast. Is Norah coming down? How is she this morning?"

Olga blushed, she knew not why. "No," she answered with incomprehensible evasiveness. "She isn't dressed yet. She . . . she hasn't got up, in fact. She's sleeping so soundly. I think . . . in fact, I fancy . . . Dr. Hazleby must have given us something to make us sleep, you know."

Mrs. Tristram smiled a knowing smile. "So he did," she answered. "Indian hemp. That's what's making Norah so oversleep herself."

Olga gave a faint little shudder. "Indian hemp!" she murmured. "Always something Indian! I hate India and all that belongs to it. It seems somehow to be a sort of fatality with me that everything Indian should always bring some kind of misfortune."

"Oh, don't say that," Mrs. Tristram cried in evident alarm. Please don't. You mustn't even think it. Why, Harry's duck-boat—the boat they've both gone up the river in, you know—it's called the *Indian Princess*, Olga. Harry named it in joke after the little *Maharanee* he met last autumn down in Norfolk."

At the word, Olga suddenly dropped the knife and fork with which she was pretending to play with her breakfast, and stood staring hard before her, with the same strange far-away look in her eyes Mrs. Tristram had noticed the previous evening during the whole of those horrid mesmeric experiments. A single word rose once more to her lips. She muttered it twice—"Kalee! Kalee!"

At that very moment, the door opened, and Sir Donald Mackinnon entered unannounced.

"We old Indians are inquisitive," he said gravely, with a slight bow, "but I've come round early to inquire this morning after my friend. Miss Norah. I haven't slept a single wink tonight, with this second sight of mine, thinking about her, Mrs. Tristram. I've lain awake and listened to the owls hooting, and the waves breaking, and imagined all manner of evil things, and fancied I could hear her moaning and groaning. How is she this morning, can you tell me, Miss Trevelyan? Not up yet, ah? I hope there's nothing serious the matter with her. . Eh? what? . . . Why, what ails the lassie? You're looking uncommon pale and ill and gash yourself, too."

"Norah's asleep," Olga answered, trembling, she knew not why, and shrinking horribly from the old man's keen and searching glance. I—I thought it was best not to wake her. She seemed so very ill and weak and tired."

Sir Donald gazed at her coldly and sternly. "Young lady," he said in a harsh voice, "I'm thinking it's not all right this morning with my friend, Miss Norah. Will you go up and call her, please, Mrs. Tristram.? There's mischief, I'm afraid, in this young lady's eyes. We Highlanders know the eerie look in them, and what it portends in the way of evil!"

Mrs. Hilary Tristram ran upstairs with vague forebodings of trouble in her heart. Olga followed her, half unconscious with terror, and weighed down with some awful burden of remorse—for what, she knew not.

The room had two little cretonne-curtained beds in it. In one of them, Olga had slept that night. The curtains of the other were half drawn, and Norah's form was still lying, quite stiff and motionless, beneath the dainty coverlet.

Olga approached softly on tiptoe. "Norah!" she whispered. "Darling Norah!"

A corner of the sheet just covered her face. Norah neither stirred nor answered.

With gentle fingers, Olga drew the bedclothes from her face and neck. Then with a fearful shriek, she fell back and fainted. The shriek rang and vibrated through the whole house. It was a deathlike cry of unutterable agony.

In a moment, the awful truth had burst upon her soul. She remembered it all, all quite clearly now. Norah was dead, and she herself was her murderer. She herself was her murderer: she herself—and Kalee!

The cry roused the whole household like a tocsin. Sir Donald and the servants hurried to the room. They found Olga insensible, supported in Mrs. Tristram's arms, while Norah, stretched upon the bed, with head thrown back, lay motionless and still as a marble statue. Her pretty blue eyes stood wide open, fixed in a deathly stare on the blank ceiling; the soft dimpled cheeks showed white and ashen; and, most terrible of all, around her smooth fair neck appeared in awful distinctness a dark blue line—the livid death-mark of that fatal handkerchief.

For one solemn moment no one stirred or spoke or even breathed almost. They stood stricken and petrified at the horrid sight. Then Sir Donald, slowly awaking as if from a hideous dream, lifted the senseless Olga in his arms, and carried her off to another room unresisting.

"This is a matter for the police," he said sternly. "There's been murder done, and we know who did it."

He looked suspiciously at the little silver image on her neck—the image of Kalee that the *fakir* had hung there. A dark red smear passed across its face. He gazed closer. It was blood—blood—blood on her lips—the fresh clotted blood of a human victim!

Blood had spurted for a moment from Norah's mouth in the agony of the throttling. Kalee that night had drunk of her sacrifice.

As Mrs. Tristram, unable yet to realise the terrible truth, stood wringing her helpless hands by Norah's bedside, a servant came in with a message from the boatmen.

"Something about Master Harry," she whispered soft below her breath. "They're afraid he's lost. The boatmen say the *Indian Princess* has come floating down the river with the tide this morning . . . empty, quite empty, and bottom upward."

Mrs. Tristram answered never a word. Her cup was full already. Nothing else would make much difference. She merely stood and rocked herself idly backward and forward, in the impotent recklessness of utter misery.

Next minute, Olga glided to her side. She had come back to herself, and stood now erect and pale and tremulous and beautiful.

"Send for the police," she said in a stony tone. "I know I did it. I give myself up. I have nothing to say for myself—Norah is dead. It was I who killed her—Alan is dead. I have heard the message—I loved them both. I shall be glad to die. I have nothing to live for. I deserve it! I deserve it!"

Once more a servant entered in hot haste, and held a telegram which she handed half hesitatingly on the salver to Olga. The girl dashed it aside with an imperious wave of her white hand.

"Perhaps," Mrs. Tristram murmured in a low voice, "it may be from

Harry or Mr. Tennant."

Sir Donald opened it mechanically and read it aloud:

"Congratulations, dear Olga, and best wishes for your future happiness. You have chosen well.

"Everard and Marion Trevelyan."

It was an Indian telegram! Always India! What mockery it seemed at such a moment! Surely, surely Kalee had sent it! It was Kalee's appropriate greeting to her votary.

CHAPTER 12

An Aquatic Excursion

Meanwhile, where were Harry Bickersteth and Alan Tennant?

Up the river in the *Indian Princess*, they had had an easy voyage, lazily paddling for the first hour or two. The mud-banks of the Thore, ugly as they seem at first sight, have nevertheless a singular and unwonted interest of their own; the interest derived from pure weirdness, and melancholy, and loneliness—a strange contrast to the bustling life and gayety of the bright little watering place whose church tower rises conspicuously visible over the dykes beyond them.

On the vast soft ooze-flats, solemn gulls stalk soberly, upheld by their broad web-feet from sinking: while among the numberless torrents caused by the ebbing tide tall long-legged herons stand with arched necks and eager eyes, keenly intent on the quick pursuit of the elusive elves in the stream below. The grass wrack waves dark in the current underneath, and the pretty sea-lavender purples the muddy islets in the side channels with its scentless bloom.

Altogether a strange, quaint, desolate spot, that Thore estuary, bounded on either side by marshy saltings, where long-horned black cattle wander unrestrained, and high embankments keep out the encroaching sea at floods and spring-tides. Not a house or a cottage lies anywhere in sight. Miles upon miles of slush in the inundated channels give place beyond to miles upon miles of drained and reclaimed marshland by the uninhabited saltings in the rear.

They had paddled their way quietly and noiselessly among the flats and islets for a couple of hours, carefully noting the marks of the wary wildfowl on either side, and talking in low tones together about that perennial topic of living interest to all past or present generations of Oxford men, the dear old 'Varsity. Alan still held a fellowship at Oriel, and Harry was an undergraduate of Queen's: so the two found plenty of matter to converse about in common, comparing notes as to the deeds of daring in bearding the proctors, feats of prowess in town and gown rows, the fatal obsequiousness of the Oxford tradesmen, and the inevitable final evolutionary avatar of that mild being under a new and terrible form as the persistent dun, to the end of their tether.

Such memories are sweet—when sufficiently remote: and the Oxford man who does not love to talk them over with the rising spirits of a younger generation deserves never to have drunk Archdeacon at Merton or to have smoked Bacon's best Manillas beneath the hospitable rafters of Christ Church common room.

At last, in turning up a side streamlet, on the southern bank—Thorborough, as everybody knows, lies to the northward—they passed an islet of the usual soft Thore slime, on whose tiny summit grew a big bunch of that particular local East Anglian wild-flower which Olga had said she would like to paint, on the day of Sir Donald Mackinnon's picnic.

"I say, Bickersteth," Alan suggested lightly, as they passed close beneath it: "don't you think we could manage to pick a stem or two of the artemisia—that feathery fluffy yellow flower there? Miss Trevelyan"—and he tried not to look too conscious—"wants to make a little picture out of it, she told me. I expect we could pull in and get near enough to clutch at a branch or so."

"No," Harry answered, shaking his head confidently. "I know by heart all the tricks and manners of the creeks and the river here. I know every twist and turn of the backwaters. No quicksand on earth could possibly be more treacherous than our Thore mud. It's a mud *per se*, quite unique in its own way for stickiness. If you try to land on it, you go on sinking, sinking, sinking, like an elephant in a bog, or a Siberian mammoth, till you disappear at last bodily below the surface with a gentle gurgle; and the mud closes neatly over your head; and they fish you out a few days later with a crooked boat-hook, as Mr. Mantalini says, 'a demd moist unpleasant corpse,' and dirty at that into the bargain. You must wait and get a bit of the stuff a little further on. There's plenty more growing higher up the backwater. We can land easier there on some of the hards, where the side creeks run deep and clear over solid pebble bottoms."

They paddled on noiselessly through the water as before, away up the silent, unpeopled inlet, among the lonely ooze and great stranded islands of salt-marsh vegetation. At every stroke, the aspect of the country grew wilder and more desolate. At last they came to a broad expansion of the tributary creek. Alan could hardly have believed any place so solitary existed in England. Some of the islands, surrounded on every side by slimy channels of deep ooze, could only be approached by a boat at high spring-tides, and even then, nowhere save at a single unobtrusive landing-place. They were thickly overgrown with rank brown hay.

"And even the owners," Harry said laughing, and pointing to one such dreary flat with demonstrative finger, "only visit them once a year in a shallow punt or low barge at hay-making time to cut the hay-crop. Sometimes the bargemen from upstream at Ponton come for a lark in the night, before the owner harvests it, and mow the crop, and carry it away down the river and out by sea to market in London; and nobody ever knows a word about it till the owner turns up disconsolate a week or so later, and finds his hay clean gone, and not a soul on earth to tell him what the dickens has ever become of it."

"It's fearfully lonely," Alan said with a shudder, looking round him in surprise at the trackless waste of ooze and sedges. "If a man were to get lost or murdered in one of these dreary channels, now, it might be weeks and weeks—ay, and years too—before anybody on earth ever discovered him."

"It might," Harry answered. "You say the truth. A capital place indeed for a murder. As De Quincey says, you could recommend it confidently to a friend. Nobody'd ever be one penny the wiser—See, there's some more of your flower nodding away on the bank over yonder—what did you call it?—artemisia, wasn't it? Well, here we can get at it, I expect, with a little trouble, if you don't mind wading. You're prepared to go through fire and water, I suppose, for Miss Trevelyan?"

Alan's face grew somewhat graver. "I'm prepared to get my bags wet through in the sea," he said, "if that's all, to do anything reasonable, for any lady. Miss Trevelyan said she'd like the flower, and I thought I might as well try to get a little bit for her."

"Well, you needn't be so huffy about it, anyhow," Harry went on, good-humouredly. "No harm in being in love with a pretty girl, that I know of: at least it doesn't say so in the Ten Commandments. Stick the pole firm into the bottom there, will you? By Jove, the stream runs fast! How deep is it? About two feet, eh? Well, we can tuck our trousers up to the thighs and wade ahead then. The channel of the stream's firm enough here. Pebble bottom! I expect it's pebble right up to the island."

They pulled off their shoes and socks hurriedly, and rolled up their trousers as Harry had suggested. Then the younger lad stepped lightly out of the boat on to the solid floor, and drove the pole deep into the slimy mud-bank beside it. The mud rose in a veritable cliff, and seemed to the eye quite firm and consistent; but it gave before the pole like slush in the street, where the brushes have heaped it on one side by the gutters. He tied the duck-boat to the pole by the painter, and gave a hand to Alan as his friend stepped out with a light foot into the midst of the little rapid channel.

"Bottom's quite solid just here," he said. "You needn't funk it. We can walk close up to the side of the island. These streams run regularly over hard bottoms, though the mud rises sheer on either side of them, till you get quite up to the head waters. There they lose themselves, as it were, in the mud: or at least, ooze out of it by little driblets from no-where in particular. Come along, Tennant. We can pick some of Miss Trevelyan's *specialité* on the far side of the island, I fancy."

They waded slowly up the rapid current, Alan pushing his stick as he went into the mud-bank, which looked as firm and solid as a rock, but really proved on nearer trial to be made up of deep soft light-brown slush. They attacked the island from every side—a double current ran right round it—but all in vain: an impenetrable barrier of oozy mud girt it round unassailably on every side like the moat of a castle.

"I shall try to walk through it" Alan cried at last in a sort of mock desperation, planting one foot boldly in the midst of the mud. "What's slush and dirt, however thick, compared with the expressed wishes of a fair lady?"

As he spoke, he began to sink ominously into the soft deep ooze, till his leg was covered right up to the thigh.

Harry seized his arm with a nervous grasp in instant trepidation. "For Heaven's sake," he cried, "what are you doing, Tennant? The stuff's got no bottom at all. Jump, back, jump back here, take my hand for it! You'll sink right down into an endless mud slough."

Alan felt himself still sinking: but instead of drawing back as Harry told him, and letting his whole weight fall on to the one foot still securely planted on the solid bed of the little river, he lifted that one safe support right off the ground, and tried with his stick to find a foothold in the treacherous mud-bank. Next instant, he had sunk with both legs up to his waist, and was struggling vainly to recover his position by grasping at the overhanging weeds on the island.

Harry, with wonderful presence of mind, did not try at all to save him as he stood, lest both should tumble together into the slough; but running back hastily for the pole, fastened the boat to his own walking-stick which he stuck into the mud, and brought back the longer piece of wood in his hands to where Alan stood, still struggling violently, and sunk to the armpits in the devouring slush. He took his own stand firmly on the pebbly bottom of the little stream, stuck the far end of the pole on the surface of the island, and then lowered it to the level of Alans hands, so as to form a sort of rude extemporised crane or lever.

Alan clutched at it quickly with eager grip; and Harry, who was a strong young fellow enough, gradually raised him out of the encumbering mud by lifting the pole to the height of his shoulders. Next minute, Alan stood beside him on the hard, and looked ruefully down at his wet and dripping muddy clothes, one malodorous mass of deep black ooze from waist to ankle.

"You must stand up to your arms in the stream," Harry said laughing, in answer to his comically rueful glance, and let the water wash away the mud a little. A pretty pickle you look, to be sure. By George, I thought for a minute it was all up with you! You won't trifle with Thore ooze again in a hurry, I fancy."

Alan pulled off his flannel boating jacket and his once white ducks with a gesture of disgust, and began scrubbing them between his hands in the discoloured water.

"I must sit on the island and let them dry," he said in no very pleasant voice, "I can't go home to Thorborough looking such a mess as this, you know, Harry."

"How'll you get on the island?" Harry asked incredulously.

"Why, you just hold the pole as you did, so, and I'll go hand over hand, like a British acrobat on parallel bars, across the mud-bank."

"And leave me to stand here in the water alone till your clothes have dried to your perfect satisfaction! No thank you, no thank you, my dear fellow."

"I can get you over when once I've got across, myself," Alan answered lightly. "Hold the pole out a little below the middle, and lift you, so, as if I were a circus man."

"I venture to doubt your gymnastic capabilities."

"Try me, anyhow. If it doesn't succeed, I'll come back at once to you."

Harry fixed the pole on the island once more, and Alan, clasping it tight with his hard grip, and lifting up his legs well above the mud-bank, made his way, hand over hand, as acrobats do along a tight rope or a trapeze, to the solid surface of the little island. There he laid out his clothes carefully to dry, and sat down, holding the pole as he had suggested, lever fashion, for Harry. By dexterous twisting, he managed to land his friend safely on the island, where they both sat down on the sun-dried top, and gazed disconsolate on the fearful waste of mud around them.

"Curious how hard the bottom is," Alan said after a while, "in the midst of so much soft ooze and slush and stuff!"

"The current washes away the soft mud, you see," Harry answered glibly, as he lighted his pipe, "leaving only the pebbles it selects at the bottom. Segregation! segregation! It's always so over all these flats. You can walk anywhere on the bottom of these streamlets."

"Well, at least," Alan said, glancing about him complacently, "we've got the flowers—any number we want of them. I should have felt like a fool indeed if I'd sunk up to my waist in that beastly ooze there, and yet never succeeded in getting what I came for. The flowers alone are the trophy of victory. It's a foreign artemisia, got stranded here by accident. Indian Wormwood or Lover's Bane the herbalists call it."

And he gathered a big bunch of the yellow blossoms from the summit of the island, tying them together loosely with a shred from his handkerchief (Men in love think nothing, it may be parenthetically observed, of tearing up a new cambric handkerchief. At a later date, it is to be feared, the person for whose sake they tear it up takes good care to repress any future outbursts of such absurd extravagance.)

They sat on the island for nearly an hour, and then, as the sun was shining hot overhead, Alan's clothes were sufficiently dried for him to put them on again in a somewhat dingy, damp, and clinging condition. The problem now was to get back again. Alan successfully lifted down his friend at the end of the pole, in true acrobat fashion: but just as Harry touched ground in the centre of the little stream, the pole creaked and gave ominously in the middle.

"Take care of it, Tennant," the young man cried, as he fixed it once more across his shoulder. "Don't trust the weak point in the middle too much. Glide lightly over the thin ice! Hand over hand as quick as you can manage!"

"All right," Alan cried, suiting the deed to the word, and hastily letting himself glide with a rapid sliding motion along the frail support.

As he reached the middle, with a sudden snap, the pole broke. Alan did not hesitate for a minute. If he fell where he was, he would sink helplessly into the engulfing mud. He had had enough of that, and knew what it meant now. With the impetus of the breakage, he sprang dexterously forward, and just clearing the mud, fell on his hands and knees upon the hard, right in front of Harry.

"Hurt yourself, eh?" his friend asked, picking him up quickly.

"Not much," Alan answered, flinging the broken pole angrily into the stream. "Barked my knees a little: that's about all. We're unfortunate to day. The stars are against us. There's a trifle too much adventure to suit my taste, it strikes me somehow, in your East Anglian rivers!"

"Here's a nice fellow!" Harry retorted, laughing. "Adventures are to the adventurous, don't they say. You first go and try a mad plan to pick a useless little bunch of fluffy small flowers for a fair lady, quite in the most approved romantic fashion, for all the world like the *London Reader*; and then when you fall and bark your knees over it, you lay the blame of your own mishaps on our poor unoffending East Anglian rivers!"

"I've got the flowers still, anyhow," Alan answered triumphantly, holding them up and waving them above his head, crushed and dripping, but nevertheless perfectly intact, in his bleeding hand. He had knocked his fist against the bottom to break his fall, and cut the skin rather badly about the wrist and knuckles.

"Well, it's high time we got back to the boat," Harry continued carelessly. "If we don't make haste, we shan't be back soon enough for me to dress for dinner. I must get home before seven. Aunt's got the usual select dinner-party stirring this evening."

They turned the corner, wading still, but through much deeper water than that they had at first encountered (for the tide was now steadily rising), and made their way to the well-remembered spot where they had loosely fastened the light duck-boat.

To their annoyance and surprise, no boat was anywhere to be seen in the neighbourhood. Only a mark as of a pole dragged by main force out of the mud—the mark left by Harry's walking-stick.

They gazed at one another blankly for a moment. Then Alan burst into a merry laugh.

"Talk about adventures," he said; "they'll certainly never be ended today. The duck-boat must have floated off on its own account quietly without us."

But Harry, instead of laughing, turned deadly pale. He knew the river better than his companion, and realized at once the full terror of the situation.

"Tennant," he cried, clutching his friend's arm nervously and eagerly; "we're lost! we're lost! The duck-boat *has* floated off without us: there's no getting away, no getting away anyhow! No living power on earth can possibly save us from drowning by inches as the tide rises!"

CHAPTER 13
Lost

Alan stared at his friend in blank dismay. It was some time before he could fully take in the real seriousness of their present position. But he knew Harry was no coward, and he could see by his blanched cheek and bloodless lips that a terrible danger actually environed them.

"Where's she gone?" he asked at last tremulously.

Harry screened his eyes from the sun with his hands.

"Downstream, at first," he said, peering about in vain, "till tide rose high enough; then up, no doubt, heaven knows where, but out of sight, out of sight anyhow!"

Alan examined the bank closely. He saw in a moment how the accident had happened. Harry, in his haste to fetch the pole to save him, had driven his own walking-stick carelessly into the larger and looser hole left by the bigger piece of wood; and the force of the current, dragging at the boat, had pulled it slowly out of the unresisting mud-bank. It might have been gone a full hour: and where it had got to, no earthly power could possibly tell them.

"Can't we swim out?" he asked eagerly at last. "You and I are both tolerable swimmers."

Harry shook his head very gloomily. "No good," he said. "No good at all, I tell you. The river's bounded by mud for acres. It's six miles at least down to Hurdham Pier, the very first place there's a chance of landing. If you tried to land anywhere else before, you'd sink in mud like the mud you stuck in just now at the island. We're bounded round by mud on every side. We stand on a little narrow shelf of pebble, with a vast swampy quagmire of mud girding it in for miles and miles and miles together."

"Can't we walk up to the source.?" Alan enquired despondently, beginning to realise the full terror of the situation. "It may keep hard till we reach *terra firma?*"

"It may, but it doesn't, I'm pretty sure," Harry answered with a groan. "However, there's no harm anyhow in trying. Let's walk up and see where we get to."

They waded on in silence together, feeling the bottom cautiously at each step with their sticks, till the stream began to divide and sub-divide into little finger-like muddy tributaries. Choosing the chief of these, they waded up it. Presently the bottom grew softer and softer, and a firm footing more and more impossible. At last, their feet sank in ominously. Harry probed a step, in advance, with the broken end of the pole that Alan had dug away. The next step was into the muddy quagmire. Land still lay a mile distant apparently in that direction. The intervening belt was one huge waste expanse of liquid treachery.

They tried again up another tributary, and then a third, and a fourth, and so on through all the radiating minor streamlets, but still always with the same disheartening result. There was no rest for the sole of their foot anywhere. Above, the streams all ended in mud; below, they slowly deepened to the tidal river. A few hundred yards of intervening solid bottom alone provided them with a firm foothold.

"I wish to goodness," Alan cried petulantly, "we'd never got out of that confounded duck-boat!"

"It's too late wishing now," Harry murmured half to himself, with a remorseful glance at the ill-omened flowers. "We've got to face the very worst. The tide's rising. It rises above the level of the mud. Not enough for us to swim in, though. We'll have to stand here as well as we can on the hard till we can stand no more, and then swim or float for dear life as far as our strength or chance will carry us."

Alan bit his lip in utter despair. He had but one thought now. That thought was for Olga. Olga would miss them! Olga would be frightened! Should he try the riskiest course of all, and swim if possible, the long six miles to the pier at Hurdham? No, no. That after all would he sheer suicide. Better hang or to the last wild chance at all hazards, and wait for the possible approach up stream of a barge or row-boat.

He took out his watch. It was half-past six. They were going upstairs to dress for dinner now at the Tristram's at Thorborough.

"Couldn't we manage to get back on top of the island?" he said at last. "We might wait there then for almost any length of time, till we could signal with a handkerchief to some passing eel-boat. That'd be better at least than waiting here in the middle of the channel till the tide rises."

Harry shook his head with almost sullen despair. "No, no," he cried. "Impossible, impossible! You know how sticky you found the mud. Without the pole we could never by any chance get there. We'd only sink over head and ears in that devilish slush. You don't know the ways of the Thore as well as I do. Sinking in water's bad enough, but sinking in mud's ten thousand times more terrible. It clogs you and hampers you on every side. Struggling or swimming only makes things worse. You go down in it helplessly, suffocating as you go, and there isn't a chance of recovering even your dead body. If we drown in peace and let the tide drift us afterwards down the river, they'll bury us decently anyhow at Thorborough."

Alan went back once more to the neighbourhood of the island. He scanned it eagerly now all around. It was no longer a question of getting a handful of pretty flowers for Olga—it was a pressing urgent life-and-death necessity. But the more he looked at it, the more utterly impossible and impracticable it seemed. Only seven or eight feet of light-brown mud separated them with its gap from that haven of refuge; and yet the seven or eight feet proved a greater barrier than miles and miles of land or water could ever have done. Water you can swim through, land you can walk over, but mud is absolutely and utterly impassable.

He returned to where Harry sat crouching in the stream, hugging his knees, and gazing blankly and wildly straight in front of him.

"Sit down," Harry said: "this is the highest point. The water here perhaps may not rise above our heads. But we'll have to wait and let it rise slowly. You must sit as long as you can, till tide reaches about to your neck. Then kneel; and after that, stand up and face it. The water rises warm over these basking shallows. If it lay cold, it would be much worse for us. We shall hold out now for about six hours. If a boat comes by, well and good. If not—"

He threw his head back significantly, and closed his eyes, gurgling low with his throat in a speaking pantomime.

Alan thought only of Olga.

They sat there silent in the running water, hugging their knees, for twenty minutes. Then Harry took his handkerchief slowly from his pocket, and tied it to the broken end of the pole.

"We must hold this up, turn about," he said. "Perhaps some boat may pass and see it."

For many minutes, neither spoke again. Then Alan said once more, "Hadn't we better try swimming?"

"No," Harry answered. "For—our friends' sake—no. Let us wait on the chance. If the worst comes to the worst, at last, we can swim for dear life. But hold on to the hard as long as it serves you."

"Ah, but then we shall be gradually chilled and powerless. If we swim now, we might manage to keep up for dear life—and for what's dearer than life—till we reached Hurdham."

"Impossible," Harry answered with a shake of his head. "Tide's against us by this time. If we swam up, as tide now runs, we should only be landed on worse mud-banks in the Ponton direction. Wait till midnight—the turn's at midnight. Then we might manage to float on our backs, with tide in our favour, and high water too, to one of the firmer islands a little way down towards Thorborough. At high tide, some of them are approachable."

"Till midnight!" Alan cried. "My dear fellow, do you mean to say we must stop here till midnight? All in the dark, and with the water rising everywhere around us? Oh, Harry, Harry, I'd ten thousand times rather swim for it at once and face it anyhow!"

Harry seized his arm impressively, "It's your one chance, Tennant," he said in a low firm voice. "Wait! . . . For Olga!"

In a moment Alan noticed the strangeness of the tone.

"For Olga?" he cried. "For Olga? For Olga?"

"Yes," Harry answered, almost bitterly. "Do you think I'm thinking only of myself.? What a coward you must fancy me? We young fellows always fall in love, they say, with girls older than ourselves. And do you think I haven't fallen in love with Olga Trevelyan? How could I help it? Who could help it? As much as you have, I tell you, Tennant: every bit as much as you have. For her sake, you've got to get back; and for her sake I've got to help you. What's the use of making secrets between us now? I know you love her. I know she loves you. If you don't come back, it'll break her heart. She's got a heart of the kind that's given to breaking. Well, I love her too. I know I'm a young fellow, and I know I shall get over it. In the end, I shall do like all the rest of us, marry some other girl younger than myself, and try to fancy she's as good and as pure and as beautiful as Olga. But while it lasts, it's as real to me as it is to you, I tell you, Tennant.

"It's Olga who's got us both into this scrape. If I hadn't aided and abetted you this afternoon, you wouldn't have got on the island there, to pick the bunch of flowers for Olga. I helped you, because I knew she'd be pleased that you'd got them for her, and that you'd taken a little trouble to get them—and risked a little danger into the bargain. And now we've both got to get you back to Olga. Never mind about me: that doesn't matter. You're taller than me: you can overtop the water a good half-hour longer. If I get drowned, you can take my body, and put it on the mud by the island yonder, and use it as a stepping-stone to get across upon. I expect it'd bear you up for a minute; enough to jump safe on to the top of the island. Somebody's sure to be up here with a boat within the next day or two. You could hold out for two or three days even without food, on top of the island, and then you could get back home at last—to Olga."

Alan could answer nothing in return. The tears stood thick in his eyes. He took the young fellow's hand in his and wrung it in silence with a long hard grip.

"Harry," he said at last in a choking voice, "you're a splendid fellow. If we've got to die, we shall die together. Nor even for her, not even for her could I ever desert you. Let's tie the flowers around our waists. Then if we die, Olga'll know we died at any rate for her sake."

"No," Harry murmured in a low soft voice. "Let's throw them away: far, far away from us. Then if we die, Olga'll have nothing at all in future to reproach herself with. She'll think we died up the creeks and backwaters looking after the wildfowl shooting for our own pleasure."

Alan answered never a word. But he felt in his heart that the young man's thought was the truest and noblest. He flung the bunch far from him into the middle of the stream. The rising tide brought it back to his hands, and then carried it vaguely up on its flood among the flats behind them.

Chapter 14
Suspense

The water had now risen up to their waists as they sat dripping in the middle current. They shifted their position, and took to kneeling. The shades began to fall slowly over the land. The stars came out overhead one by one. The gulls and rooks retired in slow procession from the purple mudflats: the herons rose on flapping wings from fishing in the streams, and stretched their long necks, free and full, homeward towards the heronry.

Nothing on earth could have seemed more awesome in its ghastly loneliness than that wide expanse under the gathering shades of autumn twilight. The water rose slowly, slowly, slowly, slowly. Inch by inch it gained stealthily but steadily upon them. It reached up to their waists, to their sides, to their breasts, to their shoulders. Very soon they would have to cease kneeling, and take to the final standing position. And after that—the deluge!

Bats began to hawk for moths in number over the mud-flats. A great white owl hooted from the open sky above. Now and again, the scream of the sea-swallows, themselves invisible, broke suddenly from the upper air. Even the clang of the hours from the Thorborough church tower floated faintly across the desolate saltings to the place where they waited for slowly-coming death.

"I should like one pipe before I die," Harry said stoically, feeling in his pockets for a box of matches. "You haven't got such a thing as a light about you, have you, Tennant?"

"I've got a flint and steel," Alan answered, pulling it out, "but I'm afraid it's wet with the mud by the island."

He opened the box. To Harry's surprise and delight, the tinder within—a long coil of yellow wick—was dry and untouched, preserved from harm by the metal covering.

"This is better than a match," he cried with new hope. "It's better than a pipe, Tennant. It's a signal: a signal! Keep the tinder alight, and hoist it on a pole, and perhaps it'll attract some one of the mud-anglers."

"Who are the mud-anglers?" Alan asked shivering.

"Men who come out fishing for eels in the streams as the tide rises," Harry answered, fired with fresh expectation. "They walk across the mud, with a lantern in their hands, and catch eels in the tidal channels."

"Walk on the mud!" Alan cried. "But, how can they? How can they? And if they can, why can't we too, Harry?"

Harry waved his hand a little impatiently. "They walk with mud-shoes," he answered with a slight cough. "Mud-shoes are thin flat pieces of board, turned up at the end and strapped on the foot, like small boats; and they glide on them across the mud as people glide with snow-shoes over the snow in Canada. In shape they're very much like the toboggans we used to slide on when I was a boy down the hills at Halifax. You've seen pictures of toboggans in the papers, haven't you? Well, that's a mud-shoe: and the mud-anglers wear them. There are pretty sure to be mud-anglers about tonight, and this light might possibly happen to attract one."

As he spoke, he tore a shred from his handkerchief, and with it fastened the smouldering wick to the broken pole. Below the sparks of light thus precariously obtained, he tied the remainder of the hand-kerchief itself. The wick lighted it up with a faint illumination, and together they served to form a slight danger-signal, sufficient to take the attention of a passing mud-angler, if any should chance to come within sight of the feeble illuminant.

The evening fell darker and darker. The tide rose slowly, remorse-lessly. The mud-flats ceased to glimmer faintly with the long reflection of the twilight afterglow. All was silent and black and invisible, save for the shrill cry of the bats as they swooped overhead, and the tiny glow of the saltpetre tinder-wick on the flapping handkerchief.

The water compelled them now to stand. Arm-in-arm they stood before it, facing together that crawling, slow, resistless enemy. If it had been waves to buffet and overcome, however fierce, even that would have been better. One would have felt then one was at least fighting them. But the utter sense of helplessness and impotence in face of that quiet, noiseless creeping flood was too appalling. Harry's teeth began to chatter with cold. The long immersion, even in that sun-warmed water, was gradually telling upon him. His limbs were stiff, and his blood coursed slowly.

They passed the pipe silently from one to the other, for Alan's last cigar was long since finished. It helped to warm and comfort them a little.

"Thank heaven," Harry said with real fervour as he took it once from his friend's mouth, "thank heaven for tobacco."

Half-past eight. Nine. Half-past nine. The bell clanged it out loudly from the Thorborough steeple, and the echoes, stole reverberant with endless resonance across the lonely intervening mudflats. How long the intervals seemed between! Twenty times in every half-hour the two young men lowered the slowly smouldering wick, and held Harry's watch up to the light, to read how the minutes went on its dial. Half-past nine, and now breast high! Ten, eleven, twelve, still to run! The water would rise far above their heads! Each minute now was an eternity of agony. Save for Olga's sake, they would have taken to swimming, and flung away the last chance of life recklessly. It is easier to swim—and die at once—than to stand still, with the cruel cold water creeping slowly and ceaselessly up you.

At twenty-five minutes to ten, they lowered the light and looked once more. As they did so, a faint long gleam streaming along the mud-flats struck Harry's eyes in the far distance. The light from which it came lay below their horizon; but the gleam itself, repeated and reflected, hit the side of the bank opposite them. Harry's quick senses jumped at it in a moment.

"A mud-angler! A mud-angler!" he cried excitedly, and waved the pole and handkerchief above with a sudden access of feverish energy.

Would the mud-angler see them? that was the question. The flicker of the wick was but very slight. How far off could it possibly be visible.? They waved it frantically on the bare chance of attracting his attention.

220

For five minutes there was an awful suspense; and then Harry's accustomed ear caught a faint noise borne dimly across the long low mud-flats.

"He's coming! He's coming!' he cried joyously. And then putting his two hands to his mouth, he burst into a long, sharp, shrill coo-ee.

"You'll frighten him away!" Alan suggested anxiously. "He'll think it's a ghost or something like one."

But even as he spoke, the gleam of a lantern struck upon the mud, and the light shone clearer and ever clearer before them.

"Hallo!" Harry cried. "In distress here! Help! help! We're drowning! We're drowning!"

A man's voice answered from above. "Ahoy! ahoy! How did yow git there?"

Thank heaven! they were saved!—Or next door to it!

The man approached the edge of the mud-bank as close as he dare (for the edges are very steep and slippery), and turning his lantern full upon them, stood looking at the two half-drowned men, as they gasped up to their breasts in water.

"How did yow git there, I say?" he asked once more sullenly.

"Can you help us out?" Harry cried in return.

The man shook his head.

"Dunno as I can!" he answered with a stupid grin. "I can't go no nearer the edge nor this. It's bad walking. Mud's deep. How did yow git there?"

"Waded up, and our boat floated off," Harry cried in despair. "Can't you get a rope? Can't you send a boat? Can't you do anything anyhow to help us?"

The man gazed at them with the crass and vacant stupidity of the born rustic.

"Dunno as I can," he muttered once more. "Yow'd ought to a stuck to your boat, yow 'ad. That's just what yow'd ought to a done, I take it."

"Is there a boat anywhere near?" Alan cried distracted, "Couldn't you put any boat out from somewhere to save us?"

"There ain't no boat," the man answered slowly and stolidly. "Leastways none nearer nor Thorborough. Or might be 'Urdham. Tom Wilkes, 'e 'ave a boat up yonder at Ponton. But that's right across t'other side o' the water." And he gazed at them still with rural indifference.

"My friend," Alan cried, h a burst of helplessness, "we've been here in the water since six o'clock. The tide's rising slowly around us. In a couple of hours, it'll rise above our heads. We're faint and cold and almost exhausted. For heaven's sake don't stand there idle: can't you do something to save two fellow-creatures from drowning?"

The man shook his head imperturbably once more.

"I dunno as I can," he murmured complacently, "Mud hereabouts is terrible dangerous. Yow'd ought to 'a stuck to your boat, yow know. There ain't no landing anywheres hereabouts. If I was to give yow a hand, I'd fall in, myself. I expect yow'll have to stick there now till yow're right drownded. I can't git no nearer yow nohow."

There was something utterly appalling and sickening in this horrible outcome of all their hopes. The longed-for mud-angler had arrived at last: they had caught his attention: they were within speaking distance of him: there he stood, on the edge of the ooze, lantern in hand, and wooden floats on feet, plainly visible before their very eyes: yet for any practical purpose of assistance or relief he might just as well have been a hundred miles on shore clean away at a distance from them. A stick or a stone could not have been more utterly or horribly useless.

The man stood and gazed at them still. If they had only allowed him, he would have gazed imperturbably open-mouthed till the waters had risen above their heads and drowned them. He had the blank stolidity of silly Suffolk well developed in his vacant features.

Alan was seized with a happy inspiration. He would use the one obvious argument adapted to the stupid sordid soul of the gaping mud-angler.

"Go back to the shore," he cried, glaring at the fellow, "and tell the others we're here drowning. Do as you're told. Don't delay. Bring a boat or something at once to save us. If you do, you shall have fifty pounds. If you don't, they'll hang you for murder. Fifty pounds if you save us, do you understand me? Fifty pounds tomorrow morning!"

The man's lower jaw dropped heavily.

"Fifty pound," he repeated, with a cunning leer.

It was too much. Clearly, he didn't believe it possible.

"Fifty pounds," Alan reiterated with the energy of despair, taking out his purse and looking at its contents. "And there's three pound ten on account as an earnest."

He tied the purse with all that was in it on to the end of the pole and pushed it up to the man, who clutched at it eagerly. Looking inside, he saw the gold, and grinned.

"Fifty pound!" he said with a sudden chuckle. "That's a powerful lot o' money. Mister."

"Go quick," Alan cried, "and tell your friends. There's not a moment to be lost, and tide's rising. If you can bring a boat or do anything to save us, you shall have fifty pounds, down on the nail, tomorrow morning. I'm a rich man, and I can promise to pay you."

The fellow turned doggedly and began to go. Next moment, a nascent doubt came over him, and clouded his mind.

"How shall I know where to find yow?" he said, staring back once more, and gaping foolishly.

"Watch the beacons," Harry cried, taking up the parable, "and mark which stream we're in as well as you 're able. Let's see. How long shall you be gone, do you reckon?"

"Might be an hour," the man answered, drawling. "Might be two hours."

"The light won't last so long," Harry said anxiously, turning to Alan, "I say, my friend, can't you leave us your lantern?"

The man shook his head with a gesture of dissent.

"Couldn't find my way back nohow without it," he said, still grinning. "Fifty pound! That's a lot o' money."

"Go!" Alan cried, unable any longer to keep down for very prudence' sake his contempt and anger. "Go and tell your other fishermen. If you want to earn your fifty pounds tonight, there's no time to spare. When you come back, we may both be dead men, if you don't go on and hurry—Harry, we can light the wick again at eleven o'clock. Let's put it out now. We can do without it. We shall hear the church clock strike the hours."

The man nodded a stolid acquiescence, and turned once more slowly on his heel. They watched him silently receding—receding. Light and reflection faded gradually away. The faint plash of his wooden mud-shoes on the flat surface was heard no more. Nothing remained save the gurgling of the water. They were left alone—alone with the darkness.

That second loneliness was lonelier than ever. Too cold to speak, almost too cold even to hope, they stood there still, linked arm-in-arm, ready to faint, with the speechless stars burning bright overhead, and the waters rising pitilessly around them. In that last moment, Alan's thoughts were turned to Olga. Beautiful, innocent, gentle-souled Olga. If he died that night, he died, on however petty an errand it might be, for Olga's sake—for Olga—for Olga. And then he relapsed into a kind of chilly stupor.

CHAPTER 15
High Tide

Ten o'clock. . . . Half-past ten. . . Eleven. Numbed and half-dead, they heard the clock strike out, as in some ghastly dream, and waited and watched for the return of the mud-angler.

It wasn't so very far to the shore. Surely, surely, he should be back by this time.

The waters in the estuary rose by slow, by almost imperceptible degrees. But still they rose. They went on rising. They were up to Harry's neck now. He rested his chin on the edge of the water. Five minutes more, and all would be up. Faint and weary, he would fall in the channel.

"Look here, Tennant," he murmured at last, grasping his friend's hand beneath the surface in a hard, long grip: "I'm going to swim now. It's no use waiting. I've only got five minutes to live. . . . I mustn't stop here. If I stop, you know, when the water rises, I shall choke and struggle. Then you'll clutch me hold, and try to save me, and that'll spoil your own last chance of living. I'm going to swim. It won't be far. But it's better at any rate than dying like a dog with a stone round its neck, still here on the bottom. Goodbye, old fellow. Goodbye forever. Never let Olga know if you get back safe, what it was we did it for!"

Alan held him hard with whatever life was yet left in him.

"Stop, stop, Harry," he cried in dismay. "There's still a chance. Every minute's a chance. Don't go, don't go. Stop with me, for heaven's sake, and if we must die, let's die together."

"No, no," Harry answered in a resolute voice. "You've got half-an-hour's purchase of life better than I have, now, Tennant. For Olga's sake, you must let me go. For Olga's sake, you must try to save yourself."

"Never," Alan cried, firmly and hastily. "Not even for Olga's sake! Never! Never!"

At that moment, a loud shout of inquiry resounded over the mud flats! A noise of men! A glimmer of lanterns! Alan seized his friend, and lifted him in his arms.

"Saved! Saved!" he cried. "Shout, Harry! Shout! Shout, shout, my dear, dear Harry!"

Harry shouted aloud with a long wild cry. It was the despairing cry of a dying man, and it echoed and re-echoed along the undulating mud-flats.

Alan lighted the wick, which he had held all this time for dryness in his teeth, and fitted it once more into the crack of the pole. Harry waved it madly about over his head. One moment more of deadly suspense. Then an answering cry told them at last that the men with the lanterns saw them and heard them.

Next instant, the men were on the brink of the mud, and the light of the lanterns poured full upon them.

A voice very different from that of their friend the mud-angler shouted aloud in a commanding tone, "Shove off the raft! Look out for your heads there!"

Before they knew exactly what it was that was happening, a great square raft, roughly improvised from two cottage doors, nailed together by crosspieces, floated on the stream full in front of them: and Alan, scrambling on to it with a violent struggle, lifted up the faint and weary Harry in his arms to the dry and solid place of safety.

The men pulled them alongside with two ropes attached to the raft; and the same voice that had spoken first said once more in kindly tones, "Brandy, hot. Take a good pull at it! Don't be afraid. Next, your turn. . . . After that, this. A pull o' soup. It'll warm your heart, man. Now, sit on the raft and recover a little."

Alan sat on the raft giddily, as he was bid, and laid Harry's head on his lap like a woman. One of the men—not their mud-angler—pulled off his dry jersey at once, and handed it over to Alan with native kindliness. Alan laid it under Harry's head. The poor fellow was half fainting, half asleep with exhaustion. They gave him more beef-tea, and more brandy. He revived slowly; and meanwhile, the raft lay idle alongside, the men in mud-shoes standing on the bank and looking over.

"We must get along soon," one of them said, after a pause. "Water's rising. Soon be over the flats. Can you walk?" kindly, to Alan. And he held up a pair of mud-shoes in his hand to explain his question.

"I never tried them," Alan answered, looking at them dubiously: "but I dare say I could. Anyhow, I'll risk it.

He sat on the raft and put them on as the man directed him. Then they reached down a pole, which the four men held; and with it they lifted him up on to the mud-bank. He took his stand there uneasily enough.

"Don't fall, whatever you do," the chief speaker said encouragingly; "and don't stumble. Glide along on 'em the same as if you was skating. Keep from stumbling, and you'll be all right. Are you getting warmer? Have another pull at the soup, and a bit o' biscuit."

Alan ate the proffered food thankfully. Thank heaven, their first mud-angling acquaintance was no fair sample of the whole fraternity.

"Now for the other one," the speaker continued. "It ain't no good giving *him* mud-shoes. He ain't in no fit state at all for walking. We must drag him along somehow on the raft, Billy. Here you, sir; hold on to the raft. Now, all together! Heave him up! heave oh!"

The four men took hold of the ropes at once, and pulled the raft, with Harry on it, over the shelving bank, now nearly level with the rising water, and on to the mud-flats. Then they tied the two ropes firmly to the pole: placed it in front of them as a sort of support or axletree, and all pulling at it, with Alan in the middle, began to make their way shoreward. They struck across the flats by the nearest way, walking slowly, on Alan's account, and dragging the raft easily behind them. It sank slightly in the mud as they went, but not much; and the men pulled it as if well accustomed to that singular conveyance.

After only a few hundred yards of mud, Alan was perfectly astonished to find that they reached the dyke and the reclaimed marshes. So, near had they been all the time to land in one direction, and yet so dangerously far and remote from it.

"We couldn't come sooner," the chief speaker explained kindly to Alan, noticing his surprise. "Billy came"—pointing to their first friend, the mud-angler—"and told us at once all about you. But I knowed it was no use going on the search till we could do something practical-like to save you; and there wasn't a minute to spare, I'll warrant you. In half an hour, the flats'll be covered: as soon as they're covered, the mud's soft, and there ain't no possibility o' walking on it.

"We'd got to hunt up two more men, and a couple o' vacant pairs o' mud shoes: and as all the lot was out on the flats, that wasn't none so easy neither. Then we'd got to take down them there two doors, and nail 'em together, and put the ropes to 'em: and it's precious lucky we thought o' doing it. For if you'd had nobody but Billy and them to help you,"—here his voice sank to a confidential whisper,—"it's my belief, in the manner o' speaking, you'd both ha' been drownded just as you stood there."

Alan saw at once in his own mind the wisdom of his new friend's well-arranged plan. To have gone out on the mere impulse, unprovided with the necessary assistance of the raft, would have been worse than useless: the men could only have gazed at them helplessly from the edge of the ooze as their stolid acquaintance Billy had begun by doing. Still, it was awful to think that they had had to stop there drowning by inches while the men on shore were quietly taking down the cottage doors and rudely knocking the extemporised raft and planks together. They might at least have sent somebody on beforehand to tell them help would soon be coming!

And then, he reflected once more on the utter loneliness of those wild saltings, with their solitary huts scattered about at long distances, and recognised immediately that the men had acted for the very best—had done the only thing possible for them. Lucky indeed that one man at least was found among the mud-anglers with a strong hand and a cool head, for if they had been left entirely to the mercy of Billy and his like-minded associates, they might, as their new friend rightly said, still be drowning by inches in the dark estuary!

The men kicked off their mud-shoes dexterously, and piled them up in a low shed, thatched with rushes, on the very edge of the drained saltings. Then without a word, and as if by signal given, they lifted up Alan and Harry between them, two and two, and carried them across the steaming fields to a small cottage. It was the home of the man who had directed the others—Tom Wilkes, the captain of the mud-anglers. Late as it was, the women were sitting up to receive them: a bright wood fire burned merrily on the kitchen hearth; and a steaming kettle hissed in the midst of it. They laid them in chairs close to the fireside, removed their wet clothes hastily, and wrapped them round as they stood in dry blankets. The fire and food soon revived Harry; and the men carried him upstairs to a bed, where he was soon asleep and comfortably settled.

As for Alan, worn out as he was, his first idea was to get back to Thorborough at all hazards. Olga would be waiting anxiously to hear about him. Could he borrow a horse and ride home alone?

Tom Wilkes shook his head in a decided negative. There wasn't a horse for three miles about—nothing but sheep and cattle on the saltings: and as to Thorborough, it was t'other side river, and river spread in fingers and fingers, with saltings between, so that there wasn't no bridge without you went round right away by Winningham.

In those lonely peninsulas of Suffolk and Essex, indeed, spots may be found more utterly isolated from the outer world than any to be seen in Wales or Scotland—saltings cut off by interminable backwaters and interlacing estuaries from any intercourse save in one long straight line, with surrounding districts. It was only six miles, as the crow flies, from Tom Wilkes's cottage to the church at Thorborough; yet the road by land led ten miles inland, and then fifteen miles more round to avoid the rivers.

There was no hope for it. Anxious as he was Alan was positively compelled to sleep at the cottage, and early next morning, he mentally resolved, he would walk with his host to the nearest "hard" or landing-place, and there hire a boat to take him to Thorborough.

He went to bed, and with the aid of more brandy, poured down hot, soon fell asleep from sheer fatigue and weariness. For an hour or more he slept very soundly—the deep sleep that succeeds exhaustion. Then about two o'clock, he awoke with a sudden start. He had dreamed something. A cold perspiration seized upon his limbs. He shuddered and listened. In his dream he fancied he had heard some noise! A stifled cry! A suppressed groan! A faint utterance! he knew not what. It seemed to come, not from the room where he slept, but, vaguely floating, from the air above him. He sat up in bed and listened again. It was only the beating and fluttering of his own heart.

"I hope to goodness nothing's the matter with Olga," he said to himself wearily. "I felt as if something—something terrible, were happening over yonder to Olga! Poor child! she'll be half dead with fright at our stopping away. How absurd of me to wake and feel like this! I'm almost superstitious myself tonight! No wonder, either, after such an adventure on death's brink as that one!

In five minutes more, the shudder had passed away entirely: he turned round, fell asleep again, and slept soundly till eight in the morning.

Chapter 16
The Bubble Pricked

At eight o'clock, Alan rose and dressed himself, in a shirt and jersey and pair of sailor trousers, coarse, indeed, but dry and warm, lent him by their kindly host and rescuer of last evening. Sleep had done him a world of good. Accustomed to exposure in his student days, he rallied fast with food and warmth; and when he went down at last to the simple breakfast in the cottage living-room, he was ready to do full justice to the smoking rasher, homemade bread, and hot coffee, that Tom Wilkes's wife set temptingly before him.

Harry, however, had suffered far more. Exhaustion and chill had told severely upon him. He was hot and feverish. It would be impossible to move him from the cottage for the present. He must clearly stop there till he got well again. There was no danger, but need for nursing. Meanwhile, Alan felt, for his own part, he must go back at once to Thorborough to report to Olga. Poor Olga, she would be wondering sadly what fate on earth could possibly have befallen them!

After breakfast, he said a temporary goodbye to Harry—not without many regrets—and walked briskly with his host by the salting footpath as far as Hurdham. There, at the little wooden pier, they found a boat, and sailed with a lucky wind against the rising tide to the well-known landing-place at Thorborough Haven. In ten minutes from their arrival, Alan was up at the hotel, had written out a cheque for the promised reward (not that Tom Wilkes himself cared so much for that), and had settled once more with infinite comfort into his proper garments. Then, without waiting for anything else he hurried along the Shell Path with eager footsteps till he reached Mrs. Hilary Tristram's door. His heart bounded as he rang the bell! One moment more, and he would be with Olga!

The servant opened the door to him with a scared face.

"You can't see Miss Trevelyan," she answered at once, in reply to his twice repeated question. "She's upstairs. . . . I don't think anybody at all can see her. She's with Mrs. Tristram. I b'lieve Sir Donald has sent out for the policeman."

"For the policeman!" Alan cried, aghast at the words, still more at the manner in which they were spoken. "Sent for the policeman! For Miss Trevelyan! Oh no, oh no! There must be some mistake. What in heaven's name do you mean to say girl?"

The girl drew back, half offended, at his words, and held the door ajar cautiously.

"I mean what I say," she answered with a slow and distinct intonation. "Miss Norah's murdered! She's lying dead on the bed upstairs. There's a great black ring round her poor neck. And they say it was Miss Trevelyan herself as did it. As true as life, Miss Trevelyan's choked her."

While she yet spoke, Olga's face appeared, pale as death, with sunken eyes and haggard cheeks, at the top of the staircase. She had heard Alan's voice as he stood at the door, and even in that hour of anguish and despair, she rushed down wildly to fling herself and her griefs upon his strong bosom.

"Alan! Alan!" she cried, as she clasped him with mad energy in her arms. "You're safe! You're safe!—Yes, I did it! I did it! It was Kalee—Kalee! Kalee bid me! I am Kalee's, Kalee's: I belong to Kalee! That's why I always sleep with my eyes open! My *ayah* told me so when I was a baby!"

Alan looked down at her in a sudden agony of pity and terror. His practised eye needed no long detail of her present symptoms to read the true secret of the ghastly story. She was half in a trance even now—even now—still comatose and frantic from the last effects of that hateful mesmerism.

"Olga, Olga, my darling," he cried, holding her off at arm's length and gazing at her for a moment. "I know it all! I see it all! What have they been doing to you? Did the creature mesmerize you?"

Mrs. Tristram approached them gently from behind.

"Olga," she said, in a calm low voice, with her red eyes looking only tenderness at the frantic girl, "come with me, love. Mr. Tennant, you will find Sir Donald and Mr. Keen over yonder in the breakfast-room. They will tell you all about our terrible trouble. Norah is dead. Where is Harry?"

She said it simply, with the infinite calmness of pure despair. Her heart was broken. Those two had been more to her than son and daughter. Yet she took Olga's hand gently in her own. She owed her no grudge for that unconscious act. Her grief was far too profound and sacred for petty thoughts of bitterness or recrimination.

"Harry is safe!" Alan answered eagerly. "He will soon be back. We were delayed all night. I left him going on well in a cottage on the saltings. . . . This cannot be true, Mrs. Tristram. It cannot be true. She is not dead. There is some error somewhere."

Mrs. Tristram led the passive Olga upstairs once more, shook her head sadly, and pointed with her hand in solemn silence to the door of the breakfast-room. She could not explain. It was too, too painful.!

Alan entered the breakfast-room with a sinking heart. Sir Donald and Mr. Keen were conversing low by themselves at the bow-window.

They turned at once as Alan entered.

"This is a bad business, Mr. Tennant," Sir Donald said solemnly as the young man looked at him with accusing eyes. I feared as much. I told you so before. The curse has worked itself out. There's mischief come of it."

"Sir Donald Mackinnon," Alan said in a stern voice, not offering the grey old man his hand, but standing bolt upright like a denouncing spirit before him, "answer me one thing first of all! Is it true you have dared to send for the police for Miss Trevelyan?"

Sir Donald stared at him in blank surprise.

"Not yet, not yet," he answered evasively as soon as he could find his voice again:—"though I feel as a magistrate I ought to have sent for them much earlier. There's been murder done, and we should hand the culprit over impartially to justice. She may have known it, or she may not have known it: but that's for a jury of her countrymen to try. *We* mustn't go and settle it for them beforehand. I meant. . . I meant to send Mr. Keen shortly to get the police here."

The young man eyed him with a calm disdain. Sir Donald quailed a little tremulously before him. He looked so stern, and cold, and judicial.

"Sir Donald Mackinnon," he said again, in a hard, dry tone, "answer me one more question, will you? Were you a party in my absence last night to mesmerising (as they call it) Miss Trevelyan?"

Sir Donald shuffled somewhat in his shoes.

"Mr. Keen," he said, with an attempt at *hauteur*, "will tell you all about it."

The mesmerist smiled feebly out of the wrinkled corners of his cold glazed eyes—those expressionless grey-blue eyes of his—and murmured with an apologetic and exculpatory wave of his long thin fingers.

"I don't understand Hindustani myself. There was Hindustani spoken at the experiment. I think Sir Donald, who knows it, had better tell you."

Neither of them, on second thoughts, felt particularly proud of his own share in the transaction, it was evident. However, Alan somewhat saved them the trouble by catching instinctively at the fatal tell-tale word Hindustani.

"Hindustani!" he cried. "Then there was Hindustani spoken! Before you venture, sir, to send for the police to this house, have the goodness to tell me, pray, who spoke Hindustani?"

"I did," Sir Donald replied nervously. He twirled his watch-chain, and cast down his eyes, ill at ease no doubt with his own conscience.

"Tell me all you know about the circumstances," Alan said, in a low tone of quiet authority.

The old civilian bridled up for a moment. Who was this young doctor that he should order and cross-examine an officer of the Crown? Then, seeing the stern look still glaring in the young man's eyes, he changed his mind, began his tale, and ran rapidly through the whole pitiful story, as it figured itself as of course to his superstitious Highland imagination.

Alan faced him in silence, flushed and angry. The mesmerist stood behind, with a furtive glance, folding his long thin hands a little nervously one over the other. Sir Donald hummed and hawed occasionally, but told his terrible story on the whole without demur, in plain and straightforward soldierlike language.

Alan drank in every word as he uttered it with eager attention, noting it all down, point after point, as the superstitious Highlander unconsciously unfolded the rise and outgrowth of that deadly tragedy in his own excited and preoccupied brain.

At last, when the old man had fully finished speaking, Alan drew back a pace or two in wrath, and said in a low, distinct voice,

"Sir Donald Mackinnon and Mr. Keen: you do well to stand there covered with confusion. This is a very bad business indeed for you. There has been a conspiracy—perhaps an unconscious one, but still a conspiracy—between you two to work this mischief. If murder has been done, it is you who are the murderers! . . . You, you, not that innocent young girl! . . . You, sir, and you; *You who are the murderers!*"

Sir Donald fell back a step, astonished and dismayed.

"Me!" he repeated, vacantly and half-angrily. "Me the murderer! Me, did you say, Mr. Tennant? Why, what in heaven's name do you mean by that, sir?"

Alan answered slowly and distinctly, crossing his arms, and gazing at him with relentless accusation.

"Miss Trevelyan is a very nervous and excitable person. Her temperament is too highly overstrung. She suffers from a peculiar affection of the eyes—due no doubt, as you say, to an operation performed on her in infancy by some Thug priest over in India, which renders her particularly liable to occasional fits of hysterical somnambulism. I myself have seen her walk in her sleep since I came to Thorborough. You too, I now for the first time learn, also saw her on that same occasion. Those two facts put together suggested to your mind a hideous delusion.

"For weeks you have talked to her about India and her childhood. You have filled her head with wild and horrible ideas about Thuggee. Having a very timid and delicate nervous organisation to work upon, you have worked upon it mercilessly—unconsciously, I know, but none the less mercilessly—by endless details about the practice of assassination and the worship of Kalee. You have recalled to the poor girl's terrified mind all that she ever heard or guessed or picked up accidentally from servants in India in her childish days about the ghastly Thugs and their detestable goddess. You have roused her to such a pitch of abnormal excitement that snatches of Hindustani, long since forgotten, came back to her of themselves in her disturbed sleep, and horrible images dogged her and terrified her in her waking moments. All this you have done under my very eyes: I knew it all and saw it all:

232

but because you were an old man, and I was a young one, I foolishly forbore to warn you and expostulate with you. I wish to heaven, now, I had had the courage to do so earlier."

He paused a moment, to gain more breath; and as he spoke, a faint gleam of nascent comprehension seemed to rise slowly in the dull, glazed, boiled-fishy eyes of the professional mesmerist.

"So much you had done, and so far, you had gone, Sir Donald Mackinnon," Alan went on bitterly, holding up his finger to enforce silence, "up to last evening. Had I been here, you should have gone no further. I warned Miss Bickersteth not to allow your guest over yonder to mesmerise my future wife on any account. I meant myself to have seen that the prohibition was carried into effect had I been here. I knew that in her existing nervous state—shattered as her health has been by so many recent occurrences—to trifle with her constitution would be little short of deliberate criminality.

"But, driven on by your puerile superstition—a superstition of the lowest Indian fanatics—you thought nothing of that—you thought nothing of her—you thought nothing of me—you thought nothing of anything but your own wild fancies. You only wished to bring about evil, in order that you might have the feminine delight of wagging your head sapiently, when all was over, and saying, as you now say, 'Ah, well, I told you so.' That foolish delight you have actually exhibited to me here this morning. And I stand in front of you as your accuser this moment, telling you plainly, if murder has been done, as I fear it has been done, that I charge you with the murder. You, you, you are the murderer!"

Sir Donald grasped the back of a chair with trembling lingers. His head swam. The young man's words were very bitter, but the provocation was indeed terrible. It began to dawn upon his dull, superstitious, heavy mind that he had richly deserved them.

"Me," he muttered once more, with feeble reiteration. "Me the murderer! Me the murderer! Oh, Mr. Tennant, don't, don't accuse me!"

"Yes," Alan went on, with increasing sternness, unable to spare the quivering old man one single drop from the full cup of his overflowing misery. "I was detained last night by a terrible accident, which kept young Bickersteth and myself lingering for hours between life and death in the rising tide in unspeakable suspense and long-drawn agony. I come back, this morning, trembling with fear for the effect of our absence on Miss Trevelyan, to find that you two, with your infernal tricks, and your mesmeric devilry, have driven my future wife, in her unnatural sleep, into committing a horrible but unconscious crime. You two have done it, and you two only. You, sir," turning fiercely upon Mr. Keen, "put her first into a mesmeric trance, without one moment's inquiry into her character or constitution or previous state of health. To do so was nothing short of wickedness.

"You are a practised mesmerist. You know that your whole art really consists in playing with edge-tools. Yet you play with them unconcernedly, on an innocent young girl, for a moment's applause at an evening party. You, Sir Donald Mackinnon, then proceed to suggest by your vague words and obscure hints to Miss Trevelyan's excited fancy the commission of a horrible and tragic crime; and you suggest it at the very moment and in the very condition when as you well know and had just seen in another case, the wildest and most impossible of all conceivable suggestions is immediately acted out with unquestioning faith by the involuntary agent.

"You knew her will was in temporary abeyance. You knew her conscience was in your safe-keeping. You knew she must do whatever you suggested to her. Yet you dimly suggested the commission of an atrocious murder, borrowed from the rites of a half-civilized race, with every circumstance of horror and stealth and blood-thirstiness, on the person of a friend whom she loved devotedly.

"You saw her carry out your half-hints to the very letter, and only refrain from the last fatal act and step of all because you roused her just in time from her mesmeric trance to prevent its taking place in your own presence. You saw her wake, horror-stricken and agonised, at the faint recollection of the unnatural crime you had deliberately forced upon her. I know it, because I hear you say it. You have told me all this in your own words and with your own prepossessions. Out of your own mouth, I condemn you as a murderer."

He wiped the cold sweat tremulously from his brow. Then he continued once more with his merciless exposition.

"You were so full of your foolish supernatural explanation," he said, "that you never once thought of the natural and true explanation. Believing in the real existence of Kalee, it seems, quite as genuinely as the wretched Thugs themselves who worship her, you accepted Kalee's orders as the moving power of what was really brought about in the sleeping girl's mind by your own terrible and unearthly suggestion. Miss Trevelyan went to her room only half aroused, under the influence of the ghastly delusion your hints had created in her. You never asked whether any precaution had been taken or was to be taken to prevent the final catastrophe you had so nearly seen consummated. You were satisfied to leave it all to Kalee—that is to say, to the unconscious working out of your own wild hints and hideous imaginings.

"By an unfortunate error of judgment—a thousand times less serious and criminal than yours, but still a terrible error,—the medical man, who ought to have known better, administered a drug which kept up instead of allaying the abnormal excitement. It rendered the delusion more fixed and permanent. That delusion still survives. I saw it at once in Miss Trevelyan's eyes the moment I entered. We must try to overcome it. But for it and for everything you, you are to blame. I say it once more, soberly and seriously, Sir Donald Mackinnon, *you are the murderer!*"

Sir Donald sank back faintly into a chair. The young doctor's words smote him to the heart. In a vague, nascent, half-doubting way, he began to feel now that he had done it all. There was no Kalee! There had never been a Kalee! There could be no Kalee! Superstitious as he was, the old man shrank from admitting even to himself when brought thus face to face with that ultimate question, the existence and power of the strange gods.

"I didn't mean it!" he muttered feebly in an undertone. "I never meant to suggest anything. I only said she was noosing a *roomal*. I thought the girl was a votary of Kalee!"

"You admit the charge," Alan cried bitterly. "You confess! You admit it! That is well, so far. But what will a common-sense English jury say to it? Will they listen to reason? Will they ever acquit her? Do you know what ordeal you have brought upon my Olga?"

He could contain himself no longer. All his force and wrath was spent and gone. The terrible possibility of a trial for murder for the woman he loved best in the world overcame him at last. He realized the thing vividly in its full awfulness. Bowing his head, broken hearted, upon the table, he wept bitterly.

Chapter 17
Hope

The mesmerist paced the room alone. "If a murder has been done," he said slowly, "we two are the murderers. I admit it. I see it. I know my art. The young man is right. Mackinnon led her into it. But *has* a murder been done at all? Eh? Who knows? I don't feel sure of it. That's just the question."

Alan raised his head in an agony of suspense. "Who has seen Miss

Bickersteth?" he asked hurriedly. "Does Dr. Hazleby give up all hope? In cases of suffocation, it's so easy at times to confound death with temporary asphyxia. Has everything been tried—every possible restorative? What has been done for her? tell me! tell me!"

"Nothing, nothing!" Sir Donald Mackinnon exclaimed with a glimpse of hope. "Hazleby's out—gone over to Hurdham. Nobody's seen her but Keen and myself and Mrs. Tristram. We thought she was dead! She looked it, certainly. She's almost cold, and her pulse isn't beating."

Alan leaped excitedly at once to his feet.

"Do you mean to tell me," he cried in surprise and horror, "that you've given her up before any medical man has even seen her? A case of strangulation! Fools! Idiots! I must go this moment! Where is she? Where is she?"

They hurried upstairs with him to Norah's room, where Olga and Mrs. Tristram sat hand-in-hand, tearless, by the bedside, absorbed in that most devouring and grinding of griefs, the grief that cannot find relief in weeping.

Olga shrank with horror from her lover's gaze as he entered the room.

"Oh, Alan, Alan," she cried, gasping, "don't come near me! Don't touch me! Don't touch me! I know I did it! I think I did it; I killed Norah, and I belong to Kalee!"

Alan motioned her gently aside with his hand. He knew it was no time now to soothe her. A servant led her, obedient and unnerved, into the next room. She followed the girl, silent but tearless.

The young doctor felt the pulse and heart a moment. Then a great joy flushed bright in his eyes.

"There is hope! There is hope!" he cried. "Artificial respiration! Aflutter! Aflutter! The heart may yet be made to beat. Quick, quick. Brandy! Lay her down on the floor here! Lift her arms! So, so! Now again! Do as I tell you. There is hope! There is hope! She is *not* yet dead, though just next door to it! We may revive her still! Heaven grant us success in it."

They waited anxiously for twenty minutes, trying every restorative that Alans skill and knowledge could possibly suggest; and at the end of that time, Norah slowly drew one long faint breath . . . and then another . . . and another . . . and another . . . and another.

Great heavens! What an eternity of suspense it seemed, the second's pause between each of those almost imperceptible, inhalations!

236

Alan poured some brandy hastily down her throat. It seemed to rouse her. Her heart beat now with regular pulsations. She was coming to! She was coming to again!

They watched and waited, watched and waited, watched and waited till one o'clock. Then Norah opened her eyes faintly.

"Is she here? Is she here?" she cried, staring wildly around her. "The black woman! The black woman! the terrible black woman!"

"Hush! Hush!" Alan whispered. "There is no black woman. We are all here. We are taking care of you. See, this is your aunt!—Hold her hand, Mrs. Tristram. Let her see your face now.... Norah! Norah!"

But Norah gazed still wildly in front of her.

"Kalee! Kalee!" she cried in terrified accents. "The snakes! The snakes! The handkerchief! The black woman! Her great eyes! Her cruel black mouth! Her pearly white teeth, that smiled so horribly!"

Alan turned with a stern look to Sir Donald Mackinnon.

"See, see," he said, "with your own very eyes, the harm you have done here! You have put it into both their minds at once—the tool and the victim. It's a fixed idea, and we can't get rid of it. They've acted their parts, each as you suggested to them—one the Thug, the other the sacrifice. They're both of them still half in the mesmeric state, and the *haschish* has had the effect of prolonging the delusion. If she keeps this infatuation, in her present weak state, for another hour, she'll die of terror! She'll die of terror! We shall save her from one death only to hand her over powerless to another!"

Mr. Keen, who had been helping to promote the artificial breathing, stood forth once more with a fixed look of contrition. He was deeply moved, in spite of his livid eyes: he knew and felt to the very bottom of his soul the harm he had been instrumental in doing.

"Let *me* try," he said, holding out his long thin hands persuasively. "They were both very hard to wake last night. I expended, perhaps, too much energy in mesmerising them. They were only very partially awakened. She's still more or less comatose, I can see at a glance. I'll try a few passes. Perhaps they'll rouse her."

He waved his hand slowly and gently above the prostrate form of the pale young girl, and fixed his eyes quietly on hers. For a moment, Norah's face grew still more painfully excited: then the muscles gradually and gently relaxed, beginning to assume a more peaceful expression. As he continued his passes, the eyes ceased to stare wildly. The eyelids closed by slow degrees above them. Her head fell back into a natural restful attitude on the pillow.

"You haven't waked her," Alan said with a long-drawn sigh of profound relief: "but you've done better; you've put her into a sound and normal sleep. Leave her alone now till she wakes of herself. Nothing on earth could possibly be better for her."

Chapter 18
Fulfilment

"Where's Olga?" Alan asked, at last, turning with a sigh to Mrs. Hilary Tristram.

"In the next room, I suppose," the poor woman answered low, holding Norah's white hand gently in her own. "Oh, Mr. Tennant, Mr. Tennant, how can we ever sufficiently thank you! Twice, twice, you've given us back our darling!"

Alan held her other hand a moment with friendly pressure.

"We have all been saved," he said, "from a terrible calamity. I myself from the most terrible and unspeakable of all. I dare not think of it. I dare not speak of it. What man could even contemplate it without a shudder of horror?"

For that haunting mental picture of Olga, his own beautiful, tender-hearted, delicate Olga, standing up deadly pale, in a common felon's dock, and arraigned alone, before a stern judge and twelve stolid jurymen, for the most hideous crime known to vile humanity, had floated all those hours wildly before his excited brain, and had almost unmanned him for the task of saving her. He had thought it out, as in times of anguish one *will* think out one's coming misery, down to the pettiest details, the most sordid and horrible and sickening possibilities.

In those few short hours he had died of grief and shame a thousand times over. Last night's suspense, as he stood waiting for the slowly crawling and creeping tide, was as nothing to the agony and horror of soul he had known since he returned to find Olga—in fact if not in intention, at law if not in equity—a murderer! A murderer! If he had spoken harshly and angrily to Sir Donald Mackinnon, he had ample grounds for it. The crime that the old Highlander by his superstition and folly had forced upon Alan's own beautiful innocent Olga was enough to make any man stern and revengeful.

For Alan Tennant knew—knew beyond the shadow or possibility of a doubt—that Olga herself in her waking moments was utterly incapable of hurting in any way the feeblest or tiniest of living creatures. He knew that she loved Norah devotedly. He knew that in that condition of will to which the mesmerist by his mere bodily power can reduce some of the most delicate and highly-strung of human organisations, no living being, however pure or good or true or holy, can resist the most hideous or ghastly or wicked of suggestions distinctly presented to it.

He knew that under such circumstances the agent becomes but a puppet in the hands of the operator, working out unconsciously as in a vivid dream, without sense of right or wrong, without effort or deliberation, without will or motive, the wildest fancy or maddest impulse of the more active intelligence. He knew all that—knew it to the point of absolute certainty: but what hope or chance or prospect was there that he could ever make twelve hard-headed British jurymen, with a hard-hearted English judge to direct them, see the matter in the light that he saw it?

Woe betide the innocent man or woman whose actions, however righteous or however unconscious, sin against the hard-and-fast technical puerilities of English lawyers. Though their souls be as fair and white and pure as Olga Trevelyan's, though all that is wise or good in the life of England stand aghast at the hideous threatened injustice, those implacable pedants, with their clogging precedents and their hair-splitting distinctions, will nevertheless tie a noose so tight round the culprit's neck that the common conscience and common justice of the whole startled English nation will never, never serve to unfasten it.

Alan walked slowly into the next room.

"Where is Miss Trevelyan?" he asked of the servant.

"Here!" the girl said, with her finger on her lip, pointing vaguely to the bed. "Asleep. Don't wake her. She fell asleep the minute that gentleman with the long fingers began to walk up and down the passage, muttering."

"Let her sleep," Alan said, sitting down on the couch. "Better let her sleep the whole effect off. This mesmeric trance has been very terrible in its intensity and duration."

Olga slept soundly, as usual, with her eyes staring wide open. For a while, she lay motionless and quiet on the bed, but presently, the servant beckoned uneasily to Alan, who rose at once, and gazed with anxious eyes down upon her. Her face was beginning to be horribly distorted, and a terrible fixed look of fear and agony seemed to grow with each moment in her glaring eyeballs. It was clear that another paroxysm was coming on. Alan stood and watched it closely from hard by in breathless excitement.

At last, moved as if by some strength not her own, she started to her feet, quivering like an aspen leaf, and stood on the hearth-rug, wildly facing him. With clasped hands, and bent head, she paused there for a moment in deathly silence, her great eyes fixed in awful earnestness on some ghastly object which seemed to float invisible in the air before her. A deep voice appeared to ring unheard in her ears. She leant forward in awe as if to catch its accents.

"Kalee, Kalee," she murmured low, in a faint tone: "I hear you. I hear you."

Then she drew herself up suddenly into an imposing attitude, sublime, tragic, as if another soul inspired her, and cried aloud in implacable accents:—

Choose; choose; between me—or Death. You have scorned me! You have betrayed me! This choice alone, this choice alone remains! Obey! Obey me!

Alan started back with a thrill of horrible recognition. Sir Donald's pale face, looking in from the passage at the half-open door, answered it back mutely. Both at once read aright her mysterious action. Carrying on the impulse of the mesmeric state, she was dramatising the ideas that floated through her mind: acting in her sleep both her own part and the part of Kalee.

She dropped her head submissively once more. A cold chill ran visibly across her shapely shoulders. Through a mist of horror that seemed to obscure her vision she groped with her hands feebly for some one.

"Alan," she cried, "help me! help me!"

Alan restrained himself with a terrible effort. To wake her now would be no less than homicidal.

She drew herself up again proudly to her full height. Her voice a second time rang cold and majestic. She spoke still as the mouthpiece of the pitiless Kalee:—

While your eyes remain open forever in sleep, you shall have no other help but mine—but Kalee's. You shall see me floating like a black Terror for ever before you. You shall worship me and serve me all your life long. Mystical, awful, bloodthirsty, implacable, I shall stand beside you and watch over you always.

Then she pealed out a few sonorous words of rolling Hindustani. Sir Donald alone knew what they meant:—

I am Kalee, Kalee, the swarthy fury, of a hideous countenance, dripping with gore, crowned with snakes, and hung round with a garland of skulls at my girdle. I am she, the horrible, of misshapen eyes; menacing, trident-topped, riding on a tiger: the Black One, the fierce, the terrible, the bloody-toothed. My fangs are red with the flesh of my victims. Choose, choose, this day, which you will take: choose, between me and Death, my votary.

It was part of the long-forgotten litany of Kalee, sung over her cradle, years, years before, by her *ayah* in India.

Olga hung her head submissively once more. There was a short struggle—an internal struggle. Then she lifted her eyes proudly in a moment's defiance.

"Let me choose death," she said. "Let me choose death, Alan, if death means innocence."

The paroxysm was over. She sank back once more exhausted on the bed. The invisible Presence seemed to fade away, vanquished from before her. Kalee had fled—fled discomfited. But her eyes stood open, open wide as usual.

"Run quick," Alan whispered to one of the servants. "Borrow a case of instruments for me and a bottle of chloroform from Dr. Hazleby's."

The servant ran, and returned immediately, bringing the case as ordered, and a small phial. Alan chose a lancet carefully from the box, and poured a few drops of the chloroform on a corner of his handkerchief. Then he held the wet spot close to Olga's mouth. It took immediate effect. She breathed more heavily. The chloroform had stilled her.

He grasped the lancet firmly in his right hand and made a slight incision, with dexterous gentleness, first on the right, then on the left temple, a little below the two wee scars left by the flint knife of the Indian fanatic. Each cut severed a tiny branch nerve, inhibitory to the action of the small muscle which closes the eyelid. A little round drop of blood oozed slowly forth from the capillary vessels on either side, opened by the lancet. Alan brushed them away lightly with his own handkerchief.

Next, he loosed with the sharp blade the silken string that tied the silver image of Kalee round her throat. The wretched bauble should no longer remain to vex her with its memories and recall its hideous half-forgotten associations. He took out his pocket-knife, and with deliberate fingers hacked the soft metal into a thousand small pieces.

It was pure unalloyed silver, like most Indian jewellers' handicraft, and it cut easily without much resistance. He flung the shapeless fragments angrily out of the open window. They fell unseen among the grass on the lawn. Kalee was annihilated—dead and gone, for Olga Trevelyan, for ever and ever.

He returned to the bed. The action of the operation had been instantaneous. Olga's eyelids lay closed in sleep, with her head resting gently on the smooth white pillow. Her rich silken hair, thrown back in soft tangled masses from her brow, almost shrouded her temples from sight; but a tranquil smile played gently about her lips, and she looked like some Italian picture of a beautiful saint, painted in the days when saintliness was still no rare attribute among us. Her long dark lashes closed over her eyes, that were never more to be open for Kalee.

"Let her sleep," Alan said, "till she wakes of herself. Mr. Keen, come here! Undo your passes!"

The mesmerist, waving his long thin hands, went through the releasing movements once more, exactly as he had done before with Norah. The peaceful look deepened on her face as he waved them, and the gentle eyelids closed tighter and tighter.

Olga Trevelyan had ceased for ever to be a votary of Kalee.

Alan watched her, speechless, by her side, for hours together. She slept so long, he almost feared at last it was as she herself had said in her agony. Had Kalee claimed her? Was Death coming to put his seal at length upon her perfect innocence?

From time to time they stepped in noiselessly and brought him tidings of Norah Bickersteth. But Alan himself refused to move from Olga's side. He must watch still over her safety.

At six, she woke. She woke quite naturally, as if from ordinary sleep. Alan and the servants bent over her, inquiring.

"Alan, Alan!" she cried, lifting up her hands to him joyfully. "Then it's all right! You're back, you're back again!"

"Yes, yes, darling, "Alan cried, stooping down and kissing her for the first time, unabashed by the presence of others in so terrible a moment. "And Norah's alive—alive and recovering. She's just taken some nourishment this minute."

Olga gazed at him blankly with a strange look of doubt and hesitation on her beautiful countenance.

"Norah?" she said in an inquiring voice. "Norah? Recovering? From what is she recovering? . . . I seem to remember. . . . I fancy I dreamed. . . No, no. . . . I don't know anything about it. Has Norah been ill? Have I been ill? Have we slept long? What's that bottle for? Why am I on the bed here? I can't recollect it!"

Alan drew back a step, in surprise.

"Thank God! thank God!" he cried. "She was still mesmerised! She's forgotten every word, every word about it!"

As he spoke, Mrs. Tristram glided gently into the room.

"Mr. Tennant," she said in a low voice "never mention anything of all this to Norah! She's wide awake now, and she doesn't remember a moment in any way since she first fell asleep in the drawing-room last evening."

Happily, those two young lives were spared till long afterward all knowledge of the awful drama in which they had unconsciously played the part of chief actors. They only knew, for the present at least, that that horrid mesmerising had given them both a serious illness.

Olga's eyes closed automatically for a second. They opened again next instant with a burst of astonishment.

"Why, what's this?" she asked, in uncontrollable surprise. "My eyelids seem to move like a hinge of themselves, somehow."

Alan took her hand tenderly in his.

"I have cut a little nerve that held them back," he said. "Henceforth, Olga, they will close in sleep like everybody else's."

"And I shall never have those horrible, horrible dreams again?"

"Never, Olga darling; never! Never!"

She let her head fall gently back against his breast. They were left alone now for a single minute.

"Alan," she whispered, low in his ear, "my darling, my darling, I am quite, quite happy."

★★★★★★

When Olga Trevelyan and Alan Tennant were married at St. George's, some six months later, everybody said the bride was looking prettier and stronger than she'd ever looked in her life before, with that odd expression quite gone altogether from her face and eyes, and such a healthy natural girlish glow on her cheeks instead of it. And everybody considered Norah Bickersteth far the sweetest and daintiest of the four bridesmaids. So much so, indeed, that Captain Leigh-Tennant (Alan's rich brother, who inherited their Uncle Leigh's money)—that dashing young officer in the 8th Hussars—arrived at a very satisfactory understanding with her in the dance that finished up the day's festivities. And if Harry Bickersteth went away that evening with a sore heart, muttering to himself that even Alan Tennant, good fellow as he undoubtedly was, wasn't half good enough for Olga Trevelyan, it is probable that in the end he will illustrate the truth of his own vaticination, and console himself in a few years' time with some other girl more nearly his coeval.

As to Sir Donald Mackinnon, when he recovered, somewhat from his first fright, and came to think the matter over seriously, he would shake his sapient head at times and mutter in a wise voice to his friend Keen:—

"My dear sir, that young doctor-fellow explained the thing on strict scientific principles very glibly and eloquently, no doubt: but for my part, I must say, between you and me, when I come to put two and two together, I somehow fancy that in spite of everything, there must be a little kernel of truth after all in the Kalee business."

To which Mr. Keen would answer with a solemn shake of his head:—

"Nonsense, Mackinnon; that's all your pure Highland superstitiousness and nonsense. Do you want me at my time of life to begin believing in a whole pack of heathen gods and goddesses? The less said about Kalee, I think, the better. Between you and me, if it comes to that, it's a precious good thing for us two that that young doctor-fellow happened to come home in the nick of time to help us out of such a very awkward predicament. We may thank our stars the thing was all hushed up as cleverly as it was, between him and Mrs. Tristram. It'd have been a precious fishy business for you and me, I can tell you, my friend, if the girl had gone and died after all, and we'd been mixed up in the hocus-pocus. Kalee wouldn't have gone far, I fancy, to help us out of it with a coroner's jury."

"But how about her brother?" Sir Donald once objected, with a grim smile of conclusive logicality. "What do you make of the murder of her brother found in his cradle strangled, you know, as I told you that day, with a blue line right round his throat? Who on earth but that girl could possibly have murdered him?"

The mesmerist shrugged his shoulders impatiently.

"My dear Mackinnon," he said with some asperity, "how should I know how everything has always happened everywhere? Am I an Indian detective, for example? Surely the fanatic, whoever it was, who dedicated the girl herself in the first place to Kalee (as her eyes bore witness), would have been quite capable of throttling her brother into the bargain as a sacrifice to his deities? You're quite at liberty to believe in Kalee yourself, if it gives you any personal consolation to do so: but

I for my part utterly refuse to have anything to say to these strange gods."

LEONAUR

ALSO FROM LEONAUR
AVAILABLE IN SOFTCOVER OR HARDCOVER WITH DUST JACKET

MR MUKERJI'S GHOSTS *by S. Mukerji*—Supernatural tales from the British Raj period by India's Ghost story collector.

KIPLINGS GHOSTS *by Rudyard Kipling*—Twelve stories of Ghosts, Hauntings, Curses, Werewolves & Magic.

THE COLLECTED SUPERNATURAL AND WEIRD FICTION OF WASHINGTON IRVING: VOLUME 1 *by Washington Irving*—Including one novel 'A History of New York', and nine short stories of the Strange and Unusual.

THE COLLECTED SUPERNATURAL AND WEIRD FICTION OF WASHINGTON IRVING: VOLUME 2 *by Washington Irving*—Including three novelettes 'The Legend of the Sleepy Hollow', 'Dolph Heyliger', 'The Adventure of the Black Fisherman' and thirty-two short stories of the Strange and Unusual.

THE COLLECTED SUPERNATURAL AND WEIRD FICTION OF JOHN KENDRICK BANGS: VOLUME 1 *by John Kendrick Bangs*—Including one novel 'Toppleton's Client or A Spirit in Exile', and ten short stories of the Strange and Unusual.

THE COLLECTED SUPERNATURAL AND WEIRD FICTION OF JOHN KENDRICK BANGS: VOLUME 2 *by John Kendrick Bangs*—Including four novellas 'A House-Boat on the Styx', 'The Pursuit of the House-Boat', 'The Enchanted Typewriter' and 'Mr. Munchausen' of the Strange and Unusual.

THE COLLECTED SUPERNATURAL AND WEIRD FICTION OF JOHN KENDRICK BANGS: VOLUME 3 *by John Kendrick Bangs*—Including twor novellas 'Olympian Nights', 'Roger Camerden: A Strange Story', and ten short stories of the Strange and Unusual.

THE COLLECTED SUPERNATURAL AND WEIRD FICTION OF MARY SHELLEY: VOLUME 1 *by Mary Shelley*—Including one novel 'Frankenstein or the Modern Prometheus', and fourteen short stories of the Strange and Unusual.

THE COLLECTED SUPERNATURAL AND WEIRD FICTION OF MARY SHELLEY: VOLUME 2 *by Mary Shelley*—Including one novel 'The Last Man', and three short stories of the Strange and Unusual.

THE COLLECTED SUPERNATURAL AND WEIRD FICTION OF AMELIA B. EDWARDS *by Amelia B. Edwards*—Contains two novelettes 'Monsieur Maurice', and 'The Discovery of the Treasure Isles', one ballad 'A Legend of Boisguilbert' and seventeen short stories to cill the blood.